"JUST A TASTE, LOVE, THAT'S ALL."

She rarely drank from a living source. Being only half vampire, she lacked the inescapable need to hunt, but there was no denying that taking blood from mortals was a pleasurable sensation. No one had ever taken her blood. What would it be like, to be prey instead of predator? To feel Zack's fangs at her throat? Driven by curiosity, she canted her head to the side, giving Zack access to her neck, only then realizing that she was putting her life in his hands. He was older, stronger. If he decided to drain her dry, she wouldn't be able to stop him.

He must have sensed her sudden apprehension, because he said, "It's all right, Katy. You don't have to do it if you've changed your mind."

"I haven't," she said, and it was true. At that moment, she wanted nothing more than to nourish Zack with her life's blood.

Murmuring her name, he bent his head to her neck.

She had expected it to hurt, at least a little, but there was only a rush of warmth when his fangs pierced her skin, and then a flood of pleasure that was sensual beyond belief. Heat flowed through her, bringing all her senses to life, pooling deep within the very heart of her being, stealing the strength from her limbs, until all she wanted was to lose herself in his touch.

Books by Amanda Ashley

BOUND BY BLOOD

BOUND BY NIGHT

DEAD PERFECT

DEAD SEXY

DESIRE AFTER DARK

EVERLASTING DESIRE

EVERLASTING KISS

IMMORTAL SINS

NIGHT'S KISS

NIGHT'S MASTER

NIGHT'S PLEASURE

NIGHT'S TOUCH

A WHISPER OF ETERNITY

Published by Kensington Publishing Corporation

BOUND BY BLOOD

Amanda Ashley

ZEBRA BOOKS
KENSINGTON PUBLISHING CORP.
http://www.kensingtonbooks.com

ZEBRA BOOKS are published by

Kensington Publishing Corp.
119 West 40th Street
New York, NY 10018

Copyright © 2011 by Madeline Baker

All Kensington titles, imprints, and distributed lines are available at special quantity discounts for bulk purchases for sales promotion, premiums, fund-raising, educational, or institutional use.

Special book excerpts or customized printings can also be created to fit specific needs. For details, write or phone the office of the Kensington Special Sales Manager: Attn. Special Sales Department. Kensington Publishing Corp., 119 West 40th Street, New York, NY 10018. Phone: 1-800-221-2647.

Zebra and the Z logo Reg. U.S. Pat. & TM Off.

ISBN-13: 978-1-4201-2132-2
ISBN-10: 1-4201-2132-4

First Printing: October 2011

10 9 8 7 6 5 4 3 2 1

Printed in the United States of America

To Sweet Sue
I love you, Cuz

Prologue

From the Journal of Alexandru Chisca
Senior Member of the Romanian Vampire Council

I remember it well, the night that Calin Sherrad, Master of our Coven, called our people together. Calin was a tall, imposing figure, feared and respected by one and all. A proud man, never defeated in battle, he stared at those of us assembled in the Great Hall of the Carpathian Fortress. The tension within the Hall was a palpable thing as all who pledged their allegiance to Calin waited for him to speak. Most of us were related to Calin by marriage or by blood. The members of the Vampire Council, myself among them, stood to one side of the Great Hall. We all wore the long black hooded robes of our office.

A hush fell over us as Calin began to speak.

"I have called you here on a matter of grave importance."

Calin spoke quietly, yet his voice filled the room. I felt a shiver of unease as I waited for him to go on.

"For many years, we have lived in peace, carefully keeping our existence a secret from the mortal world. Occasionally, a rogue has brought the hunters down upon us, bringing danger to us all."

He spat out the word hunters *as if it left a bad taste in his mouth.*

"Not only do the humans outnumber us," he said, his voice rising, "but they have the advantage of being able to hunt during the day, when we are at our most vulnerable. Many of our people were killed in the last Great Hunt.

"It was for this reason that my father built this Fortress. It was his example that caused others of our kind to build similar places of refuge in other parts of our country. Since the last Great Hunt, we have endeavored to keep our existence a secret from the mortal world.

"For many centuries, it was believed that the vampires of Romania were the only vampires in existence. But that is no longer true. I do not know where these Others came from or how long they have existed, but they are not like us. They kill indiscriminately, feeding on men, women, and even children. Unlike our kind, they are able to create others like them. These fledgling vampires have an insatiable thirst for blood. They often leave their prey lying out in the open, drained of blood, to be found by humans."

Murmurs of disbelief ran through the crowd.

"Mortals cannot differentiate between our kind and these barbaric Others," Calin said. "Vampire hunters are out in force, killing our kind and the Others, and, in their hysteria, hunters have been known to kill those of their own kind. In some parts of the world, the ground is soaked with the blood of vampires and innocent mortals alike."

I glanced at the other members of the council, and saw my own horror reflected in their eyes.

Calin paused, his gaze again moving over the assembly. "This cannot go on," he said, his voice ringing from the walls and the rafters. "Tonight, I am declaring war on the Others! We must find them and annihilate them before they destroy our people and our way of life."

There were scattered shouts of approval from the younger vampires in the crowd.

"By my decree, every Romanian male will make this fight his own." Calin's gaze moved over the Hall, settling briefly on the face of every man. "So let it be recorded," he intoned with great solemnity. "So let it be done."

"So let it be recorded," the members of the council repeated in unison. "Done and done."

As I spoke the words, I wondered at the wisdom of our decision.

There followed a period in our history known as the Dark Times. Many Romanian vampires were killed as the war raged throughout the known world. Some were destroyed by hunters, some by the Others. Towns and cities were laid waste.

As soon as our children were old enough to understand, they were taught that the Others were the enemy. From childhood, every Romanian male was trained in the art of war. Many of our unmarried women joined our men in battle.

Peace had been taken from our land and our people. Hatred for the Others grew, instilled in the hearts of our children and our grandchildren.

The war against the Others lasted for over a hundred years. In that time, many lives were lost on both sides, including that of Calin. His oldest son, Rodin Sherrad, assumed his father's place as Master of the Coven. None challenged his right to do so.

Rodin was a fierce and fearless warrior. Ever valiant in battle, he was driven by a relentless need to avenge his father's death. His daring and determination infused our people with courage and a renewed determination to win.

Within a year, the Others had been defeated and peace was restored.

Rodin deployed our men to every part of the world to act as keepers of the peace. They were charged with the task of assuring that any Others who had survived the conflict were destroyed before they could wreak havoc among the humans, *or create more of their kind. Our people established new covens in other countries throughout the known world.*

Under his leadership, our existence has remained a secret.

The Others have been mostly forgotten.

Our way of life is safe once again.

Our people have flourished.

Long live Rodin Sherrad, Master of the Carpathian Coven. And long live those of his blood.

Chapter 1

Kaitlyn Sherrad rolled down the window of her baby blue Porsche and stared up at the log cabin set alone in the midst of a cluster of tall pines. As usual, her father had outdone himself. Last month, when he had come to the States for her graduation from college, he had asked her what kind of gift she wanted and she had said, facetiously, *Oh, nothing much, just a little summer place in the mountains.*

After pulling into the driveway and cutting the engine, Kaitlyn grabbed her suitcases from the backseat. Smiling with anticipation, she hurried up the narrow, winding, red brick path that led to the front porch. She quickly skipped up the stairs and unlocked the door.

Knowing her father, she wasn't the least bit surprised to find the living room already furnished. An off-white sofa with a high, curved back and a matching love seat faced each other in front of a rough-hewn stone fireplace. A deep mauve carpet covered the floor, flowered curtains hung at the windows. The tables were walnut, as was the large bookcase—already filled with books by her favorite authors—that took up most of one wall.

Dropping her suitcases beside the sofa, Kaitlyn explored the rest of the house—two large bedrooms with a connecting bathroom; a den, complete with desk, computer and printer, sofa and big-screen TV; a small kitchen with new appliances and a refrigerator filled with her favorite foods; a service porch equipped with a new washer and dryer.

She shook her head, a sting of tears behind her eyes. Being an only child, she had always been spoiled rotten, but this went far beyond the ballet classes and piano lessons her parents had provided when she was in grade school, the new wardrobe they had given her every year, the Porsche her father had surprised her with for her twenty-first birthday last year.

She had hoped her folks would spend the summer with her, but trouble at the Fortress had drawn them home. It wasn't always easy, having a father who was the Master of the Carpathian Coven. Sometimes, as now, his duties could not be ignored. Usually, her uncle Andrei handled things at the Fortress, but whatever the emergency had been, it had required her father's attention, which meant that her mother had gone, as well. To her knowledge, her parents rarely spent more than a few hours apart.

Kaitlyn sighed as she removed her sweater and tossed it over the back of the sofa. Someday, she hoped to find a man who would adore her the way her father adored her mother. A man who would live and die for her. A man she couldn't live without.

Picking up her suitcases, she carried them into the first bedroom and tossed them on the bed. This room was done in varying shades of green, with billowy white lace curtains. The twin windows looked out over a sparkling blue lake.

Kaitlyn shook her head. How was she ever going to express her gratitude for the love and kindness her parents had showered upon her? She had thanked them on numerous occasions in the past, but words seemed woefully inadequate. She knew they hadn't been altogether pleased with her decision to remain in California after she graduated from college, but they had accepted it without argument.

Feeling a little homesick, she opened the larger suitcase and began to unpack. Her folks had always treated her like a princess, but then, maybe that was natural, since she had been raised in an old stone castle in the heart of Romania.

She smiled as she hung her clothes in the closet.

All she needed now was a prince.

Chapter 2

Zackary Ravenscroft strolled through the main floor of the casino, stopping now and then to chat with one of the customers, pausing to answer a question here, to address a complaint there. He loved owning a nightclub, loved the excitement that filled the air, the rush of adrenaline that fired the blood of the patrons, the fact that no two nights were ever the same.

Zack had built the casino ten years ago, simply because he was bored and thought it would be a nice distraction. It was one of the best decisions he had made in the last six hundred years. Not only did the casino provide a hefty income, but the constant change in customers assured a steady supply of women. And Zack loved women—all women. Old or young, ugly or pretty, smart or not so smart, black, white, red, brown, yellow—it made no difference. He loved them all. And they loved him in every way imaginable.

Leaving the gaming tables behind, he strolled up and down the aisles of slot machines. He stopped a moment to watch an elderly woman playing one of the old dollar slots. From her shabby appearance, she appeared to be down on her luck and most likely using the last of her money in a desperate hope of hitting it big. He had seen it all before. Usually, he had no sympathy for those who plunked down their last five bucks in hopes of winning a fortune on the turn of a card. Sure, it happened from time to time, but no matter what the game, the odds were always with the house.

The old lady was muttering under her breath.

It took Zack a minute to realize she wasn't cursing but praying.

He frowned as he listened to the urgency of her words, heard the unshed tears in her voice as she sent a desperate plea toward Heaven.

Zack grunted softly. Her husband was sick. He needed an operation, and medication they could no longer afford. She had lost her job. They couldn't pay the rent.

She needed a miracle.

Murmuring a breathless "Amen," she shoved her remaining three dollars into the machine, then clasped her hands to her breast.

With a bemused shake of his head, Zack concentrated on the wheels of the slot machine.

One gold bar.

Two.

Three.

Smiling, Zack moved on as the machine lit up and bells and whistles went off, signaling that a player had hit the ten-thousand-dollar jackpot. So, he had lost ten grand, he thought, but it wasn't much to pay for a miracle.

He was still smiling when he stepped outside. It was a beautiful night. Cool and crisp. A few scattered clouds drifted across the face of the full moon.

Feeling suddenly restless, he wandered away from the casino, crossed the parking lot, and headed for the wooded hillside that began just beyond the blacktop.

He moved soundlessly through the underbrush, his

keen senses aware of the tiny night creatures that scented a predator and quickly scurried out of his way. He caught the scent of a skunk and farther on, that of a deer.

Nearing one of the cabins, he came across a black bear scavenging through a trash can. The bear reared up on its hind legs and sniffed the wind. Apparently recognizing Zack as a threat, the animal dropped back down on all fours and lumbered into the trees.

Grinning, Zack continued on until he came to the solitary cabin at the top of the hill. He paused, surprised to see there were lights on in the house. The cabin had been vacant for the last two years. He had, in fact, been thinking of buying the place for a rental.

Ah, well, too late now.

He was turning away when he caught the scent of prey. Glancing back, he saw a young woman looking out the front window. He whistled softly. He had seen a lot of beautiful women in his day, but this one—he shook his head. She was beyond beautiful. Her skin was smooth and unblemished, her eyes a deep dark blue. Hair the color of a raven's wing tumbled over her shoulders.

He frowned when her gaze found his, and then shook his head. She couldn't see him, of course. He was hidden by the darkness. And yet he couldn't shake the feeling that she knew he was there, that she was staring at him, as he was staring at her.

Curious to see her reaction, he stepped out of the darkness into a shaft of bright moonlight.

He had expected her to gasp in surprise, call 911, or hastily move away from the window and close the curtains. Instead, she tilted her head to the side, her gaze moving over him from head to heel, much the way he studied a woman he was considering as prey.

Zack was contemplating what to do next when she moved away from the window. Moments later, she was standing on the front porch, her arms folded under her breasts.

"What are you doing here?" she demanded.

Her voice was low, soft, and yet he detected a fine layer of steel underneath. He grunted softly. Most women would have been frightened if they looked out their window at midnight and found a stranger standing in the yard. But she wasn't the least bit afraid.

He had to admire that. Inclining his head, he murmured, "Good evening."

She lifted one delicate brow. "I repeat, what are you doing here?"

"Merely enjoying the night air," he replied with a smile. "And I repeat, good evening." He frowned, mystified by his inability to read her mind. It was a skill that had never failed him before and left him wondering if she was deliberately blocking him, and if so, how?

She huffed a sigh of exasperation. "Same to you."

"You're new in the area," he said.

Kaitlyn nodded. He must be a longtime resident, she thought, else he wouldn't be aware of that.

"It's a lovely house," he remarked. "I had intended to buy it myself."

"Sorry."

"No need to be sorry. Our town can always use another pretty face." He took a step forward, extending his hand. "Zackary Ravenscroft," he said. "But my friends call me Zack."

She descended the stairs. "Do you think we're going to be friends?" she murmured, taking his hand.

"I hope so."

"I'm Kaitlyn Sherrad."

He gave her hand a slight squeeze. "Kaitlyn."

She didn't know if it was the sound of her name on his lips, or the touch of his hand on hers that sent a shiver of excitement racing down her spine. Startled, she jerked her hand from his and took a step backward. Who was this guy? She had never experienced a reaction like that with any other man. Stranger still was the bewildering fact that she couldn't divine his thoughts. She supposed there were bound to be a few people whose minds she couldn't read; still, it was disconcerting. Was there something wrong with him, she wondered, or was the problem hers? She would have to ask her father about it the next time he called.

Needing time to ponder her odd reaction to Zackary Ravenscroft and her failure to read his thoughts, Kaitlyn bid him a quick good night and hurried up the stairs and into the house. She closed and locked the door, then stood there, her back pressed against the wood. Who was that guy?

Zack stared after her for several moments before he turned and headed back down the trail toward the casino.

Kaitlyn Sherrad was a puzzle, he mused, and he hated puzzles.

Zack was still trying to unravel the mystery that was Kaitlyn when she strolled into the casino shortly after dusk the next evening. Clad in a simple pale pink dress that outlined a figure bordering on perfection and a pair of white heels that did wonderful things for her long, shapely legs, she quickly attracted the admiring gaze of every man in the place, and the envy of every woman.

"Miss Sherrad," Zack murmured, going forward to greet her. "Welcome to my establishment."

"Thank you, Mr. Ravenscroft."

He made a broad gesture with his hand, encompassing the gaming portion of the nightclub. "What's your pleasure?"

"What would you suggest? I've never been in a casino before."

"Well, the slots are the easiest. The craps table is a bit confusing but probably the most exciting. Poker is a game of skill. Roulette is a game of pure chance."

She looked thoughtful a moment. "Slot machines, I guess."

He followed her to a bank of slots, stayed her hand when she delved into her handbag. Reaching into his pocket, he pulled out a fifty-dollar bill.

"First time's on me," he said with a wink.

"Really? Is this something you do for all of your customers?"

"No, ma'am, just the pretty ones."

With a toss of her head, Kaitlyn took the fifty from his hand and slid the bill into the appropriate slot. A credit meter displayed the amount deposited.

"On this machine, you can play one credit or as many as five, or you can hit the button marked PLAY MAX CREDITS," Zack explained. "After you make your choice, hit the SPIN REELS button. That's all there is to it."

Kaitlyn followed his directions, then watched breathlessly as the colorful wheels turned, then slowly came to a stop, showing three cherries across.

"I won!" she exclaimed, her cheeks flushing with excitement, as credits were added to her original amount.

Zack smiled, amused by her excitement, content to stand at her shoulder as she continued to play. As with most games of chance, the odds were always in favor of the house. The payout on slots was about ninety-three percent.

A few minutes later, a hostess clad in a ruffled, off-the-shoulder white blouse and short, wine-red skirt came by offering drinks, which were free to players. Kaitlyn ordered orange juice.

"Not a big drinker, are you?" Zack remarked.

"Not really. Aren't you having anything?"

"Maybe later." He jerked his chin toward the machine. "You won again."

Amused by her enthusiasm at winning a few dollars, he was curious to see what her reaction would be if she hit the jackpot. It was easy to manipulate the machine. A single thought, and three sevens lined up on the pay line.

"Oh! Look at that!" she exclaimed as more credits were added to the meter.

He laughed, surprised that her enjoyment pleased him so much.

The waitress arrived with her orange juice only moments later. Kaitlyn couldn't help wondering if all drink orders were filled as quickly, or if the fact that she was with the boss had anything to do with the speedy service.

She continued to play while she sipped her drink, winning more than she lost, and decided to quit while she was ahead.

"Are you sure?" he asked.

"Yes."

"Then hit CASH OUT," he directed.

She frowned when the machine spit out a bar-coded ticket.

"Only the older machines pay out in cash," Zack explained. "You can cash that in later."

"Oh, okay." She slipped the coupon into her purse and glanced around.

"Are you game to try something else?" Zack asked.

"Maybe later. Right now, I think I'd like something to eat. Is there a restaurant in here?"

"This way." Curious to see if his touch elicited the same reaction as the night before, he took her hand in his. An odd look passed over her face, but she didn't pull away this time. Pleased, he led her out of the casino and down a long, carpeted hallway. Kaitlyn glanced at the shops that lined both sides of the corridor—gift shop, flower shop, hair salon. But it was the sexy black pants and top in the window of the dress shop next to the hair salon that caught her eye. She'd never worn anything like that in her whole life.

The restaurant was at the end of the corridor. Kaitlyn glanced around. The room was rectangular-shaped, with an open beam ceiling and parquet floors. Booths lined three of the walls; tables covered with deep green cloths were arranged in the center of the floor. The lighting was subdued; soft music filtered through the sound system.

They were seated immediately, but that was no surprise. After all, it was bad form to keep the boss waiting.

"Good evening, Mr. Ravenscroft," a waitress said, offering Kaitlyn a menu. "Your usual?"

"That'll be fine, Annie."

"I'll be right back," she said, smiling.

"So," Kaitlyn said, opening the menu, "what's good here?"

"Everything," Zack replied with a grin. "We've got the best chef in the state. I'm told the lobster is excellent."

"You're told?" Her eyebrows went up in surprise. "Haven't you ever tried it?"

"No. I'm . . . allergic to seafood."

The waitress returned bearing a glass of dark red wine, which she placed on a coaster in front of Zack before turning her attention to Kaitlyn. "Do you need more time?"

"No. I'll have the lobster."

"Soup or salad?"

"Salad, with ranch."

"And to drink?"

"Just water, no lemon." Kaitlyn looked at Zack. "Aren't you having anything?"

"No. I dined earlier."

After jotting Kaitlyn's order down on her pad, the waitress picked up the menu and turned to go, but not before bestowing a dazzling smile on Zack.

"She seems quite smitten with you," Kaitlyn remarked as the waitress moved to the next table.

"Annie? Yeah, she's a good kid." He draped one arm along the back of the booth. "So, are you a working girl?"

"Not yet. I just graduated from college."

He grunted softly.

"I majored in Comparative Folklore."

"How's that workin' out for ya?" he asked, grinning.

"Not very well, actually," she admitted, her grin matching his. "Believe it or not, there isn't a lot of interest in ancient folklore these days, but"—she shrugged—"I receive a substantial allowance from my father."

Zack nodded. "Must be nice." He barely remembered his own father.

"Yes, although sometimes I feel guilty for taking it, and for knowing that if I do get into financial trouble, he's there to bail me out."

"What's wrong with that? Isn't that what fathers are for?"

"I guess so, but I'm a big girl now. Old enough to stand on my own two feet. I shouldn't be living on an allowance."

"What does your father do?"

"He's in business in Romania." It was the truth. And a lie.

"Romania? Girl, you're a long way from home."

Kaitlyn nodded. "I always wanted to see America. I have an uncle here somewhere. Of course, I have no idea where he might be. He left home before I was born." Her father was still hopeful that Stefan would one day return to the Fortress, but she thought it unlikely. Stefan had been gone for over twenty years. Surely, if he intended to return, he would have done so by now. Then again, maybe not. Twenty years wasn't such a long time when you lived for centuries.

"It's going to be hard to find him if you don't know where to start," Zack remarked.

"Well, I'm not really looking for him," Kaitlyn said with a shrug. "Although it's kind of nice to know that I have family here, somewhere." All she knew about Stefan was that he looked a lot like her father and that he had once loved a mortal woman. Even her grandmother, Liliana, rarely spoke of him.

The waitress brought Kaitlyn's dinner a few minutes later, along with another glass of wine for Zack.

"You're really not going to have anything?" Kaitlyn asked.

"No." He picked up his glass and sipped his drink. "Enjoy your dinner."

The lobster was every bit as delicious as he'd said, the rice fluffy and perfectly seasoned, the vegetables the best she'd ever had. Her enjoyment must have shown on her face because Zack grinned as she took another bite of lobster.

"Told you so," he said.

"It's wonderful." She speared another piece with her fork and offered it to him. "Are you sure you don't want to try a bite?"

"Quite sure."

"You don't know what you're missing."

That much was true, he thought. He had never tasted lobster. Or hamburgers. Or hot dogs or potato chips or so many other foods that mortals took for granted these days. In his day, the wealthy had dined on pheasant and roast pork and chicken swimming in rich sauces. The poor folk had lived on bread and cheese and an occasional deer poached from the king's forest— and been glad to get it.

These days, his was strictly a liquid diet.

Kaitlyn laid her napkin on the table and pushed her plate away. "I simply can't eat another bite."

Zack's gaze moved to the pulse throbbing in the hollow of her throat. "A bite," he murmured. The scent of her blood, the need to taste her, was driving him crazy.

"What?"

"Would you like dessert?" he asked, dragging his gaze from the smooth, slender line of her neck.

"No, thank you," she said, certain she couldn't eat anything else. Until she saw the dessert cart. Brownies. Seven-layer chocolate cake with fudge frosting. Deep-dish apple pie. Dainty strawberry tarts. Tapioca pudding topped with cherries. Cheesecake.

"Are you sure?" Zack asked with a wry grin. "Your words say no, but your eyes are saying, 'Oh, yes.'"

Kaitlyn bit down on her lower lip. Her vampire cousins were jealous because she could still eat mortal food. And because, no matter how much she ate, she never gained an ounce. "Maybe a slice of that cake," she decided. "With a scoop of ice cream."

Women and chocolate, Zack thought, amused by the nearly ecstatic expression on Kaitlyn's face as she sampled the cake.

"What?" she asked when she caught him staring.

He shook his head, but he couldn't help wondering if he could put that same look of sheer pleasure on her face.

"So," he said when she finished her dessert, "what are you in the mood for now?"

"I don't know. Did you have something in mind?"

He could think of several things he'd like to do, none

of which he thought she would agree to, since they all involved the two of them romping naked in his bed.

"Zack?"

He shook the images of the two of them from his mind. "Do you want to try your luck at craps?"

She considered it a moment, then said, "No, I don't think so."

His gaze moved over her, a caress more than a look. "We could go upstairs."

"What's up there?" she asked, her eyes narrowing with suspicion.

Zack chuckled, amused by her wary expression. Did she think he had some nefarious scheme in mind, like spiriting her away and ravishing her until dawn? Not that that was such a bad idea. He wondered what she would say if he suggested it, then chided himself for being a fool. She was a nice girl. Way too nice for a guy like him.

"The Skylight Room," he replied. "Soft music. Good champagne. Dancing under the stars."

Kaitlyn hesitated. She hadn't had a lot of experience with men. She sensed that Zack Ravenscroft wasn't like ordinary men, although she wasn't sure what there was about him that set him apart. He carried an aura of danger, but that didn't frighten her. She could take care of herself. Maybe it was the fact that she found him so attractive. Almost irresistibly so. His voice, his roguish smile, both were hard to resist. Still, there wasn't much future for them. Even though her father had repealed the laws that once forbade her people to marry mortals, she knew her parents would be disappointed if she didn't marry someone from home. There was no possibility that she could ever marry Zack.

Marry Zack! Good grief, where had that thought come from? She had just met the man.

"Kaitlyn?"

He was watching her intently, making her glad he couldn't read her mind, although she would have loved to read his. Of course, being able to eavesdrop on people's private thoughts was a mixed blessing. There had been times in college when she had lowered her guard to steal into someone's thoughts, and then heard something she wished she hadn't. Like the time Kaitlyn learned her supposed best friend forever was telling everyone that Kaitlyn was sleeping with her anthropology teacher and that was why she was getting such good grades.

"It's just a dance," Zack said in his soft, oh, so sexy voice.

And the perfect excuse to be in his arms, Kaitlyn thought as he took her hand in his and led her to a glass-sided elevator that whisked them to the top floor of the building.

The Skylight Room was lovely. The walls were white, the drapes a soft blue. Small round tables were scattered along the edge of the dance floor. A pianist, two guitarists, and a drummer provided music, which was slow, soft, and sensual. It was easy to see where the room got its name. A huge skylight took up most of the ceiling. A million stars twinkled overhead. Moonlight shimmered through the glass. It was, she thought, like walking among the stars, although it was nothing like the ballroom at the Fortress.

Zack gestured at the dance floor. "Shall we?"

"Isn't that what we're here for?" she asked with a playful grin.

He didn't answer, simply drew her into his arms.

He was a wonderful dancer, light on his feet, easy to follow. She searched her mind for something to say, but small talk eluded her. How could she be expected to think coherently with his body pressed so intimately against hers? They were, she thought, a perfect fit. The scent of his cologne tickled her nostrils, his very nearness was intoxicating, as was the scent of his blood. But that was to be expected. She was half vampire, after all, a fact that had been confirmed on her twentieth birthday.

Her father had been with her when the change occurred. He had told her she could resist it if she desired, but that doing so would make it more difficult later. Taking his advice, she had surrendered to the need that night. He had warned her that undergoing the change might be violent, that she could possibly be overcome with the need to kill, but it hadn't happened like that. A yearning for blood had been niggling at her for weeks. Surrendering to it had seemed the most natural thing in the world. Her father had taken her hunting. She had not enjoyed the hunt, but her need for blood had been easily satisfied, with little harm done to the young man who had been her chosen prey.

"You must feed often the first year," her father had told her. "If you don't, it could be fatal."

"And after that?" she had asked.

"As often as you feel the need."

He had frequently gone hunting with her during the first few months to make sure she didn't have any problems.

"You're very quiet," Zack mused, wishing he could read her thoughts. "Is something wrong?"

"No." She smiled wistfully. "I was just lost in the past."

"Anything you want to share?"

"I was thinking about my father. You remind me of him."

He grimaced. "I'm not sure I like that."

"You should be pleased. He's a wonderful man."

"I'm sure he is. He's got a wonderful daughter."

"Flatterer."

"Just callin' it the way I see it." He drew her closer, his gaze intent on her face. "Are you feeling what I'm feeling?"

She knew what he meant; she just wasn't sure she was ready to admit it to herself. Or to him. Things were moving way too fast. She had only known him for a few hours. All she knew for certain was that he was drop-dead gorgeous, danced divinely, and owned a popular casino. Hardly enough on which to base a solid relationship. But somehow, with his arms around her and his devil dark eyes gazing into hers, nothing else seemed to matter.

One song blended into another, and then another, and they continued to dance, making Kaitlyn think he was as reluctant to release her as she was for him to let her go.

They shared several long, lingering glances, though few words were spoken between them.

The other patrons all left the room.

And Zack and Kaitlyn continued to dance, just the two of them, even after the musicians called it a night.

Usually, it made Kaitlyn uncomfortable when men stared at her for too long, but it pleased her that Zack couldn't stop looking at her, because she couldn't stop looking at him, either. His eyes were like dark, mysterious pools and she longed to dive in, to swim to the bottom and discover the hidden depths of his soul.

She smiled at her fanciful thoughts.

"What are you thinking about?"

"Nothing you need to know."

"Is that right?" Zack twirled her around, dipped her once, and drew her into his arms again, his gaze lingering on her lips, sliding down to the pulse throbbing in the hollow of her throat, then back to her delectable lips.

Kaitlyn shivered with anticipation. He was going to kiss her. She could see it in his eyes.

And even then he was lowering his head, claiming her lips with his.

She had never been drunk, never been high on anything, but his kiss made her feel like she was invincible, like she was soaring through rainbow-colored clouds. Like she never wanted to come down.

And it was just one kiss.

She had been right about him, Kaitlyn thought dreamily, one hand pressed to her rapidly beating heart. He was dangerous, in more ways than one.

"Can I see you tomorrow night?" he asked, his voice husky. "Say, around eight?"

Every instinct she possessed warned her that she was treading on shaky ground. As much as she wanted to see him again, she knew she had to refuse. She meant to say no, but the word that emerged from her throat was a breathless "yes."

Chapter 3

The watcher frowned as he observed Ravenscroft walking the heir to the Sherrad throne home. When had the casino owner and the woman met? Was this just a casual encounter, or something more serious? Did it matter? And how was he to find out?

He muttered a pithy oath. With Zack Ravenscroft in the picture, things had just gotten a lot more complicated.

And a hell of a lot more dangerous.

He shook his head, then flipped open his cell phone and called home.

Chapter 4

Kaitlyn woke feeling bleary-eyed. A glance at the clock showed she had slept later than usual, and it was all Zack Ravenscroft's fault. Last night, every time she had closed her eyes, his countenance sprang to mind while her vivid imagination painted ever-more erotic scenes of the two of them making mad passionate love in her bed. On the floor. On the kitchen table. In the shower. How was a girl supposed to get any sleep with all those full-color scenarios running rampant in her head?

She would see him again tonight. The thought brought a quick smile to her face and unleashed butterflies of anticipation in the pit of her stomach. She couldn't remember ever being this excited about a date. She could hardly wait!

After showering, she pulled on a pair of sweatpants and a T-shirt and went into the kitchen. It was too late for lunch, too early for dinner. She couldn't help grinning when she poured herself a small glass of AB negative. What would Zack think if he knew she was a vampire? Would he be horrified? Shocked? Disbelieving? Intrigued? Or totally turned off. Not that it mattered, because he could never, ever, know the truth. It was forbidden to tell mortals about their kind; still, it was fun to imagine what his reaction would be to the word *vampire*.

Of course, her people weren't the monsters of myth and legend. They didn't go around ripping out people's throats or draining their victims dry. Back home, there were mortals who willingly offered their blood in exchange for food and shelter and a peaceful way of life in an Old World stone castle known as the Carpa-thian Fortress. She was certain that most ordinary people would find it appalling that men and women lived there by choice, but that was the way it was now that her father was the Master of the Coven. Before her father came to power, people had been confined in the Fortress against their will. Not mistreated, of course, but kept as a ready food supply. Once, her uncle Andrei had told her, in strictest confidence, that the captives had been called sheep.

Kaitlyn was glad that way of life was gone. She rarely hunted humans. Her need for blood wasn't all-consuming, in part, she supposed, because her mother was mortal.

Kaitlyn smiled inwardly as she sat at the table. Years ago, when her father met her mother, it had been forbidden for vampires and mortals to intermarry, and rare for their union to produce children. Rare, but not impossible, Kaitlyn mused, sipping her drink. She was proof of that.

Even though it was extremely uncommon for Romanian vampires to mingle in society with humans, her uncle Stefan had fallen in love with a mortal woman, too, and gotten her with child. Sadly, the woman and her baby had died in childbirth. Her father said Stefan had never gotten over the loss. Years later, her uncle had left the Fortress and gone to America.

Frowning, Kaitlyn sipped her drink. Maybe she could hire someone to search for him, she thought, then shook her head. She had no idea if her uncle was still in the United States, or what name he might be using now. Still, trying to locate him was something to think about.

Rising, she rinsed her glass in the sink and put it in the dishwasher. It was Monday. Laundry day. In the bedroom, she opened a suitcase stuffed with dirty sweatpants, T-shirts, and shorts. She had been in such a hurry to get here, she'd just stuffed her favorite work-out clothes into a suitcase to wash later. Gathering up her dirty clothes, she headed for the service porch. She dropped everything in the washer, added detergent and fabric softener, and hit START.

She stood there a moment, marveling at all the modern conveniences in America. Back home, in Wolf-ram Castle, washers and dryers, refrigerators and indoor plumbing were relatively new arrivals. Before her father married her mother, the castle had been pos-itively medieval, with no creature comforts to speak of.

Kaitlyn couldn't help smiling when she thought of her parents. She had never seen a couple so much in love. Even now, after more than twenty years of mar-riage, her mother and father behaved like newlyweds, at least when they thought no one was looking. But Kaitlyn had caught them in the midst of some pretty heavy-duty hugging and kissing on more than one occasion.

"I just hope that you and your future husband will feel this way when you have been married as long as your mother and I," her father had remarked when she caught them embracing in the kitchen one night. Kait-lyn couldn't have agreed more.

Thinking about hugs and kisses brought Zack Ravens-croft to mind. "Mrs. Kaitlyn Ravenscroft," she murmured, giggling like a schoolgirl. "Mr. and Mrs. Zack Ravenscroft. Mrs. Zack Ravenscroft."

Arms outstretched, she twirled around and around, wishing she could speed up time or twitch her nose and make him appear. The thought made her laugh. She had several inherent powers; she could run faster than the eye could follow, she could veil her presence from mortals, she could read their minds—well, most of them, she amended—but making people appear at will wasn't one of her talents. Sadly, since she wasn't a full-blooded vampire, she lacked her father's ability to dissolve into mist, or to transport herself wherever she wished to be. He had told her to be patient, that those abilities might come to her when she was older, but he hadn't sounded very convinced when he said it. Still, if she had to choose between being able to transport herself across great distances or being able to eat anything she wanted and being able to endure the sun's light, she thought she would take the latter two. After all, how often did she need to zap herself to another location when she had a Porsche in the driveway and her father's credit card if she needed to hop a plane?

With a shake of her head, Kaitlyn left the laundry room. As her mother had always said, the best way to make time fly was to keep busy.

Kaitlyn glanced at the clock. It was almost four. Plenty of time to fold the laundry, make the bed, vacuum the rugs, and make herself beautiful before her date arrived.

Zack rose with the setting of the sun. For the first time since he had built the casino, his first waking thought wasn't about going to work, but about a woman. Kaitlyn. She had been foremost in his thoughts since the minute she'd walked into the club. Not that he was complaining. He was more than happy to have a beautiful young woman running around in his head. In fact, he'd be happy as hell to have her take up permanent residence there.

He grinned, thinking the lovely Kaitlyn must have bewitched him. Sure, he was crazy about women. Always had been, but he had always loved them and left them, never looking back, rarely remembering their names once he told them good-bye. But Kaitlyn, she was different. And even though all they had shared so far was one mind-blowing kiss, he sensed he would never forget her.

With a shake of his head, he left his lair and went up the private stairway to his apartment where he took a quick shower and changed into a clean shirt and a pair of pants. If he didn't hurry, he would be late.

He was doing a quick walk-through of the casino floor, on his way out, when he had the sudden sense that he was being watched. Pausing near the dice table, Zack pretended to be interested in the game while he let his preternatural powers expand. Sounds grew louder, colors brighter, smells sharper and more intense.

He glanced casually around the casino, his gaze resting quickly on each patron. It was still early. The crowd was light. He had no sense of another vampire on the premises, no scent of werewolf, and yet he would have sworn there was another supernatural creature in the building, although there was no trace of it now. Had he imagined it?

He finished his walk-through, stopped to talk with a few of the pit bosses, conferred briefly with the head of security, and left the casino, bound for Kaitlyn's.

She opened the door before he knocked, a smile of welcome on her face. Dressed in a pair of white slacks and a lavender sweater, her cheeks flushed with color, she was even prettier than he remembered.

"So," she said, "what do you want to do tonight?"

"Take a walk?" he suggested. "Go for a drive? See a movie?"

"It's a nice night for a walk," Kaitlyn said.

"Then that's what we'll do."

Kaitlyn felt the same peculiar sensation she had on other occasions when he took her hand in his. Not a chill, exactly, more like a warm shiver of awareness that she felt all the way down to her toes.

She pondered her strange reaction to him as they walked down the narrow, tree-lined path toward the lake. Maybe what she felt for Zack wasn't all that extraordinary. He was an extremely handsome man, after all, and there was no denying that she was physically attracted to him. But then, what woman wouldn't be?

The night seemed to close in around the two of them as they neared the lake, which gleamed like a dark mirror in the light of the full moon.

Zack paused at the edge of the water where someone had thoughtfully placed a wooden bench just big enough for two. He waited until Kaitlyn sat down and then sat beside her, one arm resting on the back of the bench. A warm breeze, carrying the fecund scent of earth and foliage, rustled the leaves of the trees. A fish popped up in the middle of the lake, sending ever-widening ripples across the face of the water.

"It's lovely here," Kaitlyn said. "Do you ever come here to swim?"

"Now and then. Do you like swimming?"

She nodded. "My father taught me when I was a little girl." She would never forget how much fun it had been to go swimming with her dad. Of course, they'd had to go at night, but she had never been afraid, not when he was there. Before she was old enough to swim, he had let her sit on his chest while he floated in the water. The most fun had been clinging to his back while he swam swiftly, effortlessly, from one end of the lake to the other and back again.

"What else do you like to do?" Zack asked.

"Oh, lots of things. I enjoy going to movies and plays and doing crossword puzzles. I don't like to cook, but I love to bake." She smiled at him. "I make a really wicked strawberry pie," she said. "I'll have to bake you one."

Zack nodded. "Anything else?"

"I love to read."

"Me, too." He had spent many a long, lonely night in the company of a good book. "What do you like to read?"

"You'll laugh."

"Why would I laugh?"

"Because I like to read old fairy tales."

He didn't laugh, but he couldn't hold back a grin. "You mean like *Little Red Riding Hood* and *Sleeping Beauty?*"

"Yes, but my favorite is *Beauty and the Beast*. It's such a wonderful story, the way Belle learns to love the Beast in spite of his gruff attitude and fearsome appearance."

"I guess you're really into those happily-ever-after endings."

"What's wrong with that?"

"Nothing." He glanced out over the water, wondering if he would ever have a happy ending of his own. "I guess everybody wants one."

"So, what do you like to read?"

"Murder mysteries. Arthur Conan Doyle. Dashiell Hammett. Mickey Spillane."

"Blood and guts, huh?" she asked with a grin. "Death on every page."

He had to laugh at that. She had no idea.

"What's so funny?" she asked, frowning.

"I was just thinking how far apart our tastes are in books." And in food and drink and sleeping habits, he added silently.

"So, Mr. Macho Man, what do you like to do?"

"Oh, you know," he said, flexing his muscles. "The usual manly things. Watch extreme sports on TV. Gamble. Drink too much. Drive too fast."

She punched him in the arm. "Be serious."

"I know what I'd like to do right now," he said, his voice soft and seductive.

A thousand butterflies took wing in Kaitlyn's stomach. There was no mistaking the desire in his eyes. "Oh?" Her voice emerged as little more than a squeak.

His finger traced the curve of her cheek. "Shall I show you?"

She swallowed. "Will I like it?"

"I think so." He drew her closer, his voice low and husky in her ear. "I hope so," he said, and kissed her.

Her eyelids fluttered down as she turned into his embrace. Her arms went around his waist, and she hugged him tight as she lost herself in the wonder and magic of being near him, of having his mouth on hers. He smelled of sandalwood cologne and musk. The combined scents made her stomach curl with pleasure. A delightful warmth spread through her, leaving her feeling weak and exhilarated at the same time. She moaned softly when his tongue stroked hers.

Pulling away, she fanned herself with one hand.

Zack looked at her, a smug, masculine grin tugging at the corners of his mouth.

Kaitlyn blew out a breath. "I think I need a drink."

He nodded, reluctant to let her go when he wanted nothing more than to swing her into his arms and carry her to bed, to touch and taste her all night long. But maybe it was better to take it slow.

"As it happens," he said, tamping down both his desire and his hunger, "I know a place that serves a great strawberry daiquiri."

"As tempting as that sounds, I think I'd better go home."

"Are you sure?"

Kaitlyn nodded. Going home was the last thing she wanted to do, but right now, it was the safest thing. For both of them.

She was vaguely disappointed when Zack didn't argue. Instead, he took her hand and drew her to her feet.

She tried to think of something to say while they walked up the path, but words failed her. She couldn't tell him the truth—couldn't tell him she was fighting an almost desperate yearning, not only for the taste of his blood, but a hunger for his body, as well.

Better to let him think that she was a prude, or that things were moving too fast, rather than let him know the truth.

Chapter 5

After bidding Kaitlyn a reluctant good night, Zack willed himself to the city, which was roughly twenty miles from the casino. It might have been smarter to build his place closer to the general population, but he liked the club's solitary location, liked having some distance between himself and the tourists after the casino closed for the night.

It wasn't easy, being constantly surrounded by the lure of beating hearts and the coppery scent of blood. It was easier to ignore temptation when it was far away. But tonight, his hunger wouldn't be denied.

He knew it was only his imagination, but it seemed that even here, miles away from her cabin, he could still hear the beating of Kaitlyn's heart, smell the sweetness of her blood.

Hunger drew him to an all-night café. Pausing inside the door, he opened his preternatural senses and quickly scanned the room. The man at the far table was drunk. The couple in the booth was too old. The woman sitting near the window was an actress down on her luck, but she was young and smelled clean.

With an effort of will, he called to her, then stepped out onto the sidewalk to wait.

A moment later, she was there, her eyes void of expression as she waited to do his bidding. Taking her by the hand, he led her down the street and into an alley between two commercial buildings.

A search of her mind revealed her name. "Alice."

She looked up at him, her expression blank.

"Relax, Alice," he murmured, taking her into his arms. "I'm not going to hurt you."

She gazed up at him, her lips slightly parted, her heart pounding with fear.

Zack brushed her hair over her shoulder, his fingertips trailing down the length of her neck while his mind invaded hers. She was a lovely girl who had left her home in Montana, certain that having a pretty face was all she needed to make it in Hollywood. Having failed that, she was ashamed to go back home and admit defeat.

It was an all-too-familiar story. Bending his head to her neck, he took what he needed, wishing, all the time, that it was Kaitlyn in his arms, her blood chasing away the coldness within him.

When he had taken his fill, he captured the girl's gaze with his. "You will remember none of this," he said quietly. "Do you understand?"

She nodded, her eyes still blank.

"Where are you staying tonight?"

"At the hotel down the street."

"All right. I want you to go there now and go to bed." Reaching into his pocket, Zack pulled out a handful of bills and pressed them into her hand. "Tomorrow, you're going to buy a plane ticket and go home." He stroked her cheek. "You will not remember me, or this conversation."

She nodded again.

"Tell me again what you're you going to do tomorrow."

"I'm going home."

And even though she was in a trance, he heard the happiness, the relief, in her voice.

Zack sent her on her way and then, unable to resist, he willed himself to Kaitlyn's place. The house was dark, but that was no surprise. It was late.

Standing outside her bedroom window, he listened to the slow, steady beat of her heart, the quiet even sound of her breathing. Funny, he thought, how the sounds soothed him.

Assured that she was home and safely asleep in her bed, he headed down the mountain.

Chapter 6

Kaitlyn slept late, fixed a big breakfast, and then, at loose ends, wandered through the cabin trying to find something to do. The laundry was done. The dishes were done. She had vacuumed yesterday. Bored, she rearranged the dishes in the kitchen cupboards, rearranged the furniture in the living room, and then put it all back the way it had been before.

Standing in the middle of the room, she glanced around, thinking that, since she lived alone and was naturally tidy, the place would never really get dirty.

When she ran out of make-work things to do, she sat on the sofa and filed her nails and tried to decide what she should do, now that she was out of college. She didn't need money, but she did need something to keep her busy during the day. A job, she thought. That was the answer. Of course, there wasn't much call for an expert in comparative folklore these days. Still, she was reasonably intelligent—there must be something she could do.

With that thought in mind, she decided to walk down to the casino. She could buy a newspaper there and check out the want ads while she ate lunch at the restaurant.

And if she was lucky, she might run into Zack.

It took only minutes to make her way down the hill to the casino restaurant. After a short wait, she was seated at a small table near the back window. She ordered a turkey club sandwich and a strawberry lemonade, then opened the paper she had picked up in the lobby and perused the help-wanted section. She frowned as she looked at the available jobs. Waitress. Maid at one of the hotels. Babysitter. Clerk at the Pink Poodle Boutique. Dog walker. Checker at one of the local markets.

She folded the paper with a huff of exasperation. There was nothing wrong with any of those positions; they were all perfectly respectable. It was just that she had been hoping, foolishly perhaps, that she would find something where she could use her degree. Zack would probably laugh at that. She recalled his response all too clearly when she had told him she had majored in comparative folklore, the amusement in his tone when he had drawled, *How's that workin' out for ya?*

Maybe she could write a book on ancient folklore. In 1890, Sir James George Fraser had done a colossal study of comparative folklore. Originally published in two volumes and later in multiple volumes, an abridged version had been published in 1922. Considered a classic, *The Golden Bough* had greatly influenced psychology and literature, presenting, in detail, the parallels between the rites, beliefs, and superstitions of early cultures and those of Christianity.

She doubted she could pen such an important tome, but maybe she could write something a little less intense, perhaps something better suited to modern times. It was something to think about.

After finishing her lunch, Kaitlyn wandered out into the casino. It wasn't nearly as crowded or as noisy at this time of day as it had been the other night. Most of the patrons were elderly. A few people stood in front of the Wheel of Fortune, others were trying their luck at the dice table, or playing roulette. The majority seemed to be playing the slot machines.

After a moment's indecision, she took a seat at one of the quarter machines. It was an old one, with a coin slot and a handle to pull. After a few minutes of play, she found that she liked the old machine better than the new ones. It was more fun to actually put the money into the machine and pull the handle, to hear the clink of quarters falling into the tray when she won. It made it seem more like playing than merely watching.

She kept glancing over her shoulder, hoping to see Zack striding toward her, even though she knew it would be better for both of them if their relationship ended now, before it went any further.

After an hour, she was ahead by about twenty dollars. Gathering her winnings into a handy plastic bucket, she carried it to the cashier and exchanged the coins for greenbacks.

"Do come again," the cashier said, smiling as she completed the transaction.

"Thanks, I will," Kaitlyn said, stuffing the bills into her wallet. "Um, do you know if Mr. Ravenscroft is here today?"

"He doesn't usually arrive until seven or eight," the woman said. "If you'd like to leave a message, I'll be sure that he gets it."

"No. No, that's all right. Thank you."

Feeling more let-down than she should have, Kaitlyn

left the casino. She stood outside a moment, then returned to the casino and headed for the dress shop.

Zack rose with the setting sun, his first thought for Kaitlyn. Although they hadn't made plans to meet tonight, he headed for her cabin as soon as he made certain that everything was running smoothly on the casino floor.

To his surprise, she was standing on the porch looking sexy as hell in a pair of tight black leather pants, a matching midriff top, and black high-heeled sandals. Her hair tumbled over her shoulders like a fall of black silk.

He whistled softly as he climbed the stairs. "You look like a million bucks," he said with a wink. "And I know what that looks like."

She smiled, her stomach curling at his nearness.

"I hope you're out here waiting for me," Zack said, resting his hip against one of the uprights. "I know we didn't have any plans, but . . ."

She placed two fingers over his mouth, silencing him. "Who else would I be waiting for?"

"How did you know I'd show up?"

"I didn't, but a girl can hope, can't she?"

"So, what shall we do tonight?" He knew what he wanted to do, horny lecherous creature that he was, but he didn't suggest the ideas that quickly came to mind, certain that her answer would be no. His lovely Kaitlyn didn't seem the type to tumble into bed with a man unless there was a wedding ring on her finger.

"I don't care. Anything you want to do is fine with me."

He lifted one brow. "Anything?"

Kaitlyn felt a blush warm her cheeks. She didn't have to be able to read Zack's mind to know what he was thinking. Because she was thinking about it, too, and far too often for her own good. But there was no way she was jumping into bed with Zack, no matter how tempting he might be. She hardly knew the man.

"I enjoyed dancing the other night," she said.

"Dancing it is, then. Shall we walk?"

"Why not?" She stepped out of her high-heeled sandals. Holding them by the ankle straps, she swung them back and forth as she walked. "It's a lovely night."

It was indeed, Zack mused as they strolled down the narrow path that ended at the casino parking lot. The air was warm, fragrant with the scent of Kaitlyn's perfume, with the heady scent of the woman herself.

And overall, the siren call of her life's blood running through her veins like a warm red river. The rhythm of her heartbeat hummed in his ears like a symphony only he could hear.

"Watch your step," he warned when they reached the curb. He held her arm, steadying her, as she scrubbed her feet clean on the grass, then stepped into her shoes. He liked it that she wasn't overly fussy, that she didn't mind getting her feet a little dirty.

It was early Tuesday night but the casino was already crowded. With his preternatural power, Zack heard the hum of the air-conditioning, the whisper of cards being shuffled, the whirring of the Wheel of Fortune, the click-click of dice at the craps table, the high-pitched shout of a gambler who had just hit the jackpot on one of the slot machines.

"Have you had dinner?" Zack asked, raising his voice a little so Kaitlyn could hear him.

"I'm not hungry," she replied. "I had a late lunch, but I'll keep you company if you haven't eaten."

"No need. I had a bite before I came to your place."

Taking her hand, he headed for the elevator that led to the Skylight Room.

Since most people were more interested in dining than dancing at this hour, Zack and Kaitlyn had the dance floor to themselves.

Kaitlyn felt a sensual thrill when Zack took her in his arms. She marveled that they fit together so well, that his steps were so easy to follow, that the mere touch of his hand made her heart beat faster. *It isn't love,* she told herself sternly. *It's just an old-fashioned case of lust.* And who could blame her? She doubted any woman whose heart was still beating would be able to resist Zack, with his long black hair, enigmatic gray eyes, and delightfully wicked grin. His brows were slightly arched, his nose straight, his lips full, sensual. He was tall and broad-shouldered, and sexier than any man she had ever met. He looked especially handsome tonight in a pair of black slacks and a long-sleeved midnight-blue shirt.

He lifted one brow, amused by her steady regard. "Like what you see?"

Embarrassment heated Kaitlyn's cheeks. She wanted to say she had seen better, thank you very much. Instead, she shrugged and turned the question back to him. "Do you? Like what you see?"

"You know I do." He twirled her around the floor, spinning her effortlessly until she was dizzy. "And I'd like to see more of you. Much more."

She searched her mind for some witty comeback, but words failed her.

Zack chuckled as he pulled her closer. "I'm sorry if the truth makes you uncomfortable."

"I guess it does," she replied with unexpected candor. "A little anyway."

"I don't know why. A girl who's as pretty as you must get compliments from guys all the time."

"Yes, but . . ."

"But?"

She tilted her head back so she could look into his eyes. "They're usually after something."

"Can't blame them for that," he replied, his gaze drifting to the pulse throbbing in the hollow of her throat.

"What are you after, Zack?" she asked. "What do *you* want?"

"You," he answered quietly. "Every inch of you, in every way possible. I want to start at the top of your head and nibble my way down to your toes."

"Well, I'll give you this—you're more honest than most." After the image he had painted in her mind, it was an effort to keep her voice steady.

The music changed tempo, going from an oldies song to something slower and more romantic.

Zack held her closer, tighter. Straps crisscrossed the back of her top, leaving parts of her back bare to the touch of his hand. His dark eyes burned into hers, hot and hungry. Kaitlyn's heart skipped a beat. She had seen looks like that before, in the eyes of her father's people. But Zack didn't belong to her father's coven, or any coven.

Still, the look unsettled her and when the music ended, she told Zack she needed to sit down. She wasn't tired, but she needed to put some space between them. She couldn't think clearly when he was holding her, when he was looking at her like that, as if he was a hungry cat, and she a tasty mouse.

He escorted her to a nearby table, held her chair for her. "How about a drink?" he asked, and when she nodded, he pulled his cell phone from his pocket and called the bar in the casino.

"Why didn't you just order from the bar up here?" Kaitlyn asked.

"That's for the tourists. I have my own private stock downstairs."

Less than five minutes later, a waiter arrived at their table carrying a bottle of *Clos Du Mesnil* champagne and a bottle of *Dom Pérignon Rosé*. A waitress arrived moments later bearing a tray with a pair of crystal goblets and a plate of canapés.

Zack dismissed the help with a smile, then gestured at the bottles. "What's your pleasure?"

"I don't know anything about champagne."

"Well, the *Clos Du Mesnil* costs about seven hundred dollars; the *Dom Pérignon* about half that."

"Are you kidding me? Seven hundred dollars for a bottle of champagne?" She shook her head in amazement. "I have got to try that."

He filled two glasses with liquid that was straw gold in color, then handed her one. "What shall we drink to?"

"Beginnings?" she suggested.

"Beginnings," he repeated, and touched his glass to hers.

He watched her over the rim of his glass as he sipped his wine, and for one moment out of time, Kaitlyn imagined his lips pressed against the side of her neck, his tongue lightly stroking her skin.

"Katy, let's go where we can be alone."

She nibbled one of the canapés, then shook her head. "I don't think that's a good idea."

"Why not? Are you afraid of me?"

"Yes."

He sat back, his brow furrowing. "What are you afraid of?"

"The way you make me feel. We're moving way too fast. I hardly know you."

"What do you want to know?"

She sipped her drink, then set her glass aside. "Everything."

"Everything, huh?" He dragged a hand over his jaw. "My parents are dead. I'm an only child. I'm rich and single and I'm crazy about you. What else do you need to know?"

"How old are you?"

"Thirty-one."

"When's your birthday?"

"August the fourth."

"A Leo," she said, smiling.

He nodded. "You?"

"I'm an Aries."

"Both fire signs," he mused.

"Are you into astrology?"

"No, not really."

"Do you read your horoscope every day?"

"No," he said, laughing. "Why, do you?"

"No. Well, not every day."

"How old are you?"

Grinning, she said, "Don't you know it isn't polite to ask a woman her age?"

"At least tell me you're over twenty-one."

Kaitlyn laughed. "No worries. I turned twenty-one on my last birthday."

"Just a baby." He wondered what she would think if she knew how old he really was. "Do you have brothers and sisters?"

"No. My mom wanted more children, but . . ." She shrugged. "I would have liked a brother or a sister, but it wasn't meant to be. My dad comes from a really large family though, so I have lots of aunts and uncles and cousins. Of course, there was a plus side to being an only child," she said, grinning. "My parents spoiled me rotten when I was growing up." She ran her finger around the rim of her glass, her expression thoughtful. "They still spoil me rotten."

Zack nodded. He would love to pamper her, to give her everything her heart desired, to show her all the wonders of the modern world. To introduce her to the magic between a man and a woman.

"Why did you call me Katy?"

He shrugged. "Doesn't everyone?"

"No. No one." She smiled a shy smile. "I like it."

He leaned toward her, his gaze resting on her face. "Come home with me, Katy."

"Zack . . . I can't."

"Just my luck," he said with a good-natured grin. "You're a good girl."

"'Fraid so." She couldn't blame him for having thought otherwise, considering the sexy "come and get me" outfit she was wearing.

He nodded. He might be a lot of things, but he had never forced a woman into his bed, or taken advantage of a virgin, although Kaitlyn tempted him sorely. He was about to refill their glasses when his cell phone rang.

Murmuring, "Excuse me," he put the phone to his ear. "What is it?" He listened a moment, then slipped the phone back into his pocket. "I need to take care of something in the casino. I'll be back shortly."

"All right." Lifting her glass, she watched him walk swiftly toward a door marked STAIRWAY.

She sat there a moment, thinking about Zack. He wanted her; there was no doubt about that. And she wanted him. There was no doubt about that, either. She glanced at her watch, drummed her fingertips on the table as she wondered what kind of emergency— if that's what it was—had called him away. Too curious to wait any longer, she took the elevator down to the main floor.

The first thing she noticed was the silence. Standing in the doorway, she glanced around, searching for Zack. She gasped when she saw him. He was standing in front of one of the poker tables. On the other side of the table, a man wearing a Hell's Angel leather jacket stood holding the edge of a knife to the dealer's throat. The dealer's face was paper-white, a vivid contrast to the angry red flush on the face of the Hell's Angel wielding the blade.

"He cheated!" the man declared, his voice carrying throughout the casino. "He's dealing from the bottom of the deck!"

"Put the knife down," Zack said. "And we'll talk about it."

The man shook his head. "I want my money back! And I want this cheat fired!"

Zack looked at the dealer. "Were you cheating, Henry?"

Kaitlyn frowned as a ripple of power raised the hair along her arms. Was that coming from Zack? It felt much like the preternatural power her father possessed.

"No, sir," Henry said, his voice laced with fear. "He's just a sore loser."

"He's lying!" the man insisted.

Kaitlyn couldn't see Zack's face. He stood there, unmoving, as that same ripple of power washed over her.

When he spoke again, his words were slow and distinct, and there was a peculiar edge to his voice. "I want you to put the knife down, Farris, and follow me outside."

Kaitlyn frowned, wondering how Zack knew the troublemaker's name. Was he a regular at the casino?

Farris glared at Zack for stretched seconds, then he dropped the knife on the table and followed Zack out of the casino.

Kaitlyn waited until Zack and Farris were outside, then hurried after them. She paused just beyond the entrance, her gaze darting left and right, but there was no sign of either man.

How had they disappeared so quickly? Puzzled, she left the casino. She had a lot to think about and she couldn't do it here.

It took only moments to navigate the path home. Kicking off her shoes, she went into the kitchen and fixed a cup of hot chocolate, then curled up on the sofa, the cup cradled in her hands as her mind replayed the scene at the poker table. She hadn't imagined the power that rippled through the air when Zack spoke. She had felt it too often in the past to mistake it for anything but what it was—the same kind of preternatural power that her father and others of their kind were able to command. Was it possible that Zack Ravenscroft was one of them? She had never seen him eat, but that didn't prove anything. At dinner the other night, he had said he'd already eaten. She'd had no reason to disbelieve him then, and none tonight. He drank wine, but so did millions of other people. He possessed a strong aura of danger, but, again, that didn't prove anything. But that rush of preternatural power—no mortal possessed that kind of supernatural energy.

What if Zack really was a vampire?

Kaitlyn shook her head. If that was true, it changed everything.

Chapter 7

Standing in the shadows, the watcher followed Kaitlyn home. His first task was to learn all he could about her. Thus far, he hadn't accomplished much of his goal. All he knew was that she was able to abide the sun, a fact he had learned while he lurked outside her house at sunset and saw her walking up the path, a grocery sack tucked under one arm. It was obvious she had left the house earlier in the day. He presumed she was able to walk by day because of her tainted blood. The second thing he had learned was that she could still eat mortal food, something that should no longer have been possible for her.

She was also very beautiful, a dark-haired angel with pale golden skin and sky-blue eyes.

He thrust the thought away. Lovely or ugly, it mattered not. He had a job to do, and he would do it. To fail was to incur his mother's wrath, and that was worse than death itself.

Chapter 8

As soon as Zack returned to the casino, he knew that Kaitlyn had gone. Frowning, he went to the bar and ordered a drink from his special blend. Why had she left without a word?

Standing with his back to the bar, he perused the room. The patrons had returned to their games of chance as if nothing out of the ordinary had happened. He grinned inwardly. Mortals had ridiculously short memories.

With a sigh, he sipped his drink, a tasty concoction of chardonnay and type O, as his thoughts returned to Kaitlyn. Had she been bothered by the earlier disturbance? He considered that possibility a moment, then shook his head. She wasn't the type to be spooked by anything so trivial. Had she grown tired of waiting for his return? He shook his head again. He hadn't been gone that long. It hadn't taken more than a few minutes to wipe his compulsion from the man's mind and send him on his way with no memory of what had occurred. So, what had prompted her to leave without a word of farewell or explanation?

He drained his glass and left it on the bar; then, as

was his wont at least once a night, he strolled through the casino. All of his employees were mortal save for the fledgling, Scherry, who was the night bartender, and two of the dealers.

Zack had sired Scherry six months ago at her request. She had been diagnosed with a rare form of leukemia. She hadn't wanted to face a lingering death and she had told him, candidly, that she didn't have the nerve to take her own life. He had never turned anyone before, but he liked Scherry. After warning her that there were no guarantees, he had taken her up to his lair late one night and brought her across. It had been an interesting experience. Other than a desperate effort to save the life of someone he loved, he had never drained anyone to the point of death before. It had been an incredible high. He still wasn't sure where he had found the willpower to stop before it was too late. But he had. And then he had given her his blood. And watched in amazement as the color returned to her cheeks, and the spark of life returned to her eyes.

The other two—Steve Walls and Jackson Lautner— had been vampires for several years. The three of them worked at the casino with the understanding that they would not prey on his customers or hunt in his territory, and the sure conviction that Zack would destroy them without a qualm if they did.

Assured that all was well on the casino floor, Zack started toward his office on the second level, then turned on his heel and left the club. Late or not, he needed to see Kaitlyn, needed to know why she hadn't waited for him to return.

Kaitlyn was watching a late movie when someone knocked on the door. She frowned when she glanced at her watch. It was a little after one A.M. Who would come calling at such an hour?

Silly question. Since she only knew one person in town, the answer was obvious.

She ran a hand over her hair and tightened the belt on her robe before she opened the door. "Do you know what time it is?"

"Four and a half minutes after one. Can I come in?"

With a sigh, she moved out of the way, felt her heart skip a beat when he stepped inside.

He closed the door behind him, then followed her into the living room, stood there while she switched off the TV.

She turned to face him, her arms crossed. "So, what brings you here at this time of the morning?"

"I couldn't sleep."

"Take a pill."

He felt his anger stir at her flippant reply. "Why did you leave?"

"Excuse me?"

"Tonight. Why didn't you wait for me?"

She sat on the sofa, her hands folded in her lap, her head tilted back slightly so she could see his face. "It was late. I didn't know how long you were going to be gone, so"—she shrugged one shoulder—"I came home. No law against it, is there?"

"Hey, I'm sorry if I offended you or . . ." He blew out an impatient breath. "Look, I just wanted to make sure you got home all right and you did, so I'll say good night."

Kaitlyn bit down on the inside corner of her lower lip as she watched him turn and walk away. What was she doing? If she didn't say something, he would leave. Did she want him to go? What if she never saw him again?

"Zack, wait!" Jumping to her feet, she hurried after him.

He stood on the porch, his expression implacable.

"I'm sorry," she murmured, not quite meeting his gaze. "I don't know what came over me. I . . ." She tapped her foot nervously, uncertain of what she wanted to say, not knowing how to phrase it. If he wasn't a vampire and she asked him if he was, he would think she was some kind of nut. On the other hand, if he was, she wanted—needed—to know.

"Listen, Katy, you don't owe me any apologies, or anything else. We had some laughs. If you want to end it—"

"No! I mean . . . no." She clasped her hands to her chest. "Tonight, at the casino, when you were confronting that man . . ."

"Yeah, what about it?" he asked, then paused, his eyes narrowing. "How do you know about that?"

"I followed you downstairs."

"Is that right?"

She shrugged. "I got tired of waiting."

He regarded her a moment. "So, you were saying?"

"What? Oh, when you were confronting that man, I thought . . . that is, I felt something . . . peculiar."

"Peculiar? In what way?" He cursed his inability to read her mind. Knowing what she was really thinking would make everything so much easier.

"Never mind. I probably just imagined it." She slid her hands into the pockets of her robe and curled them into fists. Why was it, whenever he was close to her, all she wanted to do was wrap her arms around him? What strange power did he have, that his presence should affect her so strongly? She had dated other handsome men, been held in their arms, tasted their kisses, and been unmoved. Yet a simple look from Zack, a smile, a word, and she wanted to be in his arms, naked in his bed.

She told herself again that it was nothing more than a bad case of lust, but it was getting harder and harder to convince herself that there was nothing more to it than that. "It's late. Maybe we can talk about it tomorrow night."

"Sure, Katy, whatever you want."

She smiled, thinking her nickname sounded like an endearment when he said it. She looked up at him, waiting, hoping he would kiss her good night. Just when she had given up hope, he pulled her into his embrace and lowered his head to hers.

She folded her hands over his shoulders as his mouth claimed hers in a tantalizing kiss that aroused every cell and nerve ending in her body. She pressed herself shamelessly against him, wanting to be closer, to feel the hard length of his body against hers. He tasted so good, smelled so good. Felt so good. She was sorely tempted to exert her preternatural power over him, to invite him back inside and have her way with him, and then wipe the memory of it from his mind. She had never done such a thing before—never even considered it—but there was a first time for everything. She pondered the wisdom of it another few moments, then sighed. The fact that she couldn't read his mind gave her pause. Perhaps it wouldn't work. There was no doubt she could get him into her bed. He was a man, after all. He wasn't likely to say no. But if she couldn't read his mind, maybe she wouldn't be able to erase the memory.

When he kissed her a second time, she wondered if that even mattered.

They were both breathless when, at last, he eased away from her.

"Whoa, girl," he muttered. "Unless you want me to

ravish you on the porch, right here, right now, you'd better tell me to go."

She hesitated only a moment but then, as common sense overrode desire, she murmured, "Good night, Zack."

Stepping back inside, she quietly closed and locked the door.

And instantly regretted it.

Chapter 9

Zack's head was spinning when he left Kaitlyn's house. Who the hell had taught her to kiss like that? In his time, he had kissed hundreds, maybe thousands, of women, but none had ever affected him like Kaitlyn. He hadn't been kidding when he threatened to have his way with her right there on the front porch—although a bed would suit him better. He wanted to make love to her in every way possible, to caress every inch of her sweet flesh until she cried for him to take her. And at the same time, he wanted to fold her into his arms and make love to her gently, tenderly, all night long.

And nibble on her neck while he was at it.

Returning to the casino, he went to the bar to get a drink, but he wasn't in the mood for bottled blood. He wanted something hot and fresh. Which wouldn't be a problem. Standing with his back against the bar, he unleashed his preternatural power. He could almost see it as it flowed through the room like some irresistible, invisible lure. All he had to do was focus on the woman of his choice, and wait.

Within minutes, a buxom redhead wearing a low-cut,

skintight green dress and three-inch heels sashayed toward him, her bright green eyes slightly unfocused.

"Hi," she purred in a soft, Southern accent.

"Hi, yourself." He smiled as he ran his fingertips over the inside of her wrist. He could feel the blood flowing just below the skin, hear the nervous beat of her heart.

She returned his smile, moving closer so that her thigh brushed his. "Buy me a drink, handsome?"

"Sure, honey." Grabbing a bottle one of the bartenders had left on the bar, he took her by the hand. "Come on, let's go someplace where we can be alone."

"Whatever you want, sugar."

Zack chuckled as he led her up the stairs to his private suite.

Whatever I want, he thought as he closed and locked the door.

She had no idea.

Chapter 10

Kaitlyn woke to the bothersome sound of her phone ringing. Her first thought was that it was Zack, until she realized she had never given him her phone number, an oversight she planned to remedy as soon as possible.

She smiled when she said hello and heard her father's voice on the other end of the line.

"Kaitlyn, is everything all right?"

"Of course," she said, surprised by the worry in his tone. "Why do you ask?"

"It is probably nothing, but there are rumors circulating—"

"What kind of rumors?"

"At the moment, they are vague, with no way to ascertain if there is any truth behind them. All I know is that Nadiya's name has been mentioned a few times, and that her son, Daryn, hasn't been seen lately."

"So you had to call and check up on me," Kaitlyn interjected, smiling.

"You are my only child, after all."

"Well, I'm not hiding Daryn, if that's what you're thinking." Nadiya was one of her grandfather's many wives; Daryn was her son. Kaitlyn had only met Nadiya once, but once was enough. She had never met Daryn.

Her father's laughter reminded her of home and of how much she missed it. And him.

"Seriously, I'm fine, Dad."

"You are comfortable there?"

"Of course. The cabin is wonderful, the view is terrific. I was going to go back to my apartment in L.A., but I'm thinking of staying here indefinitely."

"I see."

"What do you see?"

"Your mother is listening. She thinks there must be a man involved."

Kaitlyn grinned. She had never been able to put one past her parents. "As a matter of fact, there is. But I just met him, so don't go making any wedding plans yet."

Her father growled on the other end of the line.

"I'm kidding, Dad." Even though her father had lifted the ban forbidding their people to marry mortals, she knew he hoped she would marry one of the Romanian vampires.

"Kaitlyn, are you still there?"

"What? Oh, yes." She chewed on her lower lip as she pondered the best way to ask the question that had been niggling at her since last night. "I was wondering—is there a way for me to tell if a man is one of us?"

"You think this man you are seeing is a vampire?"

"I don't know. But last night, I would have sworn I felt a surge of preternatural power coming from him." Her father had the ability to detect those of his own kind when they were near; unfortunately, she hadn't inherited that power.

"Explain."

She quickly told her father about the events at the casino the night before.

"What is this man's name?"

"Zackary Ravenscroft. Have you ever heard of him?"

"No. If he was of our blood, I would know it."

"Maybe I just imagined it," Kaitlyn murmured. But she didn't believe that for a second.

"Perhaps. Your mother wishes to say hello. Take care of yourself."

"I will. Love you, Dad."

"I love you, too."

Kaitlyn heard muffled whispers and then her mom's voice came over the line.

"Kaitlyn, how are you, sweetie?"

"I'm fine, Mom, really. I love it here. I wish you and Dad could have stayed longer."

"Me, too, but I guess we're stuck here at the Fortress for a while until your father gets to the bottom of these rumors."

"You don't think one of the other vampires is planning a coup, do you?"

"I hope not. I was here for the last one, and believe me, it wasn't a pretty sight. Your grandmother sends her love."

Kaitlyn grinned. Her grandmother, Liliana, wasn't fond of telephones and refused to use them.

"Listen, sweetie, I've got to go. Call if you need anything."

"I will."

"All right. I love you."

"I love you more. Give Dad a hug for me. And give Aunt Katiya and Uncle Andrei my best." Though Kaitlyn had other aunts and uncles, Katiya and Andrei had always been her favorites.

"Consider it done. And keep us informed about your young man."

Kaitlyn was smiling when she ended the call. Her young man. She very much liked the sound of that.

Shortly after sunset, Kaitlyn drove to the small convenience store her mother had told her was located on the other side of the hill. "Handy for when you're in a hurry," her mother had told her, and added that there was a supermarket in the city.

Kaitlyn only needed a few things tonight. She moved up and down the aisles, quickly picking up the items on her list. She exchanged a few pleasantries with the clerk, thanked the boy who bagged her groceries, and headed for the door, a sack cradled in each arm, only to have a man stumble in front of her, jarring her shoulder and causing one of the sacks to slip from her grasp.

The man was immediately apologetic. "I'm sorry," he said, offering her a winning smile. "I wasn't looking where I was going. Of course, if I'd known how pretty you are, I would have run into you on purpose. Here," he said, when she began gathering her groceries, "let me do that."

He quickly scooped up the bread, bananas, cheese, and candy bars and dropped them into the sack which had, miraculously, remained intact, and handed it to her.

"Thank you."

"Eddie," he said, smiling again. "Eddie Harrington."

"Kaitlyn," she replied, and took a step around him.

"Hey, hold on a minute. The least I can do is buy you a cup of coffee."

"That isn't necessary."

"Please," he said. "It would make me feel better."

She hesitated. Eddie Harrington was of medium height, young and slender, with a shock of bleached blond hair and dark brown eyes. Had she been an ordinary girl, she would have refused to go with him, but she was her father's daughter. Blessed with preternatural speed and the strength of ten men, she was confident of her ability to take care of herself.

"Come on," he coaxed. "It's just a cup of coffee."

"All right."

"Great." He took one of the bags from her arm and followed her to her car.

He whistled appreciatively when she unlocked the door of the Porsche. "Nice ride!" He put the bag he was carrying on the backseat, then placed hers beside it.

"Thanks." Kaitlyn locked the car. Wishing she had never agreed to this, she listened to Eddie make small talk as they strolled toward the coffee shop, which was a few doors down from the market.

A waitress showed them to a booth. Kaitlyn sat down and Eddie slid in beside her. It annoyed her that he didn't take the seat across from her.

Eddie ordered two cups of coffee, then sat back, one arm stretched out on the seat behind her. "So, do you live around here?"

"Yes, do you?"

"No, I'm just laying over for a few days on my way to L.A."

"Oh? Is this a business trip?"

"You could say that."

The waitress arrived with their coffee. "Will there be anything else?"

Eddie glanced at Kaitlyn, one brow raised in question.

She shook her head, wishing again that she had refused his invitation. There was something about Eddie she didn't like, didn't trust, although she had no idea what it was. He seemed nice enough. And it was, after all, just a cup of coffee. It wasn't as if she was agreeing to a lifetime commitment.

"Have you lived here long?" he asked.

"No." She added cream and sugar to her cup. "What kind of business are you in?" Not that she cared, she thought as she stirred her coffee.

"At the moment, I'm just scouting around."

"Oh." She sipped her coffee. It burned her tongue, but she kept drinking. The sooner she finished it, the sooner she could get out of here. She should have bought a half-gallon of ice cream at the store. It would have given her a good excuse to hurry home.

"So, I was thinking, maybe we could go out later, take in dinner and a movie."

"I'm sorry, I can't. I have a date."

"How about tomorrow night?"

"I'm afraid you're wasting your time. I'm seeing someone."

"Are you engaged?"

"No, but we're exclusive." She drained her cup and set it aside. "I really need to go."

He stared at her, his eyes narrowed, as if he didn't believe her, but she didn't care.

She lifted one brow. "Do you mind letting me out?"

"Sure." He wasn't smiling now.

Kaitlyn slid out of the booth. "Thank you for the coffee," she murmured over her shoulder.

It was all she could do to keep from running out the door. She didn't know who Eddie Harrington was, but he gave her the creeps.

Chapter 11

Zack stood in the shadows alongside Kaitlyn's house, debating whether to see her again. She was a nice girl, obviously a little naïve when it came to men. He had the feeling she had been sheltered most of her life until she came here to live. He sensed the strength in her, but it was more physical than emotional, and the last thing he wanted to do was hurt her. In all his existence, he had had only one long-standing relationship with a woman, and that had been over a century and a half ago. It just wasn't smart to care too deeply for mortals. At best, they lived a mere seventy or eighty years; at worst, they died in your arms at the age of twenty, like his beautiful dancer, her mind gone, her body ravaged by disease.

He rarely thought of Colette. She had been a pretty young woman, with bright red hair, a winsome smile, and a dancer's slender figure. They had spent three incredible years together and then, without warning, she took sick. Within the space of a few hours, she was out of her head with fever. He had taken her to the hospital, but the doctor shook his head and said there was nothing he could do. In a few days, she looked more dead than alive. He had begged her to let him bring her across in hopes that the change would heal her in mind and body, but she had been too far gone to decide, and when he had tried to bring her across, it was too late. She had died in his arms. The memory of her death had haunted him for years. Even now, thinking of her filled him with guilt and regret. He wasn't sure he was ready to face that kind of failure, of loss, again.

He shoved his hands into his pockets. Best to go back home where he belonged. He was about to head back to the casino when Kaitlyn appeared at the front window. One look and he knew he couldn't let her go, not yet. He had been alone too long, waited too long to feel the warm rush of desire that spiraled through him whenever she was near, a hunger not just for her blood, but for the sound of her laughter, the beauty of her smile, the chance to hold her close in his arms and feel alive again. And if she broke his heart . . . well, he would just have to live with it, because he didn't want to live without her.

Zack was leaving the cover of the shadows alongside Kaitlyn's house when he caught the scent of a stranger. It could mean nothing, he thought. It could be a tourist out for a walk, the mailman, a repairman, except there was no reason for any of them to be in this particular place at this particular hour.

He took another breath, committing the scent to memory, before making his way up to the front porch.

Kaitlyn answered his knock almost immediately, leaving him to wonder if she had been standing by the door waiting for him—or for the man whose scent he had detected only moments earlier.

The look in her eyes when she saw him, the warmth

in her voice as she invited him inside, was all the answer he needed.

Murmuring her name, he pulled her into his arms and kissed her until she protested that she needed air.

"Damn, woman," he muttered.

She smiled up at him, thinking that the awe in his voice and the heated expression in his eyes was the nicest compliment she had ever received.

Standing on her tiptoes, she folded her hands over his shoulders and pressed her lips to his.

Without breaking the kiss, Zack lifted Kaitlyn into his arms and carried her to the sofa. Still without breaking the kiss, he settled her on his lap and wrapped his arms around her. She fit into his embrace as if she had been created for no other purpose than to mold her body to his. Her skin was warm and smooth, her hair fragrant with the scent of honeysuckle, her lips soft and pliable. His body reacted as expected when a soft moan rose in her throat.

"Katy," he said, his voice thick with desire.

She fanned herself with her hand, thinking one more kiss like that and she would go up in flames. "I think I need a drink," she said. "Can I offer you something?"

His heated gaze moved over her from head to heel, leaving no doubt in her mind that she was what he wanted.

"Besides that," she said, sliding off his lap.

"Wine, if you've got it."

Nodding, she walked into the kitchen and went straight to the refrigerator where she poured herself a glass of ice water. She stood there a moment, taking deep breaths and trying to calm her racing heart. If she could harness the electricity in Zack's kisses, she could probably light up the world.

After taking one last calming breath, she found a

bottle of wine and filled two glasses, then returned to the living room.

Zack was sitting on the sofa where she had left him. He accepted the drink she offered him with a frown.

"What's wrong?" she asked, taking the seat beside him.

Zack regarded her a moment. For days, his instincts had been warning him that she was keeping something from him. "Who are you really?"

"I beg your pardon?"

"Maybe the better question would be, *what* are you?"

"I'm sure I don't know what you're talking about."

"And I'm sure you do." Opening his preternatural senses, he tried to read her mind but, again, with no success. "You're not mortal, are you?"

She stared at him, her eyes wide.

He canted his head to the side, his eyes narrowing. "So, what are you, Katy? Fairy? Werewolf? What?"

Kaitlyn's heart skipped a beat. Zack hadn't mentioned vampires, but it was obvious he suspected there was something otherworldly about her. Striving for calm, she set her glass on the end table. It was strictly forbidden for her people to tell anyone else the truth of what they were. It had been drummed into her from the time she was old enough to understand that no one else was to know. "I think you should leave."

Zack drained his glass and set it aside before gaining his feet. "Not until I get some answers."

"Are you threatening me?"

"No." Closing the short distance between them, he took hold of her wrist and pulled her to her feet.

"Let me go."

He studied her speculatively. There was no fear in her voice, and none in her expression.

"I feel the strength in you," he mused, and then frowned. No doubt he would have noticed it before if he hadn't been so smitten with her. "You don't smell like any vampire I've ever met, but I can smell blood in the house." Still holding her arm, he tugged her along behind him as he went into the kitchen and opened the refrigerator. There, amid the milk, butter, cheese, and eggs, he saw two bags of blood. He sniffed the air, then glanced over his shoulder. "Type AB negative, right?"

Kaitlyn looked at him as if she had never seen him before. "How do you know that?"

He stared at her, one brow arched. "Can't you guess?"

"You can't be one of us." And yet, deep down, hadn't she suspected that very thing? She shook her head. It was impossible. "My father's never heard of you."

"That's okay," Zack said flippantly. "I've never heard of him, either." Taking her hand, Zack led the way back into the living room. Resuming his seat on the sofa, he pulled Kaitlyn down beside him. "I guess that explains why I could never read your thoughts."

"And why I couldn't read yours." She grinned, thinking how remarkable it was that Zack was a vampire, too. She could hardly wait to tell her mom and dad. What would her dad think, when he learned that Zack was indeed one of them, and that he had managed to stay under the radar?

"How long have you been a vampire?" Zack asked. With the Undead, appearances were usually deceiving. He was a lot older than he looked.

"That's a silly question. All my life, of course. And I'm only half. My mother is human."

Zack stared at her as if she had suddenly started speaking a foreign language. "What?"

Kaitlyn felt her earlier excitement melt away like ice left too long in the sun. "You're one of them, aren't you? One of the Others."

"Others?"

"My father told me there are two kinds of vampires. Our kind, who are born that way. And the Others, who are turned into vampires by an exchange of blood. Our people call themselves the Romanian vampires, although we don't just inhabit Romania anymore."

Zack shook his head. "I've never heard of anyone being born a vampire."

"Our people are basically mortal until they turn twenty, and then the craving for human blood comes on us. Once we partake of it, we lose our humanity and our ability to eat human food and walk in the sun."

"I've seen you eat."

She shrugged. "It's because I'm only half vampire."

"Can you abide the daylight, as well?"

She nodded.

He grunted softly. Half human and half vampire. If that didn't beat all. "Can all your people walk in the sun?"

"No, although my father can be awake and active in his cat form during the day."

"Cat form?"

Kaitlyn nodded, smiling. "When he wants to be active during the day, he assumes the form of a big gray cat." One of her earliest memories of her father was watching him transform himself from man to cat and back again. She had thought it was magic until her father explained that it was a gift bestowed on those born to Liliana. Her father used to tease her, saying it was because her grandmother was really a witch. Kaitlyn had believed him until Liliana set her straight.

"I am not a witch," Liliana had told her. "But there is magic in my blood that gives my descendents the ability to change shape. There is only one real witch in the family, and that is Nadiya."

Kaitlyn had never known if that was true or not,

although it wouldn't have surprised her. Nadiya Korzha was one of the most unpleasant women she had ever met.

Zack shook his head, thinking Kaitlyn's people were the weirdest vampires he had ever heard of. He could be awake during the day if his life depended on it, but he was weak, sluggish. He could also change shape, although he preferred something larger and more intimidating than a cat. Most of his kind shifted into wolves; that was his preference, as well.

"Can your father turn into anything else?" he asked. "Something a little more menacing?"

"Not that I know of, but believe me, my father can be plenty scary when he wants to be."

"What about you?" Zack asked with a wry grin. "Can you be scary?"

"No. And I can't turn into a cat, either."

"Too bad," Zack said. "That's something I'd really like to see."

"How long have you been a vampire?"

"A little over six hundred years."

"Wow! You're even older than my father! How old were you when you became a vampire?"

"A few months on the shy side of twenty-nine."

She canted her head to the side, admiring his strong jaw, straight nose, and unlined skin. His brows were inky black, like his hair. "Our people don't age once the change occurs. Apparently yours don't, either."

"Right. We just get stronger as we get older. I'm guessing your people do, too."

She looked at his hand, lightly holding hers. "We have a lot in common," she remarked wistfully.

"And that makes you unhappy?"

She looked up at him, mute.

"What is it, Katy?" Releasing her hand, he stroked her cheek. "What's bothering you?"

"Our people are enemies."

"What the hell are you talking about? I don't have any enemies." None living, at any rate.

Kaitlyn looked at him in disbelief. "Don't you know anything? Centuries ago, my great-grandfather, Calin Sherrad, declared war on the Others in order to preserve our identity and our way of life." She had read the story of the war with the Others in the *Journal of Alexandru Chisca*, written long before her father had been born. In it, Chisca had chronicled the war and how it had started because the Others were feeding indiscriminately on human men, women, and even children. Even worse, they had left their kills in the streets and byways to be found by mortals, which had brought out the vampire hunters. Not only that, but the Others had turned mortals into vampires like themselves, causing panic in the streets. The Romanian vampires couldn't turn mortals into vampires, although an infusion of their blood prolonged mortal life. Kaitlyn's mother was proof of that. Although Elena was over forty, she still appeared to be in her twenties.

Zack grunted softly. "I don't know anything about a war."

"I thought everybody knew." She had learned it at an early age. "It was fought over a thousand years ago."

"I guess that's why I never heard of it. But what the hell, that's old history. It doesn't have anything to do with you and me."

"I wish it didn't."

Zack frowned. He might not be able to read her mind, but in this instance, it wasn't necessary. He knew what she was going to say before she spoke the words.

"I'm sorry, Zack, but I can't see you anymore."

Eyes narrowed, he stared at her and then he pulled her into his arms and kissed her, hard and long. And just as abruptly, he let her go. "So, that's it," he said, his voice harsh. "It's over between us before it's even started, and all because of some war that took place over a thousand years ago."

Kaitlyn blinked back her tears. "It's not what I want. But my father would never accept you. Or forgive me."

He regarded her for stretched seconds, the taste of her still warm on his lips, her scent permeating his senses. And then he swore a vile oath. Why the hell was he so upset? It wasn't like she was ending a long-standing relationship. Hell, he had only known the woman for a few days.

"Have it your way, Katy." Rising, he dissolved into mist and vanished from the room.

Kaitlyn stared at the place where Zack had been standing, wishing she could relive the last few minutes, that she could recall the words she had spoken. And yet, it was better to end it now, before she fell any deeper, before letting him go became impossible.

She brushed the tears from her cheeks. She wouldn't cry, wouldn't think of Zack Ravenscroft, or of what might have been. She shook her head. Just her luck. She had finally met a man she liked and he was the wrong kind of vampire.

Kaitlyn closed her eyes and took several slow deep breaths. She refused to just sit home and feel sorry for herself. She was Drake Sherrad's daughter, heir to the Carpathian dynasty. She had a destiny to fulfill, and Zack Ravenscroft had no place in it. How could she have forgotten that? In a year or two, three at the most, she would be required to return to the Fortress and seek a life mate.

After washing her face, she reapplied her makeup, grabbed her purse and her keys, and left the house. It was still early and there was a movie in town she had been wanting to see. Tonight seemed like the perfect time.

The movie had been a mistake, Kaitlyn thought as she walked toward the ice-cream parlor located down the block and across the street from the theater. She had forgotten the film was one of those chick flicks with lots of long, lingering looks and a sad ending. She had cried all the way through.

Hopefully, a banana split with extra whipped cream and a cherry would cheer her up. Her mother always said there were few miseries in life that a hefty helping of chocolate couldn't make better.

Kaitlyn had just taken her first bite of hot fudge when the last person she wanted to see dropped into the seat across from hers.

"Hey, Kaitlyn, how's it going?" Eddie asked cheerfully.

She forced a smile. "Just fine, thank you."

"I thought you had a date tonight," he said, his voice carefully casual.

"Something came up at the last minute and he had to cancel." It wasn't exactly a lie.

Eddie glanced at his watch. "Well, it's early yet. Maybe we could go out. I hear there's a nice dance floor at Ravenscroft's Casino."

"No!" The idea of running into Zack was unthinkable. "I mean, I don't feel like dancing tonight."

He looked thoughtful. "Do you like bowling? There's a new place down the street. Lois Lanes. Get it?"

She forced another smile.

"So, what do you say?"

"I don't think so." She took a bite of ice cream but it seemed to have lost its appeal and she pushed the dish away.

"I guess it's not my night," Eddie remarked.

And it never will be, Kaitlyn thought, pushing away from the table. "Sorry, Eddie, I'm just really tired." Rising, she plucked her handbag from the table. "Maybe some other time." Talk about a lie, she thought.

"The least I can do is walk you home."

"Thank you, but I have my car."

"I didn't see it parked outside."

"I left it in the parking lot behind the theater." She started toward the door, a huff of annoyance rising in her throat when Eddie followed her outside and fell into step beside her.

The silence stretched between them, but Kaitlyn didn't care. She was too upset about how things had ended with Zack to worry about what Eddie Harrington thought. She had nothing to say to him and had no interest in his company. If she didn't encourage him, maybe he would finally get a clue and leave her alone.

Apparently, he was clueless. "So, you went to the movies? How was it?"

"Very sad."

"The new sci-fi flick starts on Friday. I hear it's a good one."

"Well, I hope you like it," she said, hoping he would take the hint this time. Grateful to have reached her car, she unlocked it and opened the door. "Good night."

"Yeah, good night."

Kaitlyn slid behind the wheel and put the key in the ignition. When she glanced in the rearview mirror, she saw him standing under one of the lampposts, watching her. The surly look in his eyes sent a shiver of unease down her spine. Putting the car in gear, she drove out of the parking lot.

* * *

Zack stood in the shadows across from the parking lot, his eyes narrowed as he focused on the man who had been with Kaitlyn. Even from a distance, he recognized the man's scent. It was the same as the one he had detected outside Kaitlyn's house earlier that night. Was this guy friend or foe? Judging from the hostile expression in the man's eyes, Zack didn't think he was Kaitlyn's friend, yet she hadn't appeared to be afraid of him. She hadn't appeared to be fond of his company, either.

Zack had just decided to confront the man when he disappeared from sight.

Zack grunted softly. Either the stranger was some kind of sorcerer, or he was a vampire. He was betting on the latter. And since the man didn't smell human, and he didn't smell like one of the Undead, Zack figured the man was a blood-born vampire, like Kaitlyn.

Frowning, Zack willed himself to Kaitlyn's yard and took cover in the shadows near the front porch. She might not want anything to do with him, but he was sticking close by until he determined what was going on between her and the stranger.

Chapter 12

Zack rose to his feet and stretched his back and shoulders. It wasn't really necessary. He never grew tired. His muscles didn't get sore, didn't cramp if he stayed in one position for hours on end. But moving, stretching, itching, and blinking came naturally, instinctively, to humans. After being turned, he'd had to practice doing those things until they were second nature again, because not doing so was sure to invite unwanted attention. Unlike vampires, mortals couldn't sit unmoving or unblinking for hours at a time.

He had spent the last three nights hunkered down in the shadows outside Kaitlyn's house. He wasn't sure the stranger he had seen her with was a threat, but Zack had decided it was better to err on the side of caution, at least until he determined what the man was up to, or he left town. Zack grunted softly. It wasn't like he had anything else to do. Well, other than run the casino, but Kaitlyn was infinitely more important than a few slot machines.

Now, with dawn approaching, it was time to leave, time to seek his lair before the sun found him.

He was about to transport himself to the casino when the stranger materialized on the front porch.

Zack glanced at the sky. Only minutes until sunrise.

When the other vampire reached for the doorknob, Zack flew to the porch, his hand grasping the other vampire by the arm, wrenching him around and away from the door. "What are you doing here?"

The other vampire stared at him, his eyes wide with surprise, not fear. "I'm here to see Kaitlyn," he replied smoothly.

"Before the sun's even up?" Zack asked, still gripping the other man's arm.

"We're lovers," the man said with a leer.

"You're lying. Who the hell are you?"

"My name is Eddie Harrington, not that it's any of your business." He straightened to his full height. "Now let me go. I don't want to hurt you."

Zack snorted. At six foot two, he stood a good four inches taller than Harrington and outweighed him by thirty pounds.

"I mean it," Harrington said.

Zack sensed the change in Harrington as Harrington summoned his preternatural power. Harrington's muscles tensed, his eyes went hard and cold. Power radiated from him, sizzling through the damp air, but Zack knew instinctively that his own power was older, stronger.

Confident of his vampiric strength, Harrington suddenly twisted out of Zack's grasp, then pushed him down the stairs. He flung himself after Zack, expecting Zack to be facedown on the ground, only Zack wasn't there.

Too late, Harrington realized he had badly underestimated his foe.

He landed facedown on the ground where Zack should have been, only to let out a harsh cry when

Zack twisted his right arm behind his back, his knee grinding into his spine.

"Who the hell are you?" Harrington growled.

"Zack Ravenscroft. Remember that name, because if I ever see you sniffing around Kaitlyn's house again, I'll rip your heart out. Got it?"

Harrington grunted something unintelligible.

Zack applied more pressure to the other man's spine. "Got it?"

"Yes, dammit! Now get off of me."

As soon as Zack released him, Harrington was gone.

Zack frowned thoughtfully. Harrington seemed awfully weak for a vampire, but then, maybe the vampires who were born that way weren't as strong as those who were made. Or maybe Harrington was just young. Kaitlyn had said their kind got stronger as they got older. Perhaps Harrington would, too. If he lived that long.

Zack was dusting himself off when he saw a wallet lying in the dirt. Must be Harrington's, he thought. Picking it up, he thumbed through it, then frowned when he saw the man's driver's license. The photo was Harrington's, but the name read Daryn Korzha. Zack grunted thoughtfully. Did Kaitlyn know who Harrington really was? And if not, what game was Harrington, or Korzha, playing?

Well, there was one way to find out. Materializing inside Kaitlyn's house, he dropped Harrington's wallet on the coffee table where she would be sure to find it in the morning.

A thought took Zack to his lair in the bowels of the casino. It wasn't much, just a square room with stone walls, no windows and no doors. And no lights. But artificial light was unnecessary. With his preternatural vision, he could see everything clearly, although there was little to see save the expensive polished ebony coffin in the center of the flagstone floor, and a small iron box that held a few mementos from his past—a copy of *Romeo and Juliet,* a few old English coins, a wooden toy horse one of the nuns had given him.

Stripping down to his briefs, Zack stretched out on the cool satin that had been his resting place for over six hundred years. He could have slept in a bed—and occasionally he did—but the coffin was familiar, a stark reminder of who and what he was.

Daryn Korzha paced the floor of his lavish hotel room, his outrage growing with every stride as he re-lived his encounter with Ravenscroft outside Kaitlyn's house. The man wasn't one of Sherrad's sons, or a member of any of the foreign Fortresses—Daryn was sure of that. And yet, he hadn't been able to read Ravens-croft's mind, so the stranger couldn't have been human. Besides, no mere mortal could have crept up on him unawares, or bested his preternatural strength.

Daryn muttered an oath. So, if Ravenscroft wasn't one of the Romanian vampires and he wasn't human, what the hell was he?

That question echoed in his mind as he pulled out his cell phone and called home.

Nadiya Korzha stood looking out the front window of her house, her thoughts turned inward. The house was large and well-appointed, decorated with furniture and bric-a-brac collected through the centuries. The basement was filled with things she had tired of, and with the gifts her husband had given her years ago.

She had never liked being a fourth wife. Not that he had treated her any differently from his second wife, or third, or any of the others. Except his first wife, Liliana. She had been accorded privileges and respect denied to the others. Being the first wife, and the favorite, Liliana had also been granted the right to remain at the Fortress as long as she wished, to the exclusion of all the others. A thought that still rankled in Nadiya's heart.

Staring out the window, she paid little heed to the beauty of her surroundings or to the laughter of one of her grandchildren coming from the back of the house. Her enthusiasm for life had died the night her son, Florin, was killed. She would not rest until he had been avenged, until his killer endured the same remorse that had become her constant companion, until he had shed as many bitter tears as had she. In her mind's eye, she relived her son's final moments, each one as clear as if it was happening all over again. She felt the coolness of the night, the taste of the breeze, heard the rapid beating of her son's heart as he fought for his life.

And then, as though she were seeing it all for the first time, she felt the anticipation of those watching as Drake thrust his sword through her son's heart, heard the collective sigh from the crowd as Florin's body toppled lifelessly to the ground. Knowing what was coming next, she had turned away, but she had known, by the sharp swish of the blade, the exact moment when Drake severed her son's head from his body. And now her son was dead, while Rodin's favorite son flourished at Wolfram Castle.

She refused to acknowledge her role in her son's death. Those at the Fortress had mistakenly assumed Florin was interested in avenging himself on one of Rodin's sons for a supposed misunderstanding over a woman. In reality, Florin had wanted to avenge himself on Rodin for giving the woman to Olaf, and for banishing him from the Fortress that he had long coveted. She could have prevented her son's death by forbidding him to return to the Fortress as Gerret's second. But she had been confident in his ability to accomplish his goal, eager to see her son rule the Fortress that she, too, had coveted. Eager to see Liliana ousted.

Nadiya clenched her fists. She wasn't foolish enough to send her remaining sons against Drake or Liliana. But Drake's daughter was fair game and, being half human, would be much more easily destroyed. But first the fair Kaitlyn must be made to suffer.

The ringing of her cell phone interrupted thoughts of vengeance. She smiled when she heard Daryn's voice. She listened for several moments, her eyes narrowing.

"I have never heard of Zack Ravenscroft. I do not know who he is," she said brusquely. "I do not care who he is. Get rid of him if you have to, but bring the girl to me, by force, if necessary."

She listened to his excuses for another minute, then threw the phone against the wall. If Daryn couldn't overpower the Sherrad heir, then she would find someone who could.

Chapter 13

Kaitlyn slept late, reluctant to face a new day, reluctant to admit that she missed Zack as much as she did. Which was ridiculous. She had only known him a short time, and yet he had brought a new excitement to her life, a sense of adventure, a sudden, almost irresistible urge to throw caution to the wind and follow her heart instead of her head. Would it truly be so bad to ignore her mother's teachings, to destroy her father's expectations, and take one of the Others as a lover? Just one indiscretion. And no one need ever know . . . but she would know.

After fixing a cup of coffee, she carried it into the living room. And frowned when she saw a man's wallet lying on the coffee table next to a pile of magazines. She stared at it a moment, trying to figure out whose it was and how it had gotten there.

Setting her cup on the table, she picked up the billfold. She paused before opening it, then shrugged. There was no other way to find out who it belonged to.

She stared at the face on the driver's license, and then read the name. Daryn Korzha. She blinked, and read it again. Korzha. Her father had mentioned Daryn

Korzha and his mother not long ago. Was it merely coincidence that this man had the same name, or was this Korzha related to her? And if so, why had he lied to her?

She thought about it for several minutes, but there was only one way to find out. She would confront Eddie or Daryn or whoever he was the next time she saw him, even though she hoped he would leave town and never return.

With that problem solved, Kaitlyn found herself thinking about Zack again. Had she really done the right thing in telling him good-bye? She might forget him, in time. And maybe she wouldn't.

Her mother was mortal, but she had married a vampire. Would it be so wrong for Kaitlyn the half vampire to marry Zack the Other? After all, being vampires, they had more in common than her mother and father.

Confused and lonely, Kaitlyn called home, hoping her mother could give her the answer she sought.

She had no sooner said, "Hi, Mom," than her mother asked what was wrong.

"Am I that transparent?" Kaitlyn asked.

"Are you kidding? You sound like you just lost your best friend."

"Maybe I did," Kaitlyn said, and quickly told her mother what had happened. "I miss him so much, Mom. I don't know what I should do."

"You did the right thing." Elena sighed, wondering how she could advise her daughter to stop seeing Zack Ravenscroft. So what if he wasn't one of them? She had fallen in love with someone who was not human, married him, and given him a daughter, and never regretted it for a moment.

Would Drake see it that way? As Master of the Carpathian Fortress, he was responsible for making sure the laws of the coven were upheld. But then, hadn't he changed the laws of his people in order to marry her?

"Mom?"

"Sorry, sweetie, did you ask me something?"

"I asked if you thought Dad would . . . oh, never mind. I know he wouldn't. He thinks of the Others as our enemy. I've never heard him say anything positive about any of them. I just don't understand it. They drink blood. We drink blood. They kill humans . . ." Remembering who she was talking to, Kaitlyn murmured, "Sorry, Mom."

"It's all right, dear. I know what you mean. And I know some of your father's people have killed humans to survive. But that's rare." Elena sighed again. She had lived with Drake and his people for over twenty years, and even though they accepted her and treated her with respect, there were times when she felt like an outsider. She didn't want Kaitlyn to ever feel like that.

"Well, it doesn't matter, anyway," Kaitlyn said, her voice melancholy. "I told Zack I couldn't see him anymore, and I haven't seen him since." She paused. "Mom, have you ever heard of Daryn Korzha?"

Elena's heart skipped a beat. "Did you say Korzha?"

"Yes, do you know him?"

"No. No, I don't."

"But you've heard of him?"

"I'm not sure. There are a lot of Korzhas in the world," Elena said, her mind racing. "Where did you meet him?"

"He bumped into me at the grocery store in town. He told me his name was Eddie Harrington and that he was a businessman, but his driver's license says his name is Daryn Korzha."

"How did you see his driver's license?"

"Someone left it where I'd find it." As Kaitlyn said

the words, she knew it must have been Zack and that he had been in her house without her knowledge. The thought gave her pause. "Eddie, or whoever he is, told me he was on his way to L.A., but he's still here. I saw him the other day, when I was driving home from the drugstore."

"Listen, Kaitlyn, promise me you'll stay away from this man until we know who he really is, all right? I need to talk to your father about this."

"I promise." Kaitlyn didn't even have to think about it. She'd be happy if she never saw Harrington, or Korzha, again.

"I'll talk to you soon," Elena said.

"All right. Bye, Mom. I love you."

"I love you more. And remember what I said. Stay away from Korzha."

After telling Kaitlyn good-bye, Elena went looking for Drake. She found her husband in the council chamber with his brother, Andrei.

Drake smiled and waved her forward when he saw her standing in the doorway. "Come in, wife. We are through here."

"Hi, Andrei," she said, moving toward the table where the two men sat.

"Hello, Elena." Andrei looked at Drake. "I will take care of the matter we discussed right away."

Drake nodded.

"What matter?" Elena asked when Andrei left the chamber.

Drake blew out a breath. "Northa wants a new TV for the playroom. She says there are new ones now, with something called scent-o-vision."

Elena grinned. "Did you buy one yet?"

"Andrei will take care of it." He grinned back at her. "Sometimes I am not sure freeing the sheep was a good idea. So," he said, drawing her onto his lap, "what troubles you?"

"How do you know something's bothering me? Maybe I just came in for a hug."

"Elena, we have been together over twenty years. I do not have to read your mind to know you are worried. I can see it in your eyes. So?"

"Who's Daryn Korzha?"

Drake's expression turned grim; his arm tensed around her. "What did you say?"

"Kaitlyn met him. Do you know him?"

"Yes. I know him. His mother is Nadiya, my father's fourth wife."

"Nadiya, as in Florin's mother?" Elena swallowed hard. Florin had killed Drake's sire, and Drake had killed Florin.

"The very same. Why do you ask?"

"Kaitlyn said she met a man named Korzha the other day. He accidentally bumped into her."

Drake snorted.

"You don't believe that?"

"I do not believe in accidents, or coincidence." Setting Elena on her feet, he began to pace the floor. "If there is mischief afoot, you can be sure Nadiya is behind it."

Nadiya had not spoken to anyone in the Carpathian Fortress since Drake had killed Florin, and no one here had seen her since then. Elena assumed Nadiya had gone to her own house in Bucharest to grieve for her son, but what if, instead of being in mourning, she was plotting treachery against Drake?

Elena pressed a hand to her breast. It was suddenly hard to breathe. What better way to hurt Drake than to hurt his daughter? "What are you going to do?" she asked.

"For now, I am going to make some inquiries."
Seeing her worried expression, he drew her into his
arms and kissed the top of her head. "Do not worry,
wife. I will get to the bottom of this."

Elena gazed blankly at the cards in her hand. Hoping
to distract herself, she had met Northa, Marta, and
Elnora for their weekly card game. Northa was the oldest
of the three other women. She had curly brown hair and
slanted brown eyes. Marta was a pretty brunette with
hazel eyes. Elnora was a petite redhead with a slender,
perfect figure. Elena considered the three women her
closest friends. When Drake had offered the sheep their
freedom, Marta and Elnora had stayed because they had
feelings for two of the vampires. Northa had elected to
stay because she enjoyed being bitten, and because the
Fortress was the only home she had ever known.

Elena looked up when Marta called her name.

"It's your bid."

"Oh, sorry," Elena said. It was nearly impossible to concentrate on her cards. Kaitlyn was her only child. If anything happened to her . . . She forced the thought from
her mind. Drake wouldn't let anything happen to Kaitlyn.
She had to believe that. And yet, Drake was here and Kaitlyn was in another country, alone among strangers.

"Elena, are you all right?" Northa asked, her brow
furrowed with concern.

"Fine, just a little preoccupied tonight."

Elnora laid her cards aside and leaned forward. "Anything we can do to help?"

"Not really . . . well . . . what do you know about
Nadiya Korzha?"

"Not much," Elnora said. "Except she was one of
Rodin's wives."

"I saw her a couple of times," Marta said. "Ice-cold, she was, even worse than Liliana used to be."

"Bitter," Northa added. "Very bitter. Why do you ask?"

"Her son, Daryn, might be in California. A man by that name just happened to bump into Kaitlyn."

"Oh, if it's him, that can't be good," Marta said, her eyes widening in alarm.

"Daryn fed on me once," Northa remarked, shuddering with the memory. "He reminded me of a hungry lizard."

Elena couldn't help laughing at the image but then, to her chagrin, she felt the sting of tears behind her eyes. For all that her daughter was half vampire, she was still a young woman who'd had little experience with men, whether they were human or vampire. And even though she had a vampire's increased speed and strength, would that be enough if she had to defend herself against Nadiya, who was older, stronger, and more experienced in the way of the world?

Elena slumped in her chair, suddenly certain that Drake was right. There was no such thing as coincidence.

She knew, with every fiber of her being, that Daryn Korzha was up to no good.

Elena clenched her hands in her lap. Kaitlyn had to come home—the sooner the better.

Chapter 14

It was Saturday night and the casino was in full swing when Zack entered the club. It had taken him a good long while to learn to block the myriad smells that clung to mortals, to tune out the rattle of the dice, the whirring of the games, the never-ending conversation, the raucous laughter and shouts of the winners.

Feeling restless, he wandered over to the craps table and tossed a hundred-dollar bill on eight the hard way. In the past, before he'd built his own casino, he hadn't been above manipulating the dice or the slot machines when he needed a little cash. Of course, cheating took all the fun out of winning.

The croupier tossed Zack an apologetic look when the man who had the dice rolled a five.

Shrugging, Zack left the table and strolled through the crowd, pausing to say a few words to the regulars, consoling the losers, congratulating the winners.

He stopped to watch a newlywed couple who were playing one of the old dollar slots. The husband wanted to quit, but his bride kept urging him on.

"Just one more time, honey," she coaxed. "If we win the jackpot, we could put a down payment on that house."

"Nobody ever wins the big money," her husband muttered. "These machines are all rigged."

"Please, Tom. I have a feeling we'll win."

"You and your feelings," Tom scoffed, but there was no irritation in his voice. "You haven't been right once since I've known you," he said with an affectionate smile, "except when you married me." He shook his head. "Oh, what the hell," he muttered, and dropped five silver dollars into the machine.

Zack watched the woman's face. She was a pretty thing, with short blond hair and bright green eyes. If she wanted a house, by damn, he'd see that she got one.

The wheels spun. Slowed. Stopped.

The bride squealed as three purple sevens stood side by side on the pay line. The light over the slot machine lit up and silver dollars began to pour into the tray.

Grinning, Zack moved on, his thoughts turning, as always, toward Kaitlyn and the man who had been stalking her.

After telling Scherry he was going out for a while, Zack left the casino.

The night was cool and clear and the streets were crowded with people, but he paid them little heed as he walked quickly toward Kaitlyn's place. Upon arriving, he opened his senses, searching for some sign that the Romanian vampire had been there, relieved when he didn't detect the man's scent.

Moving closer to the house, he could hear Kaitlyn moving around inside—the slam of a drawer, the sound of water running, the smell of baked chicken when she opened the oven door.

He frowned, wondering if she was having company over for dinner. Walking to the back of the house where the kitchen was located, he dissolved into mist and peered into the open window.

Clad in a pair of white shorts and a silky-looking orange-and-white striped shirt, she stood at the stove, her back toward him while she stirred something in a pot. Her legs were long and tan, her waist narrow. Her hair fell in long, loose waves down her back like a river of ebony silk.

Had he been in corporeal form, Zack was sure his mouth would have been watering, not from the smell of the food, but from the enticing scent of the woman.

Zack hovered there, content, for the moment, to simply admire the way she looked, the fluid way she moved, the lilting sound of her voice as she hummed an old rock-and-roll tune. Watching her, it was hard to believe she was half vampire. She seemed totally human. Until she put her dinner on the table and filled a goblet with a mixture of red wine and blood.

Type AB negative, he thought. Her drink of choice.

Zack was wondering if she ever drank anything else when Daryn Korzha appeared in the kitchen. What the hell? Apparently Romanian vampires didn't need an invitation to enter another's home. Or maybe that only applied to mortal dwellings. He would have to ask Kaitlyn about that. Later.

Kaitlyn whirled around, her eyes flashing with anger. "What are you doing here?"

"You stupid half-breed, you don't even know who I am, do you?"

Kaitlyn stared at him. She had rarely felt fear in her life, but she felt it now, along with a sudden certainty that he belonged to the Carpathian vampires. No one else would know of her mixed heritage. The pure-blood vampires, inherently linked by centuries, recognized each other on sight, but Kaitlyn lacked that particular talent. It also explained his ability to materialize inside her house. No human could do that.

She lifted her chin, refusing to let him see her fear. "What do you want?" she demanded with far more bravado that she felt.

"Enough talk," Korzha said with a sneer. One arm snaked out, wrapping around her waist to hold her flush against his body while he jabbed a needle in her arm.

She struggled a moment, then went limp.

In an instant, Zack was inside the house. He didn't ask questions, simply grabbed Korzha from behind and broke his neck. Kaitlyn slipped from Korzha's grasp and dropped to the floor. Zack took a moment to make sure she was breathing, then rummaged through the kitchen drawers. A broken neck wouldn't keep the vampire down for long.

Zack cussed long and loud until he found a large wooden spoon. Grabbing a knife, he quickly fashioned a point on the end of the handle and drove the makeshift stake through Korzha's heart, all the way to the floor. Dark red blood bubbled up from the killing wound.

Korzha gasped, his hand curling around the stake, but the strength was already draining out of him. He convulsed once, and then lay still, the life fading from his eyes as his skin turned a pasty gray.

Zack rocked back on his heels. It had been a long time since he'd killed another vampire, but he would gladly have dispatched this one again.

He glanced at Kaitlyn. She lay on her side, her eyes closed, her breathing shallow. Figuring she would be out for a while, he carried her into the living room, laid her on the sofa, and covered her with a blanket that had been folded over the back of the couch.

Returning to the kitchen, Zack hoisted Korzha's body over his shoulder and carried it outside.

He stood in the dark a moment, considering what to

do with the body. He grunted softly, wondering if the bodies of vampires who were born and not made disintegrated in the light of day the way his kind did.

Since he wasn't sure, burying the body seemed like the smart thing to do. Moving with preternatural speed, he found a stretch of deserted ground high in the mountains. Dropping the body unceremoniously on the ground, he quickly dug a deep hole in the soft earth. Needing to make sure Korzha didn't rise again, Zack ripped the man's heart from his chest and tossed it and the body into the hole.

Once the corpse was buried, Zack transported himself to his lair, where he washed his hands and changed his clothes.

Minutes later, he was back at Kaitlyn's house, scrubbing the blood from her kitchen floor.

Kaitlyn groaned softly as consciousness returned. She opened her eyes slowly and glanced around. What was she doing on the sofa? And why did she feel so funny?

Sitting up, she glanced around the room, her eyes widening when she saw Zack sitting in the chair across from the couch.

"What are you doing here?" She frowned as her mind cleared. "Where's Daryn?" Her gaze darted around the room, but there was no sign of Korzha. "Where is he?" She rubbed her arm. "He jabbed me with a needle."

"He's gone."

"What do you mean, 'gone'? What did you do?" She stared at Zack, weighing the curtness of his words, the icy expression in his eyes. "Did you . . . is he . . . ?"

Zack nodded. "He'll never bother you or anyone else again."

Daryn was dead. It took a moment for the cold reality of it to sink in. Zack had killed a man. She had never killed anyone and now Daryn, a member of the Carpathian Coven—one of her father's half brothers—was dead. Because of her.

"Hey, are you all right?" Zack asked. "You're looking a little pale."

"Do you know what you've done?" What would her father say? What would he think, when he found out?

"Saved your butt, that's what."

Kaitlyn nodded, then frowned, momentarily distracted. "How did he get in? That's what I want to know."

"Are you saying he was never in here before?"

"Exactly." A shiver of revulsion skittered down her spine. "I would never have invited him into my house."

Zack grunted thoughtfully. "Do your kind need an invitation?"

"The full-bloods do. I don't." She tapped her fingernails on the arm of the sofa. "Since his mother is a witch, I'm wondering if it's possible that she could have given him some sort of spell to negate the power of the threshold?"

"Beats the hell out of me," Zack said. "I don't know anything about witches, but I guess anything is possible."

Kaitlyn stood and began to pace the floor. As her mind cleared, she realized that the fact that Daryn was kin made everything worse. What would her father think when he found out Zack had killed one of their kind? Her father hated the Others; this would just make things worse. Still, Daryn had obviously been up to no good—she refused to think he had intended to kill her—and surely her father wouldn't condemn Zack for defending her.

She glanced at Zack, suddenly afraid for his future. She had seen her father when he was angry, and she had never forgotten it. She had told Zack her father in a rage was a scary sight, but that didn't begin to describe it. Her father hadn't raised his voice or anything like that, but he had suddenly seemed larger than life as he castigated one of his brothers. Preternatural power had rolled off her father, so strong, so overpowering, it seemed to suck the very air from the room. Her uncle had reeled backward, blood running from his nose and mouth as if he had been struck, even though her father had never raised his hand. She had known instinctively that, had he wished it, her father could have killed Ciprian.

And now, because of her, Zack's life might be in danger, although once she explained what had happened, she was sure her father would understand. She had to believe that.

"Why was Korzha after you?" Zack asked.

"I don't know." Sitting on the sofa again, she fidgeted with her hair. "I haven't known him very long. In fact, I met him about the same time I met you."

Zack leaned forward, his forearms braced on his knees. "He was like you, a Romanian vampire." It wasn't a question.

She nodded. "He was one of my father's half brothers."

"Go on."

"My grandfather had a lot of wives." That was an understatement; he'd had twenty. "And they had a lot of children." Another understatement. "Usually, only my grandfather's favorite wife and her children lived at the Fortress with him. The other wives all had homes elsewhere because no one really liked my grandmother back then." Kaitlyn smiled inwardly. Her mother had told her that Liliana's demeanor had changed drastically after Kaitlyn was born. Liliana had grown kinder, Elena had said, more thoughtful of others.

Zack leaned back in his chair, contemplating what Kaitlyn had said. Vampires marrying, having children, living in castles like old royalty. It was a hell of a story.

"I didn't grow up at the Fortress," Kaitlyn said, "so I don't know all of my father's half brothers and sisters, or their mothers. My grandfather's wives all kept their maiden names so he would know which children belonged to which wife."

"Sounds like he had quite a harem."

Kaitlyn laughed. "I always thought so."

"So, all things considered, it appears that Korzha was after you for some reason. Do you think he intended to kidnap you, and if so, what was his motive?"

"I don't have any idea." She chewed on her lower lip a moment. "Years ago, before I was born, my father killed one of Daryn's brothers." It was an old story, one well-known by covens throughout the world.

Zack grunted softly. "Sounds like a good, old-fashioned case of revenge to me."

"After more than twenty years?" It seemed a far-fetched idea, and yet, in the back of her mind, she remembered her father calling to check up on her not long ago. He had said something about a rumor he had heard, and almost in the same breath, he had mentioned Daryn and his mother. Was it possible Nadiya was behind it all?

When she asked Zack what he thought about it, he shrugged. "You know what they say, revenge is a dish best served cold."

"It would have to be frozen by now," Kaitlyn retorted. "Zack, you have to leave here. Or I do. If my father finds out what happened . . . You know how he feels about the Others. And if he finds out you killed one of us . . ." She shuddered, not wanting to dwell on what her father might do. She had no future with Zack.

She knew that, but she didn't want anything to happen to him.

"I'm not leaving," Zack said. "I like it here."

"Then I'll go."

"I'm not afraid of your father."

"Well, you should be!"

"Calm down, girl. There's no reason for you to be so upset. And no reason for your father to be angry with me. I haven't done anything except probably save your life. I'd think he'd be grateful for that."

He was right. She was overreacting because Zack was one of the Others. But she couldn't help it. Her father might accept her dating a mortal; dating someone he considered an enemy of her people—even if that someone had saved her life—was something else entirely.

She shook her head. She had to calm down. Zack was right. He had saved her from whatever nefarious plot Daryn had devised. Surely that would tip the scales in Zack's favor.

Besides, she loved it here and she didn't want to leave.

And she didn't want to leave Zack, either.

"Well, now that we've got that settled," Zack said, "I think it's time we got down to some serious kissing."

All thoughts of Daryn and her father disappeared at the thought of kissing Zack. "Oh, you do, do you?"

"Don't you?" He leaned forward. "Or are you going to start that whole 'I can't see you anymore' nonsense again."

"It isn't nonsense. My father's a force to be reckoned with. If . . ."

A single thought carried Zack from the chair to the sofa. "I don't want to talk about your father, or vampires, or Others," he said, drawing her into his arms. "I don't want to think about anything but you."

"Zack . . ."

"Shh."

With a sigh, she relaxed in his arms.

"That's better," he murmured. Cupping her face in his hands, he kissed her, softly, slowly. His tongue traced her lower lip, delved inside for a taste and then withdrew, moving to lave the side of her neck. Her stomach tightened when she felt the light scrape of his fangs against her skin.

"Zack . . ."

"Just a taste, love, that's all."

She rarely drank from a living source. Being only half vampire, she lacked the inescapable need to hunt, but there was no denying that taking blood from mortals was a pleasurable sensation. No one had ever taken her blood. What would it be like, to be prey instead of predator? To feel Zack's fangs at her throat? Driven by curiosity, she canted her head to the side, giving Zack access to her neck, only then realizing that she was putting her life in his hands. He was older, stronger. If he decided to drain her dry, she wouldn't be able to stop him.

He must have sensed her sudden apprehension, because he said, "It's all right, Katy. You don't have to do it if you've changed your mind."

"I haven't," she said, and it was true. At that moment, she wanted nothing more than to nourish Zack with her life's blood.

Murmuring her name, he bent his head to her neck.

She had expected it to hurt, at least a little, but there was only a rush of warmth when his fangs pierced her skin, and then a flood of pleasure that was sensual beyond belief. Heat flowed through her, bringing all her senses to life, pooling deep within the very heart of her being, stealing the strength from her limbs, until all she wanted was to lose herself in his touch.

She felt bereft when he lifted his head. "Are you done so soon?"

"I'd better stop while I can."

She touched her neck where his fangs had been. "That felt wonderful. Does it feel that way for mortals?"

"It depends on who's doing the biting. Some vampires make it pleasant, others take what they want without any thought for their prey. Haven't you ever bitten anyone?"

"Of course! Well, not often," she admitted.

"Well, I can't imagine you tearing into anybody, so they probably enjoyed it. Can you read their minds?" At her nod, he said, "Next time, listen to their thoughts."

"Can I drink from you?"

"Sure, darlin'."

She hesitated, suddenly embarrassed. It was one thing to hunt for mortal prey, to drink from a stranger and then wipe all memory of it from his mind, quite another to drink from someone you cared for, especially when that someone was a vampire.

"Having second thoughts?" he asked.

"No."

Drawing her into his arms again, he kissed her, his hands moving slowly, seductively, along her spine, traveling up and down her thigh.

His touch awakened her desire, and her hunger. She rained kisses on his cheeks, the hollow of his throat, until she found the soft, sweet place just beneath his left ear, and bit down. She had never tasted vampire blood. It was a high like no other. Or maybe it was simply because it was Zack's blood. Whatever the reason, she knew one taste wouldn't be enough. Would never be enough . . .

"Easy, girl," Zack said.

But she wasn't listening.

Muttering an oath, he grasped a handful of her hair and gave a sharp tug.

A low growl rose in Kaitlyn's throat.

Damn, maybe this hadn't been a good idea. "Katy darlin', that's enough."

It was the endearment that broke through the red haze of her hunger. Lifting her head, she stared at Zack in horror. "I didn't want to stop," she said, her voice little more than a hoarse whisper. "I could have killed you."

"I don't think so."

"What if I hadn't stopped?"

He laughed softly. "I don't want to brag, darlin', but I think I could take you down if I had to."

"You're making fun of me."

"No." He drew her into his arms and brushed the hair away from her face. "This is the first time you've really surrendered to your thirst, isn't it?"

She nodded, still embarrassed. "I don't know what came over me." When her father had taken her hunting the first time, she had been careful to keep her hunger in check, perhaps because she knew he was watching, perhaps because she was afraid of losing control, of taking too much. Whatever the reason, she had never let her hunger get out of hand. At the Fortress, she preferred to drink from Northa or one of the other women. While living at Wolfram, she had occasionally hunted in the city; since coming to America, she had survived on bagged blood.

"It's all right, Katy," Zack assured her. "No harm done."

"How do you stop when what you really want to do is take it all?"

"Willpower, darlin'. Lots and lots of willpower. And practice," he added with a grin. "Don't forget, I've got a couple of hundred years on you."

A slow smile spread over her face. "Maybe I could practice on you again sometime."

"Anytime, Katy darlin'. Anytime at all." He stroked

her cheek with his knuckles. "There's a bond between us now."

"What kind of bond?"

"A blood bond. Can't you feel it?" It bound them together. Wherever she went in the future, he would always be able to find her.

"I don't think so. What does it feel like?"

"It's hard to explain." His mind brushed hers experimentally; he still couldn't read her thoughts, but he sensed her curiosity, her trepidation. "Try reading my mind."

She sat up, her brow furrowed in concentration, and then she shook her head. "Nothing. Can you read my mind?"

"Not exactly, but I can feel the link between us," he said, pulling her into his arms again. "I'll always be able to find you. The bond between us will grow stronger every time we share blood. Perhaps one day the link will go both ways."

Nodding, she rested her head against his shoulder. It just wasn't fair, she thought. She should be the stronger one. She had been born a vampire, after all, and yet, because of her mortal blood, she lacked many of the preternatural powers the rest of her people possessed.

And if that wasn't bad enough, it seemed even the Others had stronger powers than she did.

Chapter 15

Kaitlyn dreamed of Zack that night. No surprise, considering the effect his kisses—and his blood—had had on her senses. In her dream, they were walking hand in hand near the lake, pausing now and then to kiss in the shadows. A big gray cat followed them from a distance, its yellow eyes glinting golden in the light of the moon, its tail swishing with anger.

In the way of dreams, the scene shifted abruptly and she was in Zack's bed, in Zack's arms. He was kissing her to distraction when his eyes suddenly went bloodred. She screamed when his teeth turned to fangs.

In the blink of an eye, the gray cat sprang up on the bed. Back arched, the cat lunged at Zack, but Zack rolled out of the way, his body shifting, transforming almost instantly into a large black wolf.

Fangs bared, hackles raised, ears flat, feline and canine glared at each other, and then the wolf sprang forward. . . .

Kaitlyn woke to the sound of her own screams.

Breathing heavily, her body damp with sweat, she sat up, one hand pressed to her heart.

"Just a dream," she muttered. But what if it foreshadowed a future event?

Rising, she pulled on her robe and went into the kitchen. After fixing a cup of coffee, she carried it into the living room. She needed to call her father, to tell him about Korzha's attack. It wasn't a conversation she was looking forward to.

Drake sat on the dais, his expression solemn as he glanced at the assembled council members. He had spoken to Kaitlyn on the phone earlier, listened intently as she informed him of Korzha's treachery and how the man, Zack Ravenscroft, had destroyed Korzha.

Listening carefully, Drake had been certain there was a part of the story Kaitlyn was holding back, something about Ravenscroft, but he had not pressed her on the matter. He trusted Kaitlyn's instincts, her loyalty to the coven. In due time, she would tell him the rest. He had suggested she come home immediately. She had refused, of course, but that was no surprise. He could have insisted, but something had warned him that would only make her more determined to stay.

Aware of the council watching him, wondering why he had summoned them, he stood, his gaze resting on each of the thirteen members in turn. All were related to him, bound by the blood of the same sire. The majority of the people in the Fortress were related to him.

"I have called you here this evening on a matter that concerns me personally, and perhaps the coven, as well," Drake began. "Nadiya's youngest son has been killed and she has gone missing. I have no evidence, nothing but a strong suspicion that she is plotting revenge against me, whether for the death of her youngest son, or for the death of the son that was slain in the attempted coup against my father."

"That was more than twenty years ago," Andrei said. "Why would she wait so long?"

Drake shook his head. "I have no idea. Perhaps it has taken her this long to formulate a plan, or to gather an army against me. One thing I do know, her youngest son is dead, killed by a man I do not know."

"What man?" Gregor asked.

"The one Kaitlyn is dating. When she was attacked, the man, Ravenscroft, defended her and somehow managed to kill Korzha. Kaitlyn was vague on how this was accomplished."

"You are certain young Korzha intended to do her harm?"

"Yes." Drake resumed his seat. "Elena wishes me to order Kaitlyn home."

"Do you think that is necessary?" Ciprian asked.

Drake shrugged. "I have not yet decided. I want each of you to contact the leaders of the other Fortresses. Find out if they know anything of Nadiya's whereabouts, or if they have heard anything suspicious. Marku, I want you to see if you can locate her other children. They all seem to have dropped out of sight about the same time."

Marku nodded. "It will be done."

Drake glanced at the members of the council. "I want daily reports. And until we find out what she is up to, I suggest you warn your wives and children to stay close to the Fortress. That is all. The council is dismissed."

Drake sat there for several moments. He had never cared for Nadiya. He thought her a cold, calculating woman, caring for no one but her own children. He had often wondered why his father had married her, and when he had found the courage to ask, Rodin had shrugged, then said, *She is cold. She is selfish. But she is beautiful. And no one else will have her.*

Drake's opinion of Nadiya Korzha had not changed. How far would she go to avenge the deaths of her sons? What had been her intentions where Kaitlyn was concerned? It was obvious that young Korzha had been sent to keep an eye on Kaitlyn, but why? Were his instructions merely to watch her? Given what Kaitlyn had told him, that seemed unlikely. Had Korzha intended to kidnap Kaitlyn and hold her for ransom? Or had Nadiya intended to demand his life in exchange for his daughter's? Knowing Nadiya, he thought it more likely that she planned to kill Kaitlyn, knowing the loss of his only daughter would cause him endless heartache, and more suffering than anything else she could do.

He grunted softly. Could Nadiya really be that cold-blooded? Surely she realized that if she harmed so much as a hair of Kaitlyn's head, he would hunt her down and destroy her, no matter where she went, or how long it took.

Muttering an oath, he stalked out of the council chambers.

Whether she wished it or not, he feared it was time for Kaitlyn to come home.

The nightmare was still fresh in Kaitlyn's mind when she woke the next afternoon. She hadn't told her father that Zack was one of the Others. If she was lucky, her father and Zack would never meet, and her father would never discover the truth.

Later, standing in the shower, she was overcome with guilt for her omission. She had never kept anything from her father. Not that she had ever done anything truly horrible, but from the time she was a little girl, she had confessed her misdeeds—from sneaking a cookie before dinner to sneaking out of the house for a midnight swim with her girlfriends. She had never been inclined to try drugs or cigarettes. She had been curious about sex, of course, but not curious enough to experiment with any of the boys who had offered to enlighten her.

She turned off the shower and then, after drying off with a big fluffy towel, she went into the bedroom to get dressed. She had wanted to tell her dad about Zack, but doing so could put Zack's life in danger, and that was something she simply couldn't do.

She put on clean underwear, pulled on a pair of black sweats and a pink T-shirt, then ran a brush through her hair. Maybe it wasn't just lust she felt for Zack, she mused as she went into the kitchen. Maybe it was love. She smiled as she put two slices of bread in the toaster. In love with Zack. The mere thought filled her with a delightful warmth from head to heel.

"I love him," she said, hearing the wonder in her voice. "I love him."

Hard on that realization came the unwanted thought that he might not love her in return, that he was just toying with her affection, that she was just another in a long string of women. After all, he had lived for centuries. He must have had dozens—hundreds—of women in that time. How could any woman resist him?

She shook her head. She was being ridiculous. And whether he loved her or not didn't change the way she felt about him. He was gorgeous, yes, but he was also sweet and kind, and funny in his own way. He had been the soul of patience last night, not to mention brave, to let her drink from him. Even though he had insisted he hadn't been in any danger, she might have drained him dry.

She wasn't sure exactly what had transpired between

Zack and Korzha since Zack had not elaborated, but it was obvious they had fought and Daryn had lost. Perhaps Zack had saved her life. At the risk of his own. She wondered again about Daryn Korzha's intentions. What would her fate have been if Zack hadn't come to her rescue the night Daryn drugged her? And why had Daryn attacked her in the first place?

Would she ever know?

She buttered the toast, daydreaming while she ate it—she pictured herself spending the rest of her life with Zack, maybe here, in the States, maybe in Romania, although she doubted there was much chance of that. Hatred for the Others was deeply embedded in her people. She shook her head. The war between her kind and the Others had ended centuries ago. It seemed an extraordinarily long time to carry a grudge.

She wondered if Zack liked being a vampire. What was it like, to have your whole world turned upside down?

She could relate, in a way. After all, her people were mortal for a time. Still, they knew the change was coming, knew it was normal and natural. There was no fear involved. Had Zack been afraid? Or was the change something he had wanted? If not, did he yearn to be mortal again?

Once the questions started, they just kept coming. Did he kill to survive? Did he miss the taste of food? He could tolerate wine, but what about milk and water? Had he ever been married? It was believed the Others couldn't have children. If that was true, did he regret not being able to father a child?

He was much in her mind that day, whether she was trying to watch a movie, folding a load of laundry, or fixing an early dinner since she hadn't bothered with lunch.

Time dragged. Finally, she picked up a book and settled down on the sofa to read.

She woke to the sound of someone knocking on the door. A glance at the window showed the sun was down. Smiling with anticipation, she ran a hand through her hair, then hurried to open the door.

"Zack, hi!"

He kissed her soundly. "Hi, yourself. I missed you."

"I missed you, too."

"What's on the agenda tonight?"

She shrugged. "I'm in the mood for a walk. How about you?"

"Fine by me."

Something was up, Zack mused as they strolled down to the lake. He could sense the tension in her although he had no idea what was causing it. He didn't think she was upset by what had happened last night. She had enjoyed it too much. Maybe she wanted another taste and was embarrassed to ask. No. He was pretty sure that wasn't it.

When they reached the bench, she sat down and after a moment, Zack sat beside her. "Okay, what's up?" he asked.

"What do you mean?"

"You haven't said a word since we left the house. Whatever's bothering you, just spit it out."

"Nothing's bothering me except, well, I still don't know very much about you." She raised a hand, staying his comment. "I only know you're young and single and rich. And you taste good."

"Want another bite?"

"Not right now." She stared out at the lake a moment. "Do you like being a vampire? Was it something you wanted?"

"Is that what's got your panties in a knot? You're worried about whether I'm happy being a vampire?"

"Of course not. Like I said, I just want to know more about you."

Zack shook his head. Women. "In the beginning, I hated it and I hated the vampire who turned me, but once I got the hang of it . . ." He shrugged. "It took some getting used to, but I've got no complaints now."

"Have you killed very many people?"

"Define many."

"Zack."

"I've killed a few, especially in the beginning, before I learned to control the hunger. I don't know any vampire who hasn't taken a life or two."

Kaitlyn nodded. She didn't know if her father had ever taken a life to sustain his own, but she knew he had killed at least two men. "Would you be mortal again, if you could?"

"Hell, no."

"Have you ever been married?"

"No."

"In love?"

Colette's image flashed through Zack's mind. "Once," he admitted, "a long, long time ago. How about you, Katy?" he asked, his voice suddenly silky smooth. "You ever been in love?"

She shook her head, although it wasn't entirely true, because she was in love with Zack. "Is it true you can't have children?"

"Yeah."

"Does that ever bother you?"

"Sure, but . . ." He made a vague gesture with his hand. "You've got to take the bad with the good." He stared into the darkness. "I guess that's something you're looking forward to—marriage, motherhood, the whole nine yards."

"It's expected of me."

"Expected?"

"Our women are only fertile for a short time each year."

"Is that why your grandfather had so many wives?"

"Partly. Our women outnumber the men, so it's not uncommon for Master Vampires to take more than one wife."

"I guess that makes sense," Zack muttered and then grinned. "Your grandfather must have been quite a stud."

Kaitlyn huffed a sigh of annoyance. "Do you think you'd like to have twenty wives and hundreds of children?"

"Well, I don't know about raising all those kids," he said, waggling his eyebrows, "but the begetting part doesn't sound so bad."

She punched him on the shoulder. "Men! All you ever think about is sex."

"Ow!"

"Serves you right."

Laughing, Zack pulled her into his arms. "Katy, I don't want anyone but you."

She stared up at him. Did he mean it? "Zack . . ."

"I know, I'm moving too fast. So, what do you want me to do? Back off? Go away?"

"Just kiss me, you idiot."

"You sweet talker," he murmured.

She sighed as his lips claimed hers. Falling for Zack was bound to cause nothing but trouble, but somehow, that didn't seem to matter, not when he was kissing her as if he would never let her go.

She wrapped her arms around him as his kiss grew deeper, more passionate. Maybe she was worrying over nothing. Maybe her father wouldn't object to having

Zack for a son-in-law. And maybe she was taking too much for granted. After all, no promises had been made, no words of commitment had been spoken between them.

Just because she loved him didn't mean he loved her.

Chapter 16

Eyes narrowed, hands resting on his knees, Lucien, Master of the Italian Fortress, regarded the woman standing before him. Nadiya Korzha was tall for a female, her bearing austere. Long straight brown hair fell over her rigid shoulders. Her eyes were the color of the sky on a cloudy day. He had been surprised by her request for an audience—doubly so because he had never met her. He knew who she was, of course. Rodin Sherrad's fourth wife. He had heard rumors that Sherrad's son, Drake, was interested in her whereabouts, though Lucien had no idea why.

Lucien gestured at the chair across from his. "Please, sit."

"Thank you."

"We can spend several useless minutes in small talk," Lucien said. "Or we can skip the niceties and you can come straight to the point and tell me why you're here."

"It is well-known that you have long coveted the Carpathian Fortress."

"Indeed?" Lucien lifted one brow, concerned that anyone should have such knowledge. The Carpathian Fortress was the largest of its kind. In days past, there had been those who had challenged Rodin for its possession. All had been defeated. But Rodin was no longer a threat. "Well-known by whom?"

"By myself."

"You did not come here to tell me that."

"No, I have come seeking your help in avenging my kin."

Lucien frowned. "Explain."

"Drake Sherrad killed my sons. . . ."

"That was over twenty years ago," Lucien interjected. "Wait a minute. Did you say 'sons'?"

"Yes." She had no proof that Daryn was dead, but she had not heard from him in more than a week. Only death would prevent him from contacting her. She didn't know who had killed him, but of one thing she was certain—Drake Sherrad was involved.

"What is it you want from me?"

"There are those within the Carpathian Fortress who are not happy with the changes Drake has made since his father's demise, but there are not enough of them to overpower Drake and assume control of the Fortress. They have pledged their allegiance to me."

Lucien leaned forward. "Go on."

"Together, we can overthrow Sherrad and claim the Carpathian Fortress." Lucien wasn't alone in his desire to rule Sherrad's territory. She took a deep breath. "When it is ours, we can rule it together."

He reared back, eyes wide with astonishment. "Are you proposing an alliance? Or marriage?"

"Whichever suits you best."

"If you are thinking of going to battle, you will need a strong army. Or are you suggesting that I challenge Sherrad one-on-one?" He shook his head. "I know of no one who can defeat him with the sword."

"Soon, I will have something to bargain with," Nadiya

said, her mind racing as a new strategy fell into place. "It will give us the edge we need."

"What sort of edge?"

"When I have obtained it, I will let you know."

"This is not something to be decided without a great deal of thought," Lucien remarked. "Many lives hang in the balance. I will need time to think it over."

"Take as long as you deem necessary," she said.

He nodded. She must have the patience of a saint, he mused, seeing as how she had already waited over twenty years to avenge Florin's death. He grinned inwardly. Of course, if Nadiya Korzha had a saintly bone in her body, she would not be seeking revenge.

"Where can I reach you?" he asked.

She smiled coolly. "You cannot. I will get in touch with you." Rising, she inclined her head, then vanished from his sight.

Lucien grunted softly. He would as soon put his trust in a vampire hunter as the lovely Nadiya, and yet the thought of being Master of the Carpathian Fortress, the largest vampire refuge in all the world, might be worth the risk.

Chapter 17

For Kaitlyn, the next few days were among the happiest of her life. Zack arrived at her house with the setting of the sun and stayed until dawn's first light brightened the horizon.

They took long walks in the moonlight. They swam in the lake. They went dancing until dawn at the Skylight Room. He taught her how to play poker and craps and roulette.

One evening, he took her to dinner at the restaurant in the casino, insisting she describe the taste of the lobster, the rice pilaf, the seven-layer chocolate cake she had for dessert. As far as Kaitlyn was concerned, it was impossible. How could you describe the taste of food to someone who had existed on a liquid diet for six hundred years?

Every night, when the urge to be alone together grew irresistible, they went back to her place, curled up on the sofa, and made out like randy teenagers. Though Zack had agreed they should take it slow, each night it became more and more difficult for Kaitlyn to send him home, especially on those nights when they shared blood.

Until she'd met Zack, Kaitlyn had consumed blood

because it was necessary for her survival. Given a choice, she would have shunned it. Now, having tasted Zack, she quickly found herself craving the taste of him more and more often.

Tonight was such a night. Needing to distract herself from her hunger for his blood and her desire for his body, she put her hand on his chest and gave him a little push.

He let her go without argument or comment. He might not be able to read her mind, but he recognized the hunger in her eyes.

"Sorry," she murmured.

He spread his arms out along the back of the sofa, then stretched his legs out in front of him. "No problem." Every night about this time, he remembered why he didn't date virgins, and why he left Kaitlyn's house feeling exhilarated and frustrated at the same time.

Rising, Kaitlyn went into the kitchen. She filled a glass with ice water, then returned to her place on the sofa. She sipped the water, then put the glass aside. "How did you become a vampire?"

"I took the wrong woman to bed."

"Excuse me?"

"I'd been hanging out at a local pub. One night I met a woman there. She was pretty, exotic, years older than I was." He laughed softly. "Hundreds of years older, as it turned out, but I didn't know that at the time. All I saw was a fascinating creature who was as different from the women I was used to as a queen from a scullery maid. I know now that what I saw, what I felt, wasn't real. Anyway, one night some stranger started flirting with her. When she turned him down, he got abusive."

He paused a moment, seeing it all in his mind. "At the time, I didn't realize she was more than capable of taking care of herself. Anyway, I tossed the guy out of the pub and the lady repaid my chivalry by taking me to bed. After we made love, she said she was thirsty." He shook his head ruefully. "I had no idea I was her drink of choice."

"Was it terrifying?"

"Oh, yeah. I went to bed an ignorant farmer and woke up a ravening monster."

"That's horrible."

"I thought so. It took me a while to figure out what she'd done to me. I quickly learned that the sun burned my flesh, that mortal food sickened me, that the only thing I could safely consume was blood, and that it didn't matter if it was animal or human, or if the host was dead or alive."

"Dead?" Kaitlyn grimaced.

"Yeah, well . . ." He shrugged.

"Did you ever see her again? The vampire who turned you?"

"No. I spent a year or two looking for her. I'm not sure why, or what I would have done if I'd found her. Anyway, time passed, and I learned how to be a vampire, how to hunt more efficiently, how to ease my hunger without killing my prey." He slid a glance in her direction and grinned. "How to take advantage of all the preternatural perks that were now mine."

Leaning forward, she kissed him on the cheek. "You're quite remarkable, you know?"

"Yeah, why? Because I learned to survive?"

She nodded. "I'm not sure I would have done as well in your shoes. I grew up knowing what I was. My father was there every step of the way to teach me what to do, and I had a whole flock of aunts and uncles to guide me. Not to mention my mother." Kaitlyn smiled. "She's incredible. You'd like her."

"I like you," Zack said, his voice suddenly soft and

sexy. "I like the color of your eyes, and the way they light up when you see me. I like your cute little nose," he said, kissing the tip, "and the way it twitches when you smell blood. I like your mouth, the way you taste . . ." He paused, his tongue tracing the outline of her lips.

"More," she murmured.

"I like your ears and your lovely neck. . . ." More kisses followed this declaration.

"Zack . . ."

"I know, I know." He drew back, breathing hard. "I think I'd better go before this gets out of hand."

Kaitlyn followed him to the door, rose on her tiptoes to kiss him good night. They couldn't go on like this, she thought, watching him disappear into the darkness. He had to be as frustrated as she was.

Sighing, she closed the door. Right or wrong, tomorrow night she was going to seduce Zack Ravenscroft.

Drake stared at the man standing across from him. "Are you sure of this information?"

Gregor nodded. "I overheard the end of the conversation myself."

"You are sure Lucien was speaking with Nadiya?"

"Positive."

Drake regarded Gregor for a moment. Gregor was the third son of his father's seventh wife. "What were you doing at the Italian Fortress?"

"I have been courting Lucien's oldest daughter."

Drake raised one brow. "Indeed? How long has this been going on?"

"A few months," Gregor said with a shrug.

"Do none of our women appeal to you?"

"Have you seen Rosalia?" Gregor asked with a wry grin.

"Point taken." Rosalia was one of the most beautiful

women Drake had ever seen, with her long red hair and flashing black eyes. "If you hear anything else, let me know immediately."

"Yes, my lord." Gregor inclined his head, then left the chamber.

Drake ran a hand through his hair. Gregor hadn't heard anything specific, certainly nothing useful, but the fact that Nadiya had been in contact with Lucien spoke volumes. Drake had long known that Lucien coveted the Carpathian Fortress. Not that he was alone. Nearly every Master Vampire was jealous of whoever held the Fortress in Romania. It was the birthplace of their race, the largest stronghold in the world. It had been ruled by a member of the Sherrad family for as long as their kind had existed. Many had tried to claim it—some by force, some by cunning, some by treachery—but none had succeeded.

There were those who feared the Sherrad rule would come to an end if Drake were defeated in battle. He had no son to avenge him, no son to reclaim the Fortress if it was taken. But there was Andrei. And Stefan . . .

Drake moved to the window and stared out over the valley, the current problem temporarily forgotten as he wondered yet again about Stefan's whereabouts. Stefan, his favorite brother, gone these past twenty years.

Drake braced one hand against the edge of the window. "Where are you?" he murmured. "Why have you not come home?"

Stefan Sherrad stood in the shadows outside Ravenscroft's Casino, his thoughts momentarily turning inward. More than twenty years had passed since he'd left the Carpathian Fortress, and he had missed it every single day. And yet the pain of seeing the happiness his brothers had found had driven him away, and kept him away. He did not begrudge Andrei or Drake the love they had found, wished them only continued happiness, but he could not be there to watch when his own heart remained broken. And so, like a coward, he had run away.

Rumors had sent him here. Trouble was brewing in Romania, and it involved Drake's daughter. Secrets did not long remain secrets in his world. The vampire population was not large. Gossip quickly spread from one Fortress to another. While visiting the Fortress in New England, Stefan had heard rumors of unrest in his homeland. A little discreet eavesdropping here, a little snooping there, and he had learned that Daryn Korzha had been killed in Nevada by an unknown assailant. The information had naturally piqued Stefan's interest, since he and Korzha were related. But it had been mention of Drake's daughter in the same breath that had sent Stefan to Lake Tahoe, located between Northern California and Nevada.

A little discreet snooping had turned up Kaitlyn's address, along with the fact that she was often seen in the company of Zack Ravenscroft, owner of Ravenscroft's Casino.

Moving toward the entrance, Stefan wondered what manner of man Ravenscroft was, and what his intentions were toward his niece. But it didn't matter.

He had come to take Kaitlyn home. But first, he wanted to meet Zack Ravenscroft.

Zack frowned as a tall, dark-haired man dressed in jeans and a black denim jacket over a white shirt approached him. Though the similarities were subtle, there was no mistaking the resemblance between the stranger and Kaitlyn. Could this be her father? And if so, what was he doing here?

Silly question, Zack thought. If he had a daughter, he would certainly want to meet the man she was dating. He wondered if Katy had spoken to her father recently and let it slip that he was one of the so-called Others. No doubt he would find out soon enough.

"Are you Zack Ravenscroft?" the stranger asked.

Zack nodded. "And you'd be?"

"Stefan Sherrad."

Not the father, Zack thought, but the missing brother. "What can I do for you?"

"I am Kaitlyn's . . ."

"Uncle," Zack said, finishing Sherrad's introduction for him.

Surprise flickered in Sherrad's eyes. "You know of me?"

"Kaitlyn's mentioned you once or twice. Does she know you're here?"

"Not yet."

Zack crossed his arms over his chest. "So, what brings you here?"

"I am sure you can guess."

"Did her father send you?"

"No. I have not spoken to my brother in quite some time."

Zack gestured at the bar behind him. "Can I get you something to drink?" He already knew the answer, but for the moment, he thought it better to pretend he didn't know Sherrad was a vampire.

"No, thank you." Stefan glanced at the patrons crowding along the bar. "Perhaps we could speak in private."

"Sure." Zack moved away from the bar and walked

swiftly toward the elevator. He didn't look back to see if Sherrad followed.

They were silent until they reached Zack's office.

Stefan glanced around. The room was large, sparsely furnished with a desk, a computer, a file cabinet, and a couple of chairs.

Zack took a seat behind the desk, gesturing for Stefan to take the other chair. "What do you want?"

"I would like to know what your intentions are toward my niece."

"I'm in love with her," Zack said. "Not that it's any of your business. She's a big girl, after all."

"She is her father's heir."

"So?"

"Do you know who he is?"

"She said he was a businessman in Romania. I assume he's rich," Zack said with a shrug. "But so am I."

"Is that all she told you?"

"What else is there?"

Stefan studied the other man, wondering just how much Ravenscroft really knew. It seemed unlikely that Kaitlyn would have revealed her true nature to a mortal. To do so was strictly forbidden. Yet Ravenscroft claimed to be in love with Kaitlyn, and if she was in love with him . . .

Stefan sighed, remembering Cosmina. She had been mortal, and he had broken the laws of their people when he confided in her. But what man of honor could make love to a woman and not tell her the truth? He was sorely afraid that Kaitlyn would feel the same.

"I wanted to meet you," Stefan said, "to let you know I am taking Kaitlyn home."

"Is that right?"

"Yes."

"She hasn't mentioned it to me."

"I have not yet spoken with her."

"What if she doesn't want to go?"

"I am afraid the choice is not hers. Her life is in danger here, as you well know."

"What do you mean?"

"I am talking about Daryn Korzha. I believe you killed him."

"You know about that?"

Stefan nodded once, curtly. "She is not safe here."

Rising, Zack leaned forward, hands braced against the top of the desk. "I think I've proven I can take care of her."

"Perhaps," Stefan said, also rising. "But there are things going on you are not yet aware of."

"Is that right?"

"For your own safety, I advise you not to pry into affairs that do not concern you. Good evening."

Zack frowned thoughtfully as Stefan Sherrad left his office. "That's where you're wrong," he muttered. "Anything that concerns Kaitlyn is my affair."

Kaitlyn was dressing for her date with Zack when the doorbell rang. He was early, she thought, glancing at her watch. A last look in the mirror, and she hurried down the hallway to open the front door.

And came face-to-face with a short, stocky man holding a gun. She knew, by the blank expression in his eyes, that he was under some sort of mind control.

Had Nadiya sent him? If so, had she told him to kill her?

"You. Will come. With me," he said, gesturing with the gun for her to follow him. "Now!" he added, when she didn't move.

Kaitlyn stared at him, her mind racing. She took a

step forward, intending to wrest the gun from his hand, when a dark shape rose up out of the shadows to her left and slammed into the man, knocking him off balance so that he tumbled down the porch stairs.

Without waiting to see who her champion was, Kaitlyn slammed the door and locked it, then stood there, one hand pressed to her heart. She was debating what to do next when she heard a knock at the door.

Was it the gunman? Or the man who had apparently come to her rescue? She hadn't heard any gunshots. Did that mean the intruder had been incapacitated?

She tapped her foot a moment, then peered out the front window. And into a face that looked remarkably like her father's. Could it be . . . ?

"Kaitlyn, open the door."

His words carried the sound of home and she opened the door, then stood there, too stunned to speak.

"Kaitlyn."

She stared at him a moment: Was it possible?

"I am your unc . . ."

"Stefan." It could be no one else. He looked enough like her father to be his twin. "What are you doing here? How did you know where I was?" She glanced to the left, then the right. "Who was that man? Where is he?"

"Perhaps we could discuss it inside?" her uncle suggested.

"Yes, of course, come in."

She glanced at him over her shoulder as he followed her into the living room. It was amazing, how much he looked like her father. She gestured at the sofa. "Please, sit down."

"Thank you."

She sat beside him, unable to stop staring.

"I know," he said, smiling. "Your father and I look much alike."

"You could be twins. What are you doing here?"

"I was traveling when I heard that one of the Korzhas had been killed in Lake Tahoe. I was naturally curious, since we are related." He shrugged. "A little snooping here, a few questions there, and I overheard your name. I came here to see if it was indeed you."

"Who was that man?" she asked again.

"I do not know. But he will not bother you anymore."

That could mean only one thing, but it was hard to feel sympathy for a man who had pointed a gun at her. "What do you think he wanted?"

"You do not know?"

She shook her head. "Know what?"

Before he could explain, the doorbell rang again. Startled, she glanced at Stefan.

"I will get it," he said.

Kaitlyn nodded. She told herself there was nothing to worry about. But she clenched her hands in her lap when Stefan opened the door.

A moment passed. Another. He stood there, unmoving, not speaking.

And then she heard her father's voice, thick with emotion. "Stefan!"

Hardly aware of what she was doing, Kaitlyn stood as her father threw his arms around his brother and crushed him close in a hug that would likely have crushed a mortal's ribs. "Stefan! Where have you been? What are you doing here?"

"Trying to breathe," Stefan answered with a grin.

Drake released him immediately. "Forgive me, but I am so glad to see you."

Stefan nodded. "And I you, brother."

Drake's gaze ran over Stefan. "You look well. Liliana

has missed you. You should have kept in touch with her." The unspoken words, *and with me,* hung in the air between them. "How could you stay away so long?"

"I needed time."

"Promise me you will never again stay away so long."

"I missed you, too," Stefan said.

"I will have your promise," Drake insisted.

"You have it."

Kaitlyn saw tears in her uncle's eyes, felt the sting of tears in her own eyes as the two men embraced again.

When they parted, Stefan cleared his throat. "Since you are here, I assume you know Kaitlyn is in danger."

"Yes, it is the reason I am here," Drake said as the two men moved into the living room.

"Just in time," Stefan said, and quickly told her father about the gunman who had been there earlier.

"You don't have to talk about me like I'm not here," Kaitlyn said, coming up behind the two men. "What's this all about, anyway?"

"I have come to take you home."

"But I don't want to go home!" she exclaimed.

"That decision is no longer yours. I am certain Nadiya is behind these attacks on you," Drake said. "I am not sure what she intends, only that you are involved. My guess is she is planning to use you to get to me."

"Why?" Kaitlyn asked, frowning. "You didn't have anything to do with Daryn's death."

"I believe she means to avenge herself on me for Florin's death, and also for Daryn's. She knows the best way to hurt me is to harm you. You are not safe here."

"I'm a big girl. I can take care of myself."

Stefan lifted one brow, as if to remind her of the man on the porch.

She glared at him. "I could have handled him by myself."

"This is not a matter open to discussion," Drake said. "My decision has been made. We are leaving here tonight."

"I'm not . . ." Kaitlyn began, only to be interrupted by a knock on the door, and Zack's voice, calling, "Hey, Katy, I know I'm late, but . . ."

Zack paused inside the door. Katy stood between Stefan and another man who could only be her father. "Looks like I picked a bad time to come calling."

Kaitlyn blew out an exasperated sigh. "You have no idea."

"Introduce us, Kaitlyn," the taller of the two men said.

"Dad, this is Zack, the man who saved my life. Zack, this is my father, Drake Sherrad. And this is my uncle Stefan. . . ."

"We've met," Zack said.

"Oh? I didn't know." She had a feeling there were a lot of things she didn't know.

"So," Zack said, glancing from her father to her uncle, "what's going on?"

"I have come to take my daughter home," Drake said in a voice that left no room for argument. "If you will excuse us, we are preparing to leave."

"Dad . . ."

"Tell him good-bye, Kaitlyn. We are going. Now."

"You don't have to go with him, Katy," Zack said. "You're over twenty-one."

Drake glared at him. "How dare you suggest my daughter defy me! Get out of here, now!"

"Not without Kaitlyn."

Zack reached for her, but the other vampire moved quicker.

Drake's arm snaked around Kaitlyn's waist. There was a rush of preternatural power, and Drake and his daughter were gone.

Stefan's gaze locked with Zack's for a brief moment, almost as if there was something he wanted to say, and then, he, too was gone.

Zack swore a vile oath. "This doesn't end here," he muttered angrily. "Not by a long shot!"

Chapter 18

Kaitlyn glared at her father. "How could you?"

"I did what was best for you." And in the worst possible way, Drake thought. He never should have used his preternatural power in front of a mortal, but it was too late to worry about that now, or wonder what Ravenscroft thought of their unusual leave-taking. But it didn't matter. Even if Ravenscroft was foolish enough to tell someone what he had seen, no one would believe him.

"You had no right!" Kaitlyn blinked back her tears. Turning her back on her father, she stared out the window at the valley below. Snow covered the distant mountains and dusted the leaves of the trees. She pressed a hand to her stomach. She still felt a little queasy after being transported so swiftly from her cabin in Lake Tahoe to the Carpathian Fortress. She had never really liked it here. It was too big, too cold. But it was more than that. Her father was a different man here. At Wolfram Castle, he was Dad, the man who pampered her and spoiled her, the father who had read her stories at bedtime and played Barbies on the floor with her when she was a little girl. At the Fortress, he was all business, the head of their coven, the Master of the Carpathian Fortress. It was a responsibility he took seriously and it colored everything he did, every decision he made.

"Kaitlyn, look at me."

She could have refused her father, but not the Master of the Coven. She turned to look at him, her expression sullen. "What?"

"Do you understand that you are in danger? I know you think your vampire blood makes you invincible, but it does not. Nadiya wants revenge against me. She knows you and your mother are my only weaknesses. I cannot keep you safe in America. I do not trust anyone else to do so. You may be angry with me for this. You may even hate me for a time. But until the threat to your life no longer exists, you will stay here. Do you understand?"

"Yes."

"Kaitlyn." His voice softened, along with his harsh expression.

She felt the sting of tears behind her eyes as he closed the distance between them and took her in his arms.

With a sigh, Kaitlyn rested her head on his chest. Her father loved her. Of that she had no doubt. But, danger or no danger, he had to let her live her own life. She wasn't a child anymore.

Elena smiled at Kaitlyn. "You can't blame your father for worrying," she said. "Not only about you, but about everyone in the Fortress."

"I don't understand why Nadiya has everyone so worried. Does she have that much power?"

"Of herself? No. But she has other sons, and there are rumors that she has made an alliance with the Master of the Italian Fortress. If she isn't stopped . . ." Elena's voice trailed off. Although it had happened over twenty years ago, she remembered all too clearly when the Master of the Irish Coven had challenged Drake's father for possession of the Carpathian Coven.

The two Master Vampires, both bare-chested and armed with silver-bladed swords, had met in a clearing below the Fortress under the light of a full moon. Hidden behind a tree with Stefan, Elena had watched the bloody battle, had watched, sickened by the sight, as, with one slash of his sword, Rodin had severed Gerret's head from his body. She had turned away in horror, so she had not seen what happened next. But she had heard Liliana's high-pitched scream of denial. When Elena turned back, Rodin lay dead on the ground, a long wooden stake protruding from his heart. Liliana knelt beside her husband, a look of horrified disbelief on her face. Drake had Florin by the throat.

Elena had thought the battle finished, but she had been wrong. Minutes had passed, and then Liliana rose to her feet. Eyes blazing, her cheeks streaked with scarlet tears, she had picked up her husband's sword. Standing tall and proud, she had called for a champion to avenge her husband's death. Every member of the council had taken a step forward, as had Stefan and Drake. To this day, Elena remembered the sinking feeling in the pit of her stomach when Liliana had offered the blade to Drake. Still hidden in the shadows, Elena had watched Drake take hold of his father's sword. He had defeated Florin in battle and in so doing, had become the new Master of the Carpathian Fortress.

More than twenty years had passed since that dreadful night, but the memories of that hour remained as fresh in her mind as if it had happened only yesterday.

"You're afraid for Dad, aren't you?" Kaitlyn asked. It had never occurred to her that anything could happen to her father. He was so tall and strong, always confident and in control, she had always thought him to be as indestructible as the mountain on which the Fortress was built.

Elena nodded. "If Rodin could be destroyed . . ."

Her mother didn't finish the sentence, but Kaitlyn knew what she was thinking. If Drake's father, who had lived for over a thousand years, could be destroyed, it could happen to any of them.

Lying in bed later that night, Kaitlyn pondered the conversation she'd had with her mother. She had had no idea things were so serious, or that her father's life might be in danger. Having grown up in Wolfram instead of the Fortress, Kaitlyn suddenly realized that she was ignorant of much of the history of their people. Sure, her parents had taught her the basics, taken her to the Fortress to meet her relatives, explained what was expected of her when she was old enough to take a husband. She had attended weddings and other formal functions in the company of her parents, she knew she was expected to marry, and to produce children as long as she was able. It was something she had accepted without question. Until she met Zack.

Being with him, getting to know him, she had come to the realization that she didn't want an arranged marriage, didn't want to spend her life in the Fortress doing what was expected of her. She wanted to stay in Lake Tahoe with the man she loved.

Blinking back tears, she turned onto her side. She shouldn't be thinking about herself, or missing Zack. She should be worrying about her father, about what might happen if he had to meet the Italian Master Vampire in battle to defend the Fortress.

A cold fear clutched her heart. She was her father's heir. If there was a fight and her father lost, would she be expected to meet the victor in battle? Surely not!

She had never held a sword in her life. Surely her uncle
Andrei or uncle Stefan, or one of the other brothers,
would step forward to meet the challenge.

Wouldn't they?

With Stefan's return, Elena decided they should
have a party to welcome him home.

"A party?" Drake asked. "Now?"

"Why not now?" Elena asked.

"I can think of any number of reasons," he replied
dryly.

Elena heaved a sigh of exasperation. "I think we'll
be safe for a few hours. It's not like Nadiya's going to
come here looking for Kaitlyn. And Stefan's been gone
such a long time." Rising, she moved into her husband's arms. "Please, Drake?"

"How big a party do you have in mind?"

"Just the Sherrad family."

He grunted softly. "Very well." There had never
been any doubt that she would get her way, he thought
ruefully. In all their married life, he had rarely denied
Elena anything she wished. It had pleased him to spoil
her, to grant her every wish whenever possible.

"Stefan looks good," Elena remarked, "but the sadness is still there, in his eyes. Do you think he'll ever get
over her?"

Drake stroked her hair, loving the feel of it in his
hands, the way the silky strands curled around his fingers. "I hope so."

"If only he'd fall in love again."

Lowering his head, Drake kissed her lightly. "Love
heals all?"

"Most things. And speaking of love, you must know
that Kaitlyn is in love with that man."

He nuzzled the slender curve of her throat. "I do not wish to discuss that now, wife."

"Drake . . ." Her eyelids fluttered down; whatever she had been about to say forgotten as his tongue slid seductively over her skin.

Claiming her lips with his, he swept her up in his arms and carried her into their bedroom. Some things in life changed, he thought as he lowered her onto the bed and stretched out beside her. Children grew up. Wars were fought. Dynasties rose and fell. But his love for Elena, his need for this woman above all else, remained constant now and forever.

Chapter 19

Once Zack's frustration receded and his anger cooled, he gave serious thought as to how to get Kaitlyn back. He had no idea where her father had taken her, although the Fortress she had talked about seemed the most logical destination. But whether her father had taken her there or somewhere else, locating her wouldn't be a problem. He had tasted her blood and she had tasted his. All he had to do was follow the blood bond that bound them together.

The following night, he informed Scherry he would be leaving town on Saturday for an extended vacation. Assuring her that he would keep in touch, he gave her the combination to the safe, as well as a list of bar supplies that needed to be ordered on Monday. Once he was satisfied she understood his instructions, he left the casino and drove to his favorite haunt in the city. Transporting from one country to another required a great deal of energy and concentration. Best to be well-fed before he attempted it.

After parking his car in the lot, he entered the nightclub and made his way to the bar. He stood there a moment, studying the customers, his mind touching first one and then another. Mortals all seemed to worry about the same things, he mused. The men were usually concerned with sex and how soon they could get it, or money, and how to make more of it. The women fretted over a wider variety of mundane things—their husbands, their children, their hair, their weight. He had yet to meet a mortal woman who was happy with her figure and wasn't obsessed with losing five to ten pounds, or more.

He settled on a middle-aged redhead who was standing at the far end of the bar, alone. She was pretty, she was single, and she was happy to be so. As was her wont, she had stopped in for a drink on her way home from the hospital where she worked in the admitting department.

It took little effort to draw her attention. When she met his gaze, he mesmerized her with a look. Speaking to her mind, he told her to follow him outside, which she did.

Taking her by the hand, he led her into the alley that ran between the nightclub and the building next door.

There had been a time when he'd felt guilty for luring women into the shadows and taking their blood, but the guilt hadn't lasted long. Not feeding regularly was far more dangerous for his prey. He had learned early that people died when he waited too long. It was impossible to stop feeding once discomfort turned to agony.

He spoke quietly to the woman, assuring her that he meant her no harm, and then he bent his head to her neck and drank. When he had taken all he dared, he escorted her back into the nightclub, then wiped the incident from her mind.

She blinked at him as he released her from his enchantment.

Zack smiled at her. "Can I buy you a drink?"

"What?" She looked confused for a moment.

"I asked if I could buy you a drink."

"Do I know you?"

"Zack, remember?"

She frowned at him.

Zack grinned inwardly. He knew she was trying to figure out why she felt faint and disoriented and why she didn't remember inviting him to sit with her. Since he had erased his memory from her mind, it was unlikely that she would ever recall being in an alley with a vampire. And even if the memory surfaced, no one would believe her.

"You should go home, Karen," he said.

"Yes. Yes, I should." She stared at him, her brow furrowed, and then she left the nightclub, her steps a little wobbly, due, no doubt, to the amount of blood she had lost.

Well, it had been for a good cause, Zack mused as he left the bar and drove back to the casino. Tomorrow night would find him on his way to Romania.

Zack rose with the setting sun. Time was of the essence. Being able to close his eyes and transport himself from one location to another was one of his favorite vampire perks. After he was first turned, it had taken a little getting used to, and even knowing he was nearly indestructible, it had scared the hell out of him the first few times he had tried it. And there was always the fear, at least in the beginning, that he might misjudge where he wanted to go and wind up inside a mountain or something. Thankfully, that had never happened.

At first, he had gone only short distances—from one city to another, then one state to another, then across the country. He had been a vampire for a year or so before he got the nerve to go hopping from country to country, and then he'd wondered why he had waited so long.

Of course, he had to time things just right. It wouldn't do to arrive at his destination when the sun was up. A quick check on the computer and he figured if he left in the next few minutes, he would arrive in Romania with just enough time to find a suitable place to hole up until sundown.

He took a quick shower, dressed, and left his lair. Transporting himself to the woods near Kaitlyn's cabin, he concentrated on the link between them, felt a growing surge of supernatural power stir the leaves on the trees as he opened his senses. The bond between them was like invisible strands binding them together, a sort of preternatural GPS that only he could see. All he had to do was follow it.

The sense of moving swiftly through time and space had once filled him with trepidation; now, it was a thrill like no other. A rush of cold wind, a sense of weightlessness, of being part of the very air that surrounded him.

When he came to himself again, he was standing outside a massive gray stone edifice located atop a high mountain. The structure was magnificent, with tall, narrow, leaded windows on the ground floor. Three wide stone steps led to a pair of iron-strapped doors that looked strong enough to withstand an army.

"The Fortress," he mused. It could be nothing else.

He went to ground in the midst of a stand of timber located behind the Fortress. Mortals would undoubtedly consider spending the day buried in the ground utterly morbid. But, for his kind, it was quite refreshing. He had heard of old vampires who went to ground for a year or two when they grew weary of their long existence. Others who were bored with a particular century went to ground until it was over.

Zack had never done that, but he could see how awaking in a new century might add a certain zest to one's existence. With the passage of a hundred years, there would be new inventions to explore, new dynasties, new fashions, perhaps a new language, new countries, new methods of communication and transportation.

He closed his eyes as he sensed the coming sunrise. When he was first made, the onset of the sleep of his kind had been scary as hell. It was like falling into a deep black pit, with no assurance that he would ever wake again. In the beginning, he had feared being discovered by a vampire hunter and destroyed while he slept, but that had proven to be a needless worry. Some innate vampire sense warned him when his life was in danger; if necessary, he awakened long enough to defend himself. He called it vampire adrenaline, that burst of energy that roused him from sleep.

He reached out, his senses searching for Kaitlyn, as the dark sleep overshadowed him, dragging him down into oblivion.

Chapter 20

Kaitlyn bolted upright in bed, her heart pounding, Zack's name on her lips. Sitting there, the sheet clutched to her breasts, she glanced quickly around the room. Seeing nothing, she switched on the light. Still nothing.

"Zack?" Certain he was near, she slipped out of bed, opened the door, and peered into the hallway. All was quiet. The corridor was dark and deserted.

Not surprising at this time of the morning, she thought. The vampires sought their lairs before sunrise; most of the mortals who lived here kept the same hours as their mates.

Frowning, she pulled on her robe and padded barefoot down the corridor, pausing to glance into every room she passed, but there was no sign of Zack. Or anyone else.

Still, she couldn't shake the feeling that he was nearby and so she kept searching. Moving quietly down the stairs, she peered into the kitchen, the dining hall, and the laundry room. Of course, he wouldn't be here.

The next floor was where the sheep had been kept. The dormitories and one of the dayrooms had been turned into apartments for the men and women who now willingly made their home in the Fortress. The second dayroom had been turned into a nursery/playroom for their children. Zack certainly wouldn't be there.

The vampire lairs were on the next level down. He definitely wouldn't be there.

Was it possible he was in the dungeon? She tried to link to the blood bond he said they shared. He had told her he would always be able to find her. Why couldn't she find him?

Telling herself there was nothing to be afraid of, she went down two flights of stairs, then paused at the narrow door that led to the dungeon. Her grandfather, Rodin, had not approved of her father marrying Elena. In his anger, he had imprisoned her father down here. It was a snippet of family history she wasn't supposed to know, but she had heard bits and pieces of the story while growing up, mostly from the sheep.

She opened the door, surprised that it didn't creak loudly, the way wooden doors always did in scary movies when the foolish young woman went exploring on her own, even though she knew there was a monster on the loose.

Kaitlyn grinned as she stepped into the dungeon. In this case, she was the monster.

Thanks to her preternatural vision, she needed neither candle nor lamp to find her way in the thick darkness. Iron-barred cells lined both sides of the room. Someone had obviously mopped the floors and cleaned the cells, but the air remained rank with the smell of old sweat, urine, and fear. The ceiling was low, the stark surroundings oppressive.

She was relieved to find all the cells empty.

Returning to her room on the main floor, she crawled back under the covers and closed her eyes. It must have been her imagination. She had been wanting to see

Zack so badly, she had imagined he was here. But that was just wishful thinking. Even if he knew where she was, he wouldn't be foolish enough to come after her.

When Elena decided to do something, she did it quickly, and in grand style. By Saturday night, the welcome home party for Stefan had been arranged for the following night. Of course, there was little to do when one gave a party for vampires. There was no need for an elaborate buffet. The mortals who dwelled within the Fortress had also been invited. A lavish dinner would be provided for them prior to the festivities. If they were willing, they would supply the refreshments for the vampires; if not, there would be a ready supply of bottled blood as well as a variety of wines and champagne.

Kaitlyn had mixed feelings about attending the party. She was fond of her aunts and uncles, eager to see her grandmother again, and happy that Stefan had returned. On the other hand, she was still angry with her father for whisking her to the Fortress against her will.

She had considered refusing to attend, but that seemed petty. And she knew it would hurt her mother's feelings if she stayed in her room and sulked. And so, ever the dutiful daughter, she arrived in the appointed place at the appointed time.

The ballroom in the Fortress was like nothing else in the world. The walls and ceiling, made almost entirely of glass, afforded a splendid view of the valley below and the star-studded sky above. As a child, Kaitlyn had loved to play up here when they came to visit. At night, she had pretended the ballroom was a star in the sky; during the day, she had pretended the room was an enchanted castle.

A trio of long tables covered with gold damask cloths

flanked both sides of the room. Dozens of cut-crystal decanters and delicate wineglasses sparkled on the tables.

Her aunt Miranda sat at the grand piano located on a small stage at the far end of the room. A floor-to-ceiling mirror took up most of the wall behind the piano. Miranda's bright red hair gleamed like reflected fire in the mirror. Her long, pale fingers flew effortlessly over the keys, never missing a note. She smiled when she saw Kaitlyn; a moment later, the notes of "Clair de Lune" filled the room. Kaitlyn smiled back. "Clair de Lune" was her favorite song.

Kaitlyn moved confidently among the guests, nodding at Marta and Elnora and Torrance, who stood in a group by themselves, along with their vampire mates.

Kaitlyn hugged Stefan and her grandmother, noting that Liliana looked even more radiant than usual, no doubt because her youngest son was home again. Kaitlyn spent a few minutes chatting with Andrei and Katiya, nodded at Ciprian, who was dancing with a pretty mortal girl.

Kaitlyn was thinking about having a glass of wine when she saw her mother hurrying toward her.

"Kaitlyn, there you are," Elena said, smiling. "How lovely you look!"

"Thanks, Mom, so do you." Clad in a floor-length dress made of white silk, her mother looked young enough to be Kaitlyn's sister.

Elena frowned. "You're still angry, aren't you?"

"I can't help it. He had no right . . ."

"He had every right, Kaitlyn. He's your father. Did you think he'd just ignore the danger you were in? If he hadn't brought you home, I would have."

Before Kaitlyn could reply, her father joined them. He was a handsome man, and never more so than tonight. Wearing black slacks, a gray silk shirt, and a black jacket with a velvet collar, he could easily have been a male model.

"May I have this dance, Kaitlyn?" he asked with exaggerated formality.

"Of course."

He swept her into his arms as Miranda began to play a waltz. It reminded Kaitlyn of past visits when she and her father had danced up here, just the two of them. The memory of those days made it difficult to stay mad at him.

"Are you ever going to forgive me?" he asked, twirling her around and around.

"I guess so," she said with an aggrieved sigh. "But when this trouble with Nadiya is over, I'm going back to Zack."

Drake nodded. "I see. No stopping true love, I guess, if that is what it is."

"What's that supposed to mean?"

"You are a young woman, just out of college, away from home for the first time. Hormones raging," he added with a grin. "You meet a handsome man . . ." He shrugged. "You will probably fall in love many times before you find the right man."

"You mean a man you approve of."

"No, Kaitlyn. I would not tell you who to marry. I hope you will find a mate here, among your own kind. But if you choose a mortal, how could I possibly object?"

"And what if I fell in love with one of the Others?"

His eyes narrowed. "What do you mean?"

She hadn't meant to tell him like this, but maybe now was the time. "I mean Zack is a vampire. He was turned six hundred years ago."

"Turned," Drake repeated slowly. "He is not one of us."

"I don't care what he is. I'm in love with him."

"I have indulged you your whole life," Drake said quietly. "I let you go to America when I was against it. I let you stay there after you graduated because you wished it, even though I did not approve. But this . . ." He shook his head. "As your father, I do not approve. As the leader of our coven, I cannot allow it."

Kaitlyn stared up at him. Too late, she knew she never should have said anything. And yet he was bound to find out sooner or later. "You can't keep me here forever," she said, blinking back her tears. She didn't want to have to choose between Zack and her father, fervently hoped it would never come to that. But if it did . . .

She had to talk to Zack. She couldn't call him now. She would have to wait until tomorrow, since it was still morning in Nevada. What was it like for Zack, to be drawn into darkness with the sun's rising? Most of her people also rested during the day, although those born to Liliana had the ability to be awake in their cat form when the sun was up.

"I am sorry, Kaitlyn," her father said as the music ended. "I believe Stefan is coming to ask for the next dance."

"Indeed I am," Stefan said, coming up behind them.

Drake bowed in his brother's direction, then left the dance floor.

Stefan took Kaitlyn in his arms as Miranda began to play another tune. "You've been crying," he remarked.

Kaitlyn nodded, unable to speak past the thick lump in her throat.

"You have every right to be angry with me," he said.

"It's . . ." She sniffed back her tears. "It's not you."

Stefan glanced over her shoulder to where Drake was standing. "What did he say to upset you?"

"I told him about Zack."

"What about Zack?"

"He's a vampire."

"Why would that upset your father?"

"He isn't one of us. He's one of the Others."

Stefan stared at her. Like all of their kind, he had grown up on tales of the Others, of their bloodthirsty nature, their willingness to kill mortals indiscriminately. They could not reproduce, so they did not have any family ties; instead, they lived singly, friend to neither mortal nor their own kind.

Stefan shook his head. "No wonder your father is upset."

"I love Zack. I don't care what he is."

"I felt the same about Cosmina, but take it from one who has been there. No matter how much you care for Ravenscroft, you are better off with one of your own."

"You loved Cosmina very much, didn't you?"

He nodded.

"So much that you can't bear to be with another woman?"

The sadness in Stefan's eyes deepened. "When I buried her"—he shook his head—"it was like burying my heart. My soul."

"I'm so sorry." She couldn't stay angry with her uncle for siding with her father, not now, when she knew how he felt. She couldn't blame him for wanting to spare her the kind of pain he had known.

When the song was over, he thanked her for the dance and left the ballroom.

Kaitlyn stared after him. With a sigh, she started toward her mother, who stood in a corner of the room with several other women. She stopped abruptly, suddenly overcome with the feeling that Zack was nearby, searching for her.

* * *

Zack stood on the steps of the Fortress. Earlier, he had gone hunting in the town located a few miles away. While there, he had bought a pair of black dress pants, a dark blue silk shirt, and a long black coat. It paid to look sharp when calling on your best girl.

He stared at the large double doors. There were a few drawbacks to being a vampire, one of them being that he couldn't enter a home without an invitation. With that in mind, he knocked on the door, heard the sound of it reverberate inside the building.

A few minutes later, a tall, dark-haired woman opened the door. "Yes?"

"I'm here to see Kaitlyn Sherrad."

"Is she expecting you?"

"I don't think so."

"Please wait," the woman said, and closed the door in his face.

Three minutes passed. Four. Five.

"I've got a bad feeling about this," Zack muttered. But he hadn't come this far to turn back now, not until he'd seen Kaitlyn.

When the door opened again, Drake Sherrad stood there. "You are not welcome here," he said brusquely.

"I'm not leaving until I see Kaitlyn."

"Very well. Follow me," Sherrad said, his voice cool. "We need to talk in private."

Zack felt a rush of preternatural power as he crossed the threshold, but it didn't repel him. His gaze moved from side to side as he followed Kaitlyn's father up several flights of stairs that ended at a small wooden landing.

Warning bells went off in Zack's mind as Sherrad opened a squat wooden door. Zack was about to dissolve into mist when three men materialized behind him. Before he could react, one of them—a human male—

dropped a thick silver collar around his neck. The silver burned through cloth and flesh, rendering Zack helpless. A long silver chain was attached to the collar.

Zack glared at his captor as the man dragged him through the doorway and into the room beyond. Only, it wasn't a room, but the ruins of what had once been a tower. Moonlight shone through a jagged hole in the roof.

Zack struggled against his captor as the man shackled his feet with heavy silver chains, then secured the chain dangling from the collar to a thick bolt set deep into the wall.

"The three of you may go," Sherrad said. "I trust you will say nothing of this to anyone."

With a bow of acknowledgment, the three men left the tower.

Zack glared at Sherrad. "Now what?" He glanced at the jagged opening in the roof. Come morning, moonlight would be replaced by sunlight. And while he wouldn't burst into flame and disappear as some believed, if he remained in the sun too long, it would char his flesh down to his bones. Not a pleasant prospect. Or a pretty sight.

"I am going to leave you here to think things over."

"I love your daughter," Zack said. "Nothing will change that."

"You may feel differently by tomorrow night."

"Why are you doing this?" Zack frowned. "It's more than just Kaitlyn, isn't it? It's what I am. One of the Others."

Sherrad folded his arms across his chest. "My people have sworn to destroy your kind."

"Why didn't you do it back in Lake Tahoe?"

"In front of my daughter? I think not."

"So, how are you gonna explain my absence?"

"You will simply disappear."

"She knows I wouldn't do that."

Sherrad glanced at the hole in the roof. "In a few days, it will no longer be your problem."

Zack swore. "You've really got your daughter fooled, don't you? She thinks you're wonderful."

A muscle twitched in Sherrad's jaw.

"What do you think she'll say when she finds out about this?"

"It does not matter. I will not have my daughter align herself with your kind."

"We're not that different, you and I."

Sherrad didn't answer. Instead, he stalked out of the tower.

The door clicked shut behind him with dreadful finality.

Chapter 21

Kaitlyn walked through a long black tunnel. Vampires lined both sides, their eyes red and glowing, their fangs gleaming brightly in the darkness. They hissed at her as she passed, their expressions cold, their voices angry as they shouted that she was a traitor, an outcast. She turned to her father for help, but found no succor there, only disappointment when he looked at her. Tears stung her eyes when he turned his back on her. She looked at her mother, certain her mother wouldn't reject her for loving Zack.

"I'm sorry," her mother murmured. "So sorry." And then she, too, turned away.

Tears ran down Kaitlyn's cheeks as one by one, her aunts and uncles disowned her for loving Zack.

Zack, who stood at the far end of the tunnel, his dark gray eyes filled with pain and sorrow.

All she had to do was deny her love for him and she could go back to her own people. They would forgive her. They would welcome her with open arms.

She paused, torn by conflicting emotions. She loved her parents, but she was a grown woman now. She had a right to love anyone she wished. Didn't she?

"Katy. Katy, come to me." Zack's voice, filled with grief. How could she deny him?

"Katy . . . Katy." The agony in his voice tore at her heart. He needed her.

How was she to decide between her parents and the man she loved? It wasn't fair. But Zack needed her. She could hear it in his voice.

"Ka-ty . . ." His voice, weaker now, threaded with pain. "Katy!"

She bolted upright in bed, the sound of his voice ringing in her ears. "Zack, where are you?" She glanced around the room. She hadn't imagined his voice, or the underlying agony.

Throwing back the covers, she hurried out of her bedroom and into the hallway. She paused there, listening. And then she heard it again, Zack's voice, echoing in the back of her mind. He was in pain. He needed her.

She glanced up and down the hallway, then shook her head. He couldn't be here.

Katy.

She turned toward the sound of his voice, followed it down the corridor to the small door that led up to the ballroom, then stopped. This was ridiculous. What would he be doing in the ballroom, of all places?

She opened the door and peered into the darkness, her feet climbing the stairs seemingly of their own volition. Up, up, up, until she came to the ballroom.

She tiptoed inside, and looked around, then moved toward the windows on the far wall. She had never been up here this early in the morning. The scene before her was breathtaking. A few scattered clouds hung low, drifting puffs of white against the lightening sky. The rising sun painted broad strokes of ochre and crimson across the horizon and splashed the clouds with glowing shades of pink.

Katy.

She turned away from the window as his voice sounded in her mind once again. "Where are you?" she cried in exasperation.

This was the highest room in the Fortress. If he wasn't here . . . Turning on her heel, she ran out of the ballroom and hurried up the short flight of stairs that ended on a small landing. She had never been in the room beyond. Her father had warned her to keep out, saying that the tower was in ruins, the walls crumbling, the floor unsafe.

She stared at the squat door. There was no latch. Placing her hand on the wood, she pushed, but nothing happened.

"Zack?" She pressed her ear to the door. "Are you in there?"

"Katy." Her name was a sigh on his lips.

A well-placed kick broke the barrier between them. Scrambling over the broken bits of wood, she stared at Zack, momentarily too stunned by what she saw to speak.

With a groan, he shifted his weight. The sound spurred her to action and she hurried toward him. "Are you all right?" She dropped down on her knees beside him.

It had been a foolish question. His neck was raw and blistered from the thick silver chain around it. His ankles, too.

"Who did this to you?" she demanded.

"Your father."

Kaitlyn shook her head, unwilling to believe that her father, the man she had idolized all her life, was capable of such wanton cruelty. "Why? Why would he do this?"

"I'm the enemy."

"You're not my enemy," she said, biting back her

anger. She glanced at the patch of blue visible through the hole in the roof. When the sun was overhead . . . She refused to think of what would happen then. Instead, she grabbed hold of the chain that bound his ankle and pulled with all her might.

Nothing happened.

She tried again, frowning as the silver grew warm in her hands, and then began to burn. Silver had never burned her before.

Ignoring the pain, she tugged on the chain again and yet again, but to no avail.

"Katy, stop," Zack said. "Your hands . . ."

"I don't care. I have to get you out of here."

"Stop." He took her hands in his. Her palms were red and blistering. "I think your father has infused some vampire mojo in the silver."

With a sigh, Kaitlyn sat beside him, her legs stretched out in front of her, her thigh brushing his. "I'm so sorry," she murmured. "I didn't think he'd do anything like this. What will happen when the sun is overhead? Will you . . . ?"

"Burst into flame? No. Only the dead do that."

"But it will burn you, won't it?"

"Yeah."

"I'll go get some towels and blankets to cover you with. And an umbrella, if I can find one. And something to drink . . ."

"A negative, if you've got it," he said with a tight smile.

"This is no time for jokes."

He caught her by the hand. "Stay, Katy."

"But . . ."

"Just for a little while."

She sank back down beside him, her gaze searching his face. "Do you need to feed?"

"Are you offering?"

She nodded.

Zack swore softly. It was one thing to take a taste while they were snuggling together, another to feed off of her, as if she was no more than prey. And yet, he could feel the heat of the rising sun, knew it would leech his strength as it seared his flesh.

Kaitlyn brushed the hair away from her neck and tilted her head to the side. "You need it, Zack. Just do it."

He slid his arm around her shoulders and kissed her, his lips moving over hers, trailing kisses over her cheek, down the side of her neck, back up to the soft tender place beneath her ear. He didn't want to feed off her, but the change in her breathing, the sudden thundering of her heartbeat, wiped away all thought of resisting. She moaned softly as his fangs pierced her flesh, not a sound of pain, but of pleasure.

Her blood was warm and sweet and it took every ounce of willpower he possessed to pull back. To let her go.

She smiled at him.

"Katy. Dammit . . ."

She pressed her fingertips to his lips. "Don't."

"It isn't right."

"Stop it. If I needed blood, you'd give me yours, wouldn't you?"

"Okay," he conceded. "Point taken."

"Good." She glanced at the hole in the roof. "I'd better go get those blankets."

Zack nodded. He hated to see her go, even for a short time, but blocking the sun was the only way to keep it from burning him to a crisp. He had been burned once before and it wasn't something he wanted to experience again.

Leaning his head back against the side of the tower, he closed his eyes. He had been a young vampire then, still cocky enough to think he was invincible. He had been idling in one of the pubs, flirting with one of the doxies. He could have compelled her to go with him, but that took all the fun out of it. Finally, she agreed to let him take her home. She had been a lusty wench and they had made love far into the night. Drunk on her blood, amused by her stamina, he had paid little attention to the time until it was too late, until he felt the first sharp pain skate over his skin when the morning sun filtered through the open window of her bedroom.

When he tried to leave, she grabbed hold of him with both hands, begging him to stay. Each second in the sun's light had been torture. Finally, not caring what she would think, he threw her across the room, his movements hampered by the sheets tangled around his legs.

Muttering an oath, he had dissolved into mist and fled the house.

If not for the heavy chains that bound him to the tower wall, he would have done the same thing now. But the silver negated his preternatural power, leaving him weak and vulnerable to the sun's light.

It took Kaitlyn only moments to return to her bedroom, where she gathered up an armful of blankets and quilts. Hurrying into the kitchen, she grabbed a few bags of blood from the refrigerator.

She glanced at the clock as she made her way back to the tower. The mortals who lived within the Fortress would be waking soon. Even as she ducked through the doorway that led to the tower stairs, she heard the hum of voices drifting up from the kitchen below.

Muttering, "That was close," she raced up the stairs.

When she entered the tower, Zack was pressed up against the wall as far as he could go. His eyes were closed against the sun's light. Was he already asleep?

She whispered his name, but there was no response. It was probably for the best, she thought. If he was asleep, maybe the pain wouldn't be so bad.

She quickly spread the quilts and blankets over him, making sure he was covered from head to foot. When that was done, she tucked the bagged blood under the blankets where he would be sure to find it.

"I'll get you out of here as soon as I can," she promised, her anger at her father sparking to life with renewed fury.

She was about to leave the tower when her gaze fell on the broken door. Lifting the largest piece, she angled it over Zack so that one end rested on the floor and the other rested against the wall, providing added protection from the sun.

With a satisfied nod, she left the tower.

And went directly to her parents' apartment. She knocked softly, and when there was no response, she knocked again, harder. "Mom?"

Elena opened the door and peered into the hallway. "Kaitlyn, what is it?"

"I need to talk to you."

"Now?"

"Yes, right now. It's important."

"Come on in."

"Not here. In my room."

"All right, give me a few minutes."

True to her word, Elena arrived shortly thereafter. "Is something wrong, sweetie?"

Kaitlyn closed and locked the door. "Zack is here."

"What?"

"Zack, he's here. You didn't know?"

Elena shook her head. "No. Where is he?"

"Dad locked him in the tower. I've got to get him out

of there." She blinked back her tears. "Before it's too late."

"I'm sure he'll be fine. A little uncomfortable, perhaps. I can't imagine why your father put him up there."

"Mom, Zack's a vampire. One of . . . of the Others."

"Oh, dear." Elena sank down on the edge of the mattress, and then frowned. "Where's your bedding?"

"I used it to cover Zack. Mom, you have to help me! I love Zack."

"I don't know what I can do. You know how your father feels about the Others, and from what I've heard, I can't say as I blame him."

Kaitlyn stared at her mother. "You don't even know Zack. He's wonderful." She clenched her hands, her anger and frustration growing. She had been so sure she could count on her mother for help. "If you won't help me free Zack, I'll find someone who will!"

"What do you want me to do?"

"Help me get him out of the tower before it's too late."

Elena shook her head. "I can't believe your father didn't tell me about this."

Kaitlyn sat beside her mother. "He's a monster."

"Kaitlyn, what a terrible thing to say about your father!"

"How can you defend him? Zack could die up there! He never did anything to anyone here. Dad has no right to . . ."

"Your father has every right to do what he thinks is best for us."

"And killing Zack is best?" Kaitlyn sprang to her feet and began to pace the floor. "He has no right to judge Zack. He doesn't even know him. And neither do you!"

"Kaitlyn, calm down. I'll speak to your father as soon as he wakes up."

"I can't wait that long. Will you help me?"

"I assume you tried to free Zack and failed?"

Kaitlyn nodded.

"That's what I thought. What do you think I can do that you couldn't? I don't have any superpowers."

"Maybe between the two of us, we can free him," Kaitlyn said. She didn't wait for an answer. Unlocking the door, she turned to face her mother. "Are you coming?"

"Your father won't be happy about this," Elena said. "Not happy at all . . . oh," she murmured as the door swung open and she saw her husband standing on the other side.

"What is it I will not be happy about?" he asked, glancing from his wife to his daughter and back again.

"I want you to let Zack go," Kaitlyn said angrily. "Right now."

He didn't waste time pretending he didn't know what she was talking about. "This is between me and him."

"No, it isn't."

"Drake," Elena said, taking a place between her husband and her daughter. "Why didn't you tell me about this?"

"Two against one," he muttered. "That is hardly fair."

"This isn't like you," Elena said. "If Kaitlyn loves him . . . we have to trust her judgment."

"You two can argue later," Kaitlyn said. "Dad, please get Zack down from the tower."

Drake stared at his daughter. He had rarely refused her anything she asked for, but this . . . As far back as he could remember, he had been taught that the Others could not be trusted, that they were monsters, incapable of human emotions. And yet his daughter loved

Zack. And Zack must love her in return, else why would he have come this far to find her?

"I will release him from the tower when the sun goes down . . ." He held up a hand when Kaitlyn started to speak. "But he will have to stay in the dungeon until I am sure I can trust him."

Kaitlyn nodded, knowing that was the best she could hope for.

Just when Zack thought the day would never end, he felt the shift in the atmosphere as the sun began its slow descent. The absence of its deadly rays was a welcome relief. Its light had burned his eyes, its heat had made his blood burn like liquid fire, searing his veins. He had never realized he needed to be in a dark place for the daylight sleep to overtake him. Hovering on the brink of oblivion, unable to escape the sun's heat, he had cowered under the blankets, squirming like a worm on a hot rock. It had been the worst day of his life. The only relief he had known came from the blood Kaitlyn had left for him. It had strengthened him when the pain grew unbearable. Bless the girl for her thoughtfulness.

Nightfall did nothing to ease the pain of the silver shackles. His neck and ankles were raw where the metal rubbed against his skin.

He had told Kaitlyn the sunlight wouldn't make him go up in smoke, but he wasn't sure he could survive another day in the sun.

Feeling as though he were smothering under the blankets, he jerked them away from his face. And saw Kaitlyn's father staring down at him. He recognized the man standing in the doorway as the mortal who had accompanied Drake before.

Zack glared at Drake, wondering if the vampire was about to drive a stake through his heart. Instead, the mortal stepped forward and unlocked the chain from the bolt in the wall.

"Get up," Drake said. "Torrance, bring him."

Before Zack could ask what the hell was going on, Drake turned on his heel and started down the tower stairs.

Torrance tugged on the chain around Zack's neck. Resigned, Zack followed the man, his steps hobbled by the shackles around his ankles.

When they reached the bottom of the last flight of stairs, Drake moved down the main floor hallway to a narrow wooden door that opened onto another stairway.

Zack's trepidation increased as they descended farther and farther underground. One flight. Two. Three. And they came to another door. He swore under his breath as Drake opened it.

Zack shuddered as a miasma of pain and blood and death roiled toward him through the open doorway. How many people had suffered in this place? How many had died screaming in agony or begging for mercy?

Clenching his jaw, he followed Drake and Torrance into the bowels of the dungeon.

Drake opened the door to the last cell on the right.

Tugging on the chain, Torrance forced Zack into the cell and fastened the chain around his neck to a bolt in the wall.

"Torrance, leave us," Drake said.

The man left without a word or a backward glance.

Zack flinched when Drake shut and locked the cell door. "What now?" he asked, turning to face his captor. "You gonna leave me down here to rot?"

"The thought crossed my mind."

"Listen, Kaitlyn told me about your war with the Others and how her great-grandfather took 'em out. That's got nothing to do with me."

"Does it not?"

"No. If I was the kind of inhuman, blood-sucking monster you seem to think I am, I'd have killed Katy and bled her dry by now."

"Katy." Drake spoke the word slowly, so that it came out in two syllables. Ka-ty.

"Dammit, you must have some faith in her judgment. You left her alone in Lake Tahoe."

"Where do you come from?"

"Originally? A little town outside of London that doesn't exist anymore."

"How long have you been a vampire?"

"Six hundred years, give or take a few."

"Have you made others of your kind?"

"Just one. At her request. She works for me."

"Why not more?"

Zack shrugged. "I didn't want the responsibility. What about you? Have you made other vampires?"

"We cannot turn others into what we are. What powers do you hold?"

"Just the run-of-the-mill stuff. The ability to read mortal minds. To dissolve into mist. To transport myself across the room or across the world. To change shape." He grinned. "Into something larger than a cat."

Something that might have been amusement flickered in Drake's eyes and was quickly gone.

"What about you?" Zack asked. "Any extra perks from being born a vampire?"

"None beyond what you have mentioned." Odd, he thought, that they shared the same preternatural powers, yet acquired them in totally different ways. "Can you be active when the sun is up?"

"Only if my life depends on it, and then only indoors and for a short time. You?"

"In my cat form, for as long as I wish. And in this form, for short periods, as long as I am protected from the sun."

"Kaitlyn's got the best of both worlds, doesn't she?" Zack said quietly.

Drake nodded. "You are in love with my daughter." It wasn't a question, but a statement of fact.

"Yessir, I am."

"She is my only daughter, the only child I will ever have."

"Kaitlyn told me your father had numerous wives and dozens of kids."

"That is true, but his way is not my way."

Zack shifted from one foot to the other. The pain of the silver was almost unbearable. Changing position caused the shackles to rub against his burned skin. It took all of his willpower to keep his expression impassive, to stay on his feet, to keep from rubbing the rawness around his neck. But if it killed him, he refused to let the other vampire know how badly he was hurting.

Drake studied Zack Ravenscroft through narrowed eyes. Dried blood stained Ravenscroft's neck and ankles where the silver had rubbed his skin raw. He knew the other man was in pain, yet there was no sign of it in Ravenscroft's voice or in his eyes. He stood there, tall and straight, his attitude just short of openly defiant, yet there was a trace of respect in his manner, no doubt in deference to the fact that Drake was Kaitlyn's father.

"The silver," Drake asked, though he already knew the answer. "Does it burn? Or merely drain your strength?"

"It burns like hellfire. And if it didn't weaken me, I'd

be on the other side of that door with my hands around your throat."

Drake grinned inwardly as he turned on his heel and left the dungeon. He had no doubt that Zack Ravenscroft would make a formidable enemy. The worst part was that he found himself liking the other vampire in spite of everything.

Chapter 22

Zack cursed long and loud as he sank down on the cold stone floor. If Kaitlyn's father was going to kill him, why the hell didn't he just do it and get it over with? Anything would be better than this.

He wondered again how many people—mortal or vampire—had been imprisoned here. Suffered here. Died here. The floor beneath him reeked of old blood, urine, and excrement; the very air was fetid with the scent of death.

Leaning his head back against the wall, Zack closed his eyes and tried to distance himself from the stink that surrounded him, the pain that knifed through him with every movement, every breath. Knowing it was useless, he tried to dissolve into mist, but the silver rendered him powerless, helpless.

And he hated it.

Kaitlyn had asked if he liked being a vampire. He had never really answered her, other than to say that, given a choice, he wouldn't go back to being mortal. The fact was, he loved being a vampire. He loved the physical power it gave him, the enhanced senses, the ability to read minds, to change shape, to will himself wherever he wished to go. He loved the anticipation and excitement of the hunt. He loved holding a woman in his arms, reading her thoughts, giving her pleasure even as he filled himself with her essence. And yes, if he was honest, he loved knowing that he held the power of life and death in his hands. It wasn't something he was particularly proud of, but there it was.

"Kaitlyn." He felt her presence, recognized her scent, even before he opened his eyes. And she was there, her beautiful blue eyes filled with sorrow as she looked at him.

She moved closer to the cell, her hands wrapping around the bars. "Are you all right?" It was a silly question. She could feel his pain, see it in the depths of his eyes, the tight lines around his mouth.

"Oh, yeah," he muttered, his voice laced with sarcasm. "Never better."

"I'm so sorry for all this. Zack, why did you come here?"

"I'd think that would be obvious," he said quietly.

Kaitlyn sighed, touched by the warmth in his voice. "You must have known my father wouldn't be happy to see you."

He shrugged, then winced. "I had to try, Katy. I missed you."

"My hero," she murmured.

He snorted softly. "Some hero. So, why was your father so insistent that you come home? It wasn't just to keep you from me."

"No." Grimacing, she sat cross-legged on the floor. "My father killed one of his half brothers before I was born. And then you killed Daryn . . ."

"Another brother?"

"Yes. Daryn and the brother my father killed had the

same mother. Nadiya. Apparently she's decided to avenge herself on my father for the deaths of her sons."

"And your father's afraid she might use you to get to him."

"Yes. How did you know?"

"It's not hard to figure out." Struggling to his feet, he moved closer to the bars, the shackles that bound his ankles rattling over the stone floor with every step. "He did the right thing, bringing you here."

"How can you say that?"

"It's what I would have done, in his place." Zack reached through the bars, one hand caressing her cheek. "You're his only daughter, after all, and he loves you."

"I know," she said with a sigh. What would she do if her father destroyed Zack? If that happened, she would lose the two most important men in her life, because she would never be able to forgive her father if he destroyed Zack. Never.

"How are your hands?" Zack asked, remembering how the silver had burned her skin earlier.

"Fine." She held her hands up so he could see her palms. "Silver has never burned me before."

"Like I said, I think your father infused the chains with some sort of vampire mojo to make sure I couldn't escape. He probably didn't expect you to be poking around up there."

"I knew you were nearby," she said, a note of wonder in her voice. "I could feel your presence. I heard your voice inside my mind. I could feel what you were feeling."

"Must be lots of fun now," he said, grimacing.

"It's only fair, since you wouldn't be here if it wasn't for me."

"True enough."

"Kiss me, Zack."

"Here? Now?"

"What if we never get another chance?"

"Good point."

It wasn't easy, squirming around, leaning forward far enough to be able to press his lips to hers, but it was worth it. Her lips were cool and sweet and for that brief moment, he forgot he was bound with silver and locked in a putrid cell in a dungeon, forgot that every breath might be his last.

Chapter 23

Drake sat in front of the hearth in his Fortress apartment, his fingers drumming on the arm of the chair. He had a decision to make, and for the first time in years, he wasn't certain that doing the right thing was the right thing to do.

"Are you going to tell me what's bothering you?" Elena asked, perching on the other arm. She had been watching him for the last ten minutes, waiting for him to confide in her. "Or are you going to make me guess?" Although guessing wouldn't be necessary. She knew exactly what was bothering him.

"It is Zack Ravenscroft, of course," he muttered irritably.

"Ah." No surprise there, she thought.

"Yes, ah! Dammit, I like him."

"Really? Well, that does make things more difficult, doesn't it?"

"You have no idea," he said, his voice little more than a growl. "He seems honest and forthright. If he was lying to me, I could not tell." He blew out an impatient sigh. "He claims to love Kaitlyn."

"Claims to love her? Honestly, Drake, why else would

the man come here? If he intended to harm her in any way, I'm sure he's too smart to try it here, under your very nose! Besides, if he meant her any harm, wouldn't he have done it before this?"

Drake glared at her.

"You know I'm right, so you might as well admit it."

He shook his head in resignation. In all their years together, he couldn't recall a time when she had ever been wrong. It was galling. And endearing.

Pulling her down into his lap, he kissed her soundly, then shook his head, his expression rueful. "Tell me, wife, what do you think it will cost me to make this right with our daughter?"

Kaitlyn's demands were few.

"I want you to release Zack immediately. Let him shower. Provide him with clean clothes. Give him a comfortable place to rest during the day. And get used to the idea that, for the foreseeable future, I intend to spend every possible minute with him."

"Is that all?" her father asked dryly.

"He'll need something to drink."

Drake nodded. No doubt providing fresh nourishment should be their first priority. Being in pain always heightened his own hunger. He guessed the same was true for the Others.

"I think you're getting off easy," Elena remarked.

"Hush, wife."

"Hush yourself. I think you owe Zack Ravenscroft an apology."

"I think so, too," Kaitlyn said. "Now, if you'll excuse me, I'm going to find Torrance."

* * *

With an effort, Zack gained his feet when he heard Kaitlyn's footsteps. She wasn't alone. The human, Torrance, was with her. He wondered what that meant.

Kaitlyn smiled at him as she hurried toward the cell. "I've come to get you out of here," she said as Torrance unlocked the cell door.

"What about your father?"

"I have his permission, of course." She hurried into the cell after Torrance, waited impatiently as he unlocked the shackles around Zack's ankles and removed the chain from around his neck. "Thanks, Torrance. That's all."

With a nod, the man left the cell.

"So, what changed your father's mind about me?" Zack asked.

"I don't know." She slipped her arm around his waist. "Lean on me and let's get out of here. How did you stand the smell?"

"It wasn't easy."

"I have a room for you upstairs. Once you're cleaned up, Northa has offered to let you feed from her."

Zack came to a stop. "What?"

"She won't mind," Kaitlyn assured him.

"I'm not a pet. I don't need you to bring me food."

"I'm sorry," Kaitlyn said, not sure what she had said to upset him. "The humans who stay here, it's what they do. I thought you understood that. We provide food and shelter and education for their children, and they nourish us when we need it."

"I understand that, but it's not my way."

"All right." She tugged gently. "Let's just get out of here."

It was a painful climb up three flights of stairs, but he didn't complain. Once they reached the main floor, he stopped leaning on Kaitlyn. A man had his pride, after all.

He followed her down a long corridor before they came to any doors. She opened the first door on the right.

"What's in the other rooms?" he asked.

"The room next to this one is the library. There's a music room and an art gallery across the hall. The council chambers are in that big room at the end."

Zack nodded.

"This is the guest room, I suppose you'd call it," she said, stepping inside.

Zack followed her into what was a surprisingly modern room. A little too feminine for his taste, but after the tower and the dungeon, he wasn't about to complain. A number of paintings decorated the pale yellow walls. A beige carpet covered the floor. A ceramic pitcher and a couple of glasses sat atop a three-drawer chest, along with a comb and a hand mirror. A flowered quilt covered a large brass bed. A wooden shelf held a number of books written in several different languages, as well as numerous DVDs and CDs for the TV and stereo housed in a small entertainment unit.

"There's a bathroom in there," Kaitlyn said, pointing at the door across from the bed.

Nodding, he went to the window and pulled back the heavy curtain. Although it was dark outside, he could see that the view was spectacular. The Fortress, situated on a mountain peak, overlooked a deep green valley bisected by a narrow ribbon of blue water. With his preternatural sight, he noticed several small cottages in the valley below, their windows glowing with pale yellow lamplight.

He could feel his strength returning. Before dawn, he would go out the window and hunt in the valley below.

"Zack?"

Letting the curtains fall back into place, he turned to face her.

"Is something wrong?"

"No." He glanced at his bloodstained clothes. "I need to get cleaned up."

She nodded, her smile brilliant. "I'll wait for you in the library."

Zack lingered in the shower, scrubbing away the dried blood and sweat that clung to him, along with the stink of the dungeon. From what little he had seen, the Romanian vampires lived like Old World royalty. He much preferred his own way. Unfortunately, it looked like Kaitlyn would be staying here until her father deemed it was safe for her to leave, although there was no telling when that would be.

So, he could either stay here with Kaitlyn and make the best of it, or head back to Tahoe alone. He thought about the casino. Scherry could run it without him for as long as necessary.

Zack snorted softly. Like it or not, he figured he would be staying here for the duration, however long that might be.

Stepping out of the shower, he toweled off. One of the best things about being a vampire was how quickly he recovered. His wounds were already healing. Once he fed, the healing process would speed up; by tomorrow night, he'd be as good as new.

He donned the black pants and dark blue sweater Kaitlyn had left for him. While pulling on a pair of soft black leather boots, he had the discomfiting feeling that the clothing belonged to her father, since he and Drake were roughly the same height and weight. He seemed to recall Katy mentioning that he reminded her of her father.

After running a comb through his hair, he left the

room. His footsteps made no sound as he made his way to the library. He found Kaitlyn inside, reading a book.

She looked up when he entered the room, a smile of welcome lighting her face.

"You look much better."

"Thanks. I feel better." He'd feel more like his old self again once he'd fed, but that would have to wait.

"Would you like a tour of the Fortress?" Kaitlyn asked, setting the book aside.

"Sure."

"Come on, then," she said, taking him by the hand.

He had already seen the main floor. The other levels were all downstairs. And underground. Being a vampire, he could appreciate that.

The first floor down held the kitchen, a dining hall, and a laundry room. A low hum of conversation filled the air. Two women were in the kitchen preparing dinner; another woman was folding a load of wash. They all smiled at Zack and Kaitlyn. They were all human and seemed remarkably happy.

As Zack and Kaitlyn were leaving, a woman with curly brown hair and brown eyes entered the dining room.

"Hello, Kaitlyn," she said pleasantly.

"Hi, Northa." Kaitlyn hesitated, then said, "Zack, this is Northa. She's been with us for a long time."

"Pleased to meet you," Zack said. He stared at the woman. Her name sounded vaguely familiar. And then he remembered why. This was the woman who had offered to satisfy his thirst.

Kaitlyn and Northa exchanged a few pleasantries, and then, with a last glance in Zack's direction, Northa excused herself and disappeared into the kitchen.

"I take it she knows I refused her offer," Zack said dryly.

Kaitlyn shrugged. "It's no big deal. It's probably just as well."

"Oh?" He lifted one brow. "Why is that?"

"Because she couldn't keep her eyes off of you."

"Don't tell me you're jealous?" Zack exclaimed, grinning.

"Of course not." She moved past him, walking quickly to the stairs. "This floor has been remodeled," she remarked when they reached the next level.

There were no windows down here, since this level was underground, but plenty of overhead lights to turn away the gloom.

"There used to be dormitories here and two large recreation rooms," she said. "Of course, that was before my time. The dorms and one of the rec rooms were turned into individual bedrooms when my father took over."

"You don't have any reason to be jealous, you know," Zack said when she refused to look at him.

"The second rec room is now a combination TV room and playroom."

"All right, have it your way," he said, amused by the fact that not only was she jealous of a mortal woman, but she refused to discuss it.

Zack peered into the playroom. There were rugs on the floor, boxes overflowing with toys, shelves filled with books and DVDs, a wall-mounted TV, several sofas, chairs, and tables, as well as a crib in one corner.

All the comforts of home, he thought as he followed Kaitlyn. Yet it still amazed him that there were humans willing to live among vampires, to trade their blood for a place to live. Bizarre. Totally bizarre.

"Our people live here," Kaitlyn said when they reached the fourth level down.

There were no overhead lights down here. The corridor was dark. *As dark as a tomb,* Zack thought. Which, in a way, was what it was, at least when the sun was up. He glanced at the narrow door at the end of the long

hallway and shivered in spite of himself, knowing it was
the door to the dungeon below. How many people had
died down there in ages past? It was obvious the vampires no longer kept prisoners locked up, since there
had been no scent of fresh blood—other than his own.

When they returned to the main floor, Kaitlyn's
father was waiting for them. A woman with long black
hair and beautiful brown eyes stood beside him. She
looked enough like Kaitlyn to be her older sister.

The woman took a step forward, her hand extended.
"Hello, Zack. I'm Kaitlyn's mother, Elena."

He shook her hand, his mind automatically brushing
hers. He was surprised to find a mental block between
them. Apparently, her husband had taught her how to
shield her thoughts. "Pleased to meet you, Mrs. Sherrad."

"Just Elena. We were on our way upstairs to watch a
movie. Would you care to join us?"

Zack glanced at Kaitlyn, hoping she would decline.
The thought of spending the evening with her father
was less than appealing.

Unfortunately, Kaitlyn smiled at her mother and
said, "Sure."

"Come on," Kaitlyn said, taking Zack by the hand.
"Wait until you see this."

He slid a wary glance in her direction as they passed
through the narrow doorway that led up to the tower.

"Don't worry," she said with a reassuring smile.

Right, he thought. What was there to worry about?

As they climbed the stairs, he caught the sound of excited conversation and laughter, and the scent of . . .
buttered popcorn?

He couldn't hide his amazement when they entered
a room filled with not only vampires, but men, women,
and children. The room itself was something to see.
Three of the walls and most of the ceiling were made of

glass, affording a splendid view of the valley below and the star-studded sky above. A long table held bottles of wine, cans of soda, a variety of candy bars, and an enormous tub of popcorn. Rows of chairs took up most of the floor.

Standing there, Zack overheard conversations in several languages, including English. It wasn't surprising. Vampires lived a long time. Learning new languages was a good way to while away the hours. He, himself, spoke Spanish, French, and German.

When the lights dimmed, people quickly took their seats.

Kaitlyn guided Zack to a pair of chairs in the back row. "This whole movie thing is a new addition," she whispered. "My mom's idea."

Zack nodded. The sound of so many beating hearts didn't bother him. He was used to it from spending his nights at the casino. But he could have done without the combined smells of popcorn, candy and soda, not to mention the stink of urine that came from an infant girl sitting on her mother's lap in the row ahead of him.

Someone hit a switch. Sliding doors opened on the room's one solid wall, revealing a large movie screen. A projector descended from the ceiling. The lights went out. And the movie began.

It was all Zack could do to keep from laughing out loud when he read the title. It was the old black-and-white film, *Dracula*, starring Bela Lugosi as the infamous Transylvanian count.

When the movie was over, the humans hustled their children off to bed. The vampires clustered around the table, uncorking the wine bottles which, as it turned out, didn't hold wine at all.

A few of the vampires went off with the humans, apparently in the mood for something straight from the source.

"You've got an odd look on your face," Kaitlyn remarked. "What are you thinking about?"

"How bizarre this all is."

She glanced around the room. "Is it?"

"I wouldn't expect you to think so, seeing as how you grew up here," Zack replied. "But believe me, this is like some kind of . . . I don't know . . . a fever dream, maybe." He shook his head. "It just isn't natural."

"No," she said slowly. "I guess it isn't."

Zack took her arm and they moved to the side as a couple of male vampires quickly folded up the chairs and put them away. The doors closed over the screen, the projector slid back up into the ceiling.

A woman with long red hair took a seat at the piano and began to play a waltz.

Drake took his wife into his arms and swept her onto the dance floor. Several other couples followed their lead.

Zack looked at Kaitlyn. "Shall we?"

"I'd love to."

It felt good to be in his arms, but it was hard to relax when her parents were nearby, surreptitiously watching her every move. Determined not to let it bother her, she smiled at Zack, her stomach doing a crazy flip-flop when he smiled back.

"It's like dancing among the stars, isn't it?" she asked.

"Yeah. I thought the Skylight Room was pretty amazing, but this place beats everything I've ever seen."

"You aren't . . . you're not going to leave, are you?"

"Not unless you go with me."

"I love you, Zack."

"I know, Katy darlin'." Bending down, he kissed the tip of her nose. "I love you, too, although I don't think your father will ever approve."

She couldn't argue with that, not when her father was scowling at her from across the room.

"Come on," she said, taking Zack's hand in hers. "Let's go for a walk."

It was a beautiful, clear night. Hand in hand, they strolled along a winding narrow path behind the Fortress that meandered through a copse of trees and opened into a lush green meadow.

Zack glanced back at the Fortress. It perched on the top of a craggy mountain like some medieval giant bird about to take flight. "Looks like Dracula's castle," he muttered. The only things missing were a full moon and a couple of wolves howling in the distance.

"It does not!"

"No? Take a good look. It wouldn't surprise me to see Bela Lugosi peering out of one of the upstairs windows."

"That's my home you're talking about," Kaitlyn said, punching him on the arm.

"Ow!" He lifted his head as the breeze shifted, carrying with it the scent of prey. It aroused his innate instinct to hunt and stirred his hunger. "Katy, come hunting with me."

Chapter 24

Kaitlyn stared at Zack. "What?"

"You heard me. Let's go hunting together."

She stared at him, speechless. Was he serious? A part of her was excited by the idea, another part was repelled. It was one thing to share blood with Zack in the intimacy of their relationship, quite another to feed from someone with him there, watching. Aside from sexual intercourse, which she had not yet experienced, she couldn't imagine anything as intimate or private as hunting.

"Come on," he coaxed, tugging on her hand. "It'll be fun."

"Fun!" she exclaimed. "You think hunting is fun?"

"Don't you?"

She shook her head. It was necessary, it was satisfying, but it had never been fun.

"Have you ever gone hunting?" Zack asked. "Aside from those times with your father?"

"Rarely. It seems so . . . undignified. So . . . feral." Truth be told, it embarrassed her.

He laughed softly. "Feral? Yeah, I guess hunting does tend to bring out the beast in me." He stroked her cheek with his forefinger. "You don't like that feeling of power, of being in total control?"

"Well, I've never really thought of it like that." Hunting with her father had been remarkably civilized.

"And you call yourself a vampire!" Zack chided gently. "Come on, Katy, give in to your wild side."

Hunting with Zack. How could she refuse? Just thinking about it awakened something buried deep within her, something that had been dormant for far too long.

He grinned, seeing the excitement in her eyes. "Stay close, Katy darlin'."

"Zack, wait."

"Come on, don't tell me you've changed your mind?"

"What if . . . what if I can't control myself? I don't want to kill anyone."

"Trust me. I won't let that happen."

"Some vampires turn into savage killers. How do I know that won't happen to me? Alcoholics don't know they're going to be alcoholics until they take that first drink."

"Believe me, Katy, you're not the type to turn into some ravenous monster. For one thing, you're only half vampire. I don't think you were born with a killer instinct."

"When I drank from you, I didn't want to stop."

"That was different. You'll see." He squeezed her hand again. "Are you game?"

"No, I'm the hunter."

He laughed. "Great. Let's go."

Still uncertain she was doing the right thing, she trailed behind him as he moved through the meadow, as silent as smoke. She had expected him to head for the houses clustered in the valley, but he glided past them and moved on.

It took her a moment to realize he was headed for the small town located a few miles away.

"Open your senses, Katy. Feel the darkness around you. Let it become a part of you. Smell the trees, the grass. Listen to the heartbeat of the night. Do you hear that? There's an animal in the brush just to your left. Can you hear its heartbeat?"

Katy did as he said, surprised at how different the world was when she concentrated on using her vampire senses. Her preternatural power was something she had never fully tapped into, preferring to think of herself as human.

It was as if someone had removed blinders from her eyes and unstopped her ears. The world was alive with sounds and sights and smells she had never truly appreciated until now. Everything seemed brighter, more alive. She saw things more clearly—each individual leaf on the trees in front of her, each blade of grass beneath her feet, each rock, the cricket chirping on top of the rock. Even the air seemed to smell different, fragrant with the scent of foliage and earth and meadow. Why had she suppressed this side of herself for so long? Why hadn't her father told her it could be like this?

Lost in thought, she was surprised to see the town ahead. Only then did she realize how fast Zack had been moving, and how easily she had kept up with him.

"Close your eyes and concentrate," he said, slowing to a stop. "What do you hear?"

She frowned at him, but did as he asked. "I hear a dog barking. A man snoring. A baby crying. Music coming from down the street . . ." She licked her lips. "Hearts beating," she murmured, and felt her own speed up with anticipation. Why had she never noticed before how seductive that sound was? The scent of fresh blood moving through veins and arteries, the rhythmic beating of hearts, jolted through her like electricity.

Opening her eyes, she stared at Zack.

He grinned at her, as if he knew exactly what she was feeling. And maybe he did.

"Come on." Taking her by the hand, Zack led her down the dark streets. With each step she took, the steady thrumming grew louder, stronger.

"Where are we going?" she asked.

"There's an after-hours nightclub on the next block. Easy pickin's."

They were passing by an alley when Zack came to an abrupt halt.

"What is it?" Kaitlyn asked.

"Hear that?"

She cocked her head to the side. "Someone's crying in the alley."

Zack nodded. "It's a woman."

"We've got to help her," Kaitlyn said.

Before he could stop her, Kaitlyn darted into the passage.

With a shake of his head, Zack followed her.

The woman was curled up in a ball in front of two Dumpsters about halfway down the alley. Judging from the smell, neither Dumpster had been emptied lately.

Kaitlyn hurried toward the woman. "Are you all right?" she asked, kneeling beside her.

"He beat me up," the woman sobbed.

Kaitlyn looked up at Zack. "We have to do something."

"Yeah." Zack darted forward, one hand closing around the throat of the man who had stepped out of the shadows behind the nearest Dumpster, his other hand plucking the gun from the man's fist.

The woman sprang to her feet and took off running.

"Get her!" Zack said.

Kaitlyn stared at Zack, speechless. "What?"

"Go after her."

With a grin, Kaitlyn broke into a run. The woman was fast but she was no match for a vampire. Kaitlyn passed her easily, then stood in the mouth of the alley, blocking the way. The woman shrieked and began backpedaling.

Not certain what to do, Kaitlyn grabbed the woman's arm and led her back to where Zack stood.

"Dinner is served," he said, grinning.

Kaitlyn glanced at the woman, who stared at her through wide, frightened eyes. "You mean . . . ?"

He nodded. "Which do you want? The man, or the woman?"

Kaitlyn blinked at Zack. Did he mean for them to feed here, in the open? "What if someone comes by?"

"Don't worry about it. We'll hear anyone coming long before they see us. So, the man or the woman?"

"The man." He was of medium height, with short blond hair and brown eyes. And he was AB negative.

With a nod, Zack took the woman into his arms. She murmured, "Don't, please don't," as he brushed the hair away from her neck.

He stared into the woman's eyes. "Relax," he told her, then looked at Kaitlyn. "I mesmerized the man. He won't fight you. Just do what comes naturally, Katy. You'll know when to stop."

She couldn't stop watching Zack, noticing how gently he held the woman, how he spoke a few reassuring words to her before he bent his head to the woman's neck.

The scent of fresh warm blood drifted in the air, making Kaitlyn's mouth water.

The woman's eyelids fluttered down and she moaned softly, not with pain, but with pleasure.

A sharp stab of jealousy pricked Kaitlyn's heart. Suddenly angry, she took the man in her arms, her nostrils filling with the smell of his after-shave. Taking a deep breath, she took Zack's advice, closed her eyes, and did what came naturally.

After the first taste, she knew she would never be satisfied with bagged blood again.

"So, what do you think?" Zack asked as they walked back to the Fortress. Earlier, he had wiped the minds of the man and the woman and sent them on their way.

"It was"—she spread her arms wide—"amazing. I never knew it could be like that. I never knew I could feel like that." She twirled around, her arms still outstretched. "I feel like I could fly."

"Maybe you can," he said, laughing.

"You're making fun of me."

"Never."

"I could read his mind, only it wasn't like other times. I've always been able to read minds, but this was different. I knew what he was feeling, thinking, what he was afraid of. Is it that way for you?"

"Yeah. This is probably going to sound weird, me being a vampire and all, but I've saved a few lives in my time by planting suggestions in the minds of my prey that they didn't want to kill themselves."

"Really?" she asked, her eyes wide. "That's amazing."

He smiled, remembering the girl, Alice, who had hopes of becoming a Hollywood star. She hadn't been suicidal, just lonely and depressed. Hopefully, she had gone home and reunited with her family.

"Do you think the reason I can't dissolve into mist or do some of the other things my father can do is because

I've rarely fed on humans? Maybe I'd be stronger if I fed more."

"I don't know. Maybe. It makes sense. I mean, you can't expect to be at your full power when you're denying a basic part of what you are."

"I guess you could be right."

"I'm always right, Katy."

She stuck her tongue out at him. "I don't know why, but I've always been reluctant to embrace that side of me," she murmured, speaking more to herself than to him. "I always knew what my father was and I accepted it as normal, you know, the same way I knew and accepted what my mother was." She frowned. "Maybe I played down the vampire part because I wanted to be more like my mother, because I knew my father had chosen a mortal woman for his wife, and I wanted him to love me, too."

"I'm sure he loves you."

"Oh, I know he does. But maybe, deep down, I thought he'd love me more if I was mortal, like my mother." She laughed self-consciously. "I guess I'm being silly."

"Not at all. We all want our parents' approval."

"Did you?"

"I would have, if I'd known them. My mother died in childbirth. My father refused to have anything to do with me." Zack snorted softly. "I was raised by nuns until I was twelve, and then I ran away. I've been on my own ever since."

"Oh, Zack, I'm so sorry."

"It was a long time ago." Over six hundred years, he mused. But it still rankled that his father had dumped him off at a convent in the middle of the night.

They walked in silence for a time. Lost in her own thoughts, Kaitlyn wasn't immediately aware that Zack was no longer beside her.

Looking over her shoulder, she saw him standing as still as a stone, his eyes narrowed, his nostrils flared. "What is it?" she asked, starting back toward him.

"Shh. There's another vampire nearby. One of your kind."

Kaitlyn glanced around. Had her father followed them? But no, it wasn't her father. She didn't stop to wonder how she knew it was someone else.

She gasped when Zack grabbed her by the arm and pushed her behind him. Before she could ask what he was doing, she caught a blur of movement out of the corner of her eye. A moment later, a tall man wielding a sword materialized in front of Zack.

"Give me the woman," he demanded, "and I will let you live."

"No way." Zack rocked back on his heels, his gaze intent on the other man's face.

"You can give her to me," the man said, "or I will kill you and take her."

"You can *try* to take her," Zack replied, "or *you* can die now."

The other man's eyes narrowed.

It was obvious to Zack that the stranger had not expected any resistance. And just as obvious that he didn't know Zack was also a vampire.

The other man didn't waste time arguing. He lunged forward, his sword making a swishing sound as it sliced cleanly through the air.

Kaitlyn watched in horror as the blade cut through the place where Zack had been standing mere seconds before.

Only Zack was now behind his attacker. Kaitlyn whirled away as the stranger lunged toward her. He hadn't taken more than a few steps when Zack snatched the sword from the other man's hand and drove it through his chest.

The man staggered backward, his heart pierced, front and back, by his own weapon. He stared at Kaitlyn, his expression faintly bemused before he toppled to the ground.

Kaitlyn let out the breath she hadn't realized she had been holding, felt her stomach clench when Zack pulled the sword from the other man's body, and lopped off his head.

She turned away, sickened by the sight.

"Katy, we need to go. There may be others."

"The . . . the body. We can't just leave it. . . ."

"Yes, we can. I need to get you out of here."

Feeling numb, she started to walk. She had gone only a few steps when Zack swung her into his arms. She felt an odd sensation, as if she was flying.

When the world righted itself, they were in her room in the Fortress.

Zack set her on her feet, his hands folding over her shoulders to steady her. "Are you all right?"

She stared at him, her face pale, her body trembling. "You could have been killed."

"Yeah, well, I wasn't. Are you all right?"

"No, but I will be."

"Did you recognize that guy?"

"He was one of us, wasn't he? I mean, like me. A Romanian vampire."

Zack nodded. It seemed odd that he could sense her kind when she couldn't. Of course, he hadn't been able to detect them, either, until he identified their particular scent, which made him wonder why Kaitlyn couldn't detect it. The only thing he could think of was that her human blood somehow blocked it.

Kaitlyn blinked, her mind clearing as the initial

horror faded. "We need to tell my father about this right away."

She didn't wait for Zack's reply, just took his hand and hurried out the door.

"I've got a bad feeling about this," he muttered as they went to find her father.

Chapter 25

Drake stood in front of the hearth in the library, his arms folded across his chest, his face implacable, as Zack related what had happened.

"You took my daughter out of the Fortress," Drake said, biting off each word. "You knew her life was in danger, and yet you took her hunting." He shook his head. "I think it best if you leave here now."

"No!" Kaitlyn had been sitting on the sofa beside her mother while Zack spoke to her father. Now, she jumped to her feet. Moving to Zack's side, she linked her arm with his. "If he leaves, I'm going with him."

"You will not."

"I think we all need to calm down." Elena crossed the floor and placed her hand on her husband's arm. "Zack didn't have to come here and tell us what happened, but he did. Kaitlyn, did you recognize the man who attacked you?"

Kaitlyn frowned. "I don't think so." She smiled apologetically. She didn't know any of Rodin's sons and daughters very well; it didn't help that they all looked very much alike.

"I can take you to the body if that'll help," Zack said.

Drake nodded curtly. "Kaitlyn, stay with your mother."

"Be careful," Elena said. "There could be others out there, just waiting."

Drake kissed his wife on the cheek. "We will not be long."

Drake scrutinized the scene of the confrontation, his senses expanding, drawing in the fresh smell of blood and death. And the unmistakable scent of Marius Korzha, another of his half brothers. Did Nadiya intend to send her sons out one by one to avenge the deaths of Daryn and Florin? And when she ran out of sons, would she send her daughters and her grandchildren, as well?

He felt no sorrow for his half brother's death. Marius had made himself Drake's enemy the minute he lifted a hand against Kaitlyn. If Ravenscroft had not killed Marius, Drake would have done so without a qualm.

Drake had brought a blanket with him. Spreading it on the ground, he placed Marius's body and severed head in the middle, then wrapped the blanket tightly around the grisly remains.

"Gonna bury him?" Zack asked.

"No. I am going to send him back to his mother."

"Do you know where she is?"

Drake shook his head. "I am going to send the body to her house in Bucharest. If Nadiya is not there, one of her other children will advise her of his death." Drake looked at Ravenscroft. "You are in this now."

"I figured I was in it when I killed the first one," Zack said with a shrug. "But, hey, bring her on. The sooner we kill her, the sooner Kaitlyn and I can get out of here."

Drake regarded the other vampire a moment before asking, "Are you as powerful as you seem to think you are?"

"I don't know. I'm about a hundred years older than you are. Even so, I think your way of life makes you weak."

No sooner had Zack spoken the words than he felt a sharp blast of preternatural power. Had he been mortal, it would have knocked him off his feet. But he wasn't mortal, and he had power of his own, which he now directed at Kaitlyn's father. Supernatural energy crackled in the air between the two men, singeing the leaves of the trees, scorching the earth.

"Had enough?" Drake asked.

Zack snorted derisively. "Is that the best you've got?"

With a rueful shake of his head, Drake reined in his power. Zack Ravenscroft was truly a vampire to be reckoned with. And even though it galled Drake to admit it, he feared the other man's power was, indeed, stronger.

As soon as Drake reined in his power, Zack did likewise. He probably should have let Kaitlyn's father win their little pissing contest, he thought ruefully, but it just wasn't in him to back down.

The two men stared at each other a moment, then Drake hoisted the blanket-wrapped body to his shoulder and willed himself back to the Fortress.

Zack remained where he was, his senses sweeping the countryside. Blood was a wonderful thing, he mused. Giving Kaitlyn his blood, drinking hers, had enhanced his powers, sharpened his senses. Had it done the same for her?

Once he was certain there were no other vampires lurking in the area, Zack willed himself back to the library in the Fortress, only to find it empty.

He waited a few minutes, hoping to see Kaitlyn, then made his way to his room at the end of the corridor. Stripping down to his briefs, he stretched out on the mattress. Arms folded behind his head, he stared up at the ceiling.

It had been a strange night. He was used to being in the company of humans, but he had never seen vampires and humans mingling the way they had in the ballroom earlier that evening. Like Drake, some of the vampires had chosen to marry humans, which in itself was a rare occurrence, at least in Zack's world.

But things were different here, in the Carpathian Coven. Right or wrong, vampires and mortals had found a way to coexist, each benefiting the other. It would take some getting used to.

And then there was Nadiya. What kind of woman—vampire or human—sacrificed her living children to avenge two dead ones? Three dead now, Zack amended. And he had been responsible for two of them.

As for taking Kaitlyn hunting—he blew out a breath. All things considered, he had to admit that it probably hadn't been the brightest idea he had ever come up with. But it had sure as hell been fun while it lasted. Watching her take pleasure in her vampire nature had been a remarkably satisfying thing to see. He knew, from his own experience, that Kaitlyn would never be truly happy until she accepted the whole of who and what she was. Only then would she be comfortable with both sides of her nature—at home in her own skin, so to speak. He thought he had helped her achieve that more fully tonight. It bemused him to discover that her happiness was more important to him than life itself.

Plagued by a nightmare, Kaitlyn woke before sunrise, and then, unable to get back to sleep, she left her bed and went into the kitchen, where she fixed a cup of peppermint tea and honey, hoping it would help dispel the last vestiges of her nightmare—a horrible dream in which their attacker had been the victor and it had been Zack sprawled on the ground in an ever-widening pool of blood, his head separated from his body.

She carried her tea to one of the tables in the dining room and sat down, the cup cradled in her hands while she went over the events of the past night.

It had started off so well, being with Zack. The movie had amused him. He had laughed from time to time. Occasionally he had whispered the dialogue along with the actors. When she asked, he admitted he had seen the film dozens of times. Later, they had danced. As always, she had reveled at being in his arms, feeling his strength, seeing the love in his eyes, hearing it in his voice. Hunting with him had been exciting, an adventure like none she had ever known before. For the first time in her life, she had embraced her vampire half, and because of it, she felt stronger, more confident. Yes, it had been a wonderful night, until they started for home. And now, because of her, Zack had killed two men and his life was in danger. Or maybe the blame lay with Florin.

She knew the story of Florin's treachery. Knew it had happened the night the Master of the Irish Fortress had challenged her grandfather for control of the Carpathian Fortress. Rodin had defeated the challenger, and then Florin had darted forward and stabbed Rodin in the back with a long wooden stake. In retaliation, her father had killed Florin. The matter should have ended there. A life for a life. Now, more than twenty years later, two more of Nadiya's sons were dead. Why had Nadiya waited so long to exact vengeance for Florin's death? When and where would it end? Who else would have to die before it was over?

She stared at the cup in her hands. Lost in thought, she had forgotten all about the tea and now it was cold. Pouring it into the sink, she left the kitchen. Without conscious thought, she found herself standing outside Zack's room.

She placed her hand on the door. Was it locked? Was he asleep? It was not yet sunup. She pressed her ear to the door, but heard nothing.

She tried the knob, surprised to find the door unlocked. She slipped inside, her gaze moving immediately to the bed. He slept on his back, one arm flung over his head, the covers pooled around his hips. His chest was bare. She swallowed, her fingertips pressed to her lips lest some sound betray her. Was he naked beneath the sheet?

Mesmerized by the sight of him, she stood there, avidly admiring the spread of his shoulders, his long muscular arms, his broad chest and flat belly.

Moving closer, she brushed a lock of hair from his forehead, gasped as his hand closed around her wrist, his fingers like iron.

"Zack, it's me!"

"Katy?" He stared up at her. "What the hell are you doing here?"

"I couldn't sleep."

"So you decided to wake me up?"

"I'm sorry. I didn't think you'd be asleep already."

"There was nothing else to do." His gaze moved over her face. "Do you think it's wise, your being in here?"

"Do you want me to leave?"

"Katy, you silly girl, I think you know better than that." He lifted the covers in invitation. "Come, join me."

Kicking off her slippers, Kaitlyn slid under the blankets, sighing as Zack's arm slipped around her shoulders, drawing her close to his side. She was relieved—and disappointed—to discover he was wearing briefs.

"I could get used to this," he murmured, his breath warm against her cheek.

"Me, too." She ran her fingertips over his chest. "It'll be dawn soon. The sun's coming up."

"I know. I can feel it."

"Can you? What does it feel like?"

"I don't know how to describe it. It's sort of like liquid fire running through my veins."

She grimaced. "Sounds awful."

He shrugged. "It comes in handy." Sleeping when it was his choice was entirely different from the Dark Sleep that claimed him with every sunrise.

He stroked her cheek, then kissed her lightly. He could feel the lethargy stealing over him as the sun slowly climbed over the horizon, felt it dragging him down into a dark abyss that ended in a deep black void.

"Zack?"

"I love you," he murmured, and slid into oblivion.

Chapter 26

Nadiya Korzha's blood ran cold as she folded back the bloodstained blanket and stared at the grisly remains of her son. Grief quickly turned to rage, hardening her desire for vengeance a hundredfold. Marius had been her oldest son. And her favorite child.

Raising her head, she gazed at the people clustered around her. "Who did this?"

There was a lengthy silence before her youngest daughter, Marthe, answered, "No one knows. We found his . . . his body outside the front door of the home place and brought it here."

Nadiya lowered her head, nostrils flaring. "Sherrad," she hissed. "I should have known." Hands clenched, she stood, her body trembling with outrage. First Florin. Then Daryn. And now her favorite son. "All of you, leave me."

One by one, her sons and daughters filed out of the room.

Nadiya stood there a moment, breathing heavily as she surrendered to her grief and then, as if swaddling a newborn babe, she wrapped the blanket around his remains and carried it into her bedroom. Placing her burden on the bed, she removed his bloody clothing, and after filling a basin with warm water, she gently bathed his body, then dressed it in a clean suit of clothes. Lifting his head, she washed his face and brushed his hair.

When that was done, she carefully bundled his remains in a blanket pulled from her bed and carried it outside.

Cradling his body to her breast, she let her tears flow unchecked.

The blanket was wet with her tears when she lowered him gently to the ground beneath the branches of a towering oak. Using her own two hands, she quickly dug his grave.

"I will avenge you," she whispered, lifting him into her arms once more. "I swear it by everything I hold dear."

She held him close, reluctant to let him go as she recalled the wintry night he had been born. Her labor had been long, but the pain had faded when she saw the pride and happiness on Rodin's face.

The sun was rising when she floated, as light as a feather, down into the grave. "Rest well, my son," she murmured as she lowered him onto the ground. "Rest well."

Chapter 27

For the first time in his existence, Zack woke to find a woman in bed beside him. Had she slept beside him all day? He found the thought endearing.

He had made love to women in the past—many women—but he had never invited any of them to stay the night, nor had he ever spent the night in their beds. Caution was second nature to his kind, and only a vampire with a death wish let a mortal share his lair, or know its location. There had been times, when, for one reason or another, he had been unable to reach his lair. At such times, night had been his pillow and darkness his blanket.

Turning onto his side, he studied Kaitlyn's face. Her brows were black and slightly arched, her nose small and finely sculpted, her cheeks smooth and unblemished. Her mouth—ever so lightly, he traced the outline of her lips. They were pink and warm, as soft as velvet, and endlessly tempting.

When he drew his hand away, she murmured, "Don't stop."

"I thought you were asleep."

"No, I've been awake for hours."

"Why didn't you get up?"

"I did. I had lunch with my mom and then, when no one was looking, I came back here."

Zack shook his head. "Must have made for a long, boring day."

"Not really." She rolled onto her side, facing him. "I like it here. I like watching you sleep."

"Really? I can't imagine why."

"Me, either," she said, smiling. "But there it is." She brushed a lock of hair from his forehead. "Do you dream?"

"No, but I guess you do."

She nodded, remembering her earlier nightmare.

He gazed into her eyes, those beautiful, clear blue eyes, marveling that she was in his bed, that she loved him. "What do you dream about, Katy?"

A blush crept into her cheeks. "Making love to you."

"Just say where and when."

"Here. And now."

It was tempting, he thought, but then, everything about Kaitlyn was tempting. But it didn't seem very smart, taking her virginity here, under her father's roof, especially when her father had no love for him. The chances of getting caught were too great. And as much as he desired Kaitlyn, fighting her father was the last thing Zack wanted to do. Not that he was afraid of being defeated. On the contrary, he was afraid of being victorious, certain that, if he won, Katy would hate him forever. And vampires, whether made or born, were capable of holding a grudge for a good long time. Nadiya Korzha was proof of that.

"As nice as this is," Zack said, kissing her cheek, "and as much as I would love to keep you in my bed, I think you'd better go before your father comes looking for you."

"But I don't want to go," she said, pouting.

"I know, but it's for the best." He caressed her cheek. "I love you, darlin', but I really don't want to fight your father, or spend any more time in that tower."

When he put it like that, what could she say?

She started to rise, but he pulled her into his arms, his mouth covering hers in a long, searing kiss that made her toes curl with pleasure. Heat flooded through her, as if a thousand fireflies had taken flight in the core of her being. She pressed herself against Zack, felt the evidence of his desire against her belly.

Now, she thought. He would make love to her now.

And he might have, if someone hadn't come knocking on the door.

Kaitlyn bolted upright, then looked at Zack, her eyes wide.

"Zack? Are you awake?"

Kaitlyn's heart skipped a beat at the sound of her mother's voice. She stared at Zack, panic-stricken. What was her mother doing here?

"Zack? It's me, Elena."

He cleared his throat. "Yeah?"

"Have you seen Kaitlyn? She's not in her room, and no one's seen her since this afternoon."

"If you give me a minute to get dressed, I'll help you look."

"Thanks. I'll wait for you in the library."

"Right."

Kaitlyn collapsed on the bed. How could she have been so foolish as to spend the day here? How could she have forgotten that whenever she was home, her mother expected them to dine together.

"Relax, darlin'," Zack said. He pulled on his pants, then peered out the door. "The coast is clear. You'd better go while the going is good."

With a nod, she hurried out the door and ran to her

room, wondering all the while what she could possibly say to her mother. She had never lied to her parents before, but she needed a good fib now.

In her room, she quickly changed into a pair of jeans and a sweater, ran a brush through her hair, then hurried to the library. Pausing outside the door, she took several deep breaths, pasted a smile on her face, and stepped into the room.

"Hi, Mom."

"Kaitlyn! Where have you been?"

"I . . . was upstairs. In the ballroom."

"Whatever were you doing up there?"

Kaitlyn tucked her hands into the pockets of her jeans to keep from fidgeting. "Doing? I . . ." She cleared her throat. "Nothing. I was just . . . you know, just looking at the view. It's really pretty this time of year." She bit down on her lower lip to stop the flow of words.

Her mother didn't say anything, merely sat there, watching her.

"Don't you believe me?"

"Should I?"

"No." Kaitlyn's shoulders sagged. She had never been any good at lying. What had made her think she could get away with it now? "I'll tell you the truth, but only if you promise not to tell Dad."

"I can't promise you that."

Kaitlyn sank down on the sofa beside her mother. "I was with Zack."

Elena folded her hands in her lap. "You mean just now?"

"Yes. We didn't do anything, honest," she said quickly. "He just woke up a few minutes before you knocked on the door."

"How long were you in there?"

"All day, except for when I had lunch with you."

"I see."

"I . . . I just wanted to be near him."

"Oh, dear," Elena said, sighing. "You've got it bad, don't you?"

"I love him, Mom. More than anything."

Elena smiled wistfully. "Yes, I guess you do." She took Kaitlyn's hands in hers. "Don't do anything you'll regret later, sweetheart. Don't hurry into anything. Zack is very handsome. And vampires have an allure that's hard to resist. But you know that. Just be sure that what you're feeling for him is real, and not . . . lustful attraction."

"So, how did you know what you felt for Dad was the real thing and not just infatuation, or some kind of vampire glamour?"

"That's a good question," Elena said, smiling. "I wish I had a good answer."

"What made you love him?"

"I guess it was his goodness, his kindness." She squeezed Kaitlyn's hand. "And even though he could read my mind, he never took advantage of it. Well," she added, grinning, "not often. But the most important thing was, he let me be me. That's important in a relationship, because you can't change him, and he shouldn't try to change you."

Kaitlyn nodded. Zack knew her better than she knew herself. "You won't tell Dad where I was?"

"No. But remember this, next time it could be your father knocking on the door." Elena looked up. "Zack, come in."

"I see you found her," he said, striding into the room.

"She told me everything," Elena said, rising. "In the future, I hope the two of you will be more discreet."

Zack waited until Elena left the room, then, grinning, he took Kaitlyn in his arms. "Looks like we dodged a bullet that time."

It surprised Zack to learn that the vampires who dwelled within the Fortress spent their waking hours pretty much like everyone else. They watched satellite TV and DVDs, they read a lot, they danced up in the ballroom, they argued and bickered like most married folks, they played with their kids and made sure they were well educated.

It was all a revelation to Zack. The vampires he knew were a solitary bunch. Occasionally, one or two would band together for a while, but as a rule, the vampires of his acquaintance didn't share territory or lairs. They didn't trust each other and pretty much avoided one another whenever possible.

But this was the Carpathian Fortress, and tonight both vampires and mortals had gathered in the game room downstairs to play cards. In order for the games to be fair, the vampires and the humans played at separate tables, since the vampires could read mortal minds. Most of the women played canasta or rummy, while the men, and a few of the women, preferred poker.

Zack glanced at Kaitlyn, who stood behind his chair as he shuffled the deck. Zack rarely played cards. Being able to read human minds made winning all too easy, which took all the fun out of the game. Playing with the vampires was far more challenging. He had met a mortal or two who had what was called a "poker face" but they didn't hold a candle to the vampires. Kaitlyn's father was a natural at the game, as was another vampire known as Josef.

Zack played for an hour, scooped up his winnings,

took Kaitlyn by the hand, and excused himself from the game. He was keenly aware of Drake's narrow-eyed gaze following them as they left the room.

"What do you want to do now?" Kaitlyn asked as they climbed the stairs to the main floor.

"Doesn't matter. I just wanted to be alone with you for a while."

"Sounds good to me." She nodded as they passed a couple of young vampires. "But I don't know where we'll find a place to be alone at this time of the night."

He grunted softly. The corridor was crowded with vampires and humans.

Hand in hand, Kaitlyn and Zack checked the music room, the library, and the art gallery, but all the rooms were occupied. Zack suggested the dining room, but it was filled with teenagers chatting, listening to music, and playing with the latest electronic gadgets.

"Maybe the council chamber," Kaitlyn said. But when they opened the door, they saw a number of vampires engaged in a chess match.

"The ballroom?" Zack suggested.

"It's probably crowded, too," Kaitlyn said, "but I can't think of anywhere else."

Zack was thinking that, if necessary, he would physically eject anyone he found inside, but this time, luck was on his side and the place was empty. Empty and dark, save for the silvery moonlight that filtered through the windows.

"Ah, perfect," he murmured. Taking Katy into his arms, he kissed her. "I've been wanting to do that all night long."

"And I've been wanting you to." She glanced around, wishing there was a sofa or a love seat. The only seat for two was the piano bench, or one of the window seats that looked out over the valley. Tugging on Zack's hand, she moved toward the window at the far end of the room.

She sat down on the velvet cushion. Zack sat beside her, his arm going around her shoulders to draw her close.

"Pretty view, isn't it?" she murmured. "Especially at night."

"Very."

"You're not even looking."

"Yeah, well, you look at the view you like and I'll look at the one I like." His hand cupped the back of her head, drawing her closer. He kissed her gently, as if she might break at his touch. Gradually, his kisses grew deeper, longer, hotter. His tongue teased her lips, dipped inside to duel with hers while his hand slid slowly, seductively, up and down her back.

Kaitlyn slipped one hand under his shirt, her fingernails raking lightly over his back, while her other hand slid up into his hair.

Time lost all meaning as their kisses grew more intense, their touches more intimate. She didn't protest when he lifted her onto his lap, merely wrapped her arms around him and kissed him again. And again. The evidence of his desire sparked her own until she felt as though she was melting inside.

With desire came the urge to taste him. She bit his ear lightly. "Zack?"

He drew back, a knowing look in his eyes. "Yes, love?"

"Is it all right?"

"You don't have to ask, Katy darlin'."

With a moan that was very near a growl, she gave in to the urge to taste him. And when she'd had enough, she drew his head to her neck, reveling in his bite, in the sensual pleasure of it. She had never been intimate with a man, but she couldn't imagine anything being more wonderful than this.

Reluctantly, Zack lifted his head. His whole body throbbed with need. It was time to call it a night, time to go downstairs before he did something foolish—like make love to her there, on the floor, in the moonlight.

Kaitlyn looked up at him, her eyes wide, and he knew her thoughts were running parallel with his.

"Come on, darlin'," he said, pulling her to her feet, "let's get out of here before we get into real trouble."

"Not yet."

"Katy, I'm not made of steel. Besides, we're no longer alone."

He had barely finished speaking when the lights went on.

Zack glanced over Kaitlyn's shoulder. Her father stood in the doorway, his displeasure evident in his expression.

"Kaitlyn," Drake said sternly, "your mother is looking for you. She is waiting in your room."

"We're coming, Dad. We were just . . . uh . . . looking at the stars."

"Indeed. I will wait for you downstairs."

"Is he going to follow us everywhere we go?" Zack asked.

"I hope not," Kaitlyn muttered. "Good thing you've got so much willpower."

"Yeah. I don't even want to think about what he'd say if I'd let you seduce me."

"Very funny," Kaitlyn retorted.

"I thought so," he said with a mischievous grin. "Be a good girl, and I'll let you walk me home."

She batted her eyelashes at him. "Oh, Zackary," she said with a fake, sugary-sweet Southern accent, "ya'll are so good to me."

"Okay, Scarlett," he muttered, taking her hand in his.

Side by side, they walked down the stairs, stopping to kiss on each landing until they reached the main floor. Drake was waiting for them.

"Hi, Daddy," Kaitlyn drawled. "Don't wait up."

Drake scowled at her.

"Well done," Zack said, grinning.

When they reached Zack's room, he muttered, "I guess I should have seduced you when I had the chance."

"I guess so. Good night, Zack."

"What? No kiss?" He glanced down the hallway to where Drake stood, arms folded over his chest, watching their every move.

Zack grunted softly. What the hell. If her old man wanted to watch, he'd give him something to see. Drawing Kaitlyn into his arms, Zack kissed her slowly, his tongue teasing hers, his arm holding her body tightly against his.

She went up on her tiptoes, her arms twining around his neck as she kissed him back.

The enthusiasm of Kaitlyn's response, the heat of her nubile body, made him forget that her father was watching. Until Drake cleared his throat.

Stifling a grin, Zack released her. "See you tomorrow night, Katy."

Chapter 28

Kaitlyn was surprised to see her mother in the dining room in the morning. Usually, her mom and dad kept the same hours.

"Hi, Mom. What are you doing up so early?"

"Don't you know what day it is?"

Kaitlyn looked at her mother blankly.

Elena shook her head. "Have you forgotten today is your birthday?"

"It is? It is! Oh my gosh, I can't believe I forgot that!"

"Zack Ravenscroft must really have your head in the clouds." Grinning, Elena hugged her daughter. "Ah, young love, it's a wonderful thing. Happy birthday, sweetie."

"Thanks, Mom."

"Your dad and I are planning a party for you later tonight, but I wanted to spend today with you, just the two of us, like we used to. What would you like for breakfast?"

"Blueberry pancakes, bacon, and toast." It had been her favorite breakfast ever since she was a little girl.

"Coming right up."

Kaitlyn followed her mother into the kitchen. When

she started to help, her mother shooed her away. "Not today. Just sit over there and watch."

Rolling her eyes, Kaitlyn hopped up on the stool in the corner. "What kind of party?"

"Oh, the usual, you know. Balloons and presents and dancing under the stars." Elena put the bacon in a pan, mixed the batter, and poured it on the griddle. When the pancakes and bacon were almost done, she dropped the bread into the toaster.

"At least let me set the table," Kaitlyn said.

"Already done." Elena placed everything on a tray and carried it into the dining room.

Kaitlyn trailed at her heels. "Oh, Mom," Kaitlyn said when she saw how her mother had decorated the room. "It's lovely."

A pink cloth covered the table. A crystal vase held a dozen roses. There were colorful balloons everywhere, a dress-up silver crown beside her plate.

Kaitlyn grinned when she saw the crown. Her mother had given her one every year for as long as she could remember. It wouldn't be a birthday without it.

"Please, sit, Your Highness," Elena said. She placed the tiara on Kaitlyn's head. "The roses are from your father."

"They're beautiful."

"Best eat those pancakes while they're hot," Elena said.

"Looks good, as always." Kaitlyn helped herself to several pancakes, three strips of bacon, as well as a slice of buttered toast.

"Milk or orange juice?" Elena asked.

"OJ."

"This is nice." Taking a seat across from her daughter, Elena filled her own plate. "I've missed our mornings together."

Kaitlyn nodded. When she lived at Wolfram, she adjusted her waking hours to the ones her father kept so she could spend time with her parents. In Tahoe, her hours had been erratic. Sometimes she adhered to mortal hours; sometimes she kept vampire hours. Especially after meeting Zack.

She smiled inwardly. Zack. She could hardly wait to see him.

"So, what do you want for your birthday?" Elena asked.

"I don't know. It'll be pretty hard to top what you gave me for graduation and my birthday last year."

"True."

"I really don't need anything," Kaitlyn said.

"Well, think about it."

"I will. These pancakes are great," Kaitlyn said. "I forgot what a good cook you are."

"It's nice to have someone to cook for besides myself."

Kaitlyn ate in silence for several minutes, thinking about what her mother had just said. "Mom, do you ever regret marrying Dad?"

"Of course not. Why would you ask such a thing?"

"It must be hard sometimes, living with a vampire. Eating alone all the time. Never being able to go out together during the day. You know, stuff like that."

"No relationship is perfect. I don't always eat alone. Sometimes I dine with Northa and the other women. And your father often sits with me . . ." She paused, brow furrowed. "Kaitlyn, you've only known Zack a short time. You're not seriously thinking of marrying him, are you?"

"Why shouldn't I marry a vampire? You did."

"I know, but . . ." Elena paused. "I was about to say that the two of you are different kinds of vampires, but that argument doesn't really hold water, does it? I mean, your father and I are different and yet we've been happy together. We've had to make compromises, yes, but every couple has to make adjustments. Still, marrying a vampire isn't like marrying someone from another religion." She smiled wistfully. "I guess it would be easier for you, all things considered."

"I love him, Mom, with all my heart. I can't imagine my life without him."

Elena nodded. "You're old enough to make up your own mind, sweetheart. Whatever you decide is all right with me."

Kaitlyn reached across the table and squeezed her mother's hand. "Thanks, Mom. For everything."

After breakfast, Kaitlyn went into the library to read while her mother went to take care of some household chores.

Sitting there, an unopened book on her lap, Kaitlyn remembered how it had been, growing up at Wolfram. Before she went to school, she had kept the same hours as her parents, but that had changed when she turned five. Her mother had considered teaching Kaitlyn at home, but after thinking it over, she had decided that Kaitlyn needed to have the opportunity to play with other kids her age, that she needed to learn how to interact in a group, and to share.

And so her mother had changed her routine to accommodate Kaitlyn's schedule. Thinking about it now, she realized her father must have changed his sleeping habits, as well. It must have been hard on her mother, trying to arrange it so she could spend time with a daughter who slept at night and a husband who slept most of the day.

Kaitlyn stretched her back and shoulders. She wouldn't have to make any adjustments like that if she married

Zack. Zack couldn't have children, so it would be easy to keep the same hours he did.

Zack. She ran her fingertips over her lips as she recalled how he had kissed her last night. It was probably just her imagination, but she was certain she could still taste him.

Zack. Right or wrong, she wanted him with every fiber of her being, yearned for him with every breath. Until she'd met him, she had never believed in love at first sight, or soul mates, or that there was just one perfect man for every woman. But she believed it now.

She opened the book and tried to read, but instead of seeing the words on the page, she saw Zack's image—dark gray eyes that were sometimes enigmatic but always beautiful. She loved the shape of his mouth, his smile that was sometimes cynical but always sexy. She loved the way he kissed her, the way being in his arms made her feel loved and protected. If she could have assembled the perfect man, he would have looked just like Zack.

Setting the book aside, she left the library. The Fortress was unusually quiet as she walked down the hallway. Kaitlyn grinned. No doubt her mother was holed up with Northa and some of the other women making last-minute preparations for her upcoming birthday party.

Kaitlyn stopped in midstride when the doorbell rang. It wasn't an ordinary doorbell, of course, but a bell that resounded through the whole house.

Kaitlyn hurried toward the front entrance. She couldn't be certain, but she thought there would probably be a present waiting for her when she got there.

She paused when she reached the front door. "Who's there?" she asked, suddenly cautious.

"Victoria Galleries. I have a delivery for Kaitlyn Sherrad."

She smiled as she opened the door.

A man wearing a uniform stood on the porch beside an enormous box wrapped in brightly colored paper. "Miss Sherrad?"

"Yes."

"I need you to sign this, please." He held out a digital clipboard.

"Certainly." Wondering what on earth could be in such a large box, Kaitlyn reached for the clipboard, gasped when the man grabbed her by the wrist and pulled her outside. Before she could scream, he jabbed a needle in her arm. The effect was immediate. As if in slow motion, she watched him lift the lid on the box. She tried to scream when he picked her up, but only a whisper emerged. She tried to fight him off, but she had lost all control of her arms and legs. As if she was a rag doll, he dumped her into the box and replaced the lid.

And her world faded to black.

Zack rose with the setting of the sun, his first thought for Kaitlyn. He took a quick shower, pulled on a pair of clean pants and a gray shirt, combed his hair, and left his room.

As soon as he stepped into the corridor, he knew something was wrong. The sound of angry voices drew him toward the council chamber. He paused outside the door. It was closed and he hesitated to go inside. Until he heard Kaitlyn's name.

When he stepped into the room, all eyes swung in his direction. Zack nodded at Drake, who stood on the dais in the front of the room. Elena stood beside her husband, her face pale, her eyes swollen and red. The thirteen chairs at the horseshoe-shaped table were all occupied.

"Zack," Elena said, "do you know where Kaitlyn is?"

He shook his head. "I haven't seen her since last night. Why? Is something wrong?"

"She's missing. We've looked everywhere. No one has seen her since late this morning," Elena said. "I even checked your room while you were sleeping. . . ." She smiled apologetically.

Zack looked from Elena to Drake. "You don't think that I . . ."

"No, of course not," her father said. He sat down heavily. "There can be only one answer," he said, his voice as cold as glacier ice. "Nadiya."

"But how?" Stefan asked.

"A good question," Ciprian said. "Since Kaitlyn's return, we have placed additional wards around the Fortress to warn us of intruders."

"Maybe the intruder didn't come in," Zack remarked. "Maybe Katy went out."

Drake stared at him a moment, then nodded. "Andrei, I want you to go to the Korzha estate and see if anyone is there. Liam, go to the Russian Fortress and see if they have heard anything. Stefan, visit the Italians, Ciprian, the Fortress in Ireland. If we want to find Kaitlyn, we must find Nadiya."

Zack shook his head as he listened to Drake assign the other members of the council to Fortresses through-out the world. It was, he thought, a waste of time and energy. But he understood Drake's need to be doing something, anything.

Leaving the council chamber, Zack returned to his room and shut the door. Standing in the middle of the floor, he closed his eyes and opened his vampiric senses, searching for the blood bond that had been forged between himself and Kaitlyn.

After twenty minutes, he gave up. Either she was

dead—an option he refused to consider—or she was unconscious.

Swearing under his breath, he began to pace the floor. Whether she was dead or alive, he would find her, and God help the man or woman who had taken her.

Chapter 29

Lucien looked up, smiling, when he saw Nadiya striding toward him. "I can see by the look on your face that you have good news."

"Indeed." She took the chair beside him. "The Carpathian Fortress will soon be ours. I have a bargaining chip that Sherrad cannot ignore."

"What have you done?" he asked, suddenly wary.

"I have his daughter."

"Are you mad? He will kill you for that."

"This is no time to lose your nerve, Lucien! The Fortress is within our grasp."

"Where is the girl?"

"Heavily drugged and in a secure location."

"I see." He braced his elbows on the arms of his chair and studied her over his steepled fingers. "So, what are your plans?"

"Ready your men. I have sent a messenger to Sherrad telling him to abandon the Fortress immediately."

"And if he refuses?"

She sat back in her chair, her expression serene and confident. "He will not."

"But if he does?" Lucien pressed.

"She dies, of course. She has to die, no matter what happens." A slow smile spread over Nadiya's face. It was an event she looked forward to with great anticipation. Blood for blood, a life for a life. Her sons would be avenged.

"I don't like this," Lucien said. "You said nothing of kidnapping the Sherrad heir."

"No one is asking you to like it," she said curtly.

"You have the girl. What do you need me for?"

"In case Sherrad decides to fight. If he agrees to leave, we will have to quarter some of your men there to hold the place after he evacuates. My sons and daughters will also be there, as well as those of Sherrad's people who wish to join us."

Lucien tapped his fingers on the arm of his chair. To be Master of the Carpathian Fortress was a long-held dream. But was it worth the risk? Drake Sherrad was not a man to be trifled with. He would make a formidable foe.

Lucien was still debating the wisdom of Nadiya's plan when one of his sons entered the room. "Stefan Sherrad wishes to see you, Father."

"He is here? Now?"

"Yes. He said he will not leave until he has spoken with you."

"Tell him to wait. I will be out shortly." Rising, Lucien ran a hand through his hair. "This is a fine mess. What is he doing here?"

"Sherrad is obviously looking for his daughter," Nadiya said. "Keep your wits about you. Stefan will find nothing here. Get rid of him as soon as you can. I will be waiting for you at the Fortress, at the foot of the mountain."

"Very well." Taking a deep breath, Lucien went out to meet his guest.

Stefan was waiting in the antechamber.

"Stefan, how good to see you," Lucien said jovially. "It has been years. I heard you had gone to America."

"Yes."

"What brings you here?"

"I am looking for my father's wife, Nadiya," Stefan said, his voice cool. "I believe you know her."

Lucien cleared his throat. "Yes, of course. Lovely woman."

"We believe she has kidnapped Kaitlyn."

"They are not here." Lucien spread his hands wide. "You may search my home if you wish."

"Thank you. I will."

Drake stared at the human male standing on the porch. He was obviously in thrall to someone. His first words confirmed Drake's suspicion.

"The lady Nadiya demands that you, your family, and everyone else who dwells within these walls leave immediately."

"And if I refuse?"

The drone reached into his pocket and withdrew a scrap of bloodstained cloth. He offered it to Drake.

A muscle worked in Drake's jaw as he took it. He recognized the material immediately. It was from a dress Elena had given Kaitlyn.

The blood was also hers.

The threat was plain.

"Very well. Tell your lady that we will be gone by midnight."

Zack stared at Drake. "You're going to leave, just like that? You don't even know if Katy is still alive."

They had gathered in the council chambers once again. The council members had all returned, save for Stefan. None carried news of Nadiya or Kaitlyn. Every

Master Vampire questioned had denied knowing anything of Nadiya's or Kaitlyn's whereabouts.

"I am not going to take any chances with my daughter's life," Drake said. "Once Kaitlyn is safely with us again, we will retake the Fortress. Stefan! What news have you?"

"Lucien denies any knowledge of Nadiya or her whereabouts, but she has been to the Italian Fortress recently," Stefan said, striding toward the dais." I am sure of it." He glanced at the somber faces of the council members, then looked at Drake. "What has happened?"

"Nadiya has demanded that we evacuate the Fortress. I told her emissary we would be gone by midnight."

"So she has Kaitlyn?"

"I believe so, yes."

"You believe so?" Stefan exclaimed.

Drake held up the scrap of Kaitlyn's dress. "She has her, or knows where she is."

"How do you know she will return Kaitlyn once the Fortress is hers?"

"I do not." Drake shrugged, his expression implacable. "But my daughter's life is worth more than a pile of stone. We are leaving."

"What of the mortal families?" Andrei asked.

"Their vampire mates will care for them. Northa will go with Marta and Cullen. Elena, tell the others we are leaving, then go and pack anything you wish to take with you. Stefan, you are welcome to come to Wolfram with us." After a moment, he said, "Ravenscroft, you are also welcome to join us at Wolfram."

Zack nodded. "Thanks."

Since they were vampires with preternatural power, it didn't take them long to gather their belongings. Katiya and Andrei decided to visit with Katiya's parents. Drake's other brothers and sisters all had homes of their own in various parts of the country. Liliana also had a place of her own. She opted to go there, at least for the time being, and asked Stefan to go with her.

"Are you sure that is a good idea?" Drake asked. "I would feel better if the two of you would come to Wolfram with us."

"You are sweet to worry about me," Liliana said, patting his cheek. "But I wish to stay in my own house. Besides, I am not afraid of Nadiya Korzha. And Stefan will be with me."

An hour and a half later, everyone was gone save for Drake, Elena, Stefan, Liliana, and Zack, who were the last to leave the Fortress.

"You know you cannot trust Nadiya," Liliana said. "Her mind is rotten with her need for revenge."

Drake nodded. "I know."

"She's coming," Zack said. "And she's not alone." It hadn't taken him long to recognize the peculiar scent of the Romanian vampires. Once that was done, it was easy to distinguish between the Romanian vampires, humans, and vampires like himself.

Nadiya materialized out of the darkness. She was a pretty woman, Zack thought, if you liked women made of ice. She wore a long white dress that gave her a ghostly appearance. An odd power radiated from her, one he had never experienced before.

There were other vampires aligned behind her. Zack wasn't sure how many, perhaps fifty.

"Drake," Nadiya murmured. "So good to see you."

"I have done as you asked. Where is my daughter?"

Nadiya looked offended by his curt tone. "She is well enough, for now."

"I wish to see her."

"That was not part of our agreement."

Drake glared at her. "I have sent my people away. The Fortress is yours. Give me my daughter."

"I never said I would give her to you."

Drake took a step forward, his fingers clawlike, his eyes glowing hot as hellfire when he reached for her.

Nadiya raised one hand and it was as if Drake had hit a wall. He recoiled, his face contorting with pain.

Zack swore as residual supernatural power arced through the air, brushing his skin. It was like nothing he had ever felt before. Not painful, but uncomfortable.

He nodded to himself when Liliana murmured, "Witch." That explained it.

Elena took a step forward, one hand extended in a silent plea. "Nadiya, I know we have never been friends," she said, her voice thick with unshed tears, "but Kaitlyn has never done anything to you or your family. Please let her come home to us."

"Three of my sons are dead," Nadiya replied, her voice like acid. "No blood has been shed to avenge them."

"If you want blood, take mine!" Elena cried. "But please don't hurt my child. My only child."

"If you want blood for blood, take mine," Drake said, his voice thick with barely suppressed anger. "I am the one who destroyed Florin. Although you seem to have forgotten he deserved to die for his treachery against your husband."

Nadiya's eyes narrowed ominously. "You dare say that to my face!"

"It is the truth and you know it!"

"Be gone from here!"

"Drake?" Elena looked up at her husband, her cheeks damp with tears.

"Come, wife, let us go." Taking Elena by the hand, he started down the trail, then turned back to face Nadiya. "Know this. If you harm so much as a hair on my daughter's head, I will hunt you down and rip out your heart no matter how long it takes me to find you, no matter what the cost."

Without waiting for her reply, he stalked down the long, winding path that led to the valley below.

Lucien stood at the foot of the trail, his men stretched out behind him.

Drake paused in front of the other Master Vampire, his eyes narrowing. "I should have known you would be in on this," he said, his voice thick with contempt. "I have always known you coveted this place. It is a shame you lacked the courage to fight me for it, man to man, instead of hiding behind a woman's desire for revenge."

Vampires didn't blush with embarrassment or grow flushed with anger, but Lucien's eyes filled with shame as he stepped aside to let Drake pass.

"Be warned, Lucien," Drake continued, his voice laced with quiet menace, "if anything happens to my daughter, your life will also be forfeit." Back rigid, he swept past Lucien and the other vampires.

Stefan and Liliana followed Drake and Elena down the mountainside.

Zack brought up the rear.

As he started to pass Nadiya, she put a staying hand on his arm. Magical power rippled over his skin like tiny electric shocks. "Who are you?" she asked.

He shrugged. "Just a friend of the family."

She stared at him. "What is your name?"

"Zack Ravenscroft."

Recognition flared in her eyes. "You knew my son, Daryn."

Zack nodded. "I saw him a couple of times."

"Do you know where he is?"

"Yeah," Zack drawled. "I know."

Her eyes glittered with a fierce intensity. "Tell me."

"Sure," Zack replied affably. "Right after you tell me what you've done with Kaitlyn."

Nadiya glared at him. "All I have to do is say the word and she is dead."

Zack's hands clenched into fists. He had never hit a woman but he was sorely tempted to start with this one. "Kill her and you'll never see your son again."

Nadiya's gaze searched his. She had not seen her son's body. She grabbed at the slender thread of hope Ravenscroft's words offered. "Is he still alive?" Her voice broke on the last word.

"Is she?" It took all Zack's concentration to keep his voice even.

Nadiya straightened to her full height, her eyes flashing fire as they met his. "This is getting us nowhere."

"I heard what Drake said about hunting you down if you harm Kaitlyn. If he fails, I will find you, and I will finish it."

Anger flashed in Nadiya's eyes. She glared at him, her body quivering, her eyes narrowing in concentration.

Magick shimmered in the air as she summoned her power.

Zack felt it push against him like an invisible hand. He steeled himself against it, his own power surfacing in response. Her magick swept over him like fingernails raking across his skin, but whatever spell she was conjuring had no other effect. Her magick had worked on Drake. Zack had no idea why it didn't work on him. He frowned thoughtfully. Maybe her witchcraft was nullified because he wasn't a Romanian vampire but one of the dreaded Others.

It was the only reason that made sense.

Chapter 30

Wolfram Castle was a formidable structure, even in the moonlight, Zack mused. Large and rectangular, there were round turrets at three of the corners and a high, arched entrance. Battlements edged the flat roof. The single entry, flanked by two towers, faced the rising sun. Stone steps led to an impressive, iron-barred door made of what looked like solid oak.

Zack stood aside as Drake opened the door. The Master Vampire's expression was grim, his thoughts obviously deeply troubled.

It was Elena who invited Zack into the castle. He felt the faint brush of preternatural power over his skin as he crossed the threshold.

Wolfram Castle was as impressive on the inside as it was on the outside, he thought, taking a quick look around. If this room was any indication, the castle interior had been remodeled, perhaps several times. In spite of its massive size, the room, probably once the great hall, had a homey feel to it. A pair of flowered sofas faced each other in front of a large stone hearth, several overstuffed chairs were grouped together around an oval coffee table. He guessed the trestle table against the far wall was part of the original castle furnishings. No doubt the hearth was also part of the original structure.

"Nice place," Zack remarked.

"Thank you," Elena said. "Your room is this way."

Drake laid a staying hand on Elena's arm but his gaze was on Zack. "There are a few things I need to go over with Mr. Ravenscroft."

"What might those be?" Zack asked, faintly amused by Drake's formal tone.

"There is a small town at the foot of the mountain," Drake said. "You will not hunt there."

Zack nodded. "Your territory, your rules."

"There is a large city to the east. I ask that you be discreet when you hunt."

"Right. No bodies drained of blood left lying in the street."

Drake glared at Zack; then, his expression softening, he looked at Elena. "You will not leave Wolfram, day or night, without me."

"But . . ."

"We will not discuss this," Drake said adamantly. "Until Nadiya has been captured or destroyed, you are not to go out alone."

Elena blew out an aggrieved sigh. "All right."

Drake kissed Elena's cheek, then vanished from sight.

"We've been married over twenty years," Elena remarked, "and his ability to disappear like that still amazes me." She smiled at Zack. "Sometimes I wish I was a vampire."

"I could arrange it," Zack said with a grin. He had been joking, of course. Had expected Elena to laugh. Instead, she looked thoughtful. And then interested.

"Does it hurt, becoming a vampire?"

"No. The act itself was pleasant, although I didn't realize what was happening at the time. I woke alone the next night, terrified by what was happening to me. And hungry as hell." He shook his head. "I've never forgiven her for abandoning me, for not telling me what to expect. For not teaching me how to be a vampire . . . hey." He looked at her, his eyes narrowing. "I was only kidding about turning you, you know."

"Of course. I was just curious. I mean, Drake was born a vampire, but you weren't. Have you ever turned anyone?"

"Just once. You've given this a lot of thought, haven't you?"

"Of course not. Drake can't turn me, and I wouldn't want anyone else to do it." She made a vague gesture with one hand. "It's just that, after living with Drake's people for so long, well, you can't blame me for thinking about it."

"I guess not," Zack said. But he had the feeling that, had it been an option, she would have willingly let Drake change her.

"You won't say anything to Drake about our conversation, will you?"

"Not if you don't want me to."

"Thank you. If you're ready, I'll show you to your room."

Zack replayed their conversation in his mind as he followed her up a winding staircase to the second floor. He had the feeling that, if he offered, she would happily become a vampire. He couldn't blame her. It had to be difficult, being the only mortal in the family.

He followed her past closed doors on both sides of the carpeted hallway. Paintings of sunny landscapes graced the walls between the rooms.

Elena stopped in front of the last door on the right. "Please, make yourself at home. And please be patient with Drake. In all the years I've known him, this is the first time he's been at a loss as to what to do."

Zack nodded. He wasn't used to losing, either, and he damn sure didn't like it when it happened. But he wasn't about to give up, not now, not until Kaitlyn was back where she belonged.

"Feel free to look around," Elena said. "Now, if you'll excuse me, I need to be with Drake."

"Sure." Truth be told, he would just as soon be alone. Zack glanced at his surroundings after Elena took her leave. It was a large, rectangular room. A comfortable looking queen-sized bed was flanked by a pair of mahogany nightstands. A thick, dark green carpet covered the floor. Flowered curtains hung at the windows; a matching spread covered the bed.

He grunted softly when he saw the beveled mirror over the dresser. He wondered if Romanian vampires could see their reflections, something foreign to his kind. There were no mirrors on the floor of the casino; at night, blinds covered the windows, preventing anyone from noticing that the owner of the club didn't cast a reflection, nor did a few members of his staff.

His internal clock told him dawn was still hours away. Pulling out his cell phone, he flipped it open and called Scherry.

She answered on the first ring. "Hi, boss, when are you coming home?"

He grinned at the sassy tone in her voice. "I'm not sure. How's business?"

"Good, as usual. I'm glad you called. I was just about to call you."

"I thought everything was good?"

"Oh, it is. This has nothing to do with the club. There was a man in here night before last, asking questions about some guy named Eddie Harrington. And last night, a woman showed up asking after somebody named Daryn Korzha. I couldn't be sure but I had the feeling both the man and the woman were vampires."

"What made you think that?" Zack asked, though he was pretty sure she was right.

"Something about the way they smelled—not human, but not like us. It was weird."

"You were right. They're vampires, only a different breed. I'll tell you all about it when I see you. Everything else okay?"

"Jackson's been seeing this woman, Adele. She works the late shift at the hotel in town. He turned her earlier tonight. He was afraid to tell you."

"Smart boy."

"Do you want him to leave the club?"

"No, but let him worry about it for a few days."

Scherry laughed. "You are evil."

"Yeah. I'll call you in a day or two. If you don't hear from me, don't worry."

"I always worry about you."

"Yeah, well, stop it."

"Take care, boss."

"You, too."

Zack closed the phone. So, Nadiya was sending her people out to look for Daryn. "Well, good luck with that," he muttered.

And wondered if he would have any better luck finding Kaitlyn.

Chapter 31

Elena sat on the sofa in front of the hearth, a furry blanket wrapped around her shoulders, a cup of cocoa in one hand.

For Drake's sake—and to hang on to her own sanity—she forced herself to stay positive. She told herself over and over again that there was nothing to worry about. Drake would find their daughter and bring her home.

In an effort to keep from sinking into despair, she thought about what Zack had said the night before. He could make her a vampire. It troubled her that she found the idea so appealing. She had lived with Drake and his people for over twenty years but if the truth were known, she had never truly felt like she belonged. Oh, the people treated her well enough. They were as much a part of her life as she was of theirs. And yet she couldn't escape the fact that she was different. What would it be like, to be able to will herself into the city whenever she wished to go? To be like Drake? To share his whole life? To see the world the way he saw it? Even the blood part no longer repulsed her. She had been drinking a little of Drake's blood for years. What would he think if she told him she wanted to be a vampire? What would Kaitlyn think?

"Kaitlyn." The tears she had been holding back flooded her eyes as she murmured her daughter's name. Where was she?

Elena stared into the flames, her heart aching. She hadn't been up this early in the morning since Kaitlyn was an infant. She smiled, recalling how thrilled she had been the first time she held her baby daughter in her arms, how impatient she had been for Kaitlyn to wake up so she could hold her again. Her miracle baby. All babies were wonderful, of course, but Drake had told Elena there was little chance they could have a child, so when Kaitlyn was born strong and healthy, it had truly seemed to be a miracle.

She remembered the early years, when she had worried that Kaitlyn would get sick or hurt, and how she had prayed every day that Kaitlyn would be happy, that she would be able to accept her heritage. She recalled her bittersweet feelings when Kaitlyn went to kindergarten and how she had worried that her daughter might not fit in with the other children. So many foolish fears. None of the things she had worried about had come to pass.

She wiped her tears with a corner of the blanket. Her little girl had grown up into a beautiful young woman— sweet-natured, kind-hearted. She had never given them a moment's worry.

Until now. Of course, she wasn't responsible for the trouble with Nadiya. The blame for that lay squarely on Nadiya's shoulders.

She drew the blanket around her, cold in spite of the fire. Where was her little girl now?

* * *

Kaitlyn woke feeling groggy. There was a horrible taste in her mouth. When she tried to sit up, the world spun out of focus. Feeling like she was going to vomit, she quickly closed her eyes again.

When she opened them a short time later, she felt a little better. When she sat up, an ominous clanking drew her attention. Looking down at her foot, she saw that a thick cuff made of silver circled her left ankle. A long silver chain was attached to the shackle, which was linked to an iron bolt in the wall. Taking hold of the chain, she gave it a tug, thinking she could easily dislodge it, but nothing happened. Apparently, silver negated her preternatural power, just as it did her father's, though it didn't burn her skin.

Fighting down her fear, she glanced at her surroundings. She was sitting on a mattress in the corner of a small basement, or maybe an old wine cellar. There were no lights, no windows, and only one entrance.

Rising on shaky legs, she staggered toward the iron-barred door. The chain on her foot drew her up short. Try as she might, she couldn't reach the latch. Not that it would have done her any good. Still, pounding on it might have brought help. Now, more than ever, she wished she had her father's ability to transport herself wherever she wished to be. Or to dissolve into mist so she could slip her bonds and gain her freedom.

But wishing was a waste of time.

Returning to the mattress, she resumed her seat. Where was she? And how had she gotten there? The deliveryman . . . he had drugged her and stuffed her into a box. She remembered now. Lifting her head, she took a deep breath. Her nostrils filled with the scent of mold and dust and . . . Nadiya.

Kaitlyn fought down the chill rush of fear that rose within her at the realization that Nadiya had been there not long ago. Everyone knew Nadiya hated Drake and would never forgive him for Florin's death. Did Nadiya know that Zack had killed Daryn and Marius? Was Zack also in danger?

Kaitlyn blinked back her tears. She wouldn't cry. She wouldn't panic. Wherever she was, Zack and her father would find her.

Her heart jumped into her throat when the door opened. She had been expecting Nadiya, but it was the man who had abducted her. Seeing him now, she realized he was a drone—a creature whose mind was no longer his own.

Eyes blank, footsteps stiff and unnatural, he walked toward her. She sprang from the mattress, backing away from him, and from the needle in his hand, but there was no place to go.

He backed her into the corner, his hand circling her throat to hold her in place. Had she not been so weak, she would have fought him off, but she was helpless to resist when he jabbed the needle into her arm.

The world swam out of focus, her vision blurring as the room grew dark, darker.

She was vaguely aware of another presence in the room. Words chased themselves through the air, but they had no meaning.

"You will have to feed her soon." The drone's voice, empty of emotion.

"She does not need to eat." Nadiya's voice, filled with hatred.

"She is not a full vampire," the drone said. "She must have food or blood if you want her to survive."

"Oh, very well. Give her something to eat when the drug wears off."

"Survive." Kaitlyn mumbled the word. She had to survive. For Zack. It was her last conscious thought.

* * *

Zack woke with the setting of the sun, his thoughts turning immediately to Kaitlyn. Closing his eyes, he opened his vampiric senses and tried yet again to connect with Katy, but there was only darkness. He refused to think she could be dead. He couldn't lose her now, when he had just found her.

After showering, he dressed, absently thinking that he needed a change of underwear and clothing.

When he went downstairs, he found Drake and Elena sitting side by side on one of the sofas. It was obvious Elena had been crying.

They both looked up when he entered the room.

"Any word from Nadiya?" Zack asked.

"No." Drake's answer was curt.

"We need to find one of her kids."

"What will that accomplish?"

"You don't think she'd tell us where Katy is to save the life of one of her children?"

"Do you?"

Remembering the hint of madness in Nadiya's eyes, Zack shook his head. "No, I guess not. Dammit, where does that leave us?"

"My brothers and sisters are making inquiries at Fortresses around the world. If they hear anything of Kaitlyn, they will let me know. Until then . . ." Drake let out a sigh that came from the very depths of his soul.

"She can't be dead," Elena wailed softly. "She can't be."

Drake murmured his wife's name as he wrapped her in his arms.

Zack clenched his hands into fists. He hadn't told Drake or Elena about the blood bond between himself and Kaitlyn, nor would he, unless he was able to connect with her. What was the point in telling them unless he had good news? And right now, he feared the worst. It tore at his heart to see the pain in Elena's eyes. Unable to endure it any longer, he left the castle.

Outside, he drew a deep breath, and then he started to run. He could have easily transported himself to the city, but he needed to feel the wind in his face, needed to unleash the anger and frustration and fear that had been his constant companions ever since Kaitlyn disappeared. And he needed to blow off some steam now, before he hunted, or heaven help the man or woman he preyed on this night.

It was Friday. When he reached the city, the streets were crowded with shoppers and tourists. Zack mingled with the crowd. He ignored the couples and the elderly, the skinheads and the addicts. He wanted someone who was alone and would not be missed. He continued up the street, his senses rejecting this one for being infected with AIDS, that one for being too young. He bypassed a teenage girl heavy with child, a middle-aged man who reeked of alcohol, a woman who smelled of cocaine. Not that the drugs or the diseases or the booze would affect him. He was immune to all of it. But drugs and disease tainted the blood and left a bad taste in his mouth.

When he reached the end of the block, he crossed the main thoroughfare and strolled down a side street. There were fewer people here but he quickly found what he was looking for, a woman in her late twenties who had just stepped out of a nightclub.

She wobbled a little on her high heels as she walked down the sidewalk. She stopped beside a late-model car.

She was fumbling with her keys when Zack ghosted up behind her.

"Here," he said, "let me help you."

Startled, she looked at him, her eyes widening with alarm.

He trapped her gaze with his. "Don't be afraid. I'm not going to hurt you."

She wanted to argue, but she was helpless to resist his compulsion.

A wave of his hand opened the car door. "Get in."

Her movements were jerky, like a puppet's, as she climbed into the front seat.

Zack closed her door, then went around the front of the car and slid behind the wheel. "Give me your keys."

She handed them over without a word.

"Relax . . ." He searched her mind for her name while he put the car in gear. "Lavinia. We're going to go for a little drive, and then I'll take you home."

She stared at him, unblinking, as he drove out of the city, then turned off the highway onto a dirt road.

She was trembling uncontrollably now.

Zack swore softly as he put the car in PARK. His hand curled around her nape, drawing her toward him. "Lavinia, listen to me. I'm not going to hurt you, I promise." He ran his fingertips down the length of her neck. "Do you believe me?"

She shook her head.

She had a strong will, he thought irritably. Too strong to fully succumb to his suggestions. Well, he knew how to take care of that. He drew her closer, felt her body tense as his fangs brushed her tender skin. One bite, one taste, and she surrendered her will to his, a sigh of pleasure rising in her throat as he took what he needed.

And wished it was Kaitlyn in his arms, her blood chasing away the cold, filling the emptiness deep inside.

Chapter 32

Awareness returned slowly. Feeling as though she was swimming through a sea of thick black molasses, Kaitlyn fought her way up out of the smothering darkness, then lay there, feeling weak and disoriented.

It took three tries before she could sit up. When the dizziness passed, she noted that she was in the same room as before, on the same disgusting mattress. Her eyes felt gritty. There was a horrible taste in her mouth.

How long had she been here? Where was Nadiya? Where was Zack? Had her parents stopped looking for her? No! They would never stop looking, and neither would Zack. She had to believe that, had to keep hoping they would find her.

When she stretched her legs, her toe hit something on the floor beside the mattress. Looking down, she saw a wooden tray. A tin plate held two slices of bread and a hunk of cheese. There was also a cup of water. She had no appetite for food, but she drained the cup and wished for more.

She looked at the bread and cheese again. She wasn't really hungry but she picked up a slice of bread and took a bite. Who knew when they would offer her nourishment again? Surprisingly, she discovered she was hungry, after all, and she wolfed down the bread and cheese, then licked her fingers.

How long were they going to keep her here? How long did she have before Nadiya came to exact her revenge? And how, exactly, would she do it?

Kaitlyn bit down on her lower lip to keep from crying. She couldn't die, not now, now when she had just found Zack. She wanted more time—time to get to know him better, to discover what it would be like to make love to him all night long, to explore him from head to foot and every masculine inch in between. She had saved herself for the man she loved. Surely fate wouldn't be cruel enough to let her die before she discovered what it truly meant to be a woman.

"Zack." She whispered his name into the darkness. She was a vampire. She was strong enough to endure this. But the thought of never seeing Zack again was more than she could bear. Curling up on the mattress, she whispered his name again, and let the tears flow.

Zack was on his way back to Wolfram when he heard Kaitlyn's voice. He came to an abrupt halt. "Kaitlyn?" Dammit, had he only imagined it?

Closing his eyes, he again opened his vampiric senses, seeking the blood link that bound him to Katy. It took several minutes but gradually, the link between them stirred, solidified. Zack breathed a sigh of relief. She was alive. His mind brushed hers, seeing what she saw, feeling what she felt.

She was in a dark place. A basement. Shackled to a wall. She was cold and afraid. Crying softly.

Kaitlyn? Katy, can you hear me?

There was a long moment of silence and then her voice, filled with hope. *Zack?*

Do you know where you are?

No.

Is Nadiya there?

Not now, but she's been here.

Stay calm, Katy darlin'. We'll get you out of there, he promised. And hoped it was a promise he could keep. *I need to tell your parents you're okay, but I'll be in touch again soon. And Katy? I love you.*

I love you, too.

A thought carried him to Wolfram. He found Drake and Elena on the sofa where he had left them. Drake was staring into the hearth. Elena was asleep in his arms, her eyes red and swollen.

Drake looked up when Zack appeared in the room. "Where have you been?"

"Hunting. In the city. Listen, I found Katy. That is, I know where she is. Dammit, that's not right, either. But I think I can get to her." There was just one small flaw in his plan. He couldn't materialize inside a dwelling without having been previously invited. Usually, whoever owned the place had to do the inviting, but maybe that wasn't true with Romanian vampires. Of course, there was really only one way to find out.

"What are you talking about?" Drake demanded.

"We have a bond, Katy and I, forged by the blood we've shared. . . ."

"Why didn't you tell me about this before?"

"That doesn't matter now. I was able to link with her a few minutes ago. She's all right. I should be able to follow the link to where she's being held. There's just one problem."

Drake stared at him a moment, then nodded. "You

can't materialize inside the building if you've never been there before."

"Right. Unless Kaitlyn's invitation would work."

Drake grunted softly. "Only one way to find out."

"Yeah," Zack said, grinning. "That was my thought, too. I've never tried to enter a place where I wasn't welcome, so I'm not sure how this will play out."

"There are three possibilities." Drake ticked them off on the fingers of one hand. "One, nothing will happen. Two, we will end up outside our destination. Or three, we will find Kaitlyn."

"I'm ready to go if you are."

Drake kissed Elena's cheek, then softly called her name. "Elena."

She woke with a start, a look of alarm in her eyes. "What is it? What's wrong?"

"Nothing, love. Zack thinks he knows where Kaitlyn is. We are going to try to get her back."

"I'm going with you."

"No." He caressed her cheek with his knuckles. "You must wait here. We will be back soon."

Elena glanced at Zack, then back to her husband. "How did you find out where she is?"

"Zack and Kaitlyn have exchanged blood, much as you and I have done. There is a bond between them now. Zack thinks he can follow it to our daughter."

Elena looked at Zack. It pained him to see the hope shining in her eyes.

"Be careful," she murmured as Drake kissed her cheek. "Both of you."

"So," Drake said. "How do we do this?"

Zack shrugged. "Beats the hell out of me. Just hang on to my arm and I'll see if I can connect with Kaitlyn."

Drake nodded curtly, then grasped Zack's forearm.

Zack closed his eyes, opened his senses, and concentrated on Katy's whereabouts. He formed a picture of her in his mind, felt the link between them interlock.

Katy?

Zack?

We're coming for you. I need you to invite me into wherever you are.

Come to me, Zack. Your presence is welcome.

You'd better include your father. He's with me.

Drake Sherrad, she said, her voice rising with excitement, *you are also welcome.*

Okay, darlin', hopefully we'll see you soon.

Hurry!

Zack glanced at Sherrad. "Hang on. Here we go."

It was an experience that could not be described, the sense of moving through time and space at an incredible speed. Zack's vision blurred, the sound of air rushing past rang in his ears.

The abrupt sensation of motion was jarring.

Zack glanced at the small, two-story house located on a patch of dead grass. A six-foot chain-link fence surrounded the yard. There were bars on the windows, a security screen on the front door. The house was dark save for a light in one of the upstairs windows.

"Apparently her invitation was not sufficient," Sherrad remarked.

"So it seems. I guess we'll have to do it the hard way."

"Fine by me," Sherrad said.

Zack moved closer to the fence, his senses probing the interior of the house. "I don't sense any vampires inside, just Katy and a man and a woman."

Drake sniffed the air. "Nadiya has been here recently."

Zack nodded. Hers was a smell he wouldn't soon forget. "Let's go." He didn't wait for a reply, simply vaulted over the fence. No sooner had he reached the other side than an enormous Rottweiler came charging toward him from the backyard.

In an instant, Zack transformed himself into a wolf and growled in the dog's face. With a sharp whine, the Rott tucked its tail between its legs and ran back the way it had come.

Grinning, Zack assumed his own form once again.

"Impressive," Drake remarked.

"Yeah, well, I didn't think your pussycat would have any effect."

"Let us find Kaitlyn, shall we?"

Choking back his laughter, Zack strode up to the front door and knocked. He could feel Sherrad's gaze burning an angry hole in his back.

When there was no answer, Zack knocked again. Three minutes later, a middle-aged man wearing a pair of worn jeans and a flannel shirt opened the door. He looked harmless enough, until they saw the double-barreled shotgun in his hands.

"He's a drone," Sherrad said quietly.

"What the hell's a drone?"

"A human whose mind has been tampered with. Have you never made one?"

"Hell, no. Have you?"

"From time to time. Nadiya has left him in charge of Kaitlyn. No doubt she has ordered him to kill anyone who tries to enter the house."

Zack glanced past the man to the woman who had come up behind him. She was about the same age as the man. She also carried a shotgun. It was a ludicrous picture, the short, rotund rosy-cheeked woman wearing a long blue flannel nightgown and carrying a shotgun that was almost taller than she was.

Zack looked sideways at Sherrad. "So, what do we do now?"

"See if we can override Nadiya's compulsion." Summoning his preternatural power, Drake stared into the man's eyes. "You will forget whatever Nadiya Korzha has told you," he said firmly. "Whatever threats she has made are no longer in force. Do you understand?"

The man lifted the shotgun and leveled it at Sherrad's chest. "Go away or I will kill you."

"Uh, I don't think it's working," Zack muttered.

The man eared back the hammer on the shotgun. Unless the gun was loaded with silver and penetrated Drake's heart, the blast would be painful and messy, but not fatal.

Sherrad was little more than a blur as he reached forward and wrested the gun from the man's hand, then choked him into unconsciousness.

"Maybe you'll have better luck with the woman," Zack said dryly.

"Maybe you will shut up," Drake growled.

"Maybe I'd have better luck."

"Be my guest."

"Excuse me, madam," Zack said. "May I have a word with you?"

She looked momentarily confused, then nodded.

"My name is Zack and I've come to tell you that you don't have to be afraid of Nadiya anymore. I'm releasing you from her spell. Do you understand?"

"What spell?"

"Nadiya is a sorceress and she put a spell on you. But it isn't effective any longer. So why don't you put the gun down and take care of your husband?"

She glanced at the man sprawled facedown on the floor, then looked up at Zack.

"He needs help. If you invite me in, I'll help you carry him to bed."

The woman stared at her husband, and at the gun in her hands as if she had never seen either one before and then, with a sob, she lowered the weapon and dropped to her knees beside her husband.

When she looked up at Zack again, her eyes were clear. "Please, come in and help us."

Zack looked over his shoulder at Sherrad and smiled smugly.

"Don't say a word," Drake warned.

There was a shimmer of power as Zack stepped inside. It always amazed him that something as innocuous as a threshold had the power to keep him outside. He didn't know why it was so, but it was.

When he started past the woman, she grabbed his pant leg. "My husband . . ."

"I'll be right back, I promise. Why don't you get him a drink of water?"

He didn't wait for a reply. Opening his vampiric senses once again, he followed the blood link through a door that led down into a basement. Kaitlyn's scent was strong here, and then he saw her, sitting on a filthy mattress.

"Kaitlyn!" Sherrad hurried past Zack and enfolded his daughter in his arms. "Are you all right?"

"I am now."

Zack rocked back on his heels. It was all he could do to keep from pushing Sherrad aside, but Kaitlyn was the man's only child, after all. He contented himself with looking at her. Aside from the fact that her dress was wrinkled and her hair was tangled, she seemed none the worse for wear.

Sherrad brushed a lock of hair from Kaitlyn's cheek. "We must get you out of here before Nadiya returns."

"I am afraid it is too late for that."

Zack muttered an oath at the sound of the familiar voice.

Sherrad put Kaitlyn behind him, then slowly turned around.

"How very clever of you to find her," Nadiya said. "I am afraid I underestimated your resourcefulness."

"We're not leaving without her," Zack said. "So you can move aside and let us pass, or I'll rip your heart out. And believe me, I know how to do that."

"I did not come alone," she said imperiously.

Zack crossed his arms over his chest. "Bring 'em on, witch!"

He had no sooner said the words than Nadiya vanished from sight and a dozen men—both vampires and drones—swarmed into the room.

Chapter 33

There was instant pandemonium as Zack and Drake were surrounded by a dozen men intent on destroying them.

Zack summoned his power, felt it flow through him, making everything seem sharper, brighter, as he changed into his wolf form. Fangs bared, he sprang at the nearest vampire, felt a rush of exhilaration as he tore out the man's throat. The smell of blood and death rose in the air, exciting the beast within him. Returning to his human form, he ripped out another vampire's heart and tossed it aside. A split second later, he resumed his wolf form and attacked another man. This one was human. Easily killed.

He had no idea how Drake was doing, didn't have time to check on Kaitlyn, but he knew she was alive. He could hear the rapid beating of her heart, smell her fear above that of the men trying to kill him.

He turned to confront another man, felt his foot slip on the bloody floor, heard Kaitlyn's scream as he went down. Snarling and snapping, he sank his fangs into the man's ankle and jerked him off his feet. Before the man could recover, Zack crushed his windpipe.

Caught up in the lust for blood, Zack killed another man and destroyed another vampire.

In a momentary lull, he glanced around the room, noting that there were only three vampires still standing. He looked for Sherrad and saw him standing amid a pile of bodies at the other end of the room. Kaitlyn's father was splattered with blood from head to foot, his eyes wild, his lips drawn back over his fangs.

Zack grinned. Kaitlyn was right. Her father could be scary.

The three remaining vampires pulled back. They glanced at each other, their expressions uncertain.

Zack resumed his human form. "Come on," he said, motioning them forward. "Let's finish it."

"She can fight her own bloody battles," the tallest of the three said, and vanished from sight.

Zack grinned at Sherrad. "One for you. One for me." He lunged at the nearest vampire, his hand penetrating the man's chest, ripping out his heart, before the vampire knew what hit him.

The last vampire glanced from Sherrad to Zack and vanished from the room.

Zack took a deep breath, the urge to kill fading. He glanced at Sherrad, but the vampire was looking at his daughter.

Zack swore under his breath. Dammit! What must Kaitlyn be thinking? How would she ever think of him the same way after what she had just seen? The fighting had been brutal and bloody and he had gloried in it, would have killed a dozen more to protect the woman he loved.

Fearing what he might see, Zack turned around.

Kaitlyn stood with her back pressed to the wall, her face fish-belly white. Drops of bright crimson glistened wetly in her hair, on her face and her clothing. A drone lay at her feet, his neck broken. Had she killed him? Lord, he hoped not.

Sherrad approached his daughter. Taking hold of the iron bolt in the wall, he jerked it free, then, ignoring the chain dangling from her ankle, he pulled Kaitlyn into his arms. She sagged against him, her face buried against his chest, her shoulders shaking with the force of her tears.

Were they tears of relief, Zack wondered, or regret for killing a man? He shook his head. Whether she wanted any more to do with him or not, she was safe and that was all that mattered.

Sherrad looked at Zack. "Let us go."

"You go on. I'll take care of the bodies."

Sherrad nodded.

A moment later, Zack was alone in the basement. He picked up two of the bodies and carried them up the stairs, came to an abrupt halt when he reached the living room.

Someone—most likely Nadiya—had killed the elderly couple who owned the house. Their bodies lay side by side on the kitchen floor, both drained of blood.

Zack stared at them for several moments. He hadn't killed many people in the course of his existence as a vampire. Sure, there had been a few early on, before he learned to control his strength and his hunger. And a couple of hunters he had killed in self-defense. But he had never killed wantonly.

"You're going down, Nadiya," Zack muttered. "Sooner or later, you're going down."

Every dark cloud had a silver lining, he mused as he dropped the two dead vampires on the floor. Thanks to Nadiya's cruelty, he wouldn't have to bury the bodies. He found two cans of gas in the garage and carried them inside. He used the first can to douse the bodies of the vampires, splashed the second can on the floor of the living room and the kitchen, and set fire to the place.

He stood outside for several minutes, watching it burn, before transporting himself back to Wolfram Castle.

Kaitlyn stood in the shower, eyes closed as the hottest water she could stand sluiced over, washing away the blood and tissue that had splattered over her. Never in all her life had she imagined her father was capable of such violence, such brutality. She had seen Zack destroy Marius, of course, but still—the scene in the basement had been like something out of a slasher movie. So much blood and gore.

And she had killed a man.

She washed her hair twice, her body three times, and wondered if she would ever feel clean again.

Stepping out of the shower, she dried off, then pulled on a furry bathrobe. Too restless to sit still, she paced the bedroom floor, unable to dispel the images of Zack and her father from her mind. She had grown up among vampires and never known they were capable of such carnage. She had watched her father change from a cat to a man and back again and thought it cute. But there had been nothing cute about Zack's transformation into a wolf. She hadn't been able to take her eyes off of him as he battled one attacker after another. In wolf form or his natural form, he had fought with a kind of lethal beauty that had been as mesmerizing as it was horrible.

She was half vampire. Was she capable of such violence? The thought that she might be was frightening. She had rarely tapped into her vampire half, never tested the limits of her powers. True, she had killed a man tonight, but it had been swift and she had taken no pleasure in it. The fact that it had been self-defense made it only nominally easier to bear. She wondered if he had a wife and family, tried to tell herself it wasn't her fault, but Nadiya's. But the man was still dead, his blood on her hands.

She had collapsed in her father's arms when the battle was over. He represented home and security, but even as he had stroked her hair, she had been wishing it was Zack holding her tight, Zack whispering words of comfort in her ear.

Now, alone in her room, she tried to come to grips with her mixed emotions. It was disconcerting, knowing that Zack and her father could kill so quickly, so efficiently. Still, it was comforting to know that the two men she loved the most could protect her, even when the odds were stacked against them. She knew the horror of what she had witnessed—the grotesque images of torn flesh, the sickly sweet smell of blood and death—was forever burned into her memory. And yet, the horror of it would fade, in time.

The one thing she would never forget, she thought as she crawled into bed, the one truth that would forever remain engraved in her mind and her heart, was the knowledge that they both loved her enough to risk their lives for her.

Drake and Zack were sitting in the main hall when Elena entered the room.

"How is she?" Drake asked.

"She's asleep."

"Did you have any trouble removing the shackle from her ankle?"

"No." Elena shuddered. "I threw it away."

Drake nodded, his arm wrapping around Elena's shoulders as she took a seat beside him.

"Was it awful?" she asked.

"Awful?" Drake glanced at Ravenscroft. "What do you think?"

Zack shrugged. "I found it kind of exhilarating myself."

Elena stared at him, her eyes wide with disbelief. "Exhilarating?"

"Yeah. I guess that doesn't make me a very nice guy, but I don't care. I'll rip the heart out of anybody, male or female, who hurts Katy. And that includes Nadiya and anyone else she sends against us."

"You should have seen him," Drake said, a note of admiration in his voice. "I have never seen anyone fight like that." He clucked softly. "One minute he was a wolf, ripping out throats, and the next he was a vampire, ripping out hearts."

Elena shuddered. "Sorry, but I'm glad I missed it. Don't get me wrong," she added, looking at Zack. "I'm glad you were there, I just don't think it's something I'd want to watch . . . although that changing into a wolf thing must be something to see."

Zack looked at Sherrad, one brow raised in amusement. "Scarier than a cat, that's for sure."

Elena grinned.

Sherrad scowled at him.

"So," Zack said, "what's our next move?"

"What do you mean?" Elena asked. "Kaitlyn's home safe. It's over."

Zack glanced at Sherrad, but said nothing.

"It is not over," Drake said quietly. "It will never be over so long as Nadiya lives. She must be punished for her treachery. And Lucien, as well."

"What do you mean to do?" Elena asked.

"I mean to confront them both."

Elena stared at her husband, her lips pressed tightly together.

"I cannot let this go," Sherrad said, seeing her disapproval. "The Fortress has been governed by the Sherrad family for thousands of years. My grandfather and my father fought to defend it. I will not surrender it without a fight."

"We can leave here," Elena said. "Go somewhere else. To America. Or Canada."

"You and Kaitlyn will be no safer there than you are here as long as Nadiya wants revenge. Next time she might vent her hatred on you. We were lucky to get Kaitlyn back alive. I will not risk her safety again. Or yours." He looked at Zack. "Have you nothing to say?"

"I think you're right. I'm not sure how you plan to do it. Two against twelve wasn't so bad. Two against Nadiya and Lucien's army? I don't know. That might be a stretch, even for me."

Chapter 34

Lucien sat in what had once been Drake's chair on the dais in the council chamber of the Carpathian Fortress, his hands gripping the arms as he stared at the two men before him.

"Where is Drake now?" he asked curtly.

Gavril, the taller of the two, shook his head. "I do not know. We were lucky to get out of there alive."

Lucien's gaze shifted to Emilian. "Do you know where he is?"

Clearing his throat, Emilian shifted from one foot to the other. "I left shortly after Gavril."

"And the girl?" Lucien asked. "Where is she?"

Emilian shrugged.

Lucien leaned back in his chair. Why had he ever listened to Nadiya? What had made him think they could pull this off? They had been safe only as long as Drake believed his daughter's life was in danger. All bets were off now.

Nadiya appeared as soon as he dismissed Gavril and Emilian. "It seems we need to come up with a new plan."

Lucien shook his head. "Why should I listen to you? You had the Sherrad heir and you lost her. I doubt we will get another chance at her." He stood and began to pace the floor. "I thought you were going to kill her," he muttered, talking more to himself than to Nadiya. "But it is better this way. Sherrad will be angry, but since his daughter is unharmed, he might . . ."

"Stop babbling, you coward!"

"This was a stupid idea from the beginning," he snapped. "I never should have let you talk me into it."

"You wanted this place as much as I!"

He stopped pacing. "I say we get out of here while we still can."

"And I say we stay!"

Lucien shook his head. "Sherrad has his daughter back, but he will not just forget what we have done. Sooner or later, he will return and demand retribution."

Nadiya took several slow deep breaths. "And you will give it to him."

"Are you out of your mind? You do not expect me to meet him in combat? One-on-one?"

"Of course not," she said, smiling. "I will make sure you have plenty of backup."

Chapter 35

Kaitlyn tossed and turned, unable to get comfortable, unable to relax. Every time she closed her eyes, she imagined herself back in that horrible basement, her ankle shackled to the wall, helpless to do anything but watch as Zack and her father fought a dozen men. At the time, she had given little thought to the man she had killed. True, it had been in self-defense, but her main thought had been that his death meant one less man for Zack and her father to defeat. Now, his face haunted her.

Once they had returned to Wolfram, she hadn't had a chance to talk to Zack. Her mother had followed her up to her room, making soft mothering noises as she helped her out of her bloodstained clothes, found the tools necessary to remove the shackle from her ankle. Kaitlyn knew her mother was worried about her. After all, that's what mothers did. They worried. Assured that Kaitlyn was fine, Elena had gathered up her daughter's clothes, together with the long chain, kissed her on the cheek, and left the room.

Kaitlyn had been certain all she wanted was to go to bed and forget the whole terrible nightmare, but once in bed, sleep wouldn't come. She wanted to be held, only it wasn't her father's arms she needed, but Zack's.

After another moment of indecision, she slipped out of bed and pulled on her robe. Her bare feet whispered on the carpet as she tiptoed down the hallway toward Zack's room. Dawn was still a few hours away. She opened the door as quietly as she could, in case he was asleep, and stepped inside. Even in the dark, she could see that the bed was empty.

She stood there a moment, wondering where he was. Had he gone hunting? She had no sooner thought of where he might be than she knew. Turning on her heel, she knew he was downstairs.

She paused in the doorway of the great hall. He was sitting on one of the sofas, apparently lost in thought. Maybe he wanted to be alone. Maybe he didn't want her there.

"I want you," he said, his voice a low rumble. Glancing over his shoulder, he beckoned for her to join him.

It was all the invitation she needed. She sighed as his arm curled around her shoulders, drawing her close. "What are you doing here?" he asked, a lilt of surprise in his voice.

"I couldn't sleep."

"Me, either."

Her gaze moved over him. "Are you all right? You could have been killed."

He snorted softly. "Piece of cake, darlin'. But, not to worry. I'm too mean to die." He grinned at her. "Of course, if your father finds you here, with me, at this time of the night . . ." There was no need to finish the sentence.

"I think he'd better get used to the idea of you and me," she retorted with a toss of her head. "Because I'm here to stay, unless you tell me to go."

His arms tightened around her. "No, not now." He brushed her hair away from her neck, then rained soft kisses down the length of her throat. "Not ever."

"Zack . . ."

"Shh. Just a little taste, okay?"

She nodded, her heart suddenly beating triple time as his fangs brushed her skin. She wrapped her arms around him, her eyelids fluttering down as pleasure spread through her, hot and sweet, like honey warmed by the sun.

When he drew back, she moaned softly. "That feels so wonderful." She ran her fingertips along the side of his neck, her eyes taking on a faint red glow. "My turn?"

"I've created a monster," he said, grinning. "Just remember you can't take it all."

Zack stroked Kaitlyn's hair. Sharing blood with her was an extraordinary experience. She sighed softly in her sleep, a slight smile playing over her lips. She was curled up in his arms dreaming, he thought, dreaming of something nice, and he was just arrogant enough to believe he was the one who had put that smile on her face.

Filled with a tenderness he had never felt before, Zack kissed her cheek, the curve of her throat, her eyelids. He toyed with the idea of carrying her up to his room and seducing her. It would be easy, so easy. If only she wasn't a nice girl. If only he didn't love her with every fiber of his being. But someday—someday she would be his, body and soul.

A sudden heaviness in his limbs told him the sun would soon be chasing the night from the sky. His eyelids grew heavy, his breathing slowed.

Time to put Kaitlyn to bed and seek his rest. Cradling

her in his arms, he carried her up the stairs. He had just reached the door to her room when her mother appeared at the other end of the hallway.

"Put your mind at ease, Elena. Everything's okay. We were downstairs, talking, and she fell asleep on the sofa, that's all."

"I believe you. I was just coming to make sure she's all right. I guess I'm being overprotective, but with everything that's happened . . ." She shrugged. "I can't help it."

She opened the door to Kaitlyn's room, then turned down the covers on the bed.

Zack lowered Kaitlyn to the mattress, drew the covers over her, then bent down and kissed her cheek. "Sweet dreams, Katy darlin'," he whispered.

Elena regarded him a moment, then said, "I can never repay you for what you did. I don't know what we'd have done without you."

"You don't owe me anything. I'm in love with her."

"I know. She loves you, too." It was easy to see why. He was tall and strong and handsome, loyal, willing to risk everything for the woman he loved.

"How do you feel about that?"

"I'm not sure," Elena replied honestly. "Everything would be so much easier if she'd fallen in love with one of her own people. But I trust her judgment."

Zack nodded. "Good night, Elena."

"Good night."

Elena stood there a moment, gazing down at her daughter. How quickly the years had gone by. Her little girl was all grown up. Once upon a time was past. She just hoped Kaitlyn would find her own happily-ever-after.

* * *

Kaitlyn woke in her own bed with no recollection of how she had gotten there. The last thing she remembered was falling asleep in Zack's arms. She had hoped to wake up there—which probably wouldn't have been very smart. No doubt her parents would go ballistic if they thought she was sleeping with Zack—an idea that grew more appealing with every passing day.

She glanced at the clock on the nightstand—five P.M. She was the only one in the family who didn't know instinctively what time it was, though she was able to internally discern whether it was night or day.

Zack would be awake soon. She grinned, thinking how surprised he would be if she was in his bed when he awoke.

Pleased by the idea, she threw back the covers and went into the bathroom, where she took a quick shower and washed her hair. After drying off, she applied her makeup and a dash of perfume, then spent the next twenty minutes trying to decide what to wear. Although she had taken all her favorite clothes to California, her closet at Wolfram was nowhere near empty.

She decided on a pair of black skinny jeans and a cranberry-colored cashmere sweater. A nightgown would have been her first choice, but she didn't have enough nerve to hop into his bed wearing something that blatantly said come-and-get-me.

Barefooted, she padded down the hallway to Zack's room, opened the door, and peeked inside.

He was still asleep. She stood in the doorway, her gaze moving appreciatively over his broad shoulders and strong arms. A sheet covered him from the waist down; his bare feet poked out from under the covers. The thought that he might be naked under the sheet brought a rush of heat to her cheeks.

Her flush deepened when the man she thought was

asleep said, "Are you coming in? Or are you going to stand there gawking at me all night?"

Kaitlyn closed the door behind her, then hurried across the room and slipped under the covers.

Zack's arm went around her, drawing her close. "So, what brings you here?" he asked, a note of amusement in his voice.

"I can always leave."

His arm tightened around her. "Wanna bet?"

"I never bet against a gambler," she retorted, hiding her smile.

"Smart girl." He brushed a kiss across her cheek. She smelled of lavender soap and toothpaste. And woman.

Kaitlyn grinned as the sheet suddenly tented above Zack's groin.

"Sorry," he muttered. "Some things just can't be hidden. Or controlled."

She laughed and blushed at the same time. "I guess you carried me back to my bed."

He nodded. "Yeah. About that—"

She propped herself up on one elbow. "What about that?"

"Your mother caught me carrying you to your room just before dawn."

Kaitlyn's eyes widened in alarm. "Does my dad . . . ?"

"No. Just your mom."

Kaitlyn slumped back down on the bed, her head resting on Zack's shoulder. Had her mother told her dad? She considered that a moment, then shook her head. Her mother hadn't snitched on her the last time. Besides, if her father knew, she would have heard about it by now. Big time.

"Katy."

She looked up at him, alarmed by his solemn tone. "Yes?"

"You know I'm in love with you."

"Yes." A thrill of excitement fluttered deep inside her.

"And you love me."

She smiled. "Yes."

He blew out a sigh. "I never thought I'd say this to anyone, but will you marry me?"

"Marry you?" She sat up, wondering if she looked as stunned as she felt.

Zack sat up, too. "I know your father won't approve, but . . ."

"Oh, Zack!" She threw her arms around him. "Of course I'll marry you!"

He grinned at her. "I thought you'd say no."

"Why would you think that?"

He shrugged. "I'm an outsider. One of the Others. Your father hates me. I'm not sure about your mother." He paused. "I can never give you children."

"It doesn't matter. Nothing matters, as long as you love me."

"Never doubt it, Katy darlin'," he murmured. Falling back on the bed, he carried her with him. Cupping her face in his hands, he kissed her long and slow and deep. He might have made love to her then, in spite of his vow not to defile her, but the decision was taken out of his hands when the bedroom door flew open and an angry father stormed into the room.

Kaitlyn bolted upright, her heart racing even as she told herself to calm down. She hadn't done anything wrong. And even if she had, she was a big girl now, old enough to make her own decisions, her own mistakes. But all her inner arguments melted away in the face of her father's fury.

Zack kissed Kaitlyn on the cheek, then gained his feet. "It's customary to knock before entering someone's bedroom."

Drake snorted. "You are lucky I do not drive a stake into your black heart."

"You can try."

"Dad . . ."

"Keep out of this Kaitlyn Liliana," her father said. "This is between me and Zack."

"Why don't you calm down?" Zack suggested. "She hasn't done anything wrong. If you'll notice, she's fully dressed."

A muscle twitched in Drake's cheek. "I am grateful for your help last night, but I think you should leave here. Now."

Kaitlyn leaped off the bed to stand beside Zack. "If he goes, so do I."

"Am I missing something?" Elena asked, coming into the room.

Kaitlyn smiled at her mother. "Zack asked me to marry him, and I said yes."

"You will not!" Drake roared.

"Yes, I will!" Kaitlyn replied, her tone as irate as his. "I don't need your permission."

All the anger seeped out of Drake's expression. "Perhaps not," he said quietly. "But what about my blessing?"

Kaitlyn's shoulders sagged. Tears stung her eyes.

Zack put his arm around her waist and gave her a squeeze. "I don't want to come between you and your family, Katy. I won't make you choose."

She looked up at him, her gaze searching his as she tried to hold back her tears. And failed. "What are you saying?"

"I withdraw my proposal."

"Enough!" Elena moved to stand in front of her husband, more angry with him than she had ever been in her life. "Are you happy now? Look at your daughter's face. She loves him, Drake. And he loves her. Have you forgotten how that feels? How you would have done anything to be with the one you loved?"

"Elena . . ."

"Don't 'Elena' me. You went against your father and your people to marry me, remember? Everyone thought it was a terrible idea, but you didn't listen to them. You even changed your laws. And now you're acting just like your father!"

As always, when he wanted to silence her, Drake did the only thing that worked. He took her in his arms and kissed her.

"Not this time," Elena said, pushing him away. "Our daughter's happiness is on the line. What are you going to do about it?"

Drake looked over Elena's head to where Kaitlyn stood beside Zack. "You love him?"

Kaitlyn nodded.

Drake turned his gaze on Zack. "And you love her?"

"You know I do."

Drake blew out a sigh of resignation. "All right," he said with as much good grace as he could muster. "I know when I am outnumbered."

"Thank you, Dad!" Kaitlyn hurled herself into her father's arms. "Thank you, thank you, thank you!"

Drake slid his arm around Kaitlyn's waist. "Just one thing. Whatever plans you have already made or hope to make will have to wait until Nadiya is no longer a threat."

Kaitlyn went into Zack's arms as soon as her mom and dad left the room. "You didn't really change your mind about marrying me, did you? I mean, it was just a bluff. Wasn't it?"

"What do you think?"

Canting her head to one side, she looked up at him through the veil of her lashes. "I'm not sure," she said with a teasing grin. "I guess you'll just have to propose again."

"Is that right?" In a single fluid move, he dropped down on one knee. "Kaitlyn Liliana Sherrad, will you do me the honor of being my wife?"

She would have thought he was teasing except for the serious expression on his face, the intensity that blazed in the depths of his eyes. "Yes, Zack, I will."

Rising to his feet, he drew her into his arms and kissed her. It was a kiss like no other he had ever given her—achingly tender and sweet, a kiss of commitment meant to bind two hearts and two souls together. Forever.

There were tears in her eyes when he broke the kiss.

"I love you, Katy, with all my heart. I'll do my best to make you happy."

"I am happy," she said, her voice thick with emotion. "Happier than I've ever been in my whole life."

"And I intend to see that you stay that way." *Or die trying.*

Chapter 36

Elena sat on Drake's lap. She tried to pretend she was calm, but her voice betrayed her.

"When?" she asked tremulously. "When are we leaving for the Fortress?"

"*We* are not leaving," he said, kissing her cheek. "I am leaving. You will stay here with Zack and Kaitlyn."

"No!" She slid off his lap, then whirled around to face him, her hands fisted on her hips. "I am not staying behind!"

"Elena. Wife. You will do as I say, or I will lock you in your room."

"That's not fair!"

"Fair or not, I will not put your life in danger. You will stay here with Kaitlyn. Zack will be here to protect you."

"You can't face Lucien and Nadiya alone."

"I can and I will," he said. "This is my fight. I cannot let Lucien think he has won."

"That's just your pride talking. I don't care what anyone thinks."

"The Fortress is my ancestral home. I will not give it up without a fight. Nor will I let Nadiya go unpunished for what she did."

"Please, Drake." Elena placed her hands on Drake's shoulders. "I'm afraid. What if . . ." She couldn't say the words. What if saying them made them so? She wasn't brave; she didn't care what happened to the Fortress. Her only concern was for her husband. He was her courage. Her life. Without him . . . "Drake."

"I know." He put his arms around her waist and drew her close, his head resting in the vee between her breasts.

"What if Lucien won't meet you?" she asked hopefully.

"I will not give him a choice. Day after tomorrow, I will summon my brothers and the husbands of my sisters. We will meet at the Fortress."

"Not Andrei," Elena said.

Drake lifted his head. "Why not Andrei?"

"Because Katiya is pregnant again."

"Who told you that?" he asked, frowning.

"Katiya sent me a letter. I got it a few days ago but with everything that was going on, I forgot to tell you."

Drake nodded. "Not Andrei, then."

"So you won't be alone," Elena said, relieved to know that his brothers would be there with him.

"I will meet Lucien alone. My family will be there to assure it is a fair fight."

"Isn't there another way?" She knew what his answer would be, but she had to try one more time.

"No." He cupped her face in his hands. "Do not worry, wife. I will come back to you."

Elena forced a smile, but inside, her heart was breaking. And then, not wanting him to think her weak or cowardly, she forced a smile. Taking him by the hand, she urged him to his feet. "Let us go upstairs and make the best of what time we have left before you must go."

* * *

Kaitlyn shook her head. "Can't you change his mind?"

"I tried," Elena said. "But you know how your father is, once he's made a decision."

Kaitlyn reached for her mother's hand. It was late on a rainy afternoon and they were sitting side by side on one of the sofas in the main hall. A fire crackled cheerfully in the hearth. A flowered teapot and matching china cups sat on the coffee table, along with a batch of freshly baked sugar cookies. They had dined earlier.

"Can he win?" Kaitlyn asked.

"If Lucien and Nadiya play fair, it's no contest. Your father will win easily. But you know Nadiya won't play by the rules. Even if your father defeats Lucien, I know Nadiya will have a back-up plan to make sure your father doesn't survive."

"We have to be there," Kaitlyn said.

"I agree, but I don't know how we'd manage it. We'd have to go by plane, and by the time we get there, it'll all be over."

Kaitlyn heaved a sigh of exasperation. More and more lately, she found herself wishing she was a full-fledged vampire like her father. Like Zack . . . Zack. Of course! He could take them to the Fortress.

Kaitlyn gave her mother's hand a squeeze. "I know a way. Shh, they're coming." She looked up, smiling as Zack and her father entered the room.

"You're up early," Elena said, smiling at her husband.

"I wanted to spend as much time with you as I could," Drake said, kissing his wife's cheek. "What have you two been up to?"

"Talking about the wedding, of course." Kaitlyn moved to the other sofa so her parents could sit together. She smiled at Zack as he took a place beside her.

"In a hurry to tie the knot?" Zack took her hand in his and raised it to his lips.

The touch of his mouth sent a shiver of longing straight to the center of her being. "Of course."

He grinned at her, a wicked gleam in his eyes. He knew exactly the effect he had on her.

"Zack, I have a favor to ask of you," Drake said.

"Sure, anything."

"I am going to meet Lucien at the Fortress tomorrow night. I would appreciate it if you would stay here with Elena and Kaitlyn."

"Are you sure you don't want me to go along to watch your back?"

"My brothers will be there. I need someone I can trust to stay here."

"Whatever you want."

"If anything happens to me . . ."

Elena quickly put her hand over her husband's mouth. "Don't say it! Don't even think it!"

Drake stood and pulled Elena to her feet. "If you two will excuse us, I want to spend the rest of this night with my wife."

Kaitlyn nodded. After her parents left the room, she turned toward Zack. "Let's go outside."

"I don't think your father would approve."

"Just out into the backyard."

"It's raining."

She shrugged. "Afraid you'll shrink?"

Laughing, he followed Kaitlyn into the kitchen and through a small door that led into a large garden surrounded by a high stone wall. He glanced around. He imagined the garden had once been beautiful, but no one had cared for it while Drake and Elena had been at the Fortress. The flowerbeds that lined the footpaths were filled with weeds. A small round fountain bubbled cheerfully in the middle of the yard; an ancient wrought-iron bench was located under a towering oak.

He followed Kaitlyn to the bench, which was surprisingly dry, and sat down beside her. "You're worried about your father."

"If anything happens to my dad . . ." She loosed a deep, shuddering sigh. "I don't know what my mom would do without him."

"I fought beside your dad," Zack reminded her. "I wouldn't worry about him."

"I wouldn't worry, either, if I thought Lucien would fight fair. But my mom's worried that if Dad wins the fight, Nadiya will make certain he never leaves the Fortress alive."

Zack grunted softly. It was a legitimate concern. Elena wasn't the only one to think of it. "What do you want me to do?"

"Go with him."

"No way. I'm not leaving you and your mother here alone."

"I'm not afraid."

"Forget it, Katy. I'm not leaving you here, not with Nadiya running loose."

"But . . ."

"No buts. And don't think those tears will sway me. I don't want to face your old man if anything happens to you or your mom. Besides, he told me he's calling his brothers for backup."

"He told you that?"

"We discussed his plans earlier. With all his brothers, half brothers, and brothers-in-law, he should be all right, even against the Korzha contingent."

Knowing further arguments wouldn't get her anywhere, Kaitlyn rested her head on Zack's shoulder. "I hope you're right."

He winked at her. "I'm always right, Katy darlin'. And now that that's settled, I think we should get down to some serious huggin' and kissin'."

"Oh, you do, do you?"

"Don't you?" He made a sad face. "Your lack of interest cuts me to the quick."

"Oh, shut up and kiss me, you fool."

"You're so romantic," Zack muttered. "Is it any wonder that I love you?"

In a move that left her gasping with surprise, he lifted her onto his lap and kissed her, a long lingering kiss that started off feather-light and gradually grew in intensity until it was an effort for her to think, to breathe. His hands—those cunning, clever hands—slid seductively over her back, along her hips and thighs. She leaned into him, wanting to feel his skin on hers, wanting to drag him down to the ground and explore every inch of him.

Zack lifted his head, his eyes hot. "I'm willing if you are."

"What?" She stared at him. "Are you reading my mind?"

"So it would seem."

"But . . . how is that possible?"

"I told you, the more often we share blood, the stronger the link becomes."

She blinked at him, her mind racing. "Zack . . . could you turn me?"

"What?"

"Make me a vampire like you are."

"Why on earth would you want that? You've got the best of both worlds now."

"I know, but I want to be able to zap myself across the street or across the world. I want to be able to dissolve into mist. Or turn into a wolf."

"If you want to zip across the country, I'll take you. As

for dissolving into mist . . ." He shrugged. "It comes in handy now and then, I'll admit, but mostly it's overrated."

"But being able to turn into a wolf, now that's cool. I watched you when you were fighting Nadiya's men. It gave you a real advantage."

"I can't argue with that."

"So, will you?"

"I don't know. I don't even know if it's possible to change from one kind of vampire to another. Even if was possible, what would your parents think? What would your father think?"

"That's a silly question. We both know he'd be against it. I'm not sure about my mom." Kaitlyn bit down on her lower lip. Maybe it wasn't such a good idea. If she was a vampire like Zack, there would be no more shared meals with her mom, no more going out to lunch together and then on a shopping spree, no more balmy days by the lake. Of course, when she married Zack and they went back to Tahoe, she wouldn't be doing those things very often anyway.

"Think about what you'd be giving up," Zack said.

"The sunlight," she said, thinking aloud. Would she be happy, living in a world of darkness? Never seeing the sun again, or feeling its warmth on her face? "And food." She would miss real food—apples and oranges, artichokes and tomatoes, a good steak. Chicken and rice. And chocolate . . .

"Once it's done, darlin', you can't undo it."

Kaitlyn nodded, He was right, of course. She needed to think it through. And there was no hurry. In the meantime, she was wasting precious moments with the man she loved.

She smiled a slow, seductive smile, her fingertips trailing across his lower lip. "So, where were we?"

His mouth closed around her finger. He sucked it

gently. Heat shot straight through her. With a moan, she wrapped her arms around him, her breasts pushing against his chest.

Zack bit down on her finger, then covered her mouth with his. She was driving him crazy. His hands moved restlessly over her back as he deepened the kiss. He needed to stop, now, before stopping became impossible. Instead, he held her closer, tighter.

"Katy . . ." He struggled for control, but it wasn't easy, not when she was wriggling on his lap, not when the scent of her desire and her blood made it difficult to think of anything else. Not when he knew that she wanted him as badly as he wanted her.

Moaning softly, she slid her hands under his shirt, her nails raking his chest. "Zack." He heard the desperation in her tone, the urgency. The need.

"I know," he said, his voice hoarse. "Believe me, baby, I know." He pulled back, putting some space between them. He took several deep breaths. "I can't do this," he muttered. The bench was metal. The ground was wet. "Not here."

She nipped at his ear. "Then let's go somewhere else."

It would be easy to take her in his arms and transport them to a hotel in the city. Easy, but not smart.

"No one will know," she said.

"I'm not going to take you out here, in the mud," Zack said. "And leaving Wolfram could be dangerous."

"My bedroom?" she suggested.

"And have your mother or father walk in on us?"

"We could lock the door."

He laughed. "Yeah, like that would fool your folks. Or keep your father out."

"Don't you want me?"

"More than you know." He snorted softly, unable to believe he was turning her down. He had bedded a lot of women in a lot of places, but Kaitlyn was a forever woman, not a quick roll in the hay. He wouldn't take her out in the open, like some rutting stag, or defile her in her father's house. And while he was pretty sure they'd be safe at a hotel in town, he wasn't going to take a chance on putting her life at risk.

"Zack."

"Sorry, darlin'," he muttered. "But one of us has to stay rational."

"Why? I've always been a good girl," she said, her voice smoky with desire. "Can't I be bad, just once?" He was weakening; she could see it in the sudden heat in his eyes, feel it as his arm tightened around her waist. A thrill of excitement shot through her. Tonight, she thought, tonight she would be his in every sense of the word.

The thought had no sooner crossed her mind when she suddenly found herself standing in Zack's arms in the main room of the castle.

"I guess you really meant no," she said sulkily.

"I smelled one of your kind out there, just beyond the wall."

"What?"

Before he could explain, Drake appeared in the room, bare-chested and barefooted. His gaze moved quickly over Kaitlyn. "Are you all right?"

"Yes, fine." -

"You smelled him, too," Zack said.

Drake nodded. "Stay here. I am going out to have a look around," he said, and vanished from the room.

Just then, Elena came hurrying down the stairs, tying the sash on her bathrobe. "What's going on? Where's Drake?"

"He went out to have a look around," Zack explained. "Someone's out there."

"Nadiya?" Elena asked, worry furrowing her brow.

"No."

Elena wrapped her arms around her waist. "I wish this was over."

Kaitlyn looked up at Zack. "Me, too."

He grinned as he pulled her against his side. "So do I, darlin'," he whispered for her ears alone.

"I don't like this," Elena said. "Drake should have been back by now."

She had no sooner spoken the words than he appeared at her side. "Whoever it was is gone," he said, slipping his arm around her shoulders. "I think he was just checking to see if we were still here."

Zack nodded. "Was it anyone you recognized?"

"No. It was most likely one of Lucien's kin. I would have recognized the scent if we shared the same blood." Drake paused a moment, then said, "You and Kaitlyn were outside earlier. Stay inside."

Zack nodded. It galled him to take orders from another vampire, especially when that vampire was younger, but in this case, Drake was right. Another vampire couldn't enter the castle without an invitation, but that restriction only extended to the house itself. Anyone, friend or foe, could have come over the garden wall.

Drake came forward to kiss his daughter good night, then he swung Elena into his arms and carried her swiftly up the stairs.

Zack stared after them, wishing he had the right to sweep Kaitlyn into his arms and into his bed, to make love to her until the sun chased the moon from the sky. And he would, just as soon as she was rightfully his.

He wasn't sure where this newfound code of honor came from, but it was sure as hell playing havoc with his love life.

* * *

Zack prowled the halls and corridors of Wolfram Castle long after everyone else had gone to bed. He paused outside Kaitlyn's door just to listen to the even sound of her breathing, to assure himself that she was safe.

Now and then, he heard an errant sound from her parents' bedroom that told him Drake was making love to his wife, perhaps for the last time.

Returning to the main hall, Zack paced the floor in front of the hearth. He needed to call Scherry and check on things at the club. He needed to feed.

He needed Kaitlyn. Needed her as he needed blood to survive. Needed her goodness in his life. That knowledge, combined with the fear that he might lose her, scared him right down to his socks. He had never needed anyone before. Not even Colette. He had loved his pretty dancer, though his love for her, when compared to what he felt for Kaitlyn, was like comparing a match to a forest fire. He had grieved when Colette died, but her passing had barely made a ripple in his existence. He had laid her to rest and moved on. But if he lost Kaitlyn . . . He stared into the cold ashes of the hearth. Kaitlyn. She had insinuated herself into his heart, into his very soul. If he lost her . . . He shook his head. Without her, his life would no longer be worth living.

As if his thoughts had conjured her, Kaitlyn floated down the stairs toward him, a raven-haired vision in a long white gown that billowed behind her. Her bare feet made no sound as she closed the distance between them.

Standing on tiptoe, she kissed his cheek. "What is it that troubles you so?" she whispered, her gaze searching his.

He wrapped his arm around her and pulled her up

against him. "Are you reading my mind now, Katy darlin'?"

"Not exactly, but I felt your distress. What's bothering you, Zack?"

"I've never been afraid of anything before," he said, his voice so low she could scarcely hear it. "But I'm afraid of losing you. Afraid of what it would do to me." He lifted a lock of her hair, let it sift through his fingers. "I love you, Katy."

"I know." She cupped his face between her palms and kissed him lightly. "Don't be afraid. In life or in death, I'll always be with you." She pressed his hand to her cheek. "Come to bed with me, Zack. Let me hold you until you fall asleep."

He shook his head. "I don't think that's a good idea," he muttered, but he didn't resist when she tugged on his hand. Like a man in a trance, he followed her up the stairs and down the hall to her room.

He stood in the center of the floor while she closed and locked the door. Stood there, hardly daring to breathe, as she removed his shirt, unbuckled his belt, unfastened his trousers, then climbed up on the bed and slipped under the covers.

Expelling a deep breath, he heeled off his boots, pulled off his socks, stepped out of his trousers, and left them all in a heap on the floor.

"Are you sure about this?" he asked gruffly.

"Very sure," she said.

Wearing only his briefs, he slid in beside her. "You know where this is likely to end, don't you?"

"I hope so." She wrapped her arms around him. "What has you so worried? You don't think Nadiya will come here, do you?"

"I don't know. I've just got a bad feeling about this whole mess."

"Are your premonitions usually right?"

"No. But I've never been this worried about anyone before."

She was close, too close. He could feel the heat of her body warming his, smell her desire, hear the slow, steady beating of her heart. And overall, the scent of her blood calling to him.

He muttered an oath as his honor faded away, overcome by a yearning so primal there was no denying it any longer. He groaned her name as he captured her mouth with his.

And he was lost.

One sharp yank and her gown was on the floor on top of his trousers. He crushed her close, marveling at the velvet smoothness of her skin, the warmth of her breasts against his chest. He rained kisses over her forehead, her cheeks, along the length of her neck, and then, unable to restrain himself, he closed his eyes and drank. It was the first time he had taken her blood without asking, but she didn't protest, only moaned with pleasure when his fangs pierced her flesh.

When he lifted his head, she smiled up at him. "My turn?"

"Be my guest."

She drank eagerly, careful not to take too much. Sighing with pleasure, she fell back on the bed.

"You look like the cat that ate the canary," Zack observed.

She looked up at him and grinned. "Meow."

He growled low in his throat.

"Oh, I'm scared now," she said with mock terror.

"You should be."

"Oh?" She propped herself up on one elbow, her fingers drawing figure eights on his chest. "Why is that?"

"Because everything about you tempts me."

"What's wrong with that?" She traced the ridges of his six-pack abs. "Aren't you supposed to find me tempting?" She certainly found him tempting. "We're getting married, after all. It would be awful if you didn't want me."

"Oh, I want you. The thing is, I don't know how much longer I can keep my hands off you."

"Then touch me, Zack. I don't want to wait any longer. All I could think of when I was Nadiya's prisoner was that I might die without ever having made love to you."

"Dammit, Kaitlyn. I'm not made of steel."

"Why are you fighting me?"

"For once in my life, I'm trying to do the right thing. Dammit, girl! Your father and mother are down the hall. . . ."

"I'll be very quiet," she whispered.

"Yeah? Well, I can't make that promise." Taking her in his arms, he kissed her until she gasped for breath. "When I take you the first time, I want to hear you screaming my name. And I want my ring on your finger." He kissed the tip of her nose, then slipped his arm around her shoulders. "Now, go to sleep. It's almost dawn."

He closed his eyes as he felt the tightness in his skin that meant the sun was rising. Darkness engulfed him, stealing the strength from his limbs as he tumbled gratefully into oblivion.

Kaitlyn heaved a sigh of exasperation as Zack's eyes closed and he surrendered to the dawn. Stubborn man! Even when she tried to seduce him, he refused to give in. How did he manage such self-control? She knew he wanted her.

Turning on her side, she studied his profile. Now that she had cooled off and she was thinking with her head instead of her hormones, she knew he was right. This wasn't the time or the place. When they made love the first time, she wanted it to be in their own home, not under her father's roof. Not with her parents just down the hall.

She would have suggested they go to the hotel in town, but she wasn't foolish enough to go traipsing off into the night when Zack and her father had detected the presence of another vampire lurking nearby.

She rested her head on Zack's shoulder, her fingers splayed over his chest, and prayed that the trouble with Nadiya would be over soon.

Chapter 37

Kaitlyn's yearning for a quick end to the conflict between her father and Nadiya waned as her father prepared to go to the Fortress to meet Lucien. Her father was a strong man, never defeated in battle. But Nadiya and Lucien were not to be trusted. In a fair fight, Kaitlyn was certain her father would emerge victorious. But Nadiya had already proved she didn't fight fair.

Her father spoke briefly to Zack, then strode toward her. He was, she thought, the personification of a warrior about to go to battle. If he was worried about the outcome, there was no trace of it in his bearing or his expression.

Kaitlyn blinked back her tears as her father embraced her. "Do not worry," he said, smiling. "I will be back soon."

She nodded, unable to speak past the lump in her throat.

He hugged her fiercely, kissed her cheek, and let her go.

Kaitlyn watched as her parents embraced. The love between her mother and father was a palpable presence in the room. They gazed into each other's eyes for a moment and then, between one breath and the next, her father was gone.

Unable to hold back her tears, Kaitlyn stared at the place where he had been standing and wondered if she would ever see him again.

"He'll be all right," Zack said, taking her in his arms.

"I know." She drew a deep breath. For her mother's sake, she had to stay calm and positive.

As was her wont when she was worried, Elena cleaned house. She didn't ask for help, but Kaitlyn pitched in, glad to have something to do. They mopped the floors, they washed the windows, they stripped the beds and turned the mattresses. Elena cleaned the refrigerator. Kaitlyn scrubbed the stove.

Zack watched the women with envy, wishing he had a way to expend the nervous energy building inside him. He had never liked waiting, would have preferred to be at the Fortress, in the thick of whatever was taking place there. But leaving Kaitlyn and her mother unprotected was unthinkable.

And so he paced the floor hour after hour while the women scrubbed the castle from top to bottom as if their lives, and their sanity, depended on it.

Finally, needing to do something, he went outside and spent a few minutes chopping wood for the fireplace, wishing, all the time, that the ax was a silver-bladed sword and the log in front of him was Nadiya Korzha's slender neck.

Drake stood outside the Fortress, his senses probing the night around him. His brothers and other relatives were near. He had warned them not to interfere unless he called them. He did not expect Lucien to meet him honorably; if he lost the battle in a fair fight, he had instructed Zack to flee the country with Elena and Kaitlyn and take refuge with his half sister in Russia in hopes that Nadiya would never find them. As for Liliana, he had no idea where she was. Liliana didn't carry a cell phone. Hopefully, she was safe at home. He should have insisted she stay at the Fortress, but she had been determined to go to her own house, and there had been no stopping her once she made up her mind.

Striding toward the entrance of the Fortress, Drake wiped everything from his mind but the battle ahead. He knocked on the door, hard enough that he heard it echo inside.

One of Lucien's sons bid him enter.

Drake pushed the man aside and strode down the corridor toward the council chamber.

The door stood open. Lucien sat in Drake's chair on the dais. Nadiya stood beside him, looking regal in a long black gown. The chairs at the council table were filled with Lucien's kin.

"I am here," Drake said, his hand on the hilt of the sword sheathed at his side. "Are you ready?"

Lucien looked fleetingly at Nadiya, then stood. "There is no need for us to fight."

"There is every need." Drake glanced at Nadiya, then back to Lucien again. "You have aligned yourself with a woman who is my enemy. You have usurped my rightful place by treachery. If you will not yield to me, then you will die, either on the field of battle, or now, in this room."

The air in the chamber seemed to thicken as those assembled waited for Lucien's answer.

Drake watched him through narrowed eyes. If Lucien refused to fight, he would be branded a coward, scorned by all who knew him.

"Answer him!" Nadiya hissed.

Lucien sucked in a deep breath. "I will meet you on the field of battle. Have you a second?"

"I do. He awaits outside."

With a last glance at Nadiya, Lucien left the dais.

It was a solemn procession that made its way down the side of the mountain to the clearing below. Four men clad in black cloaks, each carrying a torch, led the way. Drake and Lucien followed the torchbearers. Because Drake did not trust Nadiya at his back, he had insisted that she walk at the head of the procession. Lucien's second trailed behind.

When they reached the clearing, the four torchbearers formed a large circle. Drake and Lucien took their places in the center of the circle, facing each other.

Lucien's second took a place outside the circle. A moment later, Stefan emerged from the trees and took up his position on the opposite side of the circle.

Nadiya stood apart, her long gray cloak billowing in the faint breeze.

One of the torchbearers walked to the center of the circle and stood between Drake and Lucien. "Lucien Muscarella, Master of the Carpathian Fortress," he intoned, "be it known that Drake Sherrad, former Master of the Carpathian Fortress, has challenged your right to rule, claiming you have obtained it by treachery. He has come here this night demanding satisfaction. Should he be the victor, he will take possession of all your lands and holdings, both here and in Italy. Do you accept his challenge? Or concede?"

Lucien cleared his throat. "I accept."

"Francisco Muscarella. Stefan Sherrad. You have been chosen as seconds. Step forward."

Francisco and Stefan did as bidden, bowed to the

torchbearer, and then returned to their respective places outside the circle.

"All those required to be in attendance are here present," the torchbearer said solemnly. "Let whatever blood is shed this night be done with honor." And so saying, he returned to his place in the circle.

A low, keening wind sprang up, rattling the leaves of the trees. The torches flickered erratically, sending dancing shadows across the ground.

Drake stared at his opponent. He could almost taste Lucien's fear, his reluctance to fight. "Yield to me, Lucien, and I will spare your life."

Drake had no doubt that, had Nadiya not been present, Lucien would have surrendered.

Lucien wiped his palms on his trousers. Opened his mouth and then snapped it shut. With a mighty cry, he lunged at Drake, his sword hissing through the air.

Uttering a battle cry of his own, Drake brought up his sword, parrying Lucien's thrust. The ringing sound of metal striking metal rose in the air, along with the dust stirred by the combatants. Lucien circled Drake warily, testing the strength and mettle of his opponent. He roared with triumph when his blade found its mark and he drew first blood.

Drake paid little heed to the pain of the wound or the blood running down his arm, his only thought to destroy the man in front of him, to reclaim the Fortress that was rightfully his, to protect the women he loved. So long as he lived, they lived.

Spurred by fear, Lucien lunged and parried frantically.

Drake fought coolly, slowly wearing down his opponent. He had no thought for those who watched. No thought for his wounds. For this moment in time, Elena and Kaitlyn had ceased to exist. There was only Lucien and the need to destroy him.

Sensing defeat, Lucien made a last bold lunge, his sword coming up hard and fast, only to be deflected by Drake's blade.

Howling with fear and fury, Lucien backpedaled, his sword swinging wildly from side to side.

Certain of victory, Drake spun in a circle, feinted left, charged right, and drove his sword into Lucien's heart. Lucien staggered backward, his sword falling from his hand, a look of surprise spreading over his face as he fell to his knees, then toppled sideways to the ground.

A collective gasp rose from those watching as Drake swung his blade again, cleanly severing Lucien's head from his body.

But there was little time for victory. He had scarcely wiped the blood from his sword when Stefan shouted, "Behind you!"

Drake ducked and whirled around as a sword whistled past his head. With a cry, he plunged his sword into his attacker's heart, then spun around as another man charged toward him.

Men began to appear out of the trees on all sides. The air rang with the sounds of battle as Drake's brothers engaged Lucien's kin.

During a brief lull, Drake searched for Nadiya, but there was no sign of her. And no time to worry over her whereabouts as another of Lucien's people lunged at him.

The air reeked of blood and death by the time Stefan dispatched the last of Lucien's men.

There was little conversation as the victors made sure their foes would not rise again. One common grave served as the final resting place for the deceased.

When all was done, Drake led the way up to the Fortress. Apparently word of Lucien's defeat had preceded Drake's arrival. The massive front door stood open. None of Lucien's kin remained.

As those who had fought with him entered the Fortress, Drake thanked each of them in turn for their assistance. And then, with little thought for the wounds he had sustained or the blood dripping on the floor, he called home.

Elena sighed as she closed her cell phone. Murmuring, "He's all right, thank the Lord," she sank down on the sofa next to Kaitlyn. "He'll be home soon. He's going to stay at the Fortress until Andrei can get there. Stefan and Ciprian are notifying Northa and the others in case they want to return." She smiled through the tears of joy shining in her eyes. "The rest of his brothers are getting in touch with their families so they can all move back to the Fortress."

Kaitlyn threw her arms around her mother. "That's wonderful news!" She looked up at Zack, who had been adding wood to the fire. "What's wrong?"

"Did Drake mention Nadiya?"

"She's disappeared again." Elena's smile vanished as she looked at Zack. "You don't think she'll try something else, do you? Not after this?"

"I don't know. She doesn't seem like the kind to give up. On the other hand, she's lost three sons, and she no longer has Lucien to fight her battles."

"Well, I'm not going to worry about her anymore," Kaitlyn said. "I have a wedding to plan."

Apparently the word *wedding* possessed some kind of magical properties, Zack mused. The smile returned to Elena's face and the next thing Zack knew, the two women had their heads together, talking about dresses and veils, what kind of flowers to order for the church, and what kind of a bouquet Kaitlyn would carry. Flowers weren't part of vampire weddings, but Kaitlyn and Elena had decided to overrule Drake's objections and ignore coven tradition. Kaitlyn wanted flowers and a church wedding, and that's what she was going to have.

Zack frowned. The last time he had been inside a church had been for Colette's funeral. When he'd proposed to Kaitlyn, he hadn't given any thought to where they would get married. He had foolishly assumed they would just fly to Vegas for the weekend, get married in one of the chapels, then take an extended honeymoon in Italy or France. He grunted softly. So much for that idea. It was obvious that Kaitlyn wanted a big wedding— long white dress, flowers, bridesmaids. He grimaced. A groom wearing a tuxedo. The whole nine yards.

Looking at the excitement in her eyes, the flush in her cheeks, he figured it was a small price to pay to make her happy.

Until the next night, when he realized that, as long as Nadiya was still a threat, he was going to have to act as chaperon while the ladies went shopping.

Of course, every cloud had a silver lining, and this one came in the form of a blue Porsche Panamera 4S. The Sherrad family seemed to have a thing for Porsches, Zack mused. And this one was a beaut.

"I know you two want to gab," Zack said as he opened the rear door for them and bowed them inside.

Moving around to the driver's side, he slid behind the wheel and turned the key in the ignition. He grinned as the engine purred to life. The Panamera was a sweetheart of a ride, able to go from zero to sixty in four-point-eight seconds and reach a speed of a hundred and seventy-five miles. Although he was itching to put the car through its paces, now wasn't the time, not when Kaitlyn and her mother were in the backseat.

He put the car in gear and headed down the mountain. The Porsche took the curves with ease; the low hum of the motor like music to his ears. He couldn't help feeling a moment of regret when, all too soon, the city came into view.

At any other time, he would have dropped the women off and waited in the car, but recent events were too fresh in his mind. After parking the car, he escorted them to the bridal shop, then stood near the door, arms folded over his chest, while they picked out a dozen dresses for Kaitlyn to try on.

He opened his preternatural senses while he waited, grinned as he caught snatches of conversation from the dressing room.

"You look beautiful. . . ."

"How about this one?"

". . . need a smaller size . . ."

With a shake of his head, he stepped outside and glanced up and down the sidewalk. Only a few people were on the street, mostly couples coming from the direction of the movie theater. No scent of vampires, Romanian or any other kind. No hint of danger.

Returning to the shop, he took a seat on a chintz-covered sofa, and waited. And waited. Just when he thought he'd have to go in after them, Kaitlyn and her mother emerged from the dressing room.

Zack frowned when he saw they were both empty-handed. "No luck? Don't tell me we have to do this again."

"No." Kaitlyn kissed him on the cheek. "I found the perfect dress. Well, it'll be perfect with a little altering. The seamstress said it will be ready next week."

"Wait until you see your bride in that gown," Elena said, smiling. "She's gorgeous."

"She's already gorgeous," Zack said, winking at Kaitlyn.

"I found a veil, too. And everything else I'll need for the wedding." She smiled at him, her cheeks turning pink. "And the wedding night."

"Really?" he asked with a wicked grin. "Something black and slinky?"

"Zack!"

"Come on," he said, laughing. "Let's go home."

The next week passed peacefully. The day after the battle, Andrei, Katiya, and their children returned to the Carpathian Fortress, along with Ciprian and Liam. By right of battle, the Italian Fortress and everything in it now belonged to Drake. Four days after Lucien's defeat, Stefan and Liliana moved into the Italian Fortress, along with a number of Liliana's daughters and their families. On the fifth day, nearly everyone who had once resided at the Carpathian Fortress had returned.

Three days later, Drake returned to Wolfram Castle. He hugged Kaitlyn, shook Zack's hand, then swept Elena into his arms and carried her swiftly up the stairs to their bedroom.

"So," Zack said, looking at Kaitlyn, "what do you want to do tonight?"

"As if you didn't know," she replied with a wicked grin.

"Yeah, well . . ."

"I'll bet any other man would be happy to take me to bed."

"If any other man tries, I'll break his neck."

"Zack! You're making me crazy."

Crazy, he thought. That's exactly what he was. He

loved her. She loved him. They were getting married soon. What was he waiting for?

"Listen, Katy, I don't expect you to understand this, but I was brought up in a different era, a time when men didn't touch their brides until the wedding night."

"Are you saying men and women were all virgins back then? Because I don't believe that for a minute."

"Of course not. But men went to prostitutes before they were married. And some long after. I guess I'm more old-fashioned than I thought," he muttered ruefully.

"All right," she said with an exaggerated sigh of exasperation. "I'll stop trying to seduce you. But, mister, you'd better be worth the wait!"

They went looking at churches the following night. Zack and Kaitlyn sat in the backseat of the Porsche, stealing kisses, while Drake drove to the first church.

"This one is beautiful," Elena remarked.

"And very old," Drake said as they approached the entrance. He glanced at Zack over his shoulder. "I never thought to ask. Are churches a problem for you?"

"No."

With a nod, Drake opened the carved front door and stepped inside. Elena, Kaitlyn, and Zack followed on his heels.

It was a lovely old church, with arched ceilings and stained-glass windows. Candles burned on either side of the high altar. Baskets of fresh flowers, undoubtedly left over from a recent wedding, or perhaps a funeral, filled the air with a sweet fragrance. The wooden pews glowed with a patina of age.

"I love it," Kaitlyn said, glancing around. "Zack?"

"If you like it, I like it."

"Any point in looking anywhere else?" Elena asked.

"No." Kaitlyn shook her head. "I want to be married here."

"All right, then," Elena said cheerfully. "I'll call tomorrow and make the necessary arrangements."

Drake and Elena left the church, their heads together.

Zack caught Kaitlyn by the hand when she would have followed.

"What?" She looked up at him. "You don't want to get married here?"

"I just wanted to kiss my bride. Do you mind?"

"What a silly question." She moved into his arms, went up on her tiptoes, and pressed her lips to his. "Your bride," she murmured, smiling up at him. "I like the sound of that. Just think, soon I'll be Mrs. Zackary Ravenscroft."

"Not soon enough," he growled.

Chapter 38

The ringing of his cell phone brought Zack instantly awake. Sitting up, he grabbed the cell from the nightstand and checked the display.

"Scherry. What's wrong?"

"Zack! The club . . ."

"What about it?"

"It's gone."

"Gone? What the hell are you talking about?"

"Someone burned the place down early this morning. There's nothing left."

He frowned as he considered her words. "Are you saying it wasn't an accident? That someone did it deliberately?"

"Yes. The fire department said someone broke in shortly after dawn and torched the place. The fireman I talked to said it was the work of a pro."

"Did anybody get hurt?"

"No. The club was empty."

"All right. What time is it there?"

"Six P.M."

He grunted softly. Romania was ten hours ahead of Nevada. "All right. I'll be there sometime tomorrow night. Reserve me a room at Harrah's under an alias. Get one for yourself, too. I'll call you when I get there."

"Who do you think did this?"

"I'm not sure, but I've got a pretty good idea. Tell Walls and Lautner to lay low until they hear from me. That goes for you, too."

"All right, Zack. I'll see you tomorrow night. And Zack . . . be careful."

"You, too, kid."

Zack closed the phone and tossed it on the nightstand. He sat there a minute, lost in thought. There was no way to prove it, but he would bet his last dollar that Nadiya was behind the fire. She might not have lit the match, but he'd bet she knew who did.

He had no sooner ended the call than Kaitlyn opened the door and peeked inside. "Zack?"

"What are you doing up?"

"I heard your phone ring. . . ."

"Come on in, nosy, and close the door."

His gaze moved over her as she tiptoed toward him. Clad in a sleeveless long white gown that fluttered around her ankles, she looked like a raven-haired apparition as she glided across the floor toward him.

"I'm not nosy," she said defensively. "But good news doesn't come at four in the morning."

"You're right about that." He patted the bed, inviting her to join him. "Somebody burned down the casino this morning."

She stared at him, her eyes wide. "That's terrible! Wait a minute. Are you saying someone did it deliberately?"

"Right the first time. Any guesses on who did it?"

"You don't think Nadiya . . . ."

"Who else?"

"But why? She doesn't know you killed Daryn and Marius."

"I think she's got a pretty good idea that I had something to do with Daryn's death."

"So, you think she's in Tahoe?"

"I don't know, but I intend to find out. I'm going home tomorrow."

"How long will you be gone?"

"As long as it takes. I need to talk to the fire department, find out what they know. Get in touch with my insurance company. See about getting the mess cleaned up. Call the architect who built it the first time."

"But . . . we're getting married next Saturday."

"Right. How do you feel about getting married in Tahoe?"

She blinked at him, and then shrugged. "I guess it doesn't matter where we get married, as long as we get married. But . . . what about my mom and dad?"

"They can come with us. Hell, the whole family can come along."

"Our marriages are usually private affairs, with just the immediate family present." Of course, she'd already strayed from tradition by insisting on flowers and a church wedding.

"Really?"

Kaitlyn nodded. Weddings among her kind were not the romantic affairs of books and movies, since most marriages were arranged by the parents of the bride and groom. There was no music, no flowers, no reception afterward. At the Fortress, marriages were solemnized by the Master of the Coven. She wasn't sure if that was legal in Nevada, but it didn't matter. Wherever they were, her father would perform the ceremony.

She made a soft sound of contentment when Zack drew her into his arms. "I can't wait to be your wife."

"I'm kinda looking forward to that myself." He

hugged her close, his tongue sliding over her lower lip, slipping inside to mate with hers.

She was like a flame in his arms, igniting his desire, burning away all his good intentions. Her hands moved over his shoulders and down his arms, testing the strength of his biceps, then slipping under his T-shirt, her fingernails raking his chest, his back, sliding down to the waistband of his sweats. Every touch aroused him more.

"Katy . . ."

She covered his mouth with hers, swallowing his protest.

With a low groan, he surrendered to the need that would no longer be denied. Taking her in his arms, he kissed her fervently, his desire growing as his tongue dueled with hers. He took his mouth from hers only long enough to pull her nightgown over her head. He stared at her, speechless. She was beautiful from head to foot. Her skin was lightly tanned and perfect, her waist narrow, her hips nicely rounded, her legs long and shapely. He quickly rid himself of his T-shirt and sweats, then stretched out beside her.

"Do you have any idea how beautiful you are?" he asked.

"You are." Kaitlyn rose on one elbow, her stomach fluttering as she admired his muscular arms and chest, his long legs and flat belly. "Definitely beautiful," she murmured.

"You think so?" Slipping an arm around her, he buried his face in her cleavage. "So soft," he murmured. "So warm."

A needy moan rose in her throat as he nuzzled her breast. "Zack . . ."

He drew her into his arms, molding her body to his. The gentle abrasion of skin against skin aroused him still more. But it was the scrape of her teeth against his neck that carried him past the point of no return. Pleasure engulfed him as she drank. Only a taste, but it was enough. It heightened his desire and his thirst, made him forget everything but his need for this one particular woman above all others.

She turned her head to the side, offering him her throat. And he was lost.

Her musky scent filled his nostrils as his fangs pierced her tender flesh. She moaned softly, her hands clutching his shoulders as he rose over her. She cried out with mingled pleasure and pain as his body merged with hers.

He held her close for a moment, showering her with kisses while her body adjusted to his.

She writhed beneath him, urging him on, her hands caressing him as he moved deep inside her. She was silk and satin in his arms.

Kaitlyn clung to him, holding him so tightly it seemed as if they had melted into one another. Two made one, she thought, and felt the bond between them grow stronger even as tension built up within her.

She cried his name, desperate for release.

"Hang on, darlin'," he said, his voice husky.

One soul-shattering kiss. One last thrust, and they tumbled over the edge to paradise.

Kaitlyn spiraled slowly back to reality. Never before had she felt so complete. So content. So utterly happy.

Opening her eyes, she saw Zack watching her intently. She smiled drowsily. "Wow."

He arched one brow. "Wow?"

She kissed his chin. "It was worth the wait."

"I'm sorry I waited so long," he said, and then grunted softly. "So much for all my good intentions."

Propping herself up on her elbow, she traced his lips with the tip of her finger. He had a remarkable mouth, she thought, capable of doing remarkable things. "I'm sorry for seducing you."

He stared up at her, and then burst out laughing. "No, you're not."

"You're right," she admitted with a grin. "I'm not. In fact, I'm ready to do it all over again!"

Drake stood in front of the hearth, his arms crossed over his chest, as Zack told him the details of his phone call with Scherry that morning. "And you think Nadiya is behind it."

"She's the most logical suspect, don't you think?"

Drake shrugged. "Why you?"

"Maybe she wants to separate the two of us. Or maybe she thinks if I go back to Tahoe, Kaitlyn will go with me. Either way, I'm heading home. I know this messes up the wedding plans, and I'm sorry about that, but I need to take care of this."

"Of course you do," Elena said.

Kaitlyn glanced at Zack, who was sitting on the sofa beside her, then smiled tentatively at her mother. "We thought we'd get married in Tahoe."

Elena and Drake exchanged looks.

"Is that what you want?" Drake asked quietly.

"We want you both to be there, of course," Kaitlyn added quickly. "And Grandmother and Stefan."

"Whatever you want is fine with us," Elena said. "It isn't as though we've sent out a hundred invitations and rented a hall."

"I think Kaitlyn should stay here while Zack goes ahead and takes care of whatever he has to," Drake said.

"No way!" Kaitlyn exclaimed. "I'm going with Zack."

"I think your dad's right," Zack said. "You'll be safer

here. My lair is toast. A threshold in a hotel or a rented room doesn't offer any protection from intruders, supernatural or otherwise."

"Then you won't be safe, either," Kaitlyn said.

"I'm not going to sleep at the hotel. I'll go to ground somewhere."

"But . . ."

"It's only for a few days, Katy. I'll find a church and set the date for a week from today." He kissed her cheek, then whispered, "Just think how happy you'll be to see me again."

"I don't want to stay here without you," she said, pouting.

"Katy, I can't guarantee your safety during the day. Not in a hotel. And I'm not willing to take a chance on Nadiya getting her hands on you again."

Nadiya, she thought glumly. How had she forgotten about Nadiya?

Knowing Kaitlyn and Zack would like to spend a few hours alone before he left for Tahoe, Drake and Elena decided to go into town.

"To do a little shopping and maybe take in a movie," Elena said, giving Kaitlyn a hug. "We won't be too late."

"Ya know," Zack said when her parents had gone, "I have a feeling they know what was going on in my room this morning."

Kaitlyn stared at him, her eyes wide. "What makes you think that?"

He shrugged. "Just a hunch."

"No way. If my dad knew . . ." Kaitlyn shook her head. "Well, he would have said something. Done something."

"Are you sure about that?"

"Of course. Well . . . I don't know. Why do you think they know?"

"Like I said, just a hunch."

"Well," Kaitlyn said, grinning, "you're still alive, so they must not be too upset. And since we've already done it, and they already know"—she looked at him through the veil of her lashes—"I'm thinking—"

"Yeah," Zack said dryly. "I know exactly what you're thinking."

She jumped to her feet, her hands fisted on her hips. "Are you saying you don't want to?"

"You're a wild, wicked woman, Kaitlyn Liliana Sherrad."

"If I am, it's all your fault. I never even thought about s-e-x until I met y-o-u."

"Sure, blame me. Just like a woman."

"I am a woman, in case you've forgotten."

"Not likely," he said, grinning.

"I'm going up to my room to read. Good night, Mr. Ravenscroft. Have a pleasant trip." And so saying, she flounced out of the room.

She was something else, Zack mused as he watched her climb the stairs. His eyes lingered on the angry sway of her hips and her curvy behind. "All mine," he said. And he wanted her, now and for always.

He was sitting on her bed, legs crossed, feet bare, the pillows propped behind his back, when she opened the door.

He laughed at the look of surprise on her face, but she recovered quickly.

She closed and locked the door behind her, then kicked off her shoes. "Been waiting long?"

"Oh, yeah."

She yawned behind her hand. "I don't think I'm in the mood," she said, stifling a grin.

"No?" He patted the mattress beside him. "Come on over here, and I'll put you in the mood."

"Mighty sure of yourself, aren't you, mister?"

"Yep. No complaints so far," he said, laughing. "Of course, there was only the one time."

She stood there, her arms crossed and then, with deliberate slowness, she peeled off her sweater and tossed it on a chair. "Maybe once was enough." She stepped out of her shoes, unzipped her jeans, and slid them, ever so slowly, over her hips and down her legs. Her gaze never left his face as she kicked her jeans aside.

"Never enough," Zack said, his gaze moving over her from head to heel.

The heat in his eyes seared her skin as she removed her bra and wriggled out of her panties. "One of us is overdressed," she remarked.

"Yeah? What are you going to do about it?"

She sauntered toward him, hips swaying provocatively. "What would you like me to do?"

"Anything you want, Katy darlin'. I'm all yours."

"And don't you forget it!" She quickly removed his shirt, then tugged his jeans off and dropped them on the floor next to her own. He was beautiful, she thought, perfectly proportioned, well muscled without being bulky. And he wanted her. The evidence was unmistakable.

She was reaching for the waistband of his black briefs when he pulled her into his arms and kissed her as if he would never let her go. Which was fine with her.

Moments later, she was on her back.

"Just remember, this was *your* idea," she murmured as he rose over her. "I don't want to hear anything about me seducing you later."

He kissed her again. "You don't call that striptease seductive?"

"Well, maybe just a little," she said, running her hands up and down his chest. "But you started it."

"Me?" He nibbled on her earlobe. "What did I do?"

"What did you do?" she exclaimed. "You were in my bed!"

"Come on, admit it. You were hoping I'd be here."

"I admit nothing."

"No?" Affecting a German accent, he said, "We have ways of making you talk."

"Really?"

"Really. Your mother told me you're ticklish just here."

"No! Zack, no!" She began to thrash about as he tickled her under her arms. "Zack, quit it! I hate that! Zack!"

Laughing, he trapped both of her hands in one of his. "So, what will you give me to stop?"

"Anything," she promised, gasping for breath.

His gaze moved over her lips, then slid down to the pulse hammering in the hollow of her throat. "Anything?"

She nodded, too out of breath to speak.

"A taste?"

She nodded again, her eyes smoldering with desire as he bent his head to her neck and drank.

Kaitlyn cried when he left. She didn't want to, but she couldn't help it. For the next week, they would be miles apart. Bereft, she stood beside her parents as Zack kissed her one last time.

"Be careful," she said. "Promise me you'll be careful."

He winked at her. "You know I will. I'm getting married next week. I'd hate to miss that. And I have a lot to do between now and then. I need to find a church, rent a tux, find us a place to live." He kissed the tip of her nose. "I'm gonna be a busy man."

"You won't even have time to miss me," she said, sniffling.

"Not true, Katy. I'll miss you every minute of every night that we're apart."

"I love you."

"I know. And I love you." He looked over her head at Drake. "Take good care of my girl."

Drake nodded curtly.

"Take care of yourself," Elena said, giving Zack a hug.

"I'll see you all soon." He drew Kaitlyn into his arms and kissed her again, a long, drawn-out kiss. "That one has to last me awhile," he said.

And then he was gone.

A week, Kaitlyn thought glumly. How was she going to last a week without him?

Chapter 39

Zack stood in the dark, staring at the burnt rubble and debris that was all that remained of his nightclub. The acrid smell of smoke was still strong as he walked the perimeter of the carnage, his senses searching for some clue that would tell him who had set fire to the club, but there was no scent he recognized. Nevertheless, he was certain Nadiya was responsible for the fire. Whether or not she had set the blaze herself didn't matter. He knew in his gut that she was behind it. It didn't really matter who'd lit the match.

He blew out a sigh. Ten years of his life, up in smoke. He swallowed his anger, knowing it was a waste of time and energy, and focused on the future. He had built the place from the ground up once, and by damn, he could do it again.

Pulling his cell phone from his pocket, he called Scherry to let her know he was in town. He had talked to her before he left Wolfram to let her know he was on his way.

"Hey, boss," she said. "How's it hanging?"

Zack shook his head. "It's hanging just fine. Meet me in the lobby of Harrah's in ten minutes."

"Yessir, boss. Whatever you say, boss."

With a shake of his head, he ended the call.

Scherry was waiting for him when he arrived at the hotel. Harrah's was an impressive place, eighteen stories high, with everything a tourist could ask for—six restaurants, a luxurious pool, a spa that featured Roman baths, Turkish steam, Finnish saunas and Swedish massage, a nightclub, and a casino that offered all the latest games of chance.

"I booked you a luxury suite under the name Christopher Lee," Scherry said, giving him a hug.

"Christopher Lee?" Zack arched a brow in amusement. Lee was an actor who had played Dracula in a number of Hammer horror movies.

"The very same," Scherry said, grinning. "The concierge assured me your suite is the best the hotel has to offer."

"You're staying here, too, right?"

"Are you crazy? I can't afford to stay here on what you pay me," she teased, "especially now that I'm out of a job."

"Don't give me any sass, or you'll be permanently out of a job. Now, get yourself a room. I'm footing the bill."

"Thanks, Zack. As requested, I scheduled an appointment with your insurance man for tonight at ten. He'll meet you here, in the lobby."

Zack nodded. "Were you able to get in touch with Waters?"

"Yes. He canceled a trip out of town to meet you here at eleven."

"I should have hired you to be my personal secretary instead of my bartender."

"I used to be an executive secretary, in a former life." Reaching into her jacket pocket, she pulled out a keycard. "Here you go. Let me know if there's anything else I can do for you."

"Thanks, kid."

"Are you going to rebuild in the same place?"

Zack nodded. "Just as soon as I can. Have you been in touch with any of the other employees?"

"Yes. They're all eager to come back." She smiled at him. "Now, if you'll excuse me, I have a date."

"Yeah? With who?"

"Just a guy I met last night. His name is Wayne. He's a dealer here in the casino."

Zack nodded. "Have fun. Oh, by the way, I'm getting married."

"Married! You? I don't believe it."

"Well, it's true. She'll be here next week."

"It's her, isn't it? That woman I saw you with a couple of times."

"Yep. Thanks for taking care of things while I was away."

"No problem. I'll expect an invite to the wedding, 'cause I won't believe it unless I see it with my own eyes."

"Right."

Whistling softly, Zack took the elevator to his suite. He didn't know what it was costing him, but he had no complaints. The sitting room was grand. Two comfortable chairs stood on either side of a round table. There was a desk and a chair, should he feel the need to write a letter, a high-backed sofa and a coffee table in front of an entertainment center. Large windows on either side of the room afforded spectacular views—one of the lake, the other of the Sierra Nevada.

The bedroom was separate from the sitting room and featured a king-sized bed flanked by twin end tables, each of which held a lamp and a phone. His favorite feature was the room-darkening drapes.

There were two bathrooms—one for him, one for her. Both had TVs and phones. One bathroom had a

Jacuzzi big enough for two; the other had a walk-in shower, also big enough for two.

He smiled as he imagined himself and Kaitlyn relaxing in the Jacuzzi, making love in the shower.

Ah, Kaitlyn. He missed her already.

She was much on his mind as he left the hotel. His first stop was at a clothing store. When he had more time, he was going to have to buy a whole new wardrobe, since just about everything he owned had been burned in the fire or left behind in Romania. But for now, he only needed a few things—jeans, shirts, underwear, socks, boots. He bought four of everything, then tossed in a long black coat, not because of the weather, but simply because he liked it, and it looked good on him, judging by the admiration in the eyes of the voluptuous saleswoman. He thanked her for her help, paid the bill, and asked her to send his purchases to the hotel.

Leaving the store, he went in search of prey.

It wasn't easy to find a woman alone. They were either with husbands or boyfriends, or in groups. He strolled down the sidewalk, hands shoved in the pockets of his jeans. There was no hurry. He had three hours until his first appointment.

The sounds of an argument drew him to a restaurant parking lot. Taking cover in the shadows, he saw a man and a woman facing each other. He was a little drunk. She was angry, her arms crossed over her breasts.

"Pay up!" she demanded. "Fifty bucks, right now!"

"I can't." He swayed unsteadily. "Sorry."

"What do you mean, you can't?"

He smiled ruefully. "I mean I don't have it."

Her expression turned ugly. "I suggest you get it while you still can."

"You threatening me?" he exclaimed.

She pulled a gun from the handbag dangling from her wrist. "What do you think?"

Zack shook his head. He really didn't want to get involved in this little skirmish, but he couldn't stand by and watch one of his dealers get plugged by a hooker.

Hands still in his pockets, Zack strolled toward them.

The woman swung the gun in Zack's direction. "Get out of here!"

"Hold on there," Zack said, holding up both hands in a gesture of surrender. "That idiot's a friend of mine." Reaching into his pocket, he pulled out a handful of cash. "Turn Henry loose. I'll pay his bill."

She stared at Zack, her expression uncertain.

Henry grinned at him. "Hey, boss."

"Hey, yourself. I think you'd better go home while you can still walk."

"Sure, boss, whatever you say," Henry muttered, and staggered toward the street.

The woman's finger curled around the trigger when Zack took a step toward her. "How do I know I can trust you?"

Zack extended his hand and waved the cash at her. "Come and get it."

She hesitated, then took a wary step toward him, let out a shriek when, with preternatural speed, he closed the distance between them and plucked the gun from her grasp.

"Two mistakes in one night," she muttered. And then tried to knee him in the groin.

Zack blocked it easily, pinned her arms to her sides, then stuffed the bills into her cleavage. "For services rendered."

"Who are you?" she asked.

"No one you'll remember," he said, and lowered his head to her neck.

* * *

It was five to ten when Zack returned to Harrah's. His insurance man was waiting for him in the lobby.

"Shankman," Zack said, shaking the man's hand. "I appreciate your meeting me so late."

"Not a problem, Mr. Ravenscroft."

"Let's go into the lounge," Zack suggested. "We'll be more comfortable there."

Zack found a table for two near the back. He ordered a glass of red wine for himself, a scotch and water for Shankman.

It took less than an hour to fill out the requisite forms. Shankman assured him that the paperwork would be expedited and the check mailed as soon as possible.

The two men shook hands and Shankman left the lounge.

Leaning back in his chair, Zack sipped his wine and thought about his upcoming wedding. He had never expected to marry. It wasn't common among his kind, another major difference between vampires who were made and those who were born. His kind tended to be solitary, concerned for their own survival and little else. They tended to be jealous of their territory and rarely made friends with other vampires. By comparison, those of Kaitlyn's ilk were far more social.

Zack's meeting with his architect, Mike Waters, went quickly and smoothly.

"Just rebuild it the way it was," Zack said.

"No changes?" Waters asked. "I was thinking we should add a covered entry and extend the parking garage. Tahoe's grown quite a bit since you built the club, you know. Are you sure you don't want to add a couple of floors and include some rooms?"

"I'm not interested in running a hotel," Zack said.

"But I like the covered entry idea and the additional parking. How soon can you get started?"

"First of the month?"

"Let's do it."

"I'll draw up a contract tomorrow. Same terms as before?"

Zack nodded.

Waters shook his hand. "Nice doing business with you, Mr. Ravenscroft. I'll be in touch."

Alone again, Zack ordered another glass of wine. Closing his eyes, he brought Kaitlyn's image to mind. Tomorrow night he would find a church where they could be married. Once he made her his, he vowed they would never be parted again.

Flipping open his cell phone, he punched in her number, felt a sense of peace steal over him when he heard her voice on the other end of the line.

Three days without Zack and Kaitlyn felt like she was going stir-crazy. Her father had forbidden her and her mother to leave the castle, even when the sun was up, and although Kaitlyn slept a good part of the day— something she had being doing more and more of since dating Zack—it still left her with a lot of time on her hands and not much to do. After all, you could only watch so many movies, read so many books, play so many games of solitaire, before you felt like climbing the walls. And that's just how she felt.

Her parents did their best to keep her entertained, and she loved them for it, but she missed Zack, missed him with a hollow ache that nothing else could fill. She felt as if a vital part of her had been torn away, leaving her empty and incomplete. Was he feeling the same? Could he possibly miss her as much as she missed him?

"Oh, Zack," she murmured. She needed to see him, to hear his voice, to touch him. And be touched in return. She closed her eyes, recalling the taste of his kisses, the way her whole body came alive at the touch of his hand. She missed the sound of his voice, his smile, his laughter.

She wandered through the castle, her fingertips sliding over the back of the sofa. Zack had kissed her there. And here, in front of the hearth. And in the kitchen. And in her bedroom. And in his bed. She sighed at the memory. Making love to Zack was . . . She shook her head. There were simply no words to describe the wonder of it, the joy it brought her, the sense of belonging. In a flash of insight, she suddenly understood the shared looks between her parents, the frequent half smile on her mother's lips.

She glanced at her watch. It was almost four-thirty P.M. in California. Was Zack still asleep? Was it too early to call? God bless cell phones and the man who had invented them, she thought as she punched in Zack's number.

Her heart skipped a beat when she heard his voice, thick with sleep.

"Hey, Katy darlin'."

"Zack, I miss you so much!"

"Me, too, you. Everything okay there?"

"Yes. I just needed to hear your voice."

"You sound good, too. Listen, my business is taken care of. I found a church. I bought a tux. Tell your dad to come tomorrow night. I've got a suite at Harrah's. I'll meet you there at sundown."

"Tomorrow! You mean it? I can't wait!"

"Me, either."

She sighed, remembering how he had called last night

and vowed that once they were married, they would never be parted again. "I love you."

"I love you more. Listen, Katy . . ."

"I know. I called you too early. I'm sorry. Go back to sleep."

He murmured something unintelligible.

"Call me when you wake up."

"Will do."

She was smiling when she broke the connection. He loved her. She would see him tomorrow night.

Life was good.

Chapter 40

Kaitlyn could hardly contain her excitement as she packed a bag. Soon! Soon she would be with Zack again. She felt like dancing, singing, shouting from the rooftops that she was getting married to the most wonderful man on earth!

Arms flung out at her sides, she pirouetted around the room, then burst out laughing. How would she contain her joy when she saw him again, she wondered, but then, there was no need. She wanted Zack and everyone else in the world to know how happy she was.

She ran her hand over the garment bag that held her wedding gown and veil. What would Zack think when he saw his bride? Picturing him in a tuxedo brought a warm flush to her cheeks and turned her legs to mush. The man looked drop-dead sexy in jeans and a T-shirt. No doubt he would be lethal in a tux!

Grabbing her suitcase and her gown, she hurried down the stairs. Her parents were waiting for her.

"Are you ready?" her father asked.

"Yes! Let's go!"

"Here," her mother said, reaching for the garment bag, "let me carry that."

Her father picked up the suitcase at his feet, Kaitlyn tucked hers against her chest. She stood between her mom and dad, their arms linked together, as her father transported the three of them to Lake Tahoe.

It was an odd sensation, being swept blindly through time and space. Kaitlyn felt weightless, disoriented, almost as if her mind and body had split into two separate entities. She wondered briefly what would happen if the two halves didn't reunite. One fanciful thought turned into another and she tried to imagine what it would be like if her mind ended up in her mother's body. What a conundrum that would be!

It took Kaitlyn a minute to realize she was standing on solid ground again. When her vision cleared and her head stopped spinning, she glanced around, then looked at her father. "Where are we?"

"In the rear of Harrah's parking lot." Drake stroked Elena's cheek. "Are you all right?"

"A little shaky, but fine." Elena took Kaitlyn's hand in hers and gave it a squeeze. "Well, don't just stand there, you two. Let's go find the groom."

Zack sensed Kaitlyn's presence even before she entered the lobby of the hotel. Though it had only been a few days, it seemed much longer. His gaze moved over her, marveling again at how lovely she was. Clad in a fuzzy pink sweater and a pair of white jeans, she looked good enough to eat. Literally. Heedless of the people milling around, he hurried forward.

Kaitlyn dropped the suitcase she was carrying when she saw Zack. She ran toward him, laughed out loud when he swept her into his arms and twirled her around. "Katy!" He kissed her, long and hard. And then he kissed her again, short and sweet. "I missed you."

She grinned up at him when he set her on her feet. "As much as I hated every second that we were apart, I think that welcome was worth it."

"Drake, Elena, it's good to see you." Zack picked up Kaitlyn's suitcase. "Come on," he said, taking her by the hand, "I'll show you all to your room."

"We don't need a room," Kaitlyn said. "We can stay at my place."

"Nadiya knows where you live," Zack said. "I'm thinking it's better if you all stay here."

"But . . ."

"I think Zack is right," her father said. "Nadiya may have someone watching your house. You'd be safe inside, but not coming and going. The anonymity of the hotel is probably a good thing."

"Safety in numbers and all that," Zack remarked with a wry grin.

"Exactly," Elena said. "It'll be cozy."

Zack and Drake exchanged pained looks.

"Cozy," Zack muttered.

Kaitlyn's shoulders slumped in defeat. She had been looking forward to going home, sleeping in her own bed. Being alone with Zack.

"I asked a couple of my sisters to stay at Wolfram so that anyone sniffing around will think we're still there," Drake remarked.

In the elevator, Zack held Kaitlyn close to his side, basking in her warmth and light. Being close to her again, inhaling her scent, was like being reborn. Until they were miles apart, he hadn't realized just how much he needed her, or appreciated how the goodness she radiated chased the darkness from his soul.

He unlocked the door to the suite and ushered them inside. Drake left his suitcase by the door; Kaitlyn dropped hers on the sofa. Elena immediately went into the bedroom to hang up Kaitlyn's wedding gown.

"I'm sorry to say, there's only one bed," Zack remarked when Elena returned. "Rollaways aren't allowed in suites." He glanced at Katy. "I guess you'll have to sleep on the couch."

"What about you?" Elena asked. "If we take your room, where are you going to stay?"

"Don't worry about me. I haven't been sleeping here."

Kaitlyn frowned at him. "Why not?"

"I am guessing he felt too vulnerable to rest comfortably," Drake said.

Zack nodded. "Right."

"Have you seen any sign of Nadiya?" Drake asked.

"No."

"So, where *have* you been sleeping?" Kaitlyn asked.

"In the ground."

She couldn't help it, she grimaced. She knew her people sometimes did that, but she hadn't known the Others did it, also. She wondered if her father had ever gone to ground, as they called it. She knew it was natural for their kind, but she couldn't imagine doing it herself. It was just too . . . too morbid.

"Well, I don't know about the rest of you," Elena said. "But I'm going to unpack."

"Me, too," Kaitlyn said.

Grunting softly, Drake dropped onto the sofa and stretched his legs out in front of him.

Zack paced the floor for a few minutes, then moved one of the chairs nearer to the fireplace and sat down facing Drake. "Any chance Nadiya will just give up?"

"You are a gambler. What do you think?"

"I'd say the odds were about a thousand to one. So, what's our next move?"

"I think the next move is up to her."

"I was afraid you'd say that."

"Nadiya, Nadiya, Nadiya," Kaitlyn muttered as she reentered the room. "Can't we talk about something else?"

"Sure, darlin'," Zack said. "What would you like to talk about?"

Sitting on the arm of Zack's chair, she said, "I'd like to see the church where we're getting married."

"Me, too," Elena said.

"It's all right with me," Zack said. "I could use some exercise."

"Let's go," Kaitlyn said.

The church was about a half mile from the hotel. Arm in arm, Zack and Kaitlyn walked ahead of Drake and Elena.

"Another night or two and you'll be all mine," Zack said, squeezing her hand.

"I'm already all yours. Did you arrange it so my father can marry us?"

"About that . . . The priest I talked to said it couldn't be done."

"Then we'll just have to go somewhere else."

"I couldn't find a minister anywhere who was willing to let a complete stranger, someone who wasn't even a member of the congregation, perform a wedding. So, since the only guests will be vampires, we're just going to get married at midnight, when the church is locked up tight."

"Of course," Kaitlyn said. "Why didn't I think of that?"

"'Cause you're the pretty one," Zack said, trying hard not to laugh. "And I'm the smart one. Ouch!"

"Serves you right," she said.

"This is it." Zack paused in front of a white stone church topped by a tall golden cross. Large stained-glass windows flanked the entrance.

Holding Kaitlyn's hand, he transported the two of them inside.

Drake and Elena followed moments later.

"Oh, it's lovely," Elena said, glancing around.

Kaitlyn nodded. "It's even prettier than the one at home." Rising on her tiptoes, she kissed Zack on the cheek. "This is perfect."

Zack glanced at Drake and Elena. "Can your family be here by tomorrow night?"

"In a hurry, are you?" Drake asked.

"Probably no more than you were," Elena said, punching her husband on the arm. "I'm sure they can be here by then."

And they were.

The next night, Liliana and Stefan arrived at Harrah's just after eleven P.M.

"I was hoping Andrei would come," Kaitlyn said, hugging her grandmother and her uncle.

"They wanted to be here," Drake said, "but, all things considered, I did not think it wise for them to leave the Fortress. Ciprian and Liam are taking Liliana's place at the Italian Fortress until she returns. If you want to postpone the wedding . . ."

"No!" Kaitlyn said emphatically. "I am not waiting any longer."

Zack winked at her. "That's my girl."

Elena, ever the peacemaker, said, "All right, then. What do you say we all get dressed and meet at the church at midnight? Zack, can you find a room somewhere else? It's bad luck for the groom to see the bride before the wedding, you know."

"Sure, Elena. A friend of mine is staying here, at Harrah's. I can dress in her room. Liliana, I booked you and Stefan rooms here, too."

"Sounds like you've taken care of everything," Elena said. "Let's go."

Kaitlyn stood in front of the full-length mirror in the bathroom while her mother brushed her hair.

"You look lovely, sweetheart," Elena said. "I've never seen you looking happier."

"I've never been happier. I love Zack so much. When you fell in love with Dad, did you just know he was the right one?"

"Yes. My life might have been easier in some ways if I'd fallen in love with a human instead of a vampire. But hearts don't care about things like that."

Setting the brush aside, Elena picked up the veil and set it in place. "You look like an angel."

"Thanks, Mom, for everything."

"I can't believe my little girl is getting married." Elena shook her head. "Where did the years go? Seems like only yesterday I was holding you in my arms, and now look at you. All grown up and about to become a wife."

"Mom, don't cry."

"I can't help it. Besides, they're happy tears. You've everything a mother could ever hope for in her daughter. I'm so proud of you."

"Oh, Mom." Blinking back her own tears, Kaitlyn hugged her mother.

"Careful, sweetie, you're crushing your gown."

"I don't care."

Elena pulled a hanky from her pocket. "Here, dry your eyes. We don't want Zack to see you crying."

Kaitlyn smiled at the mention of his name, then glanced over her shoulder as her father knocked on the bedroom door and peeked inside.

"It's almost midnight. Are you . . ." His words trailed off when he saw Kaitlyn.

"Dad, are you all right?" she asked anxiously.

"I just realized I am losing my little girl."

"Oh, Daddy, I'll always be your little girl."

He held out his arms and she went to him, sighing as his arms wrapped around her. He would always be her first love. He had kissed her hurts, chased away the monster under the bed, taught her to value herself and those around her. "I love you, Daddy."

"I know. I love you, too." Putting his finger under her chin, he lifted her head. "Are you sure he is the one?"

"Without a doubt."

"We'd better go," Elena said. "We don't want the groom to think the bride changed her mind at the last minute."

Another round of hugs, and they left the hotel.

There were no lights on in the church. The only illumination came from a pair of candles near the altar.

Since Kaitlyn's father was performing the ceremony, she had asked her uncle Stefan to walk her down the aisle.

Her mother and Liliana sat side by side in the front pew. Her father stood in front of the altar. Zack stood to his right. Zack's bartender, Scherry, sat in the second pew.

Kaitlyn's heart skipped a beat when she saw her future husband. He had been born to wear a tux, she thought. The jacket, obviously hand-tailored just for him, caressed his broad shoulders, the trousers emphasized his long legs. The crisp white shirt was the perfect foil for his long black hair and dark eyes.

There was no music other than the beating of her

heart as she moved toward him. When they reached the altar, Stefan placed her hand in Zack's, then stepped back to sit next to his mother.

Drake's gaze moved over those in attendance. "Liliana Sherrad, Elena Sherrad, Stefan Sherrad, Scherry Lyons, you have been called here tonight to witness the union of Zackary Ravenscroft and Kaitlyn Liliana Sherrad, here present. Zackary, will you have this woman to be your life mate? Will you care for her and protect her so long as you both shall live?"

Zack squeezed Kaitlyn's hand as he answered, "I will."

"Kaitlyn Liliana Sherrad, will you have this man to be your life mate? Will you love him and cherish him so long as you both shall live?"

"I will."

Reaching into his jacket pocket, Drake withdrew a small golden goblet and placed it on the altar behind him. Zack looked at him askance as Drake reached for his hand.

"It is part of our ceremony," Drake explained. Using his thumbnail, he made a shallow slit in Zack's palm, then held his bleeding hand over the goblet.

He made a similar cut in Kaitlyn's palm, adding her blood to the cup.

Lifting the goblet, Drake offered it to Zack.

"You must drink," Drake said.

With a nod, Zack took a swallow.

"Now Kaitlyn," Drake said, and Zack handed the goblet to Katy.

She smiled at him, then sipped from the cup.

"By the exchange of blood and vows," Drake intoned, "and by my authority as Master of the Carpathian Coven, I hereby decree that from this night forward, Zackary Ravenscroft and Kaitlyn Sherrad are life mated. May you be blessed with happiness and may your love last throughout eternity. Zackary, you may kiss your bride."

"Katy." After lifting her veil, Zack drew her into his arms. "I will love you forever and beyond," he murmured, and kissed her, ever so gently.

Kaitlyn melted against him, happier than she had ever been in her life. She was his now, forever his. Nothing could ever part them. Not life, not death.

She was about to embrace her father when the door of the church flew open. Kaitlyn let out a cry of alarm as Nadiya and ten other vampires stormed into the church.

Fangs bared against the invaders, Zack pushed Kaitlyn behind him.

What followed was like a scene from a horror movie. Kaitlyn saw it in bits and pieces, the brutality of the attack so terrible it was hard to process it all. Added to the graphic visuals of blood and carnage were the sounds of tearing flesh and cries of pain. And overall, the heavy scent of fresh blood.

Two of the vampires attacked her father.

One of them attacked her mother, another backed Scherry against the wall.

Two of them forced her grandmother into a corner.

Two others advanced on Stefan.

Two rushed Zack.

Most horrifying of all was the fact that there was nothing she could do to help. Kaitlyn stared at the vampire who had driven her away from the others. She knew Nadiya only by sight, having seen her once at the Fortress years ago. But this Nadiya looked nothing like the beautiful woman Kaitlyn remembered. Hatred contorted her features into a hideous mask and blazed like hellfire in her eyes. Her lips were peeled back, revealing her fangs; her hands were like claws, and felt like razors as she grabbed hold of Kaitlyn's arms.

Kaitlyn glanced around, seeking help, seeking a way out, but there was nowhere to go, no one who could help her.

She cried out in anguish when she saw her mother fall beneath the weight of the vampire who had attacked her, screamed when the vampire sank his fangs into her mother's throat.

Filled with a sudden fury, Kaitlyn reached deep inside herself. Summoning the power that had long lain dormant within her, she flung Nadiya aside. But Nadiya was an old vampire. Strong. Relentless. She recovered quickly, her claws raking the length of Kaitlyn's cheek and along the side of her neck.

Kaitlyn gasped as pain exploded through the right side of her face.

"You will not get away this time!" Nadiya exclaimed, reaching for her again.

"Neither will you!"

At the sound of her grandmother's voice, Kaitlyn glanced past Nadiya to see Liliana bearing down on the two of them, a long wooden stake in her hand.

Nadiya whirled around to fight off the new threat.

Liliana drew back her arm and drove the stake into Nadiya's chest with such force that the stake sliced through her heart and protruded from her back.

With a look of disbelief, Nadiya slowly sank to the floor.

Kaitlyn stared at her grandmother, stunned by the sudden turn of events, and then she grinned.

"Stay here, child," Liliana said, and spun away to rejoin the fight.

With a shake of her head, Kaitlyn rushed to her mother's aid. Grabbing a large, decorative wooden crucifix from the wall, she broke it in half and drove the jagged end into the back of the vampire who was bent over her mother's neck.

With a gasp of pain and surprise, the vampire toppled sideways and lay still.

"Mom!" Kaitlyn shook her mother's shoulder. "Mom, answer me!"

Frantic, she looked around.

Stefan was sprawled on the floor, bleeding heavily from several wounds on his neck and chest. The vampires who had attacked him were both dead, their hearts ripped from their bodies.

Her father had destroyed one of his attackers. As Kaitlyn watched, he broke the neck of the second vampire; then, pulling a long-bladed knife from a sheath under his long black coat, he quickly decapitated his opponent.

Scherry sat on the floor nursing a broken arm that, thanks to her vampire blood, was already healing.

Where was Zack? She glanced around, then saw him near the back of the church. He moved with lethal precision as he fought off two vampires at the same time. It was like watching a beautiful, deadly dance, the way he moved. There was no fear in his eyes and she had the strangest notion that he was enjoying himself, that he could have killed his attackers at any time.

As though feeling her gaze, he glanced at her, the exultant smile on his face fading when he saw her mother, unmoving, in her lap.

At the same time, her father's roar of anguish filled the air.

Moving almost quicker than Kaitlyn's eyes could follow, Zack ripped the throat from one vampire, the heart from the other, and then he was kneeling at her side, across from her father.

"Elena!" Drake called her name, his voice thick with unshed tears. "Elena."

Her eyelids flickered open, her gaze unfocused. "Drake?"

"I am here." He clutched her hand in his. "You will be all right. I will take you to the hospital. . . ."

"I'm dying. . . ."

"No! Do not leave me!" He bit into his wrist, then held it to her lips. "Drink."

But it was too late. Her eyelids fluttered down and her head fell back against Kaitlyn's arm.

"Elena!" Eyes filled with torment, Drake looked at Zack. "I cannot turn her, but you can."

"Would she want that?" Liliana asked, coming to stand behind Drake.

"I do not care," Drake said. "I cannot lose her."

"We discussed it," Zack said. "She and I."

"What?" Drake stared at him. "When?"

"A while back. She asked me if I'd ever turned anyone. Said she was just curious."

"Do it," Drake said. "We do not have time to discuss it. She is dying."

Zack glanced up at Scherry, who was standing to his left. "I've only done it once before."

"If you fail, she will be no worse off than she is now," Drake said, his voice tinged with desperation. "I will do anything you ask of me, give you anything you desire, if you will do this for me."

With a sigh of resignation, Zack took Elena into his arms. He hesitated a moment, suddenly torn by uncertainty. He had turned Scherry and it had been hit and miss. It was one thing to drink from healthy prey, another to drink from the sick, the dying. If he took too much, and that was a risk with those who were sick, it could be fatal. Completely drained, they lacked the strength to fight their way back. Could he live with himself if he caused Elena's death? Could he live with himself if there was a chance he could save her and he didn't take it? She didn't seem to be breathing. Her heartbeat was faint, erratic.

Kaitlyn placed her hand on his arm. "Please, Zack."

Murmuring, "Forgive me," he bent his head to Elena's neck and drank.

Kaitlyn held her breath as what little color was left drained from her mother's face. Was Zack taking too much? Even with her preternatural hearing, she could barely detect her mother's heartbeat.

Looking up, she met her father's gaze. She had never seen him look so distraught, knew it would kill him as surely as a stake through the heart if her mother died.

After what seemed like forever but was only a few minutes, Zack lifted his head. Kaitlyn watched, unblinking, as he bit his wrist, then held the bleeding wound to her mother's lips.

"Drink," he said, stroking her throat. "Elena Sherrad, if you want to live, you must drink."

Kaitlyn leaned forward, her whole being focused on her mother's face, willing her to drink.

"Elena!" Drake took her hand in his. "Elena! Come back to me!"

Tears burned Kaitlyn's eyes when she looked at Zack. Zack shook his head. "The rest is up to her." He stroked her throat again. "Elena, drink." It was not a request this time, but a command.

"She isn't moving," Kaitlyn said. Had they waited too long? Had Zack taken too much?

"Dammit, Elena," Drake said, his voice thick with unshed tears. "I forbid you to leave me!"

At the sound of Drake's voice, Elena slowly licked the blood from her lips. And then she grabbed Zack's arm.

Drake blew out a sigh of relief.

"You did it!" Kaitlyn exclaimed. She threw her arms around Zack and kissed his cheek. "Thank you!"

"Yes," Drake said, never taking his gaze from his wife's face. "Thank you."

Zack nodded. Would Drake still be grateful, he wondered, if he knew that his wife and Zack now shared a bond of blood that could not be broken?

Chapter 41

"What happens now?" Drake asked, lifting Elena into his arms. After feeding, she had closed her eyes, seemingly unconscious.

"She'll sleep the rest of the night," Zack replied. "When she wakes tomorrow night, she'll be a vampire, with a new vampire's thirst."

Drake nodded.

"You'll need to watch her closely when she feeds the first few times. It's not always easy for fledglings to feed without draining their prey. Maybe you already know that."

"Indeed."

"Take her back to the hotel. I'll clean up the mess here."

"I will help you," Stefan said.

"I thought you were dead," Zack remarked, grinning.

"Not quite." Stefan glanced around the church. "We can dispose of the bodies, but I do not know how we will remove the blood from the floor."

"Yeah, that might be a problem," Zack agreed.

"I'll take care of the mess on the floor," Scherry said. "How's your arm?" Zack asked.

She stretched it out and rotated it back and forth. "Good enough to clean up the blood," she said, grinning.

"I will help you, if you like," Liliana offered.

"Great."

"We'd best get busy," Zack suggested. "We've got a lot of work to do."

"What are we going to do with the bodies?" Kaitlyn asked.

"We'll take them up in the mountains," Zack said, "and leave them there for the sun to find."

Kaitlyn looked at her father. "Who were they?"

"Three of them were Nadiya's sons. I did not recognize the others."

Kaitlyn shook her head. What a waste. Nadiya was dead, and all her sons with her. Had Nadiya survived, Kaitlyn wondered if the woman would have considered the blood of all her sons well spent.

"Revenge is a terrible thing," Stefan remarked, hoisting one of the bodies over his shoulder. "The worst of it is, Florin brought his death on himself with his treachery against our father. There was nothing to avenge."

It took several trips to transport all of the bodies to a place where they wouldn't be found before sunrise. Standing between Zack and Stefan, Kaitlyn felt a moment of remorse for those who had needlessly died, but it was quickly swept away when she recalled how close she had come to losing her mother.

"I can bury them if it'll make you feel better," Zack said.

Kaitlyn shook her head. "No. They don't deserve a decent burial."

"We'd better go," Zack said.

Kaitlyn glanced at Zack and then at Stefan. Both men were covered with blood and gore. As was she. Her beautiful wedding gown and veil were splattered with blood.

Her satin shoes were smeared with stains she didn't care to examine too closely.

"Not the way you planned to spend your honeymoon, is it?" Zack asked ruefully.

"Not quite," she admitted with a wry grin.

Stefan removed his bloodstained jacket and tossed it over one of the bodies. "The woman, Scherry," he said. "Is she . . . ?" He cleared his throat. "Is she married or engaged, or . . . anything?"

"No." Zack took off his own bloody coat and added it to the pile. "She's not married, or anything. If it helps, she thinks you're, and I quote, 'a hottie.'"

"She told you that?" Stefan asked.

"No, I read it in her mind before the ceremony."

Stefan grinned, obviously pleased. And just as obviously smitten by Zack's bartender.

"I'll put in a good word for you next time I see her," Zack said. "In the meantime, I don't know about you two, but I'd like to get out of these clothes and into a nice hot shower."

"We never even got any pictures taken," Kaitlyn wailed. "And now it's too late. My gown is ruined. I'll never get these bloodstains out."

"I'll buy you another dress," Zack promised. "And we can get married all over again."

"I'll hold you to it," Kaitlyn said as he wrapped his arm around her shoulders. "See if I don't."

A rush of preternatural power, a sense of being whisked through time and space, and Kaitlyn found herself in a room she didn't recognize.

"Where are we?"

"Harrah's."

"But this isn't our suite."

He shrugged. "It's a vacant room. Not quite as elegant as the other one, but it'll do for now." Moving around behind her, he began to unfasten the long row of buttons on the back of her dress.

Kaitlyn stepped out of her heels, shivering with anticipation as his fingers parted the fabric of her gown and slid it down over her shoulders. It pooled at her feet.

Turning her around, he eased her out of her petticoat, her lacy bra and panties. Her heartbeat increased as his gaze moved over her.

"Now you." Her fingers trembled as she removed his tie and unbuttoned his shirt. He obligingly heeled off his boots so she could remove his cummerbund and trousers.

"I think a shower is the first order of business," Zack remarked while she divested him of his briefs. "You're kind of bloody," he added, running his fingers through her hair.

"So are you."

"Come on," he said, "I'll wash your back and you can wash mine. If you're good, I'll even let you wash the front."

"As if you could stop me," she retorted with a saucy grin.

Showering with Zack was an experience like no other. He washed her hair and then, very thoroughly and slowly, he washed the rest of her, starting at her neck and working his way down. He had magical hands, she thought. His touches, his kisses, had her practically screaming with need.

Deciding that turnabout was fair play, she took the soap from his hand and washed him from head to heel. Running her hand over his stomach, she grinned, thinking he could be the poster boy for perfect six-pack abs.

He gasped when her hands slid lower, and she laughed out loud. She could hide what she was thinking and feeling. He couldn't.

The water was nearly cold when he turned it off and carried her, wet and dripping, into the bedroom. Still holding her in his arms, he fell back on the bed, carrying her with him, so that she landed on top of him. One hand cupped her nape as he kissed her brow, her nose, her cheeks.

Almost frantic with need, she wriggled against him.

"Stop that," he growled.

"Why? Don't you like it?"

"Oh, yeah, but I was hoping to draw this out a little longer."

"Next time," she said.

"Whatever you want, darlin'," he replied.

He rolled over effortlessly, tucking her neatly beneath him. He kissed her, his tongue dueling with hers while his hands stroked her damp skin, caressing her, arousing her. It was a good thing her skin was wet, she thought, or she probably would have gone up in flames. But, oh, what a way to go.

"Now, Zack." She lifted her hips to receive him. It was heaven, pure heaven, to be in his arms, to feel his skin against her own as his body became a part of hers, two halves uniquely different, yet made to be one, each half incomplete without the other, each heart unfulfilled without the other. Heat suffused her. They were bound by more than the love they shared, she thought. They were forever bound by blood.

They moved together in perfect rhythm, a mating dance as old as time, as new as the love they shared.

She clung to him, breathless, weightless, as he carried her into a world filled with moonbeams and rainbows and pleasure beyond anything she had ever known. His own climax came hard on the heels of her own. Sheened with perspiration, she closed her eyes, sated and content as she slowly drifted back to earth.

With a sigh, she trailed her fingertips over his shoulders. "Next time," she murmured, "I get to be on top."

After the next time, they took another shower, then scurried back to bed and snuggled under the covers. Zack stroked Kaitlyn's neck and shoulders. Her skin was soft and smooth, warm beneath his hand. Though she lay quietly beside him, her head pillowed on his chest, she was thinking so loudly, he had no trouble hearing her thoughts.

"Do you want to talk about it?" he asked.

She tilted her head back so she could see his face. "About what?"

"About your mother's new lifestyle."

"You must be reading my mind," Kaitlyn remarked with a sigh.

"It isn't necessary. I know you must be wondering about it."

Kaitlyn turned onto her side, facing Zack. "Will she be the same? Will she still be my mother?"

"Pretty much. Of course, there's no telling how she'll react to her new life. I imagine it's different when you're born a vampire. You know what to expect, or at least you know what's coming."

"That's true. I was nervous about the change, but I knew it was natural for us, so I wasn't afraid. I'd seen it happen to others from time to time. Of course, with me, it wasn't that big an adjustment. I could still eat and drink whatever I wanted. And my need for blood, after the first time, wasn't overpowering."

"You were lucky. It's different with my kind. Once

you're turned, your whole life changes. Everything is different. Some people accept it without a problem. Some aren't so lucky."

"What do you mean?"

"Take my bartender, Scherry, for instance. She asked me to bring her across."

"Really? Why?"

"She was dying. I'd never turned anyone before, and I was reluctant to do it, you know? I told her I was afraid I'd kill her." He laughed at the memory. "She reminded me that she had nothing to lose but a few days."

"How did she know you were a vampire?"

"I got careless one night. A customer came on to me and I kept her with me in the club after it closed. Scherry had a key and she came in while I was, ah, dining." He shook his head with the memory. "Any other woman would have freaked out, but not Scherry." He laughed. "Bold as brass, that girl. She asked me if I'd turn her when I finished eating."

"Still, it must have taken a lot of nerve for her to ask you. I mean, she had no way of knowing what you'd do. You could have been some horrible monster parading as a nice guy. You could have killed her."

"I tried to talk her out of it, but, like she said, she had nothing to lose."

"At least it turned out all right," Kaitlyn said.

"Yeah. But that first night, I thought I might have to destroy her."

"Why?"

"She was blood crazy. I brought her three men to drink from and it wasn't enough. I didn't think that girl would ever get her fill, and then I realized it was probably because of her disease. She'd had leukemia. I guess it just took a lot to fill her up that first time. She was all right, after that."

Kaitlyn stared up at the ceiling, thinking about what Zack had said. Would her mother be one of the lucky ones? Or would she be blood crazy, like Scherry?

There was a decided air of tension in the sitting room in Zack's suite the following night. It danced over Kaitlyn's skin like ants as she watched her father hover near her mother, his expression wary. Her mother was nervous and obviously on edge. Unable to sit still, she prowled back and forth between the sofa and the window. She paused now and then, shivering as if she were cold, and then she resumed pacing once again.

After watching her for almost an hour, Zack said, "Elena, you need to feed. The compulsion will only grow stronger. And the longer you put it off, the worse it will be for your chosen prey."

"I can't do that," Elena said, her fingers twisting in the hem of her sweater. "I can't . . ." She shook her head. "I can't hunt someone like they were an animal."

"Yes, you can," Zack said, his voice quiet. "It will come to you naturally. All you have to do is follow your instincts."

Elena bit down on her lower lip as she glanced at her husband and then back at Zack.

"I will take you," Drake said.

Elena shook her head. "Drake, please don't take this the wrong way, but I'd rather have Zack go with me this time."

Drake went still. Though he said nothing, Elena knew she had hurt him. "It's just that . . ." She folded her hands and pressed them against her chest. "I don't know what I'll do, or how I'll react. I don't want you to see me in case I behave badly."

Drake frowned. "What are you saying?"

"I'm her sire," Zack said. "I don't know how it works in your world. But in mine, it's natural for fledglings to look to their masters for guidance, just like it's natural for her to expect me to teach her how to hunt, how to survive her new lifestyle. It has nothing to do with her feelings for you. It's part of the bond she has with me now."

A muscle throbbed in Drake's jaw. His hands clenched and unclenched at his sides.

The tension in the room was palpable as Drake absorbed what Zack had told him. And then, suddenly, it was gone.

Drake took Elena in his arms. "I love you, wife," he said quietly. "I will be here when you return."

"Thank you for understanding."

Drake nodded. "This will take some getting used to, for both of us."

"We won't be gone long," Zack said.

Drake nodded, though it was easy for Kaitlyn to see her father was not happy with this unexpected turn of events. Not that she could blame him. Her parents had been devoted to each other for over twenty years. He kissed Elena's cheek, and then looked at Zack. "Take good care of her."

"No problem." Zack sent a reassuring look at Kaitlyn; then, taking Elena by the hand, he transported the two of them to a neighboring city.

"So," Zack asked. "How do you feel?"

They were walking down a side street, headed toward Restaurant Row.

"The same as always," Elena said with a shrug. "Maybe a little better."

He frowned. He hadn't felt anywhere near the same as always the night after he had been turned. On waking, his whole body, every fiber of his being, had been on fire with the overpowering need for blood. If he'd had someone to guide him, things might have turned out differently for the first mortal he came across. He still felt guilty for the lives he had taken before he learned he didn't have to kill to survive, but there was no going back. He'd been a new vampire and he'd done what came naturally.

"Since I feel pretty much the same, maybe it didn't work," Elena said, a note of hope in her voice. Pausing, she looked up at him. "Is that possible?"

"Only one way to find out," Zack said.

Before she realized what he meant to do, Zack bit into his own wrist.

Elena's reaction left no doubt that she was now a vampire. Her eyes went red as she stared at the bright crimson oozing from the wound. The scent of hot, fresh blood filled the air. The coppery scent surrounded her; when she breathed it in, her lips peeled back, revealing a pair of sharp white fangs.

Elena touched the pad of her thumb to the tip of one fang, gasped as the contact, slight as it was, drew blood.

"It's true," she said, her expression one of mingled surprise and horror. "I'm a vampire."

"'Fraid so."

She stared at him, trying to sort through her jumbled feelings, and not knowing where to start. First and foremost, vampire or not, she was glad to be alive. The thought of drinking blood was not repulsive; she had been taking Drake's blood for years. It was the thought of hunting for prey that was disconcerting. She was a wife, a mother, a homemaker. Women like her didn't go prowling the back alleys for sustenance. The very idea was ludicrous. And yet, there was no denying that the scent of Zack's blood was tantalizing her senses to the exclusion of all else. A taste would be welcome, maybe even necessary, but it wasn't driving her mad with need.

Zack regarded Elena thoughtfully. The red had faded from her eyes; he could no longer see her fangs.

"You're not behaving like a new vampire," he remarked. "I wonder . . ."

"What?"

"Well, you've been drinking Drake's blood for how long? Twenty years? I'm thinking that you were practically a vampire already, and the reason you're not going crazy with the need for blood is because you've got twenty years' worth of vampire blood in your veins already. I'm thinking you might need to feed tonight to make the transformation complete, and then you'll probably be like Katy, not entirely human, but not a full-fledged vampire, either."

Elena frowned and he could see her turning what he had said over in her mind, examining it from every angle. And then she grinned at him. "I can live with that."

"Good. So, let's get you fed and head for home. I'm pretty sure your husband and your daughter are going crazy worrying about you. And I'm still on my honeymoon."

"So that's it?" Kaitlyn asked, glancing from her mother to Zack and back again. "You're not like Zack and you're not like Dad. You're more like me?"

"So it would seem," Elena said, smiling happily. "Zack taught me how to call prey to me and how to drink without damaging them. It was really very easy. And quite enjoyable. But, all things considered, I think I would rather have a cup of peppermint tea."

Kaitlyn stared at her mother, then burst out laughing.

Drake frowned at Kaitlyn and Elena for several moments, and then he smiled.

Zack blew out a sigh. All was well with the Sherrad

clan, he mused. Elena's life had been saved. Kaitlyn's was no longer in danger. The long-lost brother had returned to the fold and, unless Zack missed his guess, Stefan had developed quite a crush on Scherry, which, luckily, went both ways.

Liliana had returned to the Italian Fortress, declaring that she had had enough of Lake Tahoe. "Too many people," she had complained. "Too much sunlight."

Zack's gaze lingered on Kaitlyn. His bride. She was beyond beautiful, he thought. Her cheeks were flushed with laughter, her eyes sparkling as she hugged her mother.

The only question now was where and how he and Kaitlyn would spend the rest of their lives. Would she want to return to Romania and live near her parents? Would she want to stay in Tahoe? Whatever she wanted was fine with him, as long as they were together. He had been alone for far too long, had spent a dozen lifetimes waiting for her.

And it had been worth the wait.

Epilogue

Kaitlyn stepped out of the shower. After wrapping her wet hair in a towel, she pulled on her favorite fluffy pink robe and padded barefooted into the living room. It was good to be in her own house again, to sleep in her own bed. Her parents had gone back to the Fortress a few days ago, with plans to return to Wolfram in the near future. Stefan's romance with Scherry was heating up and he had decided to stay in Tahoe indefinitely. Kaitlyn had no doubt that there would soon be another wedding in the family.

Construction had started on the new nightclub.

Life was back to normal, and she was blissfully happy.

"What are you smiling about?" Zack asked as she curled up on the sofa beside him.

"Nothing much. You still owe me another wedding, you know."

"Yeah, yeah. How about waiting until our anniversary?"

"Don't you want to marry me again?"

"Sure, but, let's wait until the club's built. We can have a grand opening, get married, and go away for a few weeks, anywhere you want to go."

She pretended to think it over, then nodded. "All

right." She grinned at him. "Maybe we'll have a double wedding."

Zack chuckled. Stefan had fallen head over heels in love with Scherry. A blind man could see that.

"You've lived a really long time," Kaitlyn remarked thoughtfully.

"Yeah."

"Even longer than my dad."

Zack nodded, wondering where this conversation was heading.

"Existing for such a long time, you must have seen everything, done everything. Do you ever get bored with it all?"

"From time to time, but, hey, who doesn't?"

"That's true." She slipped her hand under his shirt and ran her fingertips over his chest and across the rock-hard ridges in his abdomen. If he wasn't a vampire, he would have made a great underwear model. "Zack?"

"Yes, love?"

"Six hundred years," she murmured. "There must have been a lot of women in your life in that time."

"One or two," he admitted with a wicked grin.

"More like one or two hundred, I'll bet," she said with a pout.

"Kind of late in the game for you to be jealous, isn't it?"

"Yes. No. I don't know. Maybe. Were there a lot of women?"

"Not near as many as you seem to think," he said with a grin.

"Even one would be too many." She knew it was unrealistic to think he had lived like a monk for six hundred years, but still, she hated the thought of him with another woman. Any woman.

"Darlin', even if there were thousands—which there weren't!—they're all gone now."

"You're laughing at me."

"I'm sorry, love, but, really, what brought this up?"

"I found an old copy of *Romeo and Juliet* when I was putting some of your things away. It was signed 'I will always adore you, and no one else. Colette.'"

"Ah." Not everything had been destroyed in the fire. The construction crew had discovered his casket, intact, along with the iron box he had kept in his lair.

Unable to think of a plausible way to explain why there was an empty coffin in a cement underground vault beneath the club, Zack had wiped the memory of his lair and its contents from the minds of all those who had seen it. He had destroyed the coffin and thrown away all the contents of the box, save for the book.

He ran a hand over his jaw. "Do you remember when we first met and you asked me if I'd ever been in love?"

Kaitlyn nodded.

"And I said once? Well, it was Colette."

"You must have loved her very much to have kept that book all this time."

He shrugged. And then he cupped Kaitlyn's face in his hands. "Think about it, Katy. In six hundred years, I never married. Why do you suppose that is?"

"I don't know." He was a remarkably handsome man. Sexy as all get out, with a smile that could melt iron. He was fun to be with. And great in bed. And . . . She frowned. "Why haven't you ever married?"

"Don't you know, Katy darlin'?" Swinging her into his arms, he carried her swiftly into the bedroom, lowered her gently to the bed, and stretched out beside her. "I was waiting for my Juliet. I was waiting for you."

Did you miss the companion story to this novel?
BOUND BY NIGHT is available now . . .

A VAMPIRE'S KISS IS FOREVER . . .

Once featured in a horror movie, the crumbling
Wolfram estate is said to be haunted by ghosts,
witches, and worse. But Elena doesn't believe
a word of it—until she spends the night
and wakes up in the arms
of a compelling stranger . . .

Tall, dark, and disturbingly handsome,
Drake is the most beautiful man Elena has ever seen.
For centuries, he has lived alone, and Elena
is the first woman to enter his lair—and survive.
And Drake is the first man to touch her heart and
soul. By the time she discovers who he really is—
and what he craves—it's too late.
Blood lust has turned to love, and Elena
is deeply under Drake's spell.
But forever comes at a price for each of them . . .

Books by Bestselling Author
Fern Michaels

Nail-Biting Romantic Suspense from Your Favorite Authors

Romantic Suspense from
Lisa Jackson

See How She Dies	0-8217-7605-3	$6.99US/$9.99CAN
Final Scream	0-8217-7712-2	$7.99US/$10.99CAN
Wishes	0-8217-6309-1	$5.99US/$7.99CAN
Whispers	0-8217-7603-7	$6.99US/$9.99CAN
Twice Kissed	0-8217-6038-6	$5.99US/$7.99CAN
Unspoken	0-8217-6402-0	$6.50US/$8.50CAN
If She Only Knew	0-8217-6708-9	$6.50US/$8.50CAN
Hot Blooded	0-8217-6841-7	$6.99US/$9.99CAN
Cold Blooded	0-8217-6934-0	$6.99US/$9.99CAN
The Night Before	0-8217-6936-7	$6.99US/$9.99CAN
The Morning After	0-8217-7295-3	$6.99US/$9.99CAN
Deep Freeze	0-8217-7296-1	$7.99US/$10.99CAN
Fatal Burn	0-8217-7577-4	$7.99US/$10.99CAN
Shiver	0-8217-7578-2	$7.99US/$10.99CAN
Most Likely to Die	0-8217-7576-6	$7.99US/$10.99CAN
Absolute Fear	0-8217-7936-2	$7.99US/$9.49CAN
Almost Dead	0-8217-7579-0	$7.99US/$10.99CAN
Lost Souls	0-8217-7938-9	$7.99US/$10.99CAN
Left to Die	1-4201-0276-1	$7.99US/$10.99CAN
Wicked Game	1-4201-0338-5	$7.99US/$9.99CAN
Malice	0-8217-7940-0	$7.99US/$9.49CAN

Available Wherever Books Are Sold!
Visit our website at **www.kensingtonbooks.com**